By Loyalty Torn

Shawn Lamb

Allon Books

By Loyalty Torn
by Shawn Lamb

Published by Allon Books
6829 Valley Brook Trace
Utica, Kentucky 42376-5005
www.allonbooks.com

Cover design by Robert Lamb
"Unexpected Visitors" 1894
Painting by Ernest Crofts – Wikimedia Commons
Woman image used under license from Shutterstock.com.

International Standard Book Number: 978-0-9964381-7-9

Other Books by Shawn Lamb

Young Adult Fantasy Fiction

For Young Readers – ages 8-10
Allon – The King's Children series

Historical Fiction

CHARACTERS

FOXGLEN MANOR & VILLAGE

Lady Samantha O'Malley Hedgepeth
Reverend Howard Cunningham
Anne Cunningham
Henry Wyatt, bailiff of Foxglen
Master Godwin, steward of Foxglen
Master Duffy, innkeeper
Mayor Walcott

ROYALISTS

Major Lawrence Hedgepeth
Captain Wallace
Captain William Hawkins
Sergeant Nathan Strickland
Lieutenant Hodges
Lord Kyle Hedgepeth
Prince Rupert
King Charles I

PARLIAMENTARIANS

Duncan O'Malley, Duke of Rutherford
Rory O'Malley, Lord Wiltshire
Oliver Cromwell
Sir Thomas Fairfax

Chapter 1

WALCOTT LED THE BELEAGUERED GROUP THROUGH THE FOREST. Haste was required, but stealth also necessary. Three women encouraged four frightened children, the smallest a female toddler of two years. Her mother carried her as she offered soft words of comfort; the women's skirts and bodices torn and smudged. Two children were boys, ages seven and ten. Their pale grimy faces fought to hide anxiety. The eldest boy held the hand of a four-year-old girl. When she sniffled in fear, he scooped her up to keep pace with the others.

Two other men aided the women and children in following Walcott. The man in the rear had only one arm. The left sleeve of his tattered doublet tucked in his belt to keep it from swaying. In his right hand, he held a flintlock pistol. The man behind Walcott wore a bloody bandage on his head that covered his left eye. His clothes soiled and stained.

At the forest edge, Walcott signaled a halt. He crouched down to view a grand Tudor manor bathed in early morning light. A circular gravel drive led to the front door. Elaborately carved woodwork and glass windows dominated the design. Some of the windows were etched and stained with colorful heraldic family coat of arms featuring a fox. Light frost of early spring covered the budding ivy that clung to the outer walls. Constant trimming kept the ivy under control so as not to obscure the breath-taking view of the surrounding country of Lincolnshire.

To the northeast side and rear of the manor, stood the stable and carriage house. Servants' quarters flanked the stable. At the southwest corner of the manor was a walled-off garden. More frosty ivy crept up the garden wall while the wrought iron gates kept clear of vines for easy access.

The bandaged man grabbed Walcott's shoulder. "Why are we stopping?"

"Precaution. I hoped to be here before dawn since we must cross the clearing to the house." Walcott indicated the manor.

"We can't wait!"

"Steady, Jack. I want to be certain we have not been followed."

Jack called, "Sully!"

The one-armed man raced forward. "Aye?"

"Anyone following?"

"Not that I can tell."

"Jack, how much further? The children are tired and hungry," asked the woman who held the toddler.

Jack went to comfort her. "We're here. But we need to cross the meadow." He gently caressed the toddler's face. "You will eat soon, my dear Katie." He kissed the girl's head. He spoke to the others. "We made it to Foxglen, only we must run the final leg before the sun fully rises. Bob, can you do that while holding Meg?"

"Aye," replied the lad.

Jack returned to Walcott. "Ready."

"Now!" Walcott bolted from the trees with the rest following.

Jack hung back to make certain Bob managed with Meg. When the lad faltered due to the extra weight, Jack took Meg for the final hundred yards. Sully urged the group from the rear.

Walcott led them past the stables and carriage house to the rear where the kitchen was located. The smell of food and sounds of activity came from inside. He banged on the door and shouted.

"Here now! Who's banging at this hour?" A female voice came from within just before the door opened. A healthy Irish woman of sixty appeared. "Master Walcott?"

"Aye, Cookie. There is an urgent need." Walcott ushered everyone inside.

Baffled, Cookie stepped aside. She gasped at the dismal state of those who entered. "By all the saints, what happened?"

A middle-aged man of fifty rushed into the kitchen. He hastily donned a doublet, his hair unkempt from waking. "Master Walcott, who are these people?"

"Godwin, you know Jack Bannon and Pat Sully." Walcott indicated the wounded men.

Stunned by the wretched condition, Godwin made an impulsive gasp. "Good Lord."

"They need safe haven. Alas, I cannot provide it. I must speak with her ladyship."

"Aye. Cookie, food and drink," Godwin said, then to Walcott, "Wait in the drawing room while I wake her ladyship and the Reverend."

Being early morning, Godwin held a lantern to climb the rear staircase. He paused at the first door to knock. "Reverend Cunningham. Reverend." He heard faint stirring, so he opened the door. "Reverend."

"What is it?" he asked sleepily.

"You are needed downstairs at once. I go to wake her ladyship."

The Reverend sat up and pushed back a mess of graying ash blond hair from his face. "Why? Has something happened?"

"Master Walcott will explain."

"Walcott?" he said in surprise that snapped him awake. "I'm coming." He tossed aside the covers. "Wake Anne first and let her deal with Samantha."

Godwin followed instructions. With Anne in tow, they entered Samantha's bedchamber. At the age of twenty-one, the resemblance of Anne to her Reverend father obvious in the color of her hair and shape of her face. She gently touched the shoulder of a sleeping young lady. Candlelight showed her no older than seventeen.

"Samantha. You need to wake up." At a responding negative groan, Anne motioned to Godwin. The steward threw open the curtains. A cascade of morning sun flooded the darkened room. Light splashed upon a brilliant head of red hair, that became quickly buried under a pillow.

7

"Samantha! You must wake," Anne insisted.

"What time is it?" came a muffled question from under the pillow.

"Not yet six o'clock."

"An urgent situation requires attention," spoke a male voice.

Samantha peeked out to see the Reverend. "Howard. Who could need me at this ungodly hour?"

"The war, I'm afraid."

With a gasp and sudden movement, Samantha sat up. She grimaced in pain and cradled her left arm. "Is Lawrence here?" she asked in fearful anxiety.

"No, be easy. The major has not returned," Anne spoke with tender reassurance.

Samantha's entire body relaxed when she sighed with relief.

"Walcott is here. So, the matter must be of great urgency," said Howard.

"Anne, my dressing gown." She rose. Gingerly, she put her left arm through the sleeve.

"Does your arm still hurt?" asked Anne.

"I … I slept on it wrong." At Anne's disbelieving expression, Samantha admitted, "A little." Long red hair fell over her shoulder and down the back of the dressing gown. She did a quick, loose braid to keep it manageable.

In the downstairs drawing room, they met an anxious Walcott.

"My lady, forgive this intrusion. But a dire situation has occurred that requires immediate redress. You are only one with the ability to do so."

Samantha tried to stifle a yawn. "I assume it deals with the war. At least, that is what Howard believes."

"The Reverend is correct," Walcott confirmed. "Do you remember Jack Bannon and Pat Sully? Two of the tenant farmers favorited by your father?"

"Of course. I used to play with Jack's sister whenever my father took us to visit the farmers."

Walcott tried to contain his temper when asking, "You know they were conscripted into the Royal army, correct?"

"Conscripts?" she repeated. "I know of the order, but not familiar with individuals."

"Jack and Sully are two of the Rutherford men forced to take up arms for the King."

"I did not know," she said apologetically. "I am still becoming acquainted with the management of Foxglen since my marriage." Bitterness crept into her voice on the word *marriage*.

Walcott continued in his bold speech. "The King's order has done an ill turn to the estate and village. Three men have been killed, four others maimed beyond recognition or earthly help. Both Jack and Sully suffered serious wounds."

Discomposure momentarily silenced Samantha, so Howard asked, "Where are they now?"

"Here, along with their families and Jack's sister, Penny."

"At Foxglen?" asked Samantha, still trying to digest the news.

"Aye. They came to me for aid. I hid them for as long as I could, but Royalist patrols have entered Lincolnshire to hunt for deserters. If found, they will be hung, and their families imprisoned or killed for aiding them."

"Deserters," echoed Samantha in utter surprise. Her befuddled glance found Howard.

"These are Rutherford men!" Walcott spoke in high passion to Samantha. "Families dependent upon the provision and protection of this house. Forced into service against their will and loyalty to your family. As a Member of the House of Commons for Lincolnshire, I appeal to you for aid."

Overcome, Samantha sat. Howard stood beside her in a show of moral support while scolding Walcott. "This is a brash request, Master Walcott."

"One I well understand, Reverend. I served beside the duke in Parliament and heard his impassioned speech before the King forcefully removed the Members."

"I have not Duncan's head for politics and law," Samantha rebuffed.

"I speak of your late father, Sir Patrick."

Mention of him, brought Samantha to her feet. Her blue eyes flashed anger, which prompted Howard to scold Walcott.

"Are you aware that Sir Patrick arranged her marriage to Major Hedgepeth, son of Lord Kyle Hedgepeth, Royal Keeper of the Muse?"

"Aye," Walcott replied, then returned his attention to Samantha. "Does six months of marriage negate six decades of family responsibility?"

"You are bold, sir!" Samantha chided.

"Forgive my impertinence, but war is hardly the time for delicacy and decorum. They wait in the kitchen. Will you turn them away? Or at least, speak with them?"

Samantha took a deep breath to calm her temper. "I will speak with Jack and Sully. Fetch them." She waved at both Walcott and Godwin.

Howard spoke once the door closed. "This situation places you in an awkward position."

Samantha paced. "Master Walcott is correct. Despite my recent marriage, to this I was born. Foxglen is my dowry to manage and continue the honored tradition passed to me. It is fortunate Lawrence is absent." She paused by the window. Her right hand gently rubbed her upper left arm. Speaking of Lawrence brought back images of his last visit.

Shortly after the war started, he paused for the night at Foxglen on his way to York. Recollection of his angry countenance and bitter curses against those opposed to the King. Hearing the door open, brought her mind back to the situation at hand. With a quick steadying breath, she turned from the window. She made an impulsive sob upon wretched sight of Jack and Sully.

"Good Lord," Howard murmured. He lowered his head to offer a silent mouthed prayer.

"My lady." Jack bowed. "It is good to see you again. At least, with what vision I have left."

"Jack." Moved with compassion, Samantha took his hand. "Sully. Pray, be seated."

"No, thank you," Jack graciously declined.

Katie waddled in. She held a half-eaten biscuit.

"Who is this?" asked Samantha.

"My youngest. She must have followed me. Come here, Katie," Jack beckoned.

Instead, the toddler walked to Samantha and raised her arms to be picked up. Samantha obliged. "How old is she?"

"Two."

"She is a sight." Samantha tenderly brushed aside the tangled brown locks. She smiled at Katie. "You like the biscuit? Cookie bakes wonderful goodies." Katie simply munched on it.

"How did you come by your wounds?" Howard asked.

"Near York," Sully roughly replied. "One of the numerous battles and skirmishes we were forced to fight this past year. Loss of a limb or an eye isn't enough for the King!" He struggled to keep his composure as tears blurred his vision. "We couldn't take it anymore. Death and destruction for what? Enduring threats to fight and die for a man who shows no concern or compassion for his people?" He wept.

Jack comforted his friend, as he explained to Samantha. "We deserted after the captain threatened our family with imprisonment if we refused to continue. I can barely see, while Sully only has one arm. What good are we expect to be needlessly sacrificed on the battlefield?" Emotions choked his voice.

Samantha sent a worried glance to Howard. He too softened at the tale of two desperate men. Anne gently wiped the tears from her face.

Walcott spoke. "As I told your ladyship, I hid them for as long as I could. However, they need a safer location then my barns."

After a nod from Howard, Samantha told Godwin, "Send for Henry." When Godwin left, she told Jack and Sully, "He might know of a safer location. Until he arrives, return to the kitchen, and eat your fill."

When Jack came to take Katie, the toddler shook her head in refusal.

"Let her stay with me little longer," Samantha graciously said.

"Don't give her ladyship too much trouble," Jack gently spoke to Katie before he left.

Anne tenderly touched Katie's cheek. "Food is not all they need. These clothes are badly tattered."

11

"There are some older clothes stored in a chest in the cellar. You and Howard determine what is needed and fetch them. I have some entertaining to do." She grinned at Katie. The toddler finished the biscuit and yawned. "Are you tired."

Samantha walked the drawing room, as she cradled Katie. When they passed by the hearth, Katie perked up. Uncertain as to why, Samantha paused. "You see something?"

"Hor … see." Katie spoke shyly.

"Horsey? You mean this statue?" Samantha pointed to a bronze statue on the mantle. A man dressed in Tudor style clothes seated upon on a horse. "That is my grandfather riding his favorite horse, Champ."

"Hor … see."

"You like horses? No doubt you saw them at Walcott's barn. He raises some of the finest horses in Lincolnshire." With a thought she said, "I know something you might like." She moved to the other side of the room. Still interested in the statue, Katie kept looking back.

"Hor … see." The toddler grew upset.

"Aye, horsey." Samantha carefully stooped down to open the drawer of a lower bookcase. She pulled out an old stuffed toy horse that had been well played with. She showed Katie. "This was my favorite horsey as a child. My mother kept it here for me to play with when we visited Foxglen." Katie reached for the toy. "Aye, you can have it."

Katie smiled and hugged the toy horse. She yawned and leaned against Samantha to sleep. Samantha sat in a chair to allow Katie undisturbed rest. Observing the sleeping toddler in her arms suddenly made the war real. News and rumors of battles seemed distant. Even Lawrence's foul curses and descriptions felt abstract. Sight of Jack, Sully, and Katie brought a disturbing truth to the tales they heard or read in dispatches.

Her pondering became interrupted when Henry Wyatt arrived. A tall, strong man in his mid-forties. Most of his brown hair streaked with white. He wore better clothes than the typical farmer, more akin to household servants of rank.

"You—" Henry lowered his voice when Samantha placed a finger to her lips. At her indication, he sat on the footstool beside her.

"Jack Bannon's youngest," she whispered.

"I barely recognized him and Sully when I saw them in the kitchen just now."

"Is there a place on the estate for them to hide?"

Henry cocked a grin. "Aye. However, it would be best to leave shortly after sundown. Too many eyes during the day."

"They can stay in the cellar until then. Enough time to eat and be fitted with new clothes."

"Let me take her back to Brenda." Henry took sleeping Katie from Samantha.

Chapter 2

THE REAR TERRACE OF FOXGLEN DISPLAYED A COLORFUL ARRAY of summer blooms. The frosts of spring gave way to scorching heat, just the weather for hearty roses to thrive. The manor's cellar could be accessed from inside the kitchen or an exterior door for ease of loading and unloading. Samantha waited beside a cart pulled by a single horse. Henry, and two younger men, brought up needed supplies from the exterior access. Henry put the last sack on the cart.

"That should be enough to hold them for a month," he told Samantha.

Godwin emerged from the kitchen. "My lady, I understand the need for Christian generosity, but what is being provided has considerably lessened the larder. Cookie is very cross. She is struggling to make do since the crop blight and war impact what is available."

Samantha chewed on a thumbnail, a frequent habit when thinking. She asked Henry, "What is the estimated wheat and barley yield?"

Henry briefly scowled at Godwin before he replied. "Due to lack of rain and blight, we could lose half before harvest."

The news stunned her. "That bad?"

"Add what you sent from the granary in response to the duke's request for his regiment," said Godwin.

Again, she chewed on her thumbnail for a moment. "Any suggestions?"

"Rationing," said Godwin. At her skepticism, he added, "Like your grandfather ordered in the late 1590s. I have records from the previous stewards of how they managed."

"He has a point," said Henry. "I remember my father telling me about that time. It made his management difficult. Even resulted in some evictions." He removed the sack he just placed on the cart. "We can return half to storage. I'll tell Jack about the situation. As a farmer, he'll understand. Tom, Jeremy!" He summoned the younger men and gave instructions on what stayed in the cart and what went back to the cellar.

"I will use examples from the past to create a plan. One, God willing, will help us survive the blight and the war," said Godwin.

"Bring it to me when complete." She delayed his departure to say with levity, "I am sure this will please Cookie."

He grinned. "Returning the supplies, aye. Rationing? I doubt that."

Unloading didn't take as long. Henry locked the cellar door and pocketed the key. He began to climb onto the driver's seat when a mounted patrol of Royalists approached. Tom and Jeremy lingered near the cellar door, also wary of the Royalists.

"I wonder what they want?" Henry carefully moved his hand to rest on his belt near the pistol he carried.

"Stay," she warned. "We must keep up appearance." She moved to meet the patrol.

When the Royalists halted, the lead man removed his hat in greeting. A plain looking man in his thirties yet the typical Cavalier grooming and mannerism. "My lady. I am Lieutenant Gilmore of His Majesty's Calvary. We are newly assigned to Lincolnshire."

"Why? What threat does Lincolnshire pose the King being Royalist?"

"Royalist for *now*, my lady. Our presence is to ensure it remains so. As such, may I inquire as to your name?"

Samantha flashed a wry smile. "For claiming Lincolnshire to be Royalist, you are apparently ignorant of those living here. Do you know the name of this estate?"

At the stinging rebuff, Gilmore shifted in the saddle. "I heard it is called Foxglen."

"Indeed. It has stood for over sixty years. Built by my great-grandfather as a wedding gift to his son – my grandfather."

15

"History aside, your name, please."

"I am Lady Samantha Hedgepeth."

"Hedgepeth? Any relation to a major in Prince Rupert's regiment?"

"He is my husband."

"My lady." Impressed, Gilmore removed his hat and bowed at the waist in the saddle. Upon straightened, he donned his hat. He also noticed the cart and moved his horse past her. "What is this?"

"Supplies," replied Henry.

"Who are you?" Gilmore demanded in a tone less cordial than dealing with Samantha.

"Henry Wyatt. Bailiff of Foxglen."

"Then these are estate supplies?"

Samantha rejoined Henry beside the cart. "These are contributions to the poor who have been adversely affected by the crop blight."

Gilmore dismounted to inspect the load. "The estate has amble supply to be generous."

At that moment, Godwin returned. His appearance gave Samantha a clever reply. "Only by the astute rationing of my steward, Master Godwin, are we able to share with those in need."

Henry swallowed back a chuckle and hid his face behind a gloved hand of pretended cough. Godwin simply nodded to the statement of praise.

"Who are these unfortunate people to profit from your generosity?" asked Gilmore.

To this question, Samantha balked for an answer. Godwin quickly intervened.

"Sadly, the list grows. The grain harvest may only be half of normal. As such, we anticipate more will require assistance. This," he slapped a sack on the cart, "will be carefully portioned among those in need." He cast a prompting glance to Henry.

"Aye," the bailiff agreed.

"Would there be any deserters among the less fortunate?"

A bit taken back by the question; Samantha stuttered slightly. "What made you ask that, Lieutenant?"

"One of our tasks is to recover deserters from His Majesty's army. These cowards fled the field of battle and dishonored their King!" Heavy scorn filled Gilmore's voice.

At Samantha's distress, Henry spoke. "We've heard of no deserters in the area. Now, I must go. Master Walcott, the village mayor, is expecting me. I don't want to be late." He climbed into the driver's seat.

With a snap of the reins, the horse moved. This forced Gilmore to step aside. It also gave Samantha a moment to recover her nerve.

"If there is nothing else, Lieutenant—"

"There is. Why are these able-bodied young men not serving their King?" He sneered at Tom and Jeremy.

"If all young men fought, there would be no one left to tend the farms that supply the army with food. My *husband* understands this and agreed to those I requested remain for that purpose. Now, good day, Lieutenant." She reached for Godwin's arm to enter the kitchen.

Gilmore bowed. "My lady."

Godwin paused in closing the door to watch the Royalist ride off. "They're gone."

Samantha sighed with relief. "That was too close."

"What was?" Anne entered the kitchen from the hall to the main house.

"Royalists asking about the supplies."

"We managed to throw him off the scent," said Godwin.

"For now," Samantha droned. "Where is Howard?" she asked Anne.

"In town to visit some parishioners."

"Henry might need his help if he encounters Lieutenant Gilmore."

"My lady …"

"Cookie, we must ration," Samantha spoke with impatience.

"I know. I watched from the window."

Godwin fought a wry grin to say, "That is why you did not hear a string of colorful Irish phrases when I told her."

Samantha chuckled. "I'm sorry, Cookie," she forced an apology through several attempts to curb laughter.

17

"I don't mind the surly old cock," she spoke about Godwin. "I was a girl during the last famine. My mother, the cook, did right by your grandfather. I'll do right by you now."

"Thank you," Samantha spoke with sincerity. "Godwin, tell Tom to saddle my horse."

"My lady?" said Godwin, taken aback. "It is not safe to go riding alone."

"I am going to the village not for a pleasure ride" She left the kitchen.

Anne followed. "Samantha! Why go to the village?"

"I need to get a sense of Lieutenant Gilmore." She climbed the main stairs.

"Father and Henry will do that."

Samantha stopped at the top of the stairs. "No! Master Walcott reminded me that Foxglen is my responsibility. Along with everyone who depends upon me. Jack, Sully, and others have suffered enough. Lieutenant Gilmore asked why Tom and Jeremy are not in the army. I rebuffed him with a minor falsehood," she admitted then quickly said to Anne's disapproving frown, "Don't look at me like that." She hurried to her chamber.

"I'm concerned," Anne insisted.

Samantha fetched a hat and riding gloves out of the wardrobe. From a drawer in a nightstand, she withdrew a small percussion pistol. After checking it for loading, she placed it in pocket of her skirt. "I appreciate your concern. However, I must be more involved if I am to act accordingly, and not continuously caught off guard by a worsening situation."

"What if the major learns of …" Anne stopped when Samantha's face grew hard set.

"You, of all people, should understand my position."

Anne's regret manifested in fretful tears. "I do. I tended your wounds after he left. Yet, you brush aside my concern."

Moved with compassion, Samantha embraced Anne. "That is not my intent. I struggle with how to balance what is required of me both as wife and duty to my family. Especially now. I thank God that Lawrence is not here. Christian compassion is unknown to him. It is a quality my father highly valued." She tenderly smiled in remembrance. "He said I reminded him of my mother. I recall her being a gentle creature. At least, what a five-year-old thought."

Anne fought an impulsive grin. "My companionship was to tame you."

Samantha giggled. "In some respects." Sound of horses outside the window brought her back to the current situation. "Now, I *must* leave."

As they went back downstairs, Anne asked, "What shall I do while you are gone?"

Samantha paused in the foyer. "Help Godwin and Cookie stay on task. Lord knows sparks fly between those two." She flashed a wry grin.

Outside the main entrance, Samantha found Tom holding the reins of two horses: her favorite black hunter, and a chestnut cob. He wore a sword and pistol. "What is this?"

"Father would have my hide if I let you go off alone," Tom replied.

She kindly smiled. "That would be a sight, since you are nearly as large as Henry."

He chuckled and helped her mount side-saddle.

Chapter 3

MASTER WALCOTT'S FARM LAY ON THE OUTSKIRTS OF TOWN. A small crowd of twelve gathered at the front door of the house. Loud voices alerted Henry to trouble. Walcott and Howard appeared to be engaged with several men among the townsfolk. To avoid drawing attention, Henry drove the cart behind the nearest barn. He made certain all was secure before he approached the house. He caught Howard's frustrated glance. The Reverend managed to back away to join Henry while Walcott continued to argue with the crowd.

"I don't need to ask how goes it," Henry dryly commented.

"Jimmy Oswell is stirring up trouble again," groused Howard. "Try as I might, I cannot convince him that such behavior is detrimental."

"Especially now." Henry drew Howard further from the group. "A Royalist patrol came to Foxglen looking for deserters."

"What? Do they know?" asked Howard with urgency.

Henry shook his head. "We satisfied their inquiry. Rather, mention of the major kept things civil."

"Mentioned by you or Samantha?"

"She did." Henry caught sight of movement beyond the group. "Here they come." He pointed to the patrol. "The leader is Lieutenant Gilmore."

Howard and Henry joined Walcott, just as the mayor and crowd noticed the Royalists.

"Who is Mayor Walcott?"

"I am, sir. And you?"

"Lieutenant Gilmore of His Majesty's Calvary. I am here looking for deserters. Ah, Master Wyatt. I thank you for leading us here."

Walcott scowled at Henry, which made the bailiff explain. "He came to Foxglen, and I told him about *you* waiting for *me* to bring supplies to distribute among the needy."

Walcott made a slight nod of understanding. "Just so," he said to Gilmore. "As you can see, there are many in need." He motioned to the crowd.

Gilmore moved his horse amongst the people. He keenly regarded each one. "Jack Bannon. Pat Sully." He spoke the name for reaction.

"What do you want with them?" asked a thin, wiry man, with grizzled features.

"Your name?" demanded Gilmore.

"Jimmy Oswell."

"Do you know Bannon and Sully?"

"Aye. But haven't seen them since they left for war."

Gilmore raised his voice to address the crowd. "They are deserters! Anyone found aiding or harboring them will be hung alongside them."

Howard stepped forward. "Such threats are unnecessary, Lieutenant."

Gilmore surveyed Howard's attire. "A clergyman? Wearing a sword?"

"I am servant of God. As for the sword, no man would venture out these days without some defense."

"Anglican or Puritan?" Gilmore's tone betrayed bias contempt.

"Does it matter when the Word of God is preached?"

At Gilmore's seething scorn, Walcott intervened. "Reverend Cunningham has been the village parson for over six years. He is highly respected by all who fear God regardless of affiliation. Is that not so, Jimmy?" he prodded swell.

"Aye. We may not always agree, but the Reverend is straightforward."

"Oh, no," murmured Henry. He nudged Howard's elbow and nodded toward two new arrivals: Samantha and Tom.

"My lady!" Walcott hurried to greet her.

"Master Walcott," she answered with some distraction. She focused on the Royalists. "What are you doing here, Lieutenant?"

"My duty."

"He claims to be looking for Jack Bannon and Pat Sully," Jimmy Oswell told her. "Something about desertion." He scowled at Gilmore.

The Lieutenant smacked Oswell on the back of the head so hard, he went sprawling to the ground.

The violent action made Samantha's horse shy. She steadied the animal. "Lieutenant Gilmore! Stay your hand! This man, along with all in the village, are under my protection. If you are to conduct business here, it will not be with violence."

"My lady," began Gilmore with great restraint. "Whereas I appreciate your position and that of your husband, the major, I am under orders from the *King*. Do not impede me."

"I do not impede you, sir. Only require you do so without violence. Unless you would dishonor the *King* for unwarranted action against a Royalist house? And one personally attached to the royal court!"

Muted by anger at the public rebuke, Gilmore roughly turned his horse and rode from the farm with patrol in tow.

"Well done, my lady," Walcott said with admiration.

She ignored him to ask, "Master Oswell, are you seriously injured?"

Two men helped Oswell to his feet. "A bump on the head, but I'll survive."

Howard grabbed the bridle. "What are you doing here?"

"My *duty*." She moved her arms with the indication for him to help her dismount.

Tom quickly jumped down to hold the reins of both horses. He made a low side comment to his father. "I didn't let her come alone."

"She has always been headstrong. Let's hope it serves her well now," Henry replied.

Ignorant of the exchange, Samantha spoke to Walcott. "I take it, this gathering deals with the current lack of food."

"Aye. The Reverend and me were trying to reason with them when the Royalists arrived."

"What the soldiers don't take, the weather ruins!" complained Oswell.

"I am aware of the situation, Master Oswell, which is why I am here." She spoke to the crowd. "History of Foxglen shows the last famine was managed by rationing. As such, I have ordered my steward and bailiff to implement a plan that will ensure everyone receives food. Please, bear with us as we take the necessary steps for even distribution."

"Where will the supplies be stored?" asked a woman.

"Here," replied Walcott.

"No! Your barns are not secure enough," Oswell said in dispute.

"Aye! Too close to town. Anyone can sneak in and steal what they want," said another.

"Or soldiers take it," scoffed a third man.

"Foxglen," said Henry. "It is far enough from town to be safe, and large enough to accommodate crops. Master Walcott's farm will serve for distribution on appointed days. We simply need time to refine the plan."

"How much time? My babies are hungry," spoke a distraught Maggie Reynolds.

"Two or three days at most," said Henry.

"Master Godwin is drawing up the plan as we speak. While Master Wyatt came to discuss distribution with Mayor Walcott." Sympathetic, Samantha approached Maggie. "Can you manage for three days?"

"I suppose I can stretch the porridge that long."

"Thank you." Samantha again spoke to the crowd. "I give you my word, Rutherford will again endure these hard times."

"Rutherford," Oswell scoffed. "You told the soldiers of your *royalist* ties."

"Mind your tongue!" Henry rebuffed. "Do none of you understand her ladyship's position? She is caught in the middle of this! Yet just now she protected you from the soldiers and plans to provide food for all. Show some gratitude."

Despite Oswell being younger, Henry's physical size and forcefulness made him back down.

Maggie smiled at Samantha. "I am grateful, my lady. Truly."

"Return to your homes. I will send word when there is food to distribute," said Walcott.

"Without grumbling," Howard added. "As the Lord did when faced with hardship." While the crowd dispersed, he gave Samantha a fatherly scowl. "You took a great risk coming here."

Samantha compassionately watched the people. "Coming showed me the depth of danger we face."

"You must tread carefully," Henry added his warning. "You heard Lieutenant Gilmore's determination. He won't be stayed for long by mentioning the major. Let us take the risk while you remain neutral." He spoke about himself, Howard, and Walcott.

Her friendly smile quivered slightly. "Henry, I appreciate your stalwart nature. However, I cannot stand aside. You even spoke of my position. I am the only one who can stand in the gap. Help me do so."

A brief look of hurt passed over Henry's face before he nodded.

Howard drew Samantha aside. "Henry Wyatt's loyalty runs deep. Yet, he speaks wisdom. You must shrewdly determine when, where, and how to act or not act."

"Aye." She glanced around and became curious. "Henry." She waved him over to ask in a whisper, "Where is the cart?"

"Behind the barn. When I saw the crowd, I thought best to be discrete. Sight of it could have started a riot. Especially, Jimmy Oswell."

"What cart?" asked Howard.

"Supplies for *them*," Samantha carefully replied.

Walcott joined the discussion. "Not good to be done in broad daylight. That lieutenant will probably be on the lookout for anything that comes and goes from my farm. Best wait until sunset."

"I can't remain here all day. I need to help plan rationing," said Henry.

"My business in the village will take the day. No one will be suspicious of me," said Howard.

"You don't know where they are," Henry disputed.

"Then return to guide me. Your duties should be concluded by sundown."

"It is decided then," said Samantha in conclusion.

Thwarted, Henry spoke to Walcott. "Lend me a horse. It wouldn't look right for me to walk back to Foxglen with her ladyship."

Chapter 4

THE MID-AFTERNOON SUN MADE FOR A MISERABLE DAY OF HEAT. Henry, Godwin, Samantha, and Anne gathered in the study. By the looks of them, the task had been long and frustrating. All the windows stood open along with both hall doors to allow for air circulation. Any breeze provided welcomed relief from the heat. Papers lay scattered on the desk and a table.

Henry sat near a window with his doublet unbuttoned, shirt collar loosened, and sleeves rolled up. His focus shifted between two pieces of paper he held.

Anne poured liquid from a pitcher into a tankard. "This is the last of today's cider ration." She placed the tankard on a small table beside the chair. Henry merely grunted thanks.

Samantha stood at the desk to regard the disarray of papers; Godwin opposite her. "Are you certain this is the best we can do?"

"Aye," he replied with regret. "What I read from the past stewards indicates this is best course of action."

Henry drank before he joined them at the desk. "Godwin is correct. The fall crop yield is what will dictate a tightening or loosening of present rations." He placed the papers he examined on the desk.

Weary from debate and heat, Samantha lightly groaned and massaged her neck. "If only I knew how my grandfather felt about all this from his experience."

"Why not consult his journals? Sir Patrick often did after he assumed the title and running of the estate," said Godwin

"Sir Patrick also kept a journal," Henry added.

Her ire roused, as she demanded, "Why did neither of you mention these journals before?"

Godwin and Henry exchanged perplexed glances, to which Henry replied, "We assumed you knew. Keeping a journal is commonplace."

"With father's death, my wedding, and war in quick succession, there was scarcely time to think. Much less receive instruction on the management of Foxglen." Her sarcasm high to the point of mockery.

"Samantha," Anne scolded.

Stung by the warning, Samantha crossed to an open window. She closed her eyes, took a deep breath, and exhaled to enjoy the breeze. "Do you know where these journals are kept?" she asked over her shoulder

"A locked compartment in one side of the desk where the chair would hide it. Last, I recall, the key is in the middle drawer. *If* they were not taken to Foxmoor," replied Godwin.

She moved back to the desk. Her eyes scanned the scattered papers. "We shall begin implementing the plan tomorrow. Godwin, inform the household servants. Henry, spread the word among the workers, villagers, and tenants."

"I will do so on my way back to Walcott's farm," said Henry.

It took a moment for Samantha to grasp the statement. "Oh, aye. Be careful."

He flashed a confidence smile and left.

Godwin asked, "Shall I have dinner sent to the study?"

"Aye. Anne, see to it," Samantha replied with distraction.

She found a small key where Godwin suggested. She pushed back the chair to look under the desk for a keyhole on either side of the desk. Not clearly visible, she used her hand to feel for an opening. There! On the left side. The key fit perfectly. *Click.* A break in the side showed where the compartment lay hidden. Opening the side revealed three large journals standing on edge. She carefully removed them to place on top of the papers. She closed the compartment enough to draw up the chair to sit. She began by identifying the author. The dates showed two belonged to her grandfather, while the newest to her father.

She spent the next hour researching the first of her grandfather's journals to cross-referenced entries with plans for current rationing. With a thoughtful sigh, she muttered, "Foxhill. Foxmeath?"

"Have you found something to help us?" Anne sat at the table where two plates and tankards now replaced the earlier papers.

"Grandfather's entries confirm what Godwin learned about the famine."

Anne rose to escort Samantha to the table. "Rest your eyes and come eat." Anne offered a quick blessing before she pushed a plate closer to Samantha. It contained a slice of cold roast beef, small hunk of cheese, and half a loaf of barley bread. She noticed Samantha stare at the plate. "Our evening portion." When Samantha continued to stare at the food, she concluded, "It is not the food. What else did you discover?"

Samantha slowly shook her head in befuddlement. "A few curious entries without explanation. Names of places I have never heard. Foxhill and Foxmeath. Are they connected to Rutherford or isolated places?"

"Were those names also found in Sir Patrick's journals?"

Samantha shrugged since she ate. "I have yet to read his. More concerned with what is pertinent to our situation. With the plan confirmed, I will search to learn about them." She curiously glanced back at the desk. "Why lock journals in a secret compartment?" She left the table.

"You have not finished eating," Anne insisted. When ignored, she brought the plate to the desk. Samantha concentrated on the journals. Observing the light outside fading, Anne said, "I shall fetch a lantern, so you don't strain your eyes."

Samantha barely acknowledged Anne's departure. Instead, she took her father's journal to read by natural light at the window. Upon opening it, something fell from the pages. She placed the journal on the windowsill to pick it up. A folded letter sealed with Rutherford signet.

Turning it over, she saw to whom the letter was addressed – *Dearest Samantha.*

She broke the seal. At first glance, she recognized her father's handwriting. His beginning sentences made her knees weak, so she sat on the windowsill beside the journal.

My dearest Samantha,

Since war has begun, I take pen in hand to write this most poignant letter. One, I wish to God, I did not have to write. If you are reading this, then my death has come. God knows, how diligently I sought to avoid conflict. Yet now that war has come, all my efforts must be to preserve our family. To that end, I have been forced to agree to your marriage. Please understand, it was not my desire to make such a union for you, rather one of necessity. Our family has already lost much. To avoid utter ruin, I went against my conscience. For that, I ask your forgiveness, although this may come after my death. God willing, if I survive this war, I shall seek forgiveness in person and speedily remedy that which has been forced upon us.

I dare not put to paper that which brought about this unfortunate match. I can only direct you to my father's last journal. Also, I will instruct Howard —

She gasped in horror at the abrupt end to the letter in mid-sentence. Through tear-filled eyes, she frantically searched the floor for more pages that might have fallen. "God! Help me find the answers."

Anne rushed in. She placed the lantern on the desk to join Samantha on the floor. "What is wrong? Has something happened?" She seized Samantha when ignored. "Samantha."

"My father." Samantha swallowed back passion to hold up the letter. "I must find the rest of what he had to say."

"Where did you get it?"

"It fell from his journal."

Anne did a quick search. "I see nothing on the floor. Maybe some pages remain within the journal."

Panic-stricken, Samantha snatched the journal, raced to the desk, and flipped through the pages. "No!" She slammed it shut, collapsed into the chair, and wept.

Anne knelt and held Samantha's hand. She gently asked, "Can you tell me what Sir Patrick wrote that has upset you?"

Samantha could not speak due to great distress. With a shaky hand, she gave Anne the letter.

Anne observed the broken wax signet. "Did you open the seal?" When Samantha nodded, Anne spoke with compassion, "There may not be anything more."

"There must be! Read," Samantha spoke with choked words.

After a moment, Anne covered her mouth to stifle a moan of despair. She took a deep breath to compose herself. "Have you examined the second journal as he instructs?"

Samantha shook her head. She wiped tears from her face. "I don't know if I can."

Godwin arrived and became concerned. "My lady?"

"Brandy," Anne instructed the steward.

Samantha needed two hands to accept the glass. She coughed down the strong liquor.

"I came to inquire if her ladyship needs anything more for her research," Godwin explained to Anne.

"I believed she has learned enough for one day." She spoke to Godwin, then Samantha, "Come. I shall take you to your chamber."

In a quick, sudden movement, Samantha grabbed her grandfather's second journal and her father's letter. "I will read them when I have regained my composure," she told Anne.

Unable to rest, Samantha sat on the bed against the pillows. Her grandfather's journal on her lap and the letter beside her. She barely began reading when frantic voices and sounds of a scuffle in the front yard brought her to the window. Numerous people made it difficult to discern what caused the uproar. She opened the window to inquire, "Master Godwin! What is the matter?"

"Jimmy Oswell, my lady. He is badly injured!" he replied.

"Bring him inside at once!" In the hallway, she called for Anne, who promptly emerged from her chamber. "Trouble!" They raced downstairs.

Tom and Jeremy carried Oswell. An anxious woman followed.

"In the parlor," Samantha instructed them to the closest room. "Put him on the sofa. Gently! Anne, fetch hot water, bandages, and medicine." She moved to view the injured man. He bled profusely from his head and face.

"His head is broken," Tom whispered to Samantha.

"Fetch the doctor," she told him then asked Mistress Oswell, "What happened?"

Mistress Oswell fearfully hovered over the sofa. "We were attacked just after sunset!"

"By whom?" asked Godwin.

"Royalist soldiers. They burst in, broke furniture, and scattered everything! My man tried to stop them and ..." She couldn't finish due to upset.

"Soldiers did this?" Samantha repeated, stunned.

The wife swallowed back emotion to reply. "Looking for deserters they said. He told he hadn't seen them since the war started!"

Disturbed by the report, Samantha's sympathetic gaze passed between the stricken man and his wife. "How did you get him here?"

"I drug him as far as the road, where the one who left, and this man," she indicated Jeremy, "helped me bring him here."

"We were returning from the village when we chanced upon her," Jeremy explained. "We thought this was the safest place to bring him."

Distressed, Mistress Oswell confronted Samantha. "You gave your word that Rutherford would survive the famine, but soldiers looting and killing? How can we survive that?"

The reminder made Samantha say, "Jeremy, saddle my horse. I will go to their farm."

"No, my lady! It is too dangerous in the dark."

"Aye, wait until daylight when it is safe," Godwin added.

She motioned Jeremy and Godwin from the sofa. "If, God forbid, he dies, it will be murder on Rutherford land. A fact I must deal with."

"*If* that happens, delaying until morning will not change it," Godwin argued. "Please! You must work from a position of strength by using your connections against them. The slightest hint of anything else will be to the ruin of all."

She sighed with acquiescence at the wisdom. "Aye."

Anne returned with the requested items. "I also brought a calming draught," she spoke to Samantha and sent a glance to Mistress Oswell.

Samantha understood. She fetched the draught and coaxed the wife to drink. "This will strengthen you to help the doctor when he arrives."

A half-hour later, Tom returned with the doctor. Alas, the draught did little, as Mistress Oswell remained on the brink of despair. She rose to meet the doctor and plead for her husband.

"Come, let the doctor tend him." Samantha gently guided her to one side.

Anne reported to the doctor what treatment she administered while he examined Oswell.

Suddenly, and with much vigor, Oswell woke with a cry. At first, he murmured unintelligibly. He fought restraint when the physician attempted to calm him. Then—"Soldiers! Dear God, soldiers!"

Hands clasped over her mouth; his wife anxiously watched the fit.

Tom and Jeremy tried to aid the doctor and calm Oswell, but to no avail. Oswell loudly cursed *Royalists* before his words became jumbled again. A loud gasp for air, his eyes widened, and face became deathly white. A huff of exhale, and he became still. Vacant eyes stared up.

The doctor felt for a pulse. "He's dead," he somberly pronounced.

Mistress Oswell fainted. Godwin lifted her into a chair for the doctor to tend her. Samantha's knees buckled, which forced her to sit on a footstool near the sofa. Anne muttered a silent tearful prayer.

Godwin spoke to Tom and Jeremy. "Take his body to my room for proper dispensation." He approached Samantha. "I will send for the undertaker." She simply nodded.

Anne sat on the floor beside Samantha. "We must pray for my father and Henry," she spoke in a breathy tone of grief.

Chapter 5

MEANWHILE, AT WALCOTT'S FARM, HOWARD AND HENRY prepared the wagon for departure. The sun sank behind the horizon, leaving behind the gray haze of early evening. Henry placed a three-foot pole with a hook into a slot on the front of the wagon. He hung a small brass lantern with a candle inside on the hook then used a strap to secure it to the pole.

Howard peeked around the corner of the barn. He nearly ducked back before he recognized Walcott.

The mayor carried a satchel. "There is word of Royalists scouring the countryside looking for *our* friends. I brought these. Already loaded with a single shot." He pulled out two flintlock pistols.

"We anticipated trouble after the encounter with Gilmore." Howard tucked the pistol in his belt. Henry placed one on the wagon seat.

"Not like this. Miller stopped by with news that Oswell's home was burned to the ground. There is no sign of him or his wife."

"Good Lord." Howard spoke a word of prayer. Both Walcott and Henry respectfully lowered their heads and echoed "*amen*" when Howard concluded.

"Where is Miller now?" asked Henry.

"Riding to warn others. It may be best to forego the delivery."

"No, they must be warned," said Howard. "We shall give them supplies for a journey."

"What if you encounter the Royalists and are recognized?" Walcott continued his argument.

"I thought of that. So, I bought two black scarves while in town," began Howard. "Observe the one Henry is wearing around his neck. He can pull it up to conceal the lower part of his face, while his hat drawn down over his forehead. This way, he can still see to drive."

"And you?"

"I removed my white cleric collar to appear in all black." Howard held up a black scarf with slits. "I shall use it as a mask." He removed his hat and tied the scarf around his face, so the slits allowed him to see. He replaced his hat. "If seen, we will be mistaken for highwaymen."

"We should be going." Henry pulled up the scarf then climbed onto the driver's seat. Howard mounted his horse.

"God protect you both." Walcott moved aside for them to leave.

Henry took the lead. He headed into the forest. It grew darker the further they traveled. Once safely away from Walcott's farm, he struck a match to light the candle inside the lantern. It provided enough light for him to see just beyond the horse.

Howard drew alongside the wagon. "Are you sure light is a good idea?"

"If I want to avoid ruts and obstacles."

"How far is it?"

"About twenty minutes. Longer if I can't see clearly."

Howard drew back to keep the rear guard.

Twenty minutes later, a faint glow of light shown through a thicket. Henry stopped the cart and quickly blew out the candle.

Howard reined his horse near the front of the wagon. "I smell smoke."

"Aye. That light is coming from where the cottage should be."

Howard kicked his horse to ride toward the light.

"Careful!" Henry snapped the reins for the cart horse to move quickly.

Howard roughly stopped his horse. The animal slightly reared at the suddenness. Flickering flames came from various parts of a mostly burnt cottage. He dismounted to begin a search. "Jack!"

Henry grabbed the lantern to join Howard. "Let's hope no one was inside."

"God forbid!"

Both searched the perimeter.

"Anything?" Howard called to Henry.

"Only smoldering wood at this end." Henry kicked aside burned timbers and rubble. He held the lantern to look for signs of life. He stepped on something and moved his foot to bend down for a better view. A lump rose in his throat when he picked up a fire damaged toy horse.

"What have you found?"

Henry showed Howard. "This."

Howard balked in recognition. "You don't think the little girl … they were all inside?"

"We need the light of day to determine that."

"There must be something more to tell us yea or nay!"

Henry put the toy in his pocket to continue the search. "Here!" he called over Howard. "Tracks." He knelt and held the light for closer inspection. "Foot and horse lead north."

"Which may mean they were captured and not inside," said Howard.

"Possible. Either way, it is too dangerous to stay here any longer."

As they left the area, Henry turned in the driver's seat to ask, "What about these supplies? Return them to Walcott?"

"No. I have an idea. Can you find the way to Maggie Reynold's home from here?"

"Aye."

Taking the long way around Walcott's farm, Henry steered the cart to the opposite side of the village to the blacksmith's shop. Being well past supper, the forge was closed. Dim light came from inside the house. Howard signaled Henry to stop, and both dismounted.

"Quietly unhitch the horse. We shall leave the cart," Howard whispered to Henry.

As silently as possible, they undid the harness. After he led the horse into the shadows, Henry mounted. Howard remained by the wagon. He picked up a few rocks and threw them at the front door. He grabbed the reins of his horse just as the door opened. The blacksmith appeared in the threshold with Maggie right behind him.

"Who are you?" the blacksmith demanded.

Howard vaulted into the saddle. "A gift. From those who care." He wheeled his horse around to gallop off into the darkness. He drew rein to join Henry in the woods yet still able to see the house. The blacksmith and Maggie rummaged through the cart. They heard shouts of joy and praise. The blacksmith turned in direction Howard rode to shout.

"Thank you! Whoever you are."

"At least some good happened," droned Henry.

"God always works things for good. Now, come. Our work is done this night."

Not far from the blacksmith's forge, they reached a fork in the road. Sudden shouts came from behind.

"You, there! Stop and be identified."

"Royalists," Henry said in warning. They kicked the horses into a gallop.

"Stop! In the name of the King."

Howard glanced back. "They're gaining!"

"Follow me." Henry turned his horse into the woods.

Howard veered off the road right behind Henry. A shot narrowly missed him and struck a tree. They pushed the horses through the forest. More shouts came from the soldiers. Another shot. Another near miss.

"We need to get to safety!" Howard yelled.

Henry jerked the reins to alter direction down a steep incline. When his horse hesitated, Howard snapped the reins for obedience. It slid down the incline and slightly stumbled at the bottom. He managed to stay seated and right the startled animal.

"In here!" Henry called in a harsh whisper.

Howard joined Henry under an earthen hollowed portion of the incline which they descended. The question on his lips unspoken when Henry placed a gloved finger to his lips for silence. At that moment, they heard horses overhead. Three distinct voices spoke.

"Where did they go?"

"I don't know."

"They disappeared," marvel the third voice.

"Quiet!" commanded the first. For a few moments nothing was said.

"The forest swallowed them," the third again spoke with awe.

"Nonsense. We should hear horse or terrain noise."

"I hear nothing," said the second.

"The locals are right. The woods are haunted, so they disappeared like a phantom without a trace!" insisted the third.

"You are too easily deceived," chided the first.

"Then where are they?"

"Come. We'll find them in the morning."

Henry and Howard waited ten minutes before leaving.

"How did you find this hollow so quickly?" Howard asked.

Henry chuckled. "I grew up in these woods. As grandfather used to say, *A good bailiff knows every inch of the estate he manages.* He passed that knowledge down to my father, and then to me."

Chapter 6

AN HOUR LATER, HENRY AND HOWARD DISMOUNTED AT FOXGLEN stables. Henry spoke to Jeremy while Howard headed for the house. When he entered the kitchen, the maids cried out in fright.

"Here now! Begone, you thieving bandit!" Cookie reached for a cleaver.

"Cookie! Easy!" Howard hastily said in defense.

"Reverend? Is that you?" she asked at recognizing the voice.

Henry quickly arrived to say, "The mask!"

"Oh." Howard removed his hat and took off the mask. "A little protection for our night's venture of delivering supplies," he explained. He stuffed the mask in a doublet pocket.

Relieved, Cookie set the cleaver on the table. "You missed supper, but I can bring you some soup."

"Aye, thank you. Have Samantha and Anne retired?"

"Not after the undertaker was here."

"What?" Stunned, Howard seized Cookie to stop her fetching the soup.

"It's been a frightful evening. You best speak to them. In the study."

Howard and Henry hastened to the room. Samantha paced while Anne stoked the fire. Both women turned when they entered. Each distressed.

"Father." Anne embraced him.

He felt her tremble. "What happened? Cookie mentioned the undertaker." He held Samantha's hand when she reached for him.

With a shaky voice, Samantha replied, "Jimmy Oswell was killed by soldiers searching for Jack and his family. They burned down his farm."

"But the undertaker was here?" said Henry, a bit confused.

"His wife struggled to bring him to safety. Tom and Jeremy found her and brought them here. His head ..." Samantha couldn't finish, as she motioned to the location of injury on her head.

"Is she still here?" asked Howard.

"No. She left with the undertaker an hour ago." Samantha then asked, "Did you deliver the supplies? How is Jack and the family?"

"We delivered the supplies, though not to the intended recipients," Howard tactfully replied.

His tone and foreboding expression made her wary. "What do you mean?"

"Apparently, they were found."

In dreaded anticipation, Samantha stared at Howard. Her voice barely above a whisper, "Are they—?"

"We don't know."

"We discovered the smoldering remains of the cottage. Tracks led away from it." Henry withdrew the toy from his pocket. "Alas, I found this in the ashes."

Samantha covered her mouth to stifle a sob at sight of the scorched toy she gave Katie. With trembling hands, she took it and wept. Anne comforted her.

"Tracks were made by men and beasts," said Henry.

"It means they may still be alive," Howard offered solace.

"Death and destruction by overzealous brutes! Do you know why?" Samantha hotly confronted Howard.

"Sadly, it is war."

"Not just war. Not according to my father." Samantha retrieved the letter from the desk and thrust it at him. "He wrote about giving *you* instructions. Only failed to disclose exactly what those are."

At the insistent waving of the letter, he took it to read. "I have never seen this nor any idea what he could mean. The wording *I will instruct*

Howard along with the abrupt ending of the letter, suggests an unfulfilled intention."

"Then who sealed the letter if not you?"

Howard turned it over to see the wax seal of Rutherford. "I have no access to your family's signet. Where did you find this?"

When Samantha hesitated to respond, Anne said, "Inside a journal, which was hidden in a compartment of the desk."

"Sir Patrick's journal?" asked Henry, to which Samantha nodded. "Then he sealed it."

"Unfinished?" Samantha shot back.

"The means of discovery should tell you I have no knowledge of this," Howard said.

Samantha took back the letter yet would not be put off. "Did my father ever speak to you about the circumstances surrounding my marriage?"

To this, Howard clamped his mouth shut, unwilling to answer.

"He did!" she declared.

"In general terms, nothing specific. Nor do I find it connected to our current situation."

"Oh, really? Married to a Royalist while trying to maintain a Parliament house?" she challenged with high sarcasm.

Howard's shoulders sagged, cornered by the stinging rebuff. "Please, sit, and I will tell what I know."

Samantha perched on a chair beside the hearth. Her face set, and the letter on her lap.

"I should leave." Henry headed for the door.

"No, Henry. Stay. This concerns Foxglen," Samantha said.

Howard proceeded with the explanation. "A few months prior to the wedding, Sir Patrick came to me extremely upset. For days, he had been unable to sleep or eat. His heart and mind deeply troubled."

"Aye," Samantha began in remembrance, "He seemed totally out of sorts, only dismissed it as preoccupation with the events in Parliament."

"Partly. However, the most disturbing aspect dealt with Lord Kyle."

"My father-in-law," chided Samantha.

Howard ignored her comment to continue. "I am ignorant of what took place between him and Lord Kyle. I only know the enforced agreement of your marriage had a connection to your grandfather's past."

"Father mentioned so in the letter."

Again, Howard proceeded without response to her comment. "Sir Patrick endured many sleepless nights until he sought me out for guidance on how to proceed. When I pressed him for more details, he refused to betray his father's confidence. Based upon what he did disclose, I advised him to pray, seek God, and act in the best interest of his family. A week later, he told me of his intent to annul the contract. Alas, Lord Kyle got wind of it, and took swift action to prevent the disillusionment."

Her ire stirred and she demanded, "What could he do to prevent a duke from acting in the best interest of his family?"

Howard sat in the opposite chair, his tone and face firm. "Remember, Lord Kyle is Royal Keeper of The Muse. He has the King's ear. Whatever the past event, it carries enough importance to be used as blackmail."

At the startling news, Samantha read aloud, "'*all my efforts must be to preserve our family. To that end, I have been forced to agree to your marriage. Please, understand, it was not my desire to make such a union for you, rather one of necessity. Our family has already lost much. To avoid utter ruin, I went against my conscience and heart.*'" In dreaded conclusion she said, "My marriage to keep grandfather's past buried."

"Aye. The repercussions have reached across generations. That is what deeply troubled your father. Despite ignorance of his declared desire to impart instructions to me, I have followed Duncan's request to act as guardian since your arrival at Foxglen."

"Duncan?" she asked, surprised by the revelation.

"After assuming the title Duke of Rutherford, he had to fulfill the contract. He may hold the answers since the letter bears the signet."

She scowled in annoyance. "A little late for my brother's help since I am married!"

Anne approached. Until that moment, she silently observed. "We are both here because Duncan did not want you to be left alone. To be defenseless."

Samantha held Anne's hand. "I am thankful for your presence. Both of you. I only wish I had known before." A mischievous smile appeared. "Being raised with two brothers, I am hardly defenseless. I can keep pace with them all day on a horse and cross blades."

"Do not be so arrogant," began Howard in warning. "Where politics and scheming machinations are concerned, you have not Duncan's legal education nor the Rory's military training."

Angry, Samantha rose and held up the scorched toy. "Neither of my brothers are here to protect against marauding soldiers! Such responsibility has fallen to me as mistress of Foxglen."

"We must take a different approach. One that will keep Rutherford safe while not arousing Royalist suspicion and place you in danger with your husband and father-in-law," Howard slyly countered.

"The Reverend's right, my lady. After tonight, we should be very careful," said Henry. He motioned to the toy horse.

Samantha grew visibly upset in regard of the toy. "However, we decide to proceed, I will be better prepared against the Royalists!"

Howard gently took hold of her arm. "Enough for one night. We all need rest for our minds, hearts, and spirits. Tomorrow, we shall consider actions beyond rationing."

Passing Henry on the way out, Samantha whispered to him, "Dawn. Cellar drill."

Henry made the slightest nod.

After seeing Samantha to her room, Anne hesitated to retire. "Father," she said reticent.

He gently lifted her chin. "What is it, child?"

She spoke in a low confidential tone. "If you know why Sir Patrick acted, please, tell her. She needs to know. Lives depend upon her."

"I answered truthfully about Sir Patrick."

"But you said Duncan sealed the letter. There must be more than you told," she insisted.

"I *surmised* he did so. Since Patrick did not finish what he intended, it had to be Duncan. He is the only one who could or would use the signet."

She scowled, a rare sight for Anne, which made Howard concerned.

"All this must be horribly difficult for you."

"I am concerned for Samantha. She is forced to act without complete knowledge."

He somberly sighed. "I can only provide what information I am able."

This time her expression contained anger. "Shall I tell her about a letter I saw written in your hand addressed to Duncan?"

Irked, Howard drew Anne into her chamber. "Beware, child. There are forces at work that neither you nor Samantha are aware of."

"Really? With war raging across the country and now death in Lincolnshire?"

"Anne," Howard sternly warned.

At his rebuke, her anger turned to regret. "I fear for her. For everyone at Foxglen."

He tightly held her hands. "You must trust me." He again lifted her head. "I will tell you this, Duncan is as concerned for your safety and well-being, as for his sister."

She bashfully blushed and grinned.

He smiled at the reaction. "It is difficult to fancy someone during a time of war. For both involved." When her blush deepened, her said, "Be at ease and sleep, my child." He kissed her on the forehead and left.

Instead of retiring, Samantha sat at the writing table to reread her father's letter and grandfather's second journal. Tone of the letter suggested a recent event, thus she started from the latter entries to read backwards. She stopped upon seeing the words Foxhill and Foxmeath. Reading further, her mouth gaped at one entry by her grandfather.

Although the charge is preposterous, there can be no recourse until evidence is uncovered to connect Kyle to this grievous action. Howbeit, the loss of Foxhill and Foxmeath seems enough to satisfy His Majesty. On that, I must be content, else lead the family to total ruin. If only Buckingham had not acted foolishly for the Popish queen, this whole affair could have been avoided. God help us.

She flipped back and forth through the journal for more entries to discern exactly what transpired. All proved cryptic in alluding to some scandal involving the late Duke of Buckingham, Lord Kyle, and her grandfather. With sudden thought, she snatched up her father's letter to read aloud, "'*all my efforts must be to preserve our family. To that end, I have been forced to agree to your marriage. Please, understand, it was not my desire to make such a union for you, rather one of necessity. Our family has already lost much. To avoid utter ruin, I went against my conscience and heart.*'"

The letter slipped from her hand, as she sat back to absorb the horrid thought. Under her breath she gave voice to it; "Confiscation of the estates satisfied the King, but not Lord Kyle." She swallowed back anger at a disturbing thought. "Now, he has Foxglen through me!"

She swiftly crossed to the window to look up at the stars. "Oh, Lord, help me. Let justice be done for my family." She glanced back to her wardrobe. Hastened to open it, and from a concealed compartment in the door, withdrew a sword. "For right. For truth. For all," she quoted the family motto.

Chapter 7

EARLY THE FOLLOWING MORNING, HOWARD PROCEEDED downstairs. He found neither Samantha nor Anne in their chamber. He searched the study and drawing room, yet again, found no one. At such an early hour, he knew the kitchen staff would already be hard at work. He discovered Anne seated at the kitchen table as activity of breakfast preparation took place around her.

She bolted up at sight of him. "Father! Good morning." Her voice rose and fell with nervousness.

Her skittishness made him skeptical. "You are up rather early."

"Morning ale, Reverend." Cookie offered him a tankard.

He took a drink, although his focus remained on Anne. "Where is Samantha?" He barely finished the question when the sound of clanking metal echoed in the kitchen. Not from utensils or pans. He listened to determine where the noise came from. He noticed the interior cellar door open. He put down the ale to approach the door and listen. "Sounds like swordplay. But why is it coming from the cellar?"

Anne balked at his inquiry. Unable to reply, she simply shook her head in pretense of ignorance.

"Child, you are not a good liar."

"Samantha is down there."

Howard ignored Anne's protest to descend the cellar stairs. He heard, then saw, Henry with Samantha. She wore breeches and doublet to engage Henry in swordplay.

"What is going on?"

They disengaged at the question. Howard stood braced in a fatherly stance of disapproval. A fretful Anne appeared behind him.

"I asked a question," Howard demanded of Henry.

Samantha stopped Henry from answering to reply. "A fencing lesson. Or more rightly, sharpening my skills with practice."

Howard's admonishing glare again found Henry. Samantha came to the bailiff's defense.

"Henry has helped me since childhood whenever we visited Foxglen. He also told me about eluding a Royalist patrol last night. A detail you forgot to mention."

"We emerged unscathed," Howard insisted. "Yet, this …"

"Is my duty! Something you cannot prevent." His rigid features made her amend the harsh tone. "I greatly appreciate your aid and counsel." She took Howard's hand. "Please, let us not quarrel. We must be united. Can you agree to that?"

"Aye. To that I can wholeheartedly agree."

Samantha accepted a towel from Henry to wipe the sweat off her face. "Will you meet with more parishioners today?"

"In truth, I rose early to find Henry for a trip to town. I'm sure the excitement of last night will have tongues wagging."

"Excellent idea." She then said to Henry, "I shall change for the ride to town. Have the horses ready."

While Anne followed Samantha from the cellar, Henry approached Howard. "She is good with a sword."

"Let us pray there is never a time she needs to use it for real combat."

"We prayed to avoid war. Yet since it came, there is no harm in being prepared. You have even preached on that subject."

After breakfast, Howard, Samantha, and Henry arrived at the Dove Cottage Inn. Situated on the north side, the complex consisted of a three-story main building, a large walled-in rear yard with corral, stables, chicken coop, and private well. This showed the prosperity of the village's most visited inn.

She wore a plain riding habit with hat and gloves. "Master Duffy does not appear to be in want of patrons." She accepted Howard's help to dismount from the side-saddle.

"Royalists," Henry spoke in warning. He indicated the calvary mounts.

"Their presence should not deter us," she said.

"No, merely a sign to act with caution," said Howard.

Henry held open the door. Upon sight of Samantha, Duffy, the innkeeper rushed over. A vigorous, heavy-set man with gray hair.

"My lady! This is a pleasure. Reverend." He led them to a nearby table. He quickly used a towel to wipe off the crumbs from an earlier occupant. "What can I get you? Breakfast? Morning ale?"

"Morning ale for three. Do I smell Mistress Duffy's apple bread?"

"Indeed. I will bring a loaf with the ale." Duffy widely smiled.

Others at breakfast included three soldiers. They sat opposite Samantha and her companions, though not paying attention to the new arrivals. They continued to engage in heated conversation.

"I tell you it is haunted! There is no other way to disappear like that," one insisted.

"You're daft!" chided another.

Recognizing the voices, Henry carefully nudged Howard. "Our pursuers," he whispered.

The soldiers continued speaking, still unaware of being observed.

"He may be right," the second said. "There are local tales of ghosts and phantoms."

Lieutenant Gilmore entered. At first, he didn't notice Samantha, rather spoke to the soldiers. "You three! Back to duty."

"Sir, we just came off night patrol for breakfast," said the first.

"Have you given a report to Sergeant Breck?"

"He wasn't awake, so we came to eat."

"He is awake now. Off with you."

With plates nearly empty, the soldiers left. In turning, Gilmore spied Samantha.

"Lady Hedgepeth." He presented himself with the typical Cavalier air. "What brings you to town?"

"After the deplorable actions of last evening, I came to offer reassurance."

"You heard about this rogue roaming the countryside?" he asked, intrigued.

"What rogue?"

Howard offered a stalling cough that caught Gilmore's attention. "My throat is parched from our ride," he spoke to the lieutenant's quizzical glance. "Thank you, Duffy." He accepted a tankard and took a long drink.

Gilmore again directed his question to Samantha. "What else would bring you to the village but news of this rogue?"

"To comfort Mistress Oswell. How horrible to be attacked in one's home at night by brigands." She returned his steady gaze, to boldly ask, "Have you not heard of the unfortunate incident by marauding soldiers?"

Henry choked on his drink. "I drank too fast," he said when Gilmore looked at him.

Gilmore stiffened. "My lady, there are no marauders. Only soldiers performing their duty of hunting for deserters in a time of war. Remember, I approached you about them." His voice rose above the din of those assembled in the dining room. "And warned all about the dangers of harboring fugitives from the King's justice!"

Irate, Samantha stood. "Does the King's justice include looting, burning, and murder?"

"Murder?" Gilmore repeated in stunned wariness. "What do you mean?"

Henry quickly placed himself between Gilmore and Samantha when the lieutenant took a step too close.

"Jimmy Oswell died of injuries suffered during the unprovoked attack. That, Lieutenant, is murder!" she hotly replied.

Gilmore's jowls flexed in a display of intense anger. He gripped the hilt of his sword.

Howard rose to defend Samantha. "Take care, Lieutenant. Remember to whom you speak."

Gilmore marched from the inn.

Duffy returned with the bread. Mable, his wife, accompanied him. He spoke when they settled down at the table again. "That lieutenant is a tough unfeeling sort. Since the soldiers arrived, tension in the village has escalated. What happened to Jimmy has everyone on edge."

"Except the Reynolds," said Mabel.

Samantha swallowed a bite of bread before asking, "Why them?"

Mabel eagerly answered. "Some mysterious stranger left an entire wagon of food and supplies at the forge last night. He was there one moment then disappeared into the darkness on a black horse. A phantom figure."

"Woman," scolded Duffy.

"I'm only repeating what Maggie called him. A *phantom*," she spoke the last sentence to Samantha.

Both Henry and Howard fought to keep any reaction from being seen by eating bread and drinking ale. Samantha noticed their efforts yet spoke to Mabel and Duffy.

"I came to bolster spirits. Mistress Oswell challenged my word about Rutherford," her voice slightly choked, which made her continue with determination "I want to reassure everyone that I shall carry on just as my grandfather and father did to protect and care for those in my charge."

"You will find many stanchly loyal to Rutherford. Us included," said Duffy.

Samantha's smiled filled with gratitude. "Thank you. Now, we shall finish this delicious bread and continue the purpose for which we came."

During the morning, Samantha, Howard, and Henry made various stops in the village. They first called upon the Reynolds. The couple eagerly shared the story of their good fortune. Afterward, they visited the doctor, various merchants, and finally Mayor Walcott.

Riding from Walcott's farm, Samantha spoke to Howard. "It appears word of this benevolent *phantom* has spread throughout the village. It has even provided a ray of hope amid gloom."

"Purely unintentional on our part. Yet, divinely used," Howard admitted.

"*We must take a different approach. One that will keep Rutherford safe and not arouse Royalist suspicion,*" Henry quoted. "That is what you said last night, is it not, Reverend?"

Howard's brows grew level at the quote of his own words. "Such a course as that will require much prayer and consideration."

"By the look of Gilmore, we may not have time."

Samantha raised a hand to pause Henry's argument. "If anyone realizes the importance of prayer joined with action, it is Howard."

"I shall consult Scripture immediately upon our return."

For hour upon hour, Howard searched the Scriptures. He pondered passages, prayed, and looked for more answers. Supper, followed by dinner, went untouched. Finally, near time to retire, Samantha and Anne entered the study. He appeared to be asleep in a chair by the fire.

Anne gently touched his shoulder. "Father?"

He sat up. It took a moment to realize who spoke. "Anne. I was deep in prayer." He noticed the darkness. Several candles illuminated the room. "What time is it?"

"The day is spent and servants in bed," replied Samantha. "Have you found the answer?"

He crossed to a table and picked up a Bible. "Aye. It was a topic your father and I spoke of often, and why he diligently sought to avoid war. In the book of First Samuel, God told Samuel to anoint David king of Israel, although Saul still reigned. Despite the Divine anointing, David did not usurp Saul, rather waited for his time. However, Saul pursued David to kill him and maintain the throne. During all those years of surviving confrontations, David never wanted to harm Saul. When Saul arrived in the cave, where David hid, it presented the perfect opportunity to kill him. Instead, David only cut off a piece of Saul's garment."

"So?" Samantha asked when Howard thoughtfully paused.

"Your father wanted to emulate David in his approach to King Charles. To bring the King into alignment with Parliament for the good of England. Alas, Charles would have none of it. His dismissal of Parliament, and threat of war, forced Patrick, and others, to take up arms in defense. The same as David did when Saul's forces came after his people. Like David, Patrick acted to protect, not dethrone. That would happen in God's timing. Both for David, and now."

Samantha chewed on her thumbnail as she listened. "I assume you mean for me to apply the same principle of protection and provision."

"You already started with rationing for provision and standing up to Lieutenant Gilmore to defend your people. Now, to further the cause and bring hope, *The Phantom* will join the effort to protect and provide." He picked up the black scarf that laid on the table and put it on.

Chapter 8

GROUND MIST ROSE TO MEET THE RISING SUN ON THE LATE October day. A man drove a heavily laden cart on the main road through Lincolnshire. He was a tall robust man of thirty with a thick head of flaxen hair, beard, and mustache. A pair of cobalt eyes nervously glanced at the Cavalier escort. Two rode ahead of the cart; two behind, and two alongside.

"Lieutenant! The horse is growing tired," he shouted. His accent local to Lincolnshire.

The lieutenant slowed his horse to turn in the saddle. "We will not stop until we reach the inn. It is your job to keep the beast going."

"This load needs two horses," he chided.

The lieutenant rode back to confront the driver. "You will do as your told, Miller! Or risk the consequences for failure to aid your king."

Miller bit back a reply to make a curt nod.

The lieutenant rejoined the lead. "Sergeant, how much further to the inn?"

"A mile, maybe a little more. *If* his directions are correct."

"He will be flogged if they are not."

"Let us hope we do not run afoul of The Phantom before we reach the inn."

"Six against one will see the end of this rebellious outlaw," boasted the lieutenant.

53

They only travelled a hundred yards further when two shots rang out. The lieutenant unhorsed when struck in the upper chest. A Cavalier riding alongside the cart, slumped in the saddle before he fell off wounded.

Two riders emerged from the trees with swords drawn. Both dressed in black from head to toe. One wore a masked from the bridge of his nose to under his hat. The other had a kerchief which covered his mouth and chin.

"The Phantom!" cried the sergeant. "Protect the cart!"

A Cavalier jumped from his horse onto the driver's seat. Miller wouldn't yield control. They fought. A blow to the face sent the Cavalier reeling. He managed to catch his balance and remain on the cart. He withdrew a dagger and knifed Miller, who fell to the floorboard clenching his abdomen. The Cavalier reached over a huddled Miller for the reins. He gasped when a sword sliced across his back. He fell to the road between the wagon and horse. Startled, the horse bolted. Howard brought his horse beside the cob to grab the harness to slow the cart.

"Look out!" he shouted in warning to his companion.

Henry easily repelled the sergeant's attack. A deep cut to the sword hand, and the sergeant lost his weapon. Unarmed, he sent his horse directly at Henry with the intent to ram. Keen to the effort, Henry made his horse rear. This action caused the sergeant's horse to shy and bolt. Thrown, the sergeant was rendered unconscious upon impact with the ground.

"Behind you!" Henry returned the warning.

Howard parried an attack. Before the second rear guard joined the fray, a shot rang out. He grabbed his shoulder, which pulled the reins. The horse skidded off balance and fell, which pinned him underneath and rendered him unconscious. Loosed, the horse rose and galloped off.

Howard wounded the final Cavalier.

"Are you hurt?" Henry holstered the pistol in his belt with the other one used earlier.

"No. Thanks to you."

"Help." Miller used the seat to pull himself up off the floorboard.

"Miller? What are you doing here?" asked Howard.

"How do you know my name?"

"We know all those faithful to the cause of justice."

"They threatened my family if I didn't drive the cart."

Henry lifted the canvas. "Appears to be a wagon of military supplies."

"Stolen from Parliament. Or so, I heard them say," said Miller. He groaned in pain.

"What do we do with them?" Henry asked Howard about the Royalists.

"Nothing. We must get Miller to safety and secure the wagon." Howard moved from his horse to the driver's seat. Henry grabbed the reins of Howard's horse to follow.

Almost recklessly, he drove the wagon. Nearing the outskirts of town, he steered off the road to approach the rear of the Dove Cottage inn. He stopped the wagon outside the back gate. He spied a young man collecting wood from a wood pile. "Simon!"

Simon dropped the wood to exit the gate. "What happened?"

"Royalists."

Simon stopped Howard from dismounting the wagon. "No! Some are here. They spent the night."

"Miller is wounded."

"He can hide in the tack shed." Simon motioned to a small building just inside the fence. He helped Miller down. "Move the wagon behind the stable so it can't be seen."

Howard secured the wagon before he and Henry carefully entered the tack shed. Miller lay on a small cot. Simon lit a candle.

"I'll fetch Mother." Simon gave the candle to Henry.

Henry held the light for Howard to examine Miller's wound. "How bad is it?"

"Doesn't appear too serious."

"I didn't want to do it. I swear! They threatened my family if I didn't replace the driver," Miller insisted through clenched teeth of pain.

"Why didn't one of them drive the wagon?" asked Henry.

"I don't know the details. They arrived at the mill and woke us with curses and threats."

"Are any Royalists still at the mill?"

Miller shook his head in distress, both from pain of the wound and anxiety. "No. When I agreed, they spared them."

"Enough questions," Howard told Henry, then to Miller, "Rest. Be easy of mind."

Simon returned with Mabel and Duffy.

"Miller?" asked Duffy.

"They made me," Miller repeated with deep regret.

"Hush now," Mabel said. "All of you, out. Let me tend him."

Howard and Henry carefully left the shed then exited the back gate. Duffy's question stopped their departure.

"What does he mean they made him?"

Howard sneered with a disgust. "They threatened his family if he did not replace the driver. The reason is unknown. Thankfully those drunken Royalists you housed alerted us to the stolen cargo."

"Won't do any good for them to see you here. I heard them stirring about. They're supposed to relieve the York crew to finish the journey to Leicester."

"I thought York stood for Parliament because of Fairfax?" asked Henry.

Duffy huffed with annoyance. "These days, everyone changes sides like the wind. Even here. Because of Foxglen, more Royalists patrol the shire. Didn't used to be like that under the late duke, before—"

"We understand," Howard firmly interrupted.

"I should send word to Gertie. She and the boys must be worried," said Duffy.

"Only that he is safe and will return when he can. Word of this will spread quickly. No need to add undo anxiety by having his state included in the venture," Howard sternly spoke.

"People who know Miller will assume it happened under duress," Duffy argued.

"When everyone changes sides like the wind?" Henry quoted Duffy.

Duffy frowned and nodded. "Aye, best keep his name clear." He then asked Howard, "What about the goods?"

He slyly grinned. "None will arrive in Leicester rather be diverted back to whom it belongs." He clapped Duffy's shoulder. "See Miller is well cared for."

Henry took the lead with Howard following with the cart. They headed west and skirted the edge of the forest. They turned onto a smaller road that branched off the main highway.

Howard steered the wagon to the northeast around the other buildings to the rear of Foxglen. An open, stair-stepped terrace of hedges and gardens lead to a small dock. Further south of the terrace was the manor's spring over which was built a small enclosure for the storing of butter and milk. The spring was a short walk from the manor's kitchen in the rear of the southwest wing. Skillfully, he drove the horses as close to the dock as possible. A flatboat moored to the dock. He jumped down from the driver's seat.

"Let us see exactly what we have." He and Henry untied the canvas to view the contents. "Four kegs of gun powder. No doubt for artillery. This is saltpeter. Five boxes of musket balls."

"All very useful indeed," said Henry.

"Ah!" Howard smiled. "Wheat, potatoes, and onions. These we shall keep. Fetch men to help load the boat. We must act quickly."

Howard unloaded the food supplies to make closer inspection of the items. Hearing a female voice, he bolted up from placing down the potatoes.

"What have you found?" Samantha wore a cloak with hood up.

Upon seeing her, Howard scowled at Henry. The latter heaved a hapless shrug as he and the men began transferring the military supplies from the cart to boat.

"Do not be cross with Henry." She knelt to inspect the items already unloaded. "The food will be helpful. Henry said these were captured from Parliament. I would know if there were anything personal that could bring comfort."

Howard drew her aside to speak privately. "Doubtful anything of a personal nature would be transported to a garrison."

"But—"

"We must make haste. The risk of discovery is too great. Trust me," he added when she bit her thumbnail, a sign of distress.

"I do. I long for word …" She couldn't finish due to rising emotions.

He embraced her. "There, child. God will protect them. We must remain strong and continue to aid them as best we can. Come. Henry, bring the wheat when finished here."

Howard gave Samantha a small sack of onions while he carried the large sack of potatoes. They climbed the terrace steps to the back of the great manor house. The kitchen buzzed with activity in preparation for the evening meal.

"These should keep you happy, Cookie." Howard placed the potatoes on the main preparation table beside the onions Samantha put down.

"Oh, aye, sir!" Cookie cheered.

"Use them sparingly," Samantha said.

"Aye, my lady."

In the hallway outside the kitchen, they heard commotion from the front of the house; mostly male voices, raised and angry, though followed by an uneasy female.

"Quickly! Leave," Samantha urged Howard. She threw off her cloak.

He went back to the kitchen, while she headed toward the arguing. In the foyer, Anne and Godwin debated with Lieutenant Gilmore. Two soldiers stood behind him.

"What is the meaning of this intrusion?" she demanded.

Gilmore looked at Samantha with haunter. "You are dressed for the day while your maid remains in a dressing gown?" he spoke about Anne.

"Work on such a large estate often requires early mornings and late nights. However, you have not answered my question, Lieutenant."

From a room off the foyer, Howard appeared. He carried an open book. "Here now, what is going on? Why all this ruckus? I am studying for Sunday's sermon."

Gilmore glanced up and down at Howard. "Studying with dirty boots?" he inquired with skepticism.

"I returned a short while ago from spending the night comforting a family after passing of their mother. Now, what could you want at this early hour, Lieutenant?" Howard challenged.

Gilmore's keen gaze shifted between Howard and Samantha. "I seek those responsible for an attack upon soldiers and looting of military supplies."

"When did this happen?" Howard loudly closed the book to draw Gilmore's marked attention from Samantha.

"Just prior to dawn. Perhaps, near the time you returned, Reverend."

Howard heaved a casual shrug. "I neither heard nor saw any attack or commotion on my return from the village."

"Strange. Since six soldiers were wounded."

Anne made an impulsive gasp. Samantha quickly took hold of Anne's shoulder. She spoke to Gilmore's piqued interest. "Violence, even talk of it, distresses her. Since Reverend Cunningham has given answer in this matter, it best you leave before causing more upset."

"He has, but you have not. If your ladyship will give me your word—"

"The lady asked you to leave!" chided Godwin. "Now, off with you!"

"My lady," Gilmore spoke in a tone of appeal.

"You have received sufficient answer. Good day, Lieutenant. Godwin." She nodded to the steward.

Godwin stepped between the women and lieutenant. Gilmore slapped his sword and bowed in compliance. After Godwin shut the door, he moved to the window to watch the Royalist departure.

"They are gone."

At Godwin's report, Anne let out a deep, long sigh of relief.

"Courage, Anne," Samantha soothed.

"Courage is something we both need by the look of your hands," Anne replied.

At that moment, Samantha realized she clenched her hands so tightly, the knuckles turned white.

"Let me take your boots, Reverend," Godwin said.

Howard sat on a nearby bench. He put the book aside to hold up each leg for Godwin to remove the boots and wet socks. He noticed the women's disapproval. "Much work last night with the Durants followed by our *diversion* in returning."

"Has the boat launched?" asked Samantha.

Howard nodded, more interested in his freed toes. "I need dry socks."

Godwin removed a pair of slippers from a compartment under the hall tree. "These should keep your feet from getting cold while I fetch the socks and clean shoes."

"Thank you, Godwin." Howard rose to speak confidentially. "Miller became wounded, but his family safe."

"Miller?" echoed Samantha with alarm.

"They forced him to drive the cart. Be assured, he will recover."

"What about the Durants? We should send condolences," Anne said to Samantha.

"Without their mother, the little ones can use extra food," said Howard.

"I shall have Cookie send a portion of what was recovered." Samantha sighed with lament. "The shire is becoming unsettled and divided."

"War is a nasty business. We can expect more hostility and division."

"What remedy is there for a divided heart?" she pointedly asked him.

Howard took Samantha's hand to fold them together. "Prayer. Trust God and each other." He ushered Samantha and Anne into the room from which he emerged, a quaint drawing room of warm wood paneling.

Howard read from the Psalms then lead them in prayer for mercy, courage, and strength to face the dangerous time. They finished just when Godwin returned with dry socks, shoes, and to announce breakfast.

Chapter 9

SEVERAL DAYS LATER, THE EARLY MORNING SUN BECAME OBSCURED by clouds threatening rain. Weather did not deter Howard from his appointed course. He rode to a house a mile from the manor on the road to town. By the Tudor construction and similarity to Foxglen, this house belonged to the estate. Unlike the grand manor, the roof was thatched and windows much smaller. Still, the size and location told that whoever occupied it, held an important position.

Howard's knock was answered by Tom. "Is your father awake?"

"Of course, Reverend." Tom stepped aside for Howard to enter. The downstairs consisted of four rooms: living room, dining room, kitchen, and study.

Henry sat at the table eating breakfast. "You wouldn't expect me to sleep in on rent day, would you?" he sarcastically asked Howard.

Howard chuckled. "Do not be too heavy handed with the collections. Many are barely getting by."

"Her ladyship said the same. I will bring the accounting to the manor when finished."

"I'm sure all will be in order. Yet, that is not why I'm here." Howard sat at the table. Tom brought him a tankard of morning ale. He acknowledged it with a nod, though more intent on speaking with Henry. His voice low and cautious. "Duffy sent word that more Royalists are entering the shire since *escapades* have increased. Word is that the war has taken a turn for worse against Parliament."

"Can you really believe what Royalists say?" scoffed Henry.

"Duffy can discern truth from rumor."

Henry made an assenting nod and drank.

"More harassment of folk hereabout," Tom vehemently complained.

"Mind your manners!" Henry stood to cuff his son on the head.

"No, the lad is right. More harassment. And more danger," Howard warned.

Henry resumed his seat. His expression concerned. "You're not suggesting we allow them run roughshod over our people?"

"No. We simply need to be more cautious and judicious in how we act. Samantha is in a delicate position. We must guard that above all else less or everything is lost."

"Duffy might think people of the village change sides like the wind, but not at Foxglen. My grandfather served as first bailiff. Tom will be bailiff after me. Serving the O'Malleys and Rutherford is not just our duty, it's an honor," Henry stoutly declared.

Howard kindly grinned. "There is no doubt of your loyalty or mettle, Henry Wyatt. Nor of Tom and others. I speak in the broader context. Some in the village have succumbed to Royalist coercion, and that you know right well."

"Aye," Henry grumbled. "You propose a meeting?"

Howard nodded. "Tonight. Seven o'clock."

"Same place?"

"Aye. We have been successful there so far."

"Tom, go—" Henry began when Howard interrupted.

"No, I need Tom for something else." He pulled out a sealed letter from his doublet. "As before, there is no address, and I entrust it to you for another safe delivery."

"His Grace." Tom took the letter.

"It is long past time he wrote. Only uncertain if he is back in London."

"I'll find him." Tom fetched his hat, cloak, and sword off the peg in the hall.

"Take Ginger. She's best for long distance," Henry called to his son. Tom shouted an acknowledgement and left through the kitchen door. "How much longer will this madness go on?" he chided in bitter complaint.

"As long as it takes to free us from tyranny, my friend."

"The King doesn't see it that way," Henry groused. He took the plates to the kitchen.

Howard followed. The kitchen was empty. "Where is Mistress Radley?"

Henry heavily frowned with sorrow. "Ben was killed in a skirmish outside York two days ago."

"Merciful heaven. First her husband, now her son." Howard spoke a short prayer to which Henry echoed his *amen*. "I shall call upon her while in the village."

"No, she left yesterday to stay with her daughter in Northampton. I gave her some funds from what I already collected. I noted it in the accounting."

Sounds of hooves made them look out the kitchen window. Tom rode from the stables.

"Lord, protect him," Henry softly spoke the earnest plea.

"He will. Until tonight." Howard donned his hat to leave the kitchen for the front. Banging and shouting at the door made him pause.

Henry rushed to open the door. "Lieutenant Gilmore."

Gilmore pushed past Henry to enter. "Reverend Cunningham. Why are you here?"

"On my daily rounds to visit parishioners."

Gilmore's sneer passed from Howard to Henry. "Who was that leaving just now?"

"My son. I sent him on an errand."

"At a gallop?"

"It's collection day. Some are not so eager to pay rent," Henry coolly replied. "What do you want, Lieutenant?"

"As Foxglen bailiff, you know everyone who lives and works on the estate, correct?"

"Aye, I manage the business affairs," replied Henry, wary.

"Do you also tend to legal matters where the estate is involved?"

Howard's hand on Henry's shoulder stopped the bailiff from answering. "What is the reason for this line of questioning, Lieutenant?"

"Reverend," Gilmore spoke the title with strained patience, "should you not be leaving to continue your visits?"

"When one of my parishioners is being roughly questioned, I remain for moral support." Howard removed his hat. "God pays particular attention to those being abused."

Gilmore's jowl's clenched and eyes narrowed at Howard.

"What legal matter, Lieutenant?" Henry probed.

"By order of the King, locals are to supply goods and money to the Royal army. As bailiff, you are responsible for the collection."

"I have not received such an order."

"Consider yourself informed. One third of what you collect today will be handed over to me tomorrow."

"At that time, will you provide me a copy of the order to include in my accounting for her ladyship?"

Gilmore seized Henry. "Do not press me."

"Lieutenant!" Howard loudly intervened. "Have you a copy of the order on your person to make such a demand?"

Gilmore tried to shove Henry back to confront Howard. However, such a powerful man as Henry Wyatt did not move a step. "Reverend, you try my patience with constant interference."

"I am merely serving in my ecclesiastical capacity to keep the peace. For in truth, if Master Wyatt has not seen it, then neither has Lady Hedgepeth. As wife of *Major Hedgepeth*, she would most certainly have given it to Master Wyatt for collection."

Gilmore stood rigid at the rebuff.

Having the upper hand, Howard further spoke. "You would not wish to wrongly impose upon a Royalist house without proper authorization, now would you, Lieutenant?"

"A proper Royalist house would willingly supply what is needed."

"*If* the request were known. Master Wyatt admitted this is first he heard of the order. He did not refuse, simply requested to see the order for proper implementation."

Gilmore grabbed a hat off a peg in the hall and shoved it into Henry's hand. "Come with me to see her ladyship."

"I'll fetch my horse—"

"You can ride double with me for the short distance!" Gilmore snapped.

At Foxglen, Henry quickly slipped down from behind the saddle to allow Gilmore to dismount. Howard joined them at the front door.

"Wait here," Gilmore ordered his men. He waved Howard to enter first then gave Henry a hard shove to follow. He came last.

"Godwin! Master Godwin." Howard removed his hat and cloak to place on the hall tree.

A maid hurried to greet them. She curtsied. "Reverend. Master Godwin is with her ladyship in the cellar."

Howard motioned for Henry to take the lead. Gilmore hot on the bailiff's heels. Down in the cellar, they found Samantha and Godwin inspecting casks of ale and various other supplies.

"My lady." Henry respectfully approached.

"Henry. Lieutenant Gilmore?" Her gaze briefly passed to Howard, who hung back.

"The lieutenant—" began Henry.

"I am ordered by the King to requisition supplies from the locals. Your bailiff is ill disposed to do so. Although I find ample supplies here," Gilmore rudely chided.

"I did not refuse. I simply asked to see the order. For accounting purposes. Reverend Cunningham can vouch for me," Henry defended himself to Samantha.

"A Royalist house would willingly comply," chided Gilmore.

"A Royalist house acts graciously to those who approach graciously!" Samantha scolded.

Gilmore gripped his sword to maintain decorum. "Will you order your bailiff to turn over one third of the collection or not?"

"You bellow threats at her ladyship and expect a response?" Godwin questioned.

"It appears all your servants are impertinent."

"How my servants behave is none of your concern. However, as any good soldier defends their officer, they defend me. I am sure you can appreciate such loyalty."

"Indeed. Yet you have not answered my question about the *King's* order for requisitions."

"If the King orders it, it shall be done," Samantha willingly said.

Gilmore flashed a smug smile. "So, your bailiff lied. You did receive the order."

"No, I am agreeing based upon *your* word. As for these supplies. This is only a meager portion of what should have been a bountiful harvest. Alas, foul weather, and blights have proved devastating this year. Still," she forestalled Gilmore. "Be good enough to give a copy of the order to Master Wyatt, and he shall proceed to add it to his collection duty today."

Howard's rough cough caught attention. "He has no such order on his person."

"That fact does not invalidate the order!" Gilmore rebuffed. "Hesitancy of all here shall written into my report."

Samantha's ire rose. "Your base behavior shall be included in a letter to my husband. Along with a letter about abuse of the King's order to my father-in-law, Lord Hedgepeth, Royal Keeper of the Muse!"

To this rebuke, all the color drained from Gilmore's face. "Lord Hedgepeth," he fearfully muttered. He clapped his sword and bowed. "My lady. Forgive me. Zeal for duty overshadowed my better judgement."

"That's putting it mildly," Henry made a side comment to Howard.

Samantha snatched a glance to Howard when Gilmore bowed. Howard made a slight nod. She then spoke to Gilmore. "Master Wyatt will proceed with the collection. When you come tomorrow for the King's portion, bring a copy of the order. Good day, Lieutenant." She moved to continue her task with Godwin.

Gilmore left the cellar.

Henry fought laughing.

"Do not be so amused, Henry," Samantha cautioned. "Threats of letters might have stayed him for now, but such demands for future requisitions will be costly for us."

"Aye. Even bartering is more difficult with devastated crops while the livestock grows weaker. Then add this bloody war …"

Samantha raised a hand to stop Henry's reply. "Godwin and I are revising the plan for distribution of what we are able to store."

"If we give the Royalists a third, what will be left?" Godwin asked, greatly concerned.

Henry moved closer to speak confidentially. "When the major announced his departure at the start of war, I made adjustments in the accounting."

Intrigued, Samantha asked, "How so?"

"Two ledgers. One with real figures, the other, well for a time like this. To protect Rutherford. It will be a very *small* third."

Samantha tenderly smiled. "More and more I see why my grandfather chose the Wyatt family as bailiffs. Thank you, Henry."

He grinned, donned his hat, and left.

Chapter 10

BURIED DEEP IN THE FOREST BETWEEN FOXGLEN AND VILLAGE stood an abandoned woodman's cottage. Even at night, overgrowth showed that no one had lived there for many years. However, four tethered horses stood outside. A small amount of light came from inside. Five men gathered around a table upon which sat a solitary lantern. Four wore swords along with a pistol tucked in the belt.

"Miller, you shouldn't be here," Howard mildly scolded.

"Royalists threatened my family. Where else should I be?" Miller winced; his wound still troublesome. He was the only one unarmed.

"He wouldn't let us leave without him," Duffy spoke about himself and Simon.

"He rode double with me to not aggravate his wound," said Simon.

Howard asked Henry, "Are Frank and Joe coming?"

Henry's expression turned somber. "Frank succumbed to his illness earlier today."

The news surprised Howard. "He seemed better when I visited a few days ago."

"He took an unexpected turn this morning. The doctor couldn't bring down the fever. Joe left to help his sister. Her husband was killed two weeks ago during a Royalist raid for supplies."

"God's teeth!" Howard swore. At the stunned look from the others, he apologized. "I'm sorry. There are times the senselessness of this war gets the better of me."

"Just shows you're as fallible as the rest of us, Reverend," Duffy spoke with a wry grin.

"No titles," Howard rebuked. "And my fallibilities are the not reason we meet."

"Is it because of the Royalist collection?" asked Miller.

"In part. Mostly to bolster our solidarity in the face of increasing harassment. It is enough the weather has destroyed crops and caused diseases among people and livestock. The lengthening burden of war places further constraints and pressures on us all."

"You most of all," said Miller.

"No. Her ladyship bears the greatest burden, and threat," Howard grimly said. "Satisfying the Royalists while maintaining the honor of Rutherford."

Duffy scowled with lament. "It seems like a lifetime ago the village thrived under the O'Malleys when the Dukes of Rutherford dealt kindly with us."

"Aye, hard to believe it's scarcely two years," droned Simon.

"She is standing up to the threat!" Henry warmly declared.

"Easy, Henry," soothed Howard. "They meant no offense."

"No, indeed. And you know that right well," insisted Duffy to Henry. "We wouldn't place our lives and businesses in jeopardy if we did not fully support her."

Henry recanted with a nod and murmured, "Aye."

"What more can we do?" asked Miller.

Howard pulled out several folded sheets of paper. He opened them to lay on the table. "These are copies of a code replacing symbols for words. With the Royalists presence growing, we can no longer write clear messages. Each of you take one and hide it in a secure location where only you can find it."

"I assume you have the original." Duffy stuffed a paper into his doublet pocket.

"Aye." Howard then spoke with deadly earnest. "Gentlemen, we must not leave this place without a solemn pledge to support each other,

Rutherford, and Parliament without reservation." He looked at each man. "Do you each pledge, before God, to those conditions? To uphold the pledge to very end? I so pledge." He held out a gloved hand.

"I so pledge!" Henry placed his hand on top of Howard's hand,

"I so pledge!" said Duffy, Simon, and Miller in near unison; their hands linked with Howard and Henry.

Hands remained stacked when Howard lifted his eyes to the ceiling. "Before you, O Lord, we make this pledge for the good of our earthly brethren. Strengthen us with resolve to defend the weak, provide for those in need, and protect those in our charge from unwarranted aggression. Amen."

"Amen," the others echoed.

"Thank you for coming, Miller." Howard patted the man's shoulder. "See he is returned safely," he instructed Simon and Duffy. He and Henry waited for the others to leave.

"You made Miller swear without revealing the key secret," said Henry.

Howard grinned. "What makes you think he doesn't already know? Or at least guessed." He grew deeply thoughtful. "No, it is Gilmore we must keep from making the discovery."

"That will be difficult with more soldiers coming."

"Then we shall try harder and act more clever. Now, I want to visit Frank's family. He was a good godly man."

Near midnight, Howard dismounted at Foxglen stables. He and Henry parted company at the bailiff's house. He didn't bother to wake the groom and tended to the horse before he entered the kitchen. He caught a flash of light before it went dark. He reached for his sword when a female spoke.

"Thank God." Samantha removed the handkerchief she threw over the lantern. She and Anne sat at the kitchen table.

"What are you both doing up at this hour?" Howard removed his hat and cloak to hang on a hook beside the door.

"Waiting for you," replied Samantha.

He paused in removing his sword. "How did you know I went out?"

"I heard you leave," Anne replied. To the fatherly stare, she sheepishly admitted, "I could not sleep. Not after learning about Lieutenant Gilmore's threat to Samantha."

"He was put in his place." Howard sat at the table to help himself to some ale. Cookie always left a pitcher and two tankards on the table.

Banging and shouting came from the front door. Startled, both women jumped while Howard stood to made defense. More noise.

"Quick! Both of you upstairs," he said.

They hastened up the rear stairs while he took the lantern to respond to the banging. He encountered Godwin just outside the kitchen.

The steward hastily donned a dressing gown. "Reverend?"

"Take this." Howard took the pistol from his belt and gave it to Godwin.

The raised voice and command became more distinct once they reached the foyer. "Open in the name of the King!" Gilmore shouted

Howard nodded to Godwin, who in turn complied to unbar and open the door. Three soldiers stood behind Gilmore.

"Lieutenant Gilmore, this is an unwelcomed intrusion!" Godwin scolded.

Gilmore ignored Godwin to confront Howard. "Reverend, according to Sergeant Ryan you were out past curfew." He briefly motioned to one of the men with him.

"Comforting the Kern family. Frank died this evening."

"That is true, sir. We had to let the doctor pass, so he could tend the butcher," Ryan told Gilmore.

Gilmore pursed his lips. Despite the confirmation, he demanded of Howard, "Why did you not report to the night watch when arriving in town?"

"Because the last time I called upon a parishioner past curfew, Sergeant Ryan delayed me for nearly an hour! I could not risk a repeat of that, as time was critical."

"I was just doing my duty, Reverend," Ryan said in defense.

"I understand that. However, souls are of eternal importance. When one is dying, there can be no delay."

Gilmore stopped Ryan from further dispute. Instead, he continued to argue with Howard. "I do not recall you armed the last time you claimed to be visiting a parishioner late at night."

"Last time, you interrupted my study. I had time to remove my sword."

"But not muddy boots."

"That was my fault, Lieutenant," began Godwin. "Household matters diverted my attention from fetching the Reverend clean boots and dry socks as he instructed upon return."

"You too are armed," Gilmore rebuffed.

"Naturally. In such a dangerous time, no one would answer banging and shouting after midnight without arms."

"Lieutenant," began Howard sternly, "your man confirms my story. Before you wake the whole house, I bid you goodnight!"

Howard grabbed the handle from Godwin intent on closing the door. The hasty action made Gilmore take an awkwardly step out of the threshold to avoid being hit by the door. With loud emphasis, Howard drew the bolt. He waited while Godwin went to the drawing room and peeked out the window. He rushed back to report.

"They're gone."

Howard and Godwin barely stepped away from the door when Samantha and Anne descended the main stairs. Samantha held a candle.

"Frank Kern died?" she asked, disturbed.

"Aye. According to Doctor Barton, three more are at risk of succumbing from typhoid."

"Merciful heavens. What more can be done?"

Howard took hold of Samantha to steer her back upstairs. "We are doing all we can. The storehouse, rationing. The rest, is in God's hands."

"Also, give spiritual guidance as needed," Anne added.

"Aye." He smiled at his daughter.

"Sometimes I wish there was more I could do," Samantha said, weary.

"What we are doing brings *hope* to those who have little to none," Howard encouraged.

"On that score, you do more than me," she said with great lament.

"Oh, no," he insisted. "It is to you, the villagers look. Despite marriage to the major, you are sister to the Duke of Rutherford, and defender of all your family has represented these past six decades." Once they reached the top landing, he touched her cheek to look her in the eyes. "Never forget the great honor and responsibility God has given you."

Samantha smiled. "I don't. Yet there are times, I wish to do more. To somehow end this war and return to those simpler days."

"Those things are out of our control. All we can do, is continue the course placed before us. Now, it is late. I for one, am ready for bed."

Chapter 11

SIGNS OF ANOTHER LATE AUTUMN SHOWN IN THE TURNING LEAVES and brisk early November breeze. The final gray light of sunset sunk behind the western horizon. Wearing a cloak with hood up, Samantha watched from the terrace. Her attention shifted between the house and the activity at the dock. She held a sword.

"How goes it?"

The voice made Samantha whirl about, sword ready for defense. "Anne!"

"You look a frightful mess."

Samantha brushed the caked mud off the breeches. "I slipped and fell off the dock." She returned to view the progress. "The boat is launched."

The women heard Howard issue orders. He wore his Phantom disguise. When he reached the terrace, Samantha sheathed her sword.

"Another success," she said.

"You need to be more careful, young lady," he chided. "Mud will be the least of your problem if Gilmore suspects your involvement."

"I have managed to keep him off balance this past year."

"Alas, times have grown more desperate. As such, the Royalists are doggedly determined to find those behind the raids. Anne, take her inside."

"Where are you going?" Samantha asked.

"I have some unfinished business this night."

Before either could ask another question, Howard raced from the terrace.

In the kitchen, Anne told Cookie, "Bring broth and bread for after her ladyship's bath."

"Just broth. Others need the bread more," Samantha disputed.

"What about dinner? I would use the broth for the main soup," asked Cookie.

"Do we have any cider?"

"Aye."

"That will be sufficient until dinner."

"Aye, my lady."

"You really need to eat more," Anne chided, as they climbed the backstairs.

"I eat what is necessary. As for the bath, a basin of water will do for cleaning."

"Water we have plenty of," Anne wryly countered.

"But not soap. We barely have enough hogs to eat much less make soap from the tallow. And what tallow there is, we need for candles."

The statement made Anne stop lighting the third candle. "Fortunately, I started a fire in anticipation of your return. I will lay out your clothes while you undress. Leave the dirty ones on the screen."

Samantha moved behind the dressing screen. A few moments later, she stepped out wearing only her undergarments and went to the hearth.

"As you requested. A towel and sliver of soap by the basin." Anne gathered the soiled garments.

At the basin, Samantha gasped in surprise, and quickly withdrew her hands from the basin. "The water is cold!"

"It must have cooled since I filled the basin earlier." Anne gathered the soiled clothes.

Samantha flinched with each sensation of the cold water. She regarded herself in the small mirror attached to the basin. She touched a few smudges of mud on her face and brushed red strands of fallen hair behind her ears. "I do look a mess."

After washing, she moved to the vanity to sit and brush her hair. She paused to regard the pearl necklace she always wore, only removed for the earlier venture. It lay on the vanity where she left it. Three strands of pearls came together in front held by a large pearl in a silver setting from which hung a teardrop pearl. When she picked it up, vivid memories appeared, as if replaying in the mirror. Only a week married when Lawrence received an urgent summons to duty. She would leave the family home of Foxmoor in a rush. Her dowry to be sent to Foxglen when ready. Despite the urgency of departure, her two older brothers found time to give her gifts. Duncan, the eldest at five years her senior, gave her a horse. Rory, the one closest to her in age, at sixteen months older, gave her the pearl necklace.

Rory held one hand behind his back when he approached. He smiled and said, "I wanted to give you this in private." He brought his hand forward to show he held a round craved box.

Opening the box, she discovered the pearl necklace. "Oh, Rory. It is beautiful. How did you manage to find so magnificent a gift?"

"With father's help. I know Grandmother gave you the single strand you wear when you were five. Only you broke it several times due to daring antics," he teased. "I wanted to give you one more fitting for a woman."

Tears fell. "Oh, Rory, I miss you so."

"Samantha?"

Hearing Anne, Samantha put on the necklace. "Now to dress. The water gave me a chill."

Anne finished lacing the gown when Cookie arrived with a tray.

"There are two biscuits left from yesterday. They will soften up nicely with dunking in the warm cider." Cookie smiled at Samantha. "My lady." She curtsied and left.

Anne served the cider. "Do not underestimate your people. They are more for Rutherford than Hedgepeth."

Samantha sat to accept the cup. "I know. This war has shown a depth of loyalty I could scarcely imagine." She noticed two biscuits on the tea saucer. "You will take one."

"Of whom were you thinking that caused tears? Your husband or brothers?"

Samantha fingered the necklace "My brothers. One week married, the next war." She put down the tea and crossed to the window. "Two years ago, abundant crops and livestock covered the shire. Now, Foxglen barely yields enough to support us and the tenants." She partially glanced back to

Anne. "Howard warned us of rising hostility and deep division. Since then, I have endeavored to maintain the Rutherford name and honor. Yet, I fear no matter who wins, England will never be the same."

Anne comforted Samantha. "Duncan would be proud of you."

"If only I could be sure of that. We left so abruptly. Scarcely any word from him since."

"I am sure," insisted Anne.

"Dear Anne, always the optimist." When Anne shyly smiled, Samantha asked, "How often do you think of Duncan?"

"Perhaps, as often as you," came the demure answer.

"Then every day. While longing for word." Samantha kindly grinned when Anne again grew timid. "Be not shy with me about your feelings for Duncan."

"You speak rightly that we have received little correspondence. As such, I dare not give it more voice than is proper between a maid and duke."

"Oh, posh! You are not a servant. You are my friend. A better one, I could not imagine. Loyalty of heart and purity of character are not solely qualities of rank or station. In fact, I know they are not. My husband and his father prove that." Her tone grew bitter. She shivered and drew her arms around her for comfort.

"Do not dwell on them." Anne paused to listen to a chime. "Come. I hear the clock. Cookie will have dinner ready. I wonder what creative dish she has prepared for us tonight."

In the dining room, the normal three places set and ready. Godwin and Cookie put the food on the table.

"Godwin, has Howard returned?"

"Not yet, my lady. Though knowing the Reverend, he won't until certain of discharging his duty."

"Cookie, take a portion for the Reverend's return."

"Aye, my lady." Cookie did as instructed, then left.

Samantha's prayer for the meal became interrupted by banging at the front door. Upon the steward's departure, she passed a bowl to Anne. Shouts grew louder.

"They are at supper." Godwin loudly insisted.

The dining room door burst open.

"Lieutenant Gilmore!" Samantha said, startled. "Why are you here?"

"Stolen munitions."

Anne gasped and attempted to disguise her reaction.

"What has that to do we us?" Samantha demanded, though also a bit unnerved.

"The pattern of these raids occurs very near to Foxglen."

"So?"

"Your marriage to Major Hedgepeth notwithstanding, you are sister to the Roundhead Duke of Rutherford!"

Samantha swallowed back a rising lump in her throat to respond. "Indeed. That fact is well known since my family has been here for generations. I'm surprised it has taken you this long to learn of it."

"I have known for months. Only withheld information until such time as needed. Wagon and horse tracks lead to Foxglen!"

"Naturally. Both come and go frequently."

"To the back of the manor?"

"That is where the kitchen and outer access to the cellar are located."

Gilmore's brows leveled in regard of the women and food. "Where is your feast for the number of wagons that are see coming and going?"

Samantha's initial surprise and defensiveness gave way to annoyance. "As I have told you repeatedly, Foxglen acts as a storehouse for the equal distribution of what is available to avoid starvation and conflict! You have seen for yourself the limited supplies in the cellar. Witness, *again,* our meager meal of leek soup and a small portion of fish."

"Where is Reverend Cunningham?"

"Tending to the comfort and encouragement of parishioners, who are under constant harassment!"

Gilmore's mustache twitched in a sneer. "Perhaps there is an ulterior motive to these visits? To aid those disloyal to the Crown?"

Anne bit back an unintended sob. She covered her mouth with a napkin.

"Tell me where your father is, Mistress Cunningham."

When Anne paled with fright, Samantha rose to speak sternly. "I have already given answer to his absence."

"Rather convenient answers, my lady."

"Take care, Lieutenant!" Godwin strongly warned.

Gilmore ignored Godwin. "I am certain Major Hedgepeth would not condone recent activities swirling about this house."

Samantha fought back a cold shiver at the threat to vehement dispute the implication. "My husband is aware of my duties as mistress of Foxglen. Just as those in his regiment depend upon him to keep them fed and supplied, so do those around Foxglen depend upon me for their livelihood. Good night, Lieutenant!"

Gilmore shook off Godwin, marching from the room with the steward as escort.

Samantha did not resume her seat until Godwin returned. When she sat, the adrenal surge of emotion gave way to a shiver of relief. She took a deep breath followed by a long exhale to regain her composure.

"Thank you," Anne spoke to Samantha with low disquietude.

"A sip of brandy for you and Mistress Anne, my lady?" Godwin asked with a confident intonation.

"From your secret stash, no doubt."

"Always kept for times of need. None more so than now."

Near midnight, Samantha sat at a window in her bedchamber and stared out into the darkness. She wore a dressing gown over her nightclothes. In a long braid, her hair hung over one shoulder. Confrontation with Gilmore made it difficult to sleep. She bravely withstood the deep chill that shot through her body at his threaten to tell Lawrence. Sadly, an all too familiar sensation whenever she thought of him or heard his name. She wrapped her arms about herself.

Despite the fifteen-year age difference, nothing about Lawrence repelled her at first. He was comely with light blue-grey eyes that could dazzle when he smiled. She learned about his rough manner after their arrival at Foxglen. She rose to retrieve her father's letter from a drawer in the small writing desk.

Ever since its discovery, she reread it, and continually compared it to the secret journals. The only determination she made regarded Foxhill and Foxmeath, is that both were Rutherford estates confiscated by the Crown due to some scandal involving her grandfather. Each time she reviewed the journal, she heard Howard's voice speak of Duncan holding the answers. Unfortunately, there had been little correspondence between them since the war started. Nor was this a topic for written communication. Silence on behalf of her brothers pained her. Silence from Lawrence ...

Another shiver wracked her in recalling his last visit. Although eight months ago, the haunting memories felt like yesterday. The eyes that could make a woman swoon in a good mood, also flashed with cold anger when his temper aroused. Commanding in their piercing gaze, few withstood him. His voice coarse and face screwed in contempt. He spouted callous words for those in opposition to King Charles.

Divided loyalties and divided families made the task difficult. She needed to adapt quickly to maintain an estate during war time. Through it all, she leaned upon her faith and advice from Howard.

Thought of Howard made her consider a different problem. He had yet to return. When out past curfew, he spent the night at the Dove Cottage Inn or another's home. Yet, he always sent word. Not tonight. It took much convincing, and two glasses of brandy, for Anne to retire.

Even with an active mind, Samantha fought a yawn. Nothing would be accomplished by waiting up all night. She climbed into bed and just settled down when multiple raised voices and running feet made her rise. She snatched her dressing grown. The voices came from the hallway. She withdrew the pistol from a nightstand. She carefully opened the door to peek out, ready for action should it be needed.

Godwin held a lantern to lead Henry, Tom, Miller, and Jeremy who carried—

"Howard?" she muttered; a bit confused.

"In here." Godwin directed the men to Howard's bedchamber.

Anne emerged from her room. "What is wrong? Why are they going to father's room?"

"I don't know." Samantha took Anne's hand to enter Howard's room.

The men gently laid Howard on the bed. Blood stained the entire front of his black doublet. His face deadly pale.

Anne screamed. She rushed to the bed and grabbed his shoulders. "Father!"

He blinked. "Anne," he could barely speak her name.

"Father." She sobbed and gently caressed his face.

"Henry?" Samantha asked with frightful concern.

"I fear it is mortal," he somberly whispered in reply.

Samantha swallowed back sorrow to ask, "What happened?"

"A riot in town."

"The Royalists are to blame!" spat Miller.

"What?" asked Samantha in confusion.

Henry gripped Samantha's arm. "Too much to explain, and little time to do so. Soldiers will be here very soon."

"He needs a doctor!" Anne sobbed.

"No," Howard weakly refuted. "It is too late."

"Please, don't say that," Anne pleaded through tears.

Howard reached for Samantha. She sat on the bed, opposite Anne, and take his hand.

"I will send for the doctor—" she began.

"No. I am done." His eyes wearily shifted to his daughter then back to Samantha. "Look after Anne."

"Of course." Samantha battled tears.

"And your people." His voice began to fade.

"Do not concern yourself with them …"

He squeezed her hand and spoke with urgency. "They need you! Before God, promise me to keep them safe."

"I promise," she tearfully said.

Howard looked at Anne one last time and became still.

Henry leaned down to speak in Samantha's ear. "I don't wish to be insensitive, but he cannot be found like this."

"I will see to Anne. You and Godwin take what needs disposal." In soft words, she coaxed Anne from the bed, although Anne refused to leave the room.

Miller humbly approached the women. "The Reverend, your father, was a good, godly man, miss. He thought of others before himself."

Anne could only nod.

"Thank you, Miller," Samantha said.

"If I may, my lady. It could go badly for all of us after this." He motioned to the bed.

"We can discuss that another time. Tom, Jeremy, take Miller out the back. See he is away safely."

It took ten minutes for Godwin and Henry to strip Howard of cloak, doublet, and boots. They just finished when raised voices came from the hallway.

Samantha looked out the door. Jeremy and Tom argued with Gilmore, as they moved from the main stairway towards the room. She quickly shut the door. "Henry, take those things and hide in the antechamber!"

Henry hastened to comply. With Henry's hands full, Godwin opened and closed the anteroom door. He stepped away from the door the moment Gilmore burst into the room.

"Sorry, my lady. Jeremy and I tried to stop him," said Tom.

Samantha nodded to Tom yet confronted Gilmore. "Why are you here?"

"Catching a fugitive! A *Phantom* to be precise."

"Have you quelled the riot that you barge in here making wild accusations?" Godwin felt the sting of Gilmore's backhand across his face.

"Lieutenant! How dare you?" exclaimed Samantha.

"Have your servants keep a civil tongue, or all will be arrested!"

"On what charge?"

"Aiding a fugitive."

"Take care, Lieutenant. My husband will not accept false accusations."

"This *Reverend* is responsible for countless raids against the Crown. He showed up tonight during an illegal assembly and incited a riot. He fought one of my men and became gravely wounded."

"My father is dead! A result of the riot," Anne passionately argued.

"How he died is the question. By blade or shot?"

Godwin stepped in front of Gilmore to stop him from approaching the bed. Gilmore shoved Godwin aside. He threw off the sheet that covered Howard from the waist down, though he still wore the shirt and pants. Gilmore inspected the fatal wound.

"Musket shot. Close range by the powder burns," said Godwin.

Gilmore straightened. His expression perplexed.

"Killed by your soldiers! Who terrorize innocent people!" Anne passionately shouted. Overcome by grief, she collapsed to her knees sobbing. Samantha held her.

"Get out!" Samantha commanded Gilmore. "Never show your face here again. Or my husband shall hear of this disrespectful effrontery!" She tightly held onto Anne and rocked her in attempted comfort.

Her raised voice brought Tom and Jeremy to shield the women. Their stern expression fixed on Gilmore.

Embarrassed into humility, Gilmore clasped the hilt of his sword and offered a quick bow. He departed with Godwin on his heels.

Henry emerged from the antechamber. He squatted near Samantha and Anne. He spoke sympathetically to Anne. "I tried to save him, miss."

"We know you did," Samantha quietly said. "Take care of the clothes. And yourself, dear Henry."

"We'll watch out for them," Tom spoke to Henry about the women. He and Jeremy quietly waited for Samantha to calm Anne.

"Tom, you and Jeremy prepare—" she looked to the bed, but unable to finish the thought, instead, "In the morning, fetch Master Seager." Samantha coaxed Anne to return to her chamber.

Godwin arrived at Anne's chamber with Cookie. The later carried a tray with two tankards of steam beverages. She gave each woman a tankard.

Cookie whispered to Samantha, "I made it extra strong so she will sleep. Now, to make you comfortable." She placed pillows on the lounge chair for Samantha. "Just warm cider for you." She and Godwin left.

Silent tears fell, as Samantha kept watch over Anne. They became friends six years ago when her father engaged Howard as local reverend for Foxglen. Each wealthy estate sponsored a reverend or bishop depending upon whether the family was Anglican or Puritan. Being a widower with a daughter, Patrick arranged for Anne to be Samantha's companion at Foxmoor. The commonality of being deprived of their mothers early in life, helped them bond. Anne and Howard shared in Samantha's grief at the unexpected loss of Patrick.

Anne accompanied Samantha to Foxglen. At the start of the war, Howard moved from the estate rectory to Foxglen. Through tragedy and conflict, they became like family: a sister, and substitute father.

She realized she could not even inform her brothers of Howard's death. She had no idea where to send a letter. If she did, would it arrive safely? The war caused so much confusion and mistrust among the local populace. News of what happened outside their corner of England proved slow in coming, and often brought conflicting accounts. The covert launches to send supplies down river to London notwithstanding, it became difficult to keep the peace and provide for those around Foxglen. Howard's death meant the responsibility fell solely to her.

She closed her eyes and prayed, "God, help me. Grant me wisdom, courage, and strength not to fail those depending upon me."

Chapter 12

LARGE WET SNOWFLAKES SWIRLED IN THE HOWLING WIND before finally coming to rest on the frozen earth. Within moments, the dry and brittle grass became a blanket of white. The wind chilled to the bone. Coupled with heavy snow and occasional ice pellets, made for a miserable day from which both men and beast would be wise to flee. Trees bore the brunt of the winter's blast. Once stalwart branches bent then broke under the endless onslaught of the storm. Older trees stiff with age suffered worse than the younger trees and saplings that yielded to the mighty winds. Birds buried themselves beneath the branches. Small animals huddled together in any tiny crack for shelter.

A half-frozen, heavily laden company of Cavaliers made painfully slow headway against the storm. To provide warmth and protection from the harsh elements, metal cuirasses were exchanged for heavy buff coats. Plumed hats tied securely by scarf or sash. Some men wore cloaks, but with such a fierce wind one could hold either the cloak closed or tightly on the reins to steer a weary horse through the blizzard.

Sight of a troop traveling in such wretched conditions was surprising, yet more disturbing were the weather-beaten expressions and tattered, disordered state of each Cavalier. They moved in a huddled mass and not as an orderly military troop. Even the Blue Royal Standard of Prince Rupert's famed regiment displayed frayed edges and faded colors. The bearers did not carry their flags proudly, rather let their duty sag. Their appearance made bold confirmation of what malady the Royal Army suffered of late.

For three bloody years, civil war raged across the length and breadth of England. At first, the Cavaliers zealously set out to teach a harsh lesson to the fiery and undisciplined upstarts in Parliament. After defeating Parliament at Edgehill, Prince Rupert and the King's Generals announced that the war would only last six months, and King Charles would again reign supreme. Unfortunately, what the King and generals failed to appreciate was the strong will and determination of Lord Essex, John Pym, Henry Ireton, John Hampden, Sir Thomas Fairfax, and Oliver Cromwell.

It became a most unfortunate day when Charles walked out of Parliament. In that singular moment, an act of royal belief in divine right to rule, would divide the country. It set brother against brother, father against son, and a people against their king.

For the moment, all these bone-chilled and desperately hungry men thought about was a warm place to sleep and a morsel of food to quiet their growling stomachs. Parliament commanded all the seaports and trade routes. Supplies were smuggled by loyal supporters of King Charles. Alas, with barely enough to feed the infantry, Cavaliers scoured the countryside for sustenance while awaiting the next summons to battle.

Even in this moving mass of disorder, one could distinguish a leader. He rode slightly ahead of his company. Strains of sable hair peeked out from beneath the hat and sash. Ice formed on the major's small beard and mustache. His usual tawny complexion whipped red and chapped by the wind. Despite all these indignities, unquestionable authority and confidence shone from the strong squared face. His mouth firmly set in grim determination against the storm. He strained to see through the blinding whiteness. Bearing showed Lawrence Hedgepeth as a man of intelligence and breeding, accustomed to being obeyed.

He turned his troop northeast to Lincolnshire and his home on the Trent River. The blizzard abated, as twilight grew nigh. Gray clouds appeared on the horizon. Threat of a new storm or smoke from warm and inviting fires? When the twilight gave way to a starry evening sky, the smoke remained. The smell of fire floated on the breeze.

"Not much further to hearth and food!" he shouted.

At his announcement, a spirit of hope lifted the Cavaliers straight in their saddles. They would approach the major's house with dignity.

Once through a small grove of ice-encrusted trees, Foxglen stood a gleaming white meadow. Smoke spiraled from almost every chimney, battling its way against the dense cold air to push upward and outward. The yellow warmth of candles glowed from behind tall narrow windows. For mile after endless mile the troop saw only small cottages or burnt-out farms incapable of housing and feeding fifty men. Foxglen appeared as a beautiful oasis from the desolate winter and harsh realities of war.

Godwin hurried from the house. "This is a surprise, Major."

"No doubt." Hedgepeth tossed him the reins. "Wallace! Hawkins!" The officers quickly appeared. His eyes narrowed upon the younger Hawkins. Despite the age difference, Hawkins matched Hedgepeth in height, yet broader in shoulders. Just as dark in hair and mustache, yet lighter eyes. He returned Hedgepeth's stare.

"This is my home, Hawkins. Mind your manners and your words!" With a curt wave, Hedgepeth motioned for them to follow him inside.

Hawkins lingered a moment. The warning made his teeth clench and jowls tighten. In that brief pause, Nathan Strickland appeared next to him. He was a half-head shorter and slender in comparison. Both the same age, but Nathan's face round and clean shaven. His fair complexion reddened by the cold. Eyes of mossy green shifted between the vanishing of Hedgepeth entering the house and Hawkins.

"Will? What did Hedgepeth say?" Nathan anxiously whispered.

"To mind myself, of course," William bitterly complained.

"Do you think he knows?" To William's curious glance, Nathan added, "About your past connection here?"

"Hush," William harshly whispered. Nathan cocked a contrary brow at the mild rebuke. This prompted William to sigh. "Doubtful. It's been years." He went inside.

By the frenzied sounds, the major's arrival sent everyone into a tizzy. William reached Hedgepeth just as Anne arrived. Her eyes gaped with apprehension. "Major Hedgepeth," she said with a quick curtsey.

"Is my wife about?"

"Aye, Major. I shall fetch her if you wish."

"Send her to me in the study." Hedgepeth moved off with the officers.

Hedgepeth warmed himself by the fire. Wallace and William waited until Hedgepeth motioned for them to proceed. They removed their cloaks to place over chairs beside the hearth before warming their hands over the fire. Hedgepeth sat at the desk.

Samantha entered. She clasped her hands tightly yet spoke in calm steady voice. "To what do we owe this unexpected visit, sir?"

"Necessity, pure necessity."

"How long will this necessity last?" She tried to mask the anxiety in her voice.

"As long as I desire."

Samantha barely moved a muscle, save a furrowed brow. "How many men have you?"

"Fifty."

To this, she showed the greatest emotion: surprise. "Our provisions cannot sustain that number for long." She looked to the officers, who remained beside the hearth.

He noticed. "My senior officers. Captains Wallace and Hawkins."

Her eyes only flashed an icy glance at Wallace. A stout foreboding Scottish Highlander in his middle thirties with rugged features, black hair, amber complexion, and insubordinate gleam. Upon William, her gaze lingered. He had the appearance of a war veteran with strong broad shoulders and powerful arms. Still, there remained a marked genteelness to his countenance not visible in either Hedgepeth or Wallace. Clear hazel eyes vividly peered out from storm-ruddy cheeks. The glistening of melting ice on his brown hair and mustache completed the man. Not all his twenty-five years were hardened or dampened by war. He made the slightest nod to her inspection of him.

"Welcome to Foxglen, gentlemen. Excuse me, while I see what accommodations can be arranged on such short notice." She bravely tossed Hedgepeth a displeased parting glance.

Irate at the slight, Hedgepeth snapped at his officer. "See to the men then join me in two hours for supper!"

After tending to duty of billeting, William found Samantha in the cellar with Godwin. "My lady."

"Captain Hawkins."

"It used to be plain William or Will to friends and family," he said with a gentle grin.

"I remember," she said demurely. "Do you seek me or Master Godwin?"

"You, my lady, to express my gratitude for your hospitality."

She ruefully smiled. "Surely, you of all people, know my hospitality is enforced."

"Enforced though you say, it is most generous."

Samantha lightly laughed. A melodic laugh that made her blue eyes sparkle. "I had forgotten what a gallant gentleman you are, Captain."

"Wife!" Hedgepeth's voice boomed from the top of the stairs.

"Please, leave. My husband is very suspicious," she hastily told William

He withdrew by way of the outside door. He did not completely close the door nor mount the stairs, rather listened. "Wife!" he heard Hedgepeth.

"You need not bellow for me like some recruit, sir," she rebuffed with a slight tremor.

"My ways and manners are not open for debate."

"Then why do you disturb me?"

William dared a peek. Samantha bravely faced Hedgepeth with Godwin standing stalwartly behind her. Thin and small stature, Godwin hardly presented an imposing figure compared to Hedgepeth. He remained in moral support of his mistress.

Hedgepeth sneered disapproval to the unflinching steward. "Out!" he ordered.

"Master Godwin and I are tending to the supplies for *your* men. It is you who interrupt us. Continue your accounting, Master Godwin," she said, to which he silently obeyed.

Hedgepeth spoke in a lower voice, though nonetheless disagreeable. "Your behavior earlier was intolerable. While we are here, I demand more respect shown in public."

"You demand, sir?" she clamored. Her hands clenched to maintain composure.

"As your husband and lord, it is my right!"

"As husband and lord, it is also your responsibility to behave in a civil manner toward me and respect this house. Despite personal differences appearances must be maintained. Is that not so, husband?"

Hedgepeth barely contained his temper, as told by his strained voice. "You are correct, madam. For the duration of my stay, a truce is in order."

Samantha slightly nodded. "Be it so; providing your stay is short. Despite the war, peace has returned to Foxglen and done wonders for everyone."

Hedgepeth seized her arm, which caused Samantha to utter a gasp of alarm. Godwin stopped work. William stiffened in anger at the action yet resisted entering to intervene.

"Curb your tongue. You may be my wife, but I would be within my rights to give you a good thrashing for insolence!"

"No!" she lowly stammered with terror.

"Then do not press me!" He tightened his grip.

She winced at the crushing grasp. "Very well," she weakly said.

With a jerk, he released her. "We shall start by you joining myself and my officers for dinner. Your company shall provide a delightful diversion. Until tonight, dear wife." He triumphantly smiled and withdrew.

"My lady?" Godwin inquired with concern.

Samantha cradled her arm. She went upstairs without replying.

William's entrance startled Godwin. "You need not fear me."

Skeptical, Godwin picked up a sack of potatoes and headed upstairs. He muttered under his breath about Royalists.

William heard Godwin, but more concerned with what transpired between Hedgepeth and Samantha. True, he positioned himself outside the door to listen, but found Hedgepeth's behavior detestable. To intervene was impossible; so, he angrily listened to the manhandling.

Samantha paced her chamber to regain her composure. "Why did he have to return? All I want to do is forget."

"Courage," soothed Anne. "God will not abandon you."

Samantha took Anne by the hand. "What would I do without your counsel? Indeed, God promised never to forsake those who love Him. I should not be undone by that wicked man." She shivered slightly.

Anne tightened her grip of Samantha's hand. "God will deal with Major Hedgepeth in His time."

"Aye. When the war ends, there will be a day of reckoning for Lawrence Hedgepeth. Duncan will see to that." She made a low sigh of lament. "Though his old friend is also here."

"You mean Captain Hawkins?"

"Aye. What a sad turn of events this war has caused. So much heartache."

Anne's voice filled with sympathy. "Let us pray before dinner."

They placed laced kerchiefs on their heads. They knelt at a small table upon which sat a plain wooden cross, the Holy Bible, and two candles.

"Dear Lord," Samantha began. "We beseech you to look with grace and mercy upon us. The enemy of both You and this house has returned. We ask for strength and protection during the time." Her voice grew weak while her trembling hands clenched tightly together. "Lord, help us!"

Chapter 13

S PIT AND POLISH, WILLIAM WENT TO SAMANTHA'S CHAMBERS. After a knock, he announced his intentions. "Lady Hedgepeth, it is Captain Hawkins. I am here to escort you to dinner."

He heard a murmur of voices and the ruffle of skirts. With a curtsey and greeting, Anne admitted him. In brisk military step, he entered and stopped before Samantha. In evening dress, hair pampered and arrayed she was radiant. William bowed. "My lady."

Samantha slightly blushed to his admiring regard. "You stare."

William grinned with a bit of playful swagger. "Hardly the thirteen-year-old girl I remember."

In an awkward response, she said, "Oh, posh. What do you remember of me? You and Duncan were so preoccupied you had no time for anyone else."

"I recall a girl who scampered up a tree to avoid being discovered for spying on us. Which resulted in a ruined dress."

Anne covered her laugh by coughing. The reaction diverted William's attention enough for Samantha to regain her composure. Despite his dashing appearance and memories of happier times, he wore a sword. "Your gallantry is marred by your saber, Captain. A weapon is not necessary for dinner."

"War has made precaution a habit for this soldier." He offered her his arm.

Anne respectfully followed them downstairs. The dining room had two fireplaces, one at each end of the room. Wooden beams with cross-timbers braced the arched ceiling. Upon the walls hung several large portraits. A tapestry of the family coat of arms with a fox blazon hung over the center hearth. The massive oak table properly set for five. Hedgepeth and Wallace already present, also cleaned, polished, and wearing swords.

Samantha took a seat. "As I told Captain Hawkins, weapons are not needed at dinner."

William made no comment, as he assumed his place at the table. After gaining knowledge of violence, he made it a point to remain a silent observer. He noticed a pleasant smile appear when Hedgepeth answered.

"Under normal circumstances I would not permit it. However, these are unusual times, madam." He rang for the first course.

"I noticed another peculiarity, guards have been posted," she said.

"Military precaution, my lady," said Wallace.

"From whom do you fear attack, Captain? This shire is under Royalist control."

"It is a soldier's duty to be prepared for the unexpected, my lady."

"My husband has instructed you well, Captain." She made the remark with such a charming smile that Hedgepeth checked his anger. "Aren't you forgetting something, husband?" she asked when he began to eat his soup.

Hedgepeth furrowed his brow. "Am I?"

"It is custom of this house to thank the Lord for our food. More so now with provision difficult to maintain."

Hedgepeth scowled and placed aside his spoon. "Very well." He grumbled some unintelligible words followed by a forced amen. He proceeded to eat. Samantha's head remained bowed with eyes closed and hands folded. "I have concluded."

"Perhaps the Good Lord heard your thankfulness, I did not."

Hedgepeth sneered and curtly waved at her. "Proceed!"

"Good Lord, we thank Thee for the blessings bestowed upon this unworthy house. From sword and hunger Thou hast kept us safe. Thou preparest a table before me in the presence of mine enemies—"

Hedgepeth loudly cleared his throat, which forced her to stop. "Have you seen the enemy about that you mention them in your prayers?"

"No!" she quickly answered. "I merely quote the Twenty-third Psalm in praising the Lord for His Provision and Protection during a time of war."

William's gaze carefully shifted from Hedgepeth to Samantha. Despite her stern chin, her knuckles white in their grasp upon the arms of the chair.

Hedgepeth once more assumed an air of cordiality. "By the way, I see Mistress Cunningham occupies her usual place at the table. What of Reverend Cunningham? I have not seen him since my return."

Anne paled and lowered her head to avoid eye contact.

"Sadly, Reverend Cunningham is no longer with us," Samantha spoke with discretion.

"Has he gone to Foxmoor?" Hedgepeth's question caused Anne further distress.

"No, he died some months ago," Samantha somberly replied.

"Really? Of what malady?"

"No malady! Wounds." Anne dared a harsh look at Hedgepeth.

"Wounds? I did not take him for a fighting man," he scoffed.

"Enough, sir," pleaded Samantha when Anne sobbed. "Can you not see Anne still grieves for her father?"

"I am distressed, madam, that your family and retainers take up arms with traitors against the King!"

William shifted uncomfortably in his seat at Hedgepeth's accusation, though he kept focus on Samantha. He and others caught briefly by surprise when Anne bolted to her feet.

"My father was a man of God! He died of wounds suffered while protecting innocent people from marauding Cavaliers!" In tears, she fled the room.

"Now, see what you have done." Samantha rose with the intent to pursue Anne.

"Sit down, madam!" Hedgepeth ordered.

Jowls tight, Samantha resumed her seat.

William closely observed her fluid expression, as she battled emotions. Her voice strained.

"Is there anything else before you ring for the next course?" she chided.

"Since you ask. A matter deals with *my* father." The anger in his eyes like daggers.

94

The color suddenly drained from her face. The mention of Lord Kyle Hedgepeth brought a visible dread almost too powerful for words. "His Lordship? Is he also to arrive?"

"No. Wounds inflicted by Parliament cannon nearly crippled him. *That* is the issue, madam. What say you?"

She took a moment to regain her composure. "I am truly sorry. I shall pray for his complete recovery."

"Indeed? I thought you should have rejoiced," he bitterly scoffed.

"Sir!" she exclaimed in offense. "I detest this war. Death and destruction tear this country apart."

To her rebuff, Hedgepeth wryly grinned. "Well said, madam."

William noticed her ire immediately rose by a flush of her cheeks. No doubt she realized Hedgepeth entrapped her into reacting. A common tactic the major often employed. William briefly met her glance before she lowered her head. An effort to regain her composure.

A ruckus in the foyer drew their attention. Three soldiers entered and held a struggling captive. The fellow had been hastily roused from his home, for no cloak. His plain coarse doublet partly open to reveal the shirt beneath. On his feet he wore common shoes, not boots for tramping about in ankle deep snow.

Samantha uttered a low gasp of surprise, as her eyes widened with recognition of Miller. Swiftly she used her napkin to recover herself. Her reaction did not go unnoticed by William, who intercepted her glance.

"What is the meaning of this?" Hedgepeth demanded, ignorant of the visual exchange between William and Samantha.

"He was conducting a meeting of Roundheads in the cellar of his mill. Unfortunately, the others escaped," explained a soldier.

Hedgepeth gave a quick glance down the length of the table to his wife. "Precautions do have a way of rooting out trouble, madam."

Samantha sent a sympathetic eye to Miller.

"So, Miller, you breed sedition and plot against the King while I am away."

"Lady Hedgepeth—," Miller respectfully began.

"It is to me you speak!" the major snapped.

"Aye, Major." Miller again glanced down to Samantha.

Enraged, Hedgepeth stood. "Look at me when I speak to you!"

"We meet and talk like free Englishmen."

Hedgepeth slapped Miller. Samantha stiffened at the assault. She used the napkin to stifle murmur of horror. The major ignored her.

"Treasonous talk. How many were there and who are they?" When Miller remained silent, Hedgepeth struck him again. This time blood flowed from a cut lip.

William noticed Samantha's pale distress at the second assault. "Major! Is this brutality necessary in her ladyship's presence?"

His intervention surprised Samantha.

Hedgepeth cast a scrutinizing glance to William, then his wife. Her pallor pale and expression fretful. "It makes little difference. He will be shot in the morning." He sat.

Miller's eyes widened in horror and his mouth opened to protest. Yet before he could speak, Samantha exclaimed; "Without a trial?"

"This is war, and he is a traitor. A trial is not needed." He cast a probing look at Miller. "Unless he wishes to save his neck by giving me the names of his conspirators."

To this, Miller's earlier rigidity returned.

Upon meeting stubborn resistance, Hedgepeth waved for Miller to be taken away. "Go! Let me finish my meal in peace!"

The first soldier remained and waited until Miller was gone to speak. "Pardon, Major, but I believe we should double the guard on him tonight. The locals talk about a phantom rider who liberates Roundheads."

"Phantom rider?" Wallace questioned.

"The folk liken him to Robin Hood. They say he's killed three of the King's men last month while setting free a dozen Roundheads."

Samantha took a nervous drink at mention of the Phantom. William noticed, so did Hedgepeth.

"Do as you see fit." Hedgepeth addressed his wife after the sergeant left. "Strange, madam, you did not mention this phantom rider."

"Why?" she forced herself to speak. "It is idle talk. I have seen no evidence such a person exists."

"Three of the King's men are dead, my lady," said Wallace.

"This is first I have heard of any deaths, Captain. And am naturally disturbed." She looked to her husband while speaking the last sentence. She withstood his intense gaze with an air of innocent defiance, though her color slow to return to her cheeks.

After a moment, he asked, "Shall we proceed with dinner? Or are you too disturbed to continue?"

"Duty requires I remain."

William inwardly applauded Samantha's fortitude for truly the scene disturbed her. The remainder of the meal passed in relative quiet, with only occasional comments on various subjects for small talk. William only spoke when addressed, content to play his part of observer. When dinner concluded, Samantha politely asked to be excused. Hedgepeth readily agreed. He also dismissed his officers.

William retired to his chambers; a room that once belonged to Rory. Nathan prepared for his return. He ignored Nathan's greeting to sit by the fire.

Keen to the silence, Nathan said, "I know something is wrong."

"Coming here and seeing Samantha again has revived some painful memories," droned William. "I must be on my guard against those memories and Hedgepeth."

Chapter 14

A GLOVED HAND COVERED HIS MOUTH, WHICH CAUSED EVERY muscle in Henry's powerful body to stiffen, ready for action. Being in a light slumber, his eyes instantly opened upon first touch. Nothing was immediately perceivable in the dark. His pupils adjusted to the single candle to focus on the dimly lit figure in a black silk mask and costume. The black mask covered most of the face, from the bridge of the nose, across the cheeks and over the head to the nape where it was securely tied. Even the plume was dyed black.

"Come, friend. There is work to do," a familiar voice whispered.

Beneath the blankets, Henry lay fully dressed in black. He tucked his graying-gold locks under a black hat he had been holding. At the questioning glance, he grinned and said, "After hearing about a ruckus in town, I was expecting you. Who is it this time?"

"Miller. The Royalists arrested him."

"If they've taken him to the garrison, it will be difficult to free him."

"No. He is in the springhouse at Foxglen. Under guard."

"What? And you want to—"

"I must!" The Phantom stoutly interrupted. "And you know it," was added at Henry's scowl.

"Aye." Henry pulled the handkerchief up over his mouth and nose.

After extinguishing the lantern, they left the bailiff's house. Outside stood two black hunters fully saddled and ready. Their slender bodies, speed, and agility made ideal mounts for such work. Beside the hunters, waited a small cob, also saddled.

"Grab the cob and follow," The Phantom instructed.

Once mounted, they skirted Foxglen to pause at a thicket near the springhouse. Henry shifted in the saddle to observe the surroundings.

"This makes no sense. The river is easy for escape, leaving no tracks."

"Or a tempting trap." The Phantom dismounted. "Hedgepeth seeks to outfox us. Well, we shall spring the trap and free poor Miller by doing exactly what he thinks we'll do."

"Are you certain about this?"

The Phantom stared directly at Henry. "I have never been more certain about anything. Tie the cob here. We will lead the others closer to the springhouse on the riverside."

A sergeant and four men stood guard. Two posted by the river access, two more kept vigil from the landside. The sergeant guarded the springhouse door. Near the springhouse, a good size fire served for warmth and light.

At the river, a sentry spotted something floating on the current. He spoke to his companion on the other side of the small tributary that flowed from the springhouse to the river. "I saw something near on the river. I'm going to take a look."

The second sentry took up a supporting position. A moment or so later, he heard a rustling of branches. "Kent?" He moved to where the tributary emptied into the river.

"Aye," came a muffled reply. He reappeared wrapped against the cold. "What happened?"

"I tripped," was the short, mumbled response. "Look!"

The second sentry turned to see a small raft with somebody on it. He raised his musket to aim at the raft. "Halt, in the name of the King!"

Suddenly, Henry ceased his role playing and leapt upon the sentry. A hard blow to the head sent the man tumbling into the icy water of the river. At the commotion, a voice called, "Kent? Doyle?"

Henry had to act fast. "The Phantom! Help!" he shouted when two figures raced toward him. "There!" He pointed to the decoy where he bound and gagged the first sentry. Henry ducked into the thicket when the soldiers fired upon the decoy.

"Got him!" one shouted.

"Only wounded! After him!" Henry yelled from the thicket.

As the soldiers passed, Henry knocked one into the river.

The other turned. "The Phantom!" he said when Henry attacked him.

At the springhouse, the sergeant anxiously listened to the distant scuffle. Being preoccupied, he almost didn't notice the Phantom creep up behind him. The firelight changed into a shadow and made him turn in time to use his musket and block a club aimed at his head. With the musket knocked away, he reached for his sword. He could not see whom he fought behind the black mask. He retreated against the springhouse. A quick circular parry disarmed the sergeant. A naked sword hovered before his eyes.

"Yield and live," said the Phantom.

"And face Major Hedgepeth in failure? Never!" He foolishly tried to escape. The Phantom lunged and pierced the sergeant in the chest. Seriously wounded, he sank to the ground.

"You should have yielded," the Phantom said with remorse. Shouts from the manor made the Phantom open the springhouse door.

The cold of the enclosure served to keep fresh the milk and butter crocks that filled with shelves. Two ways lead into the springhouse; the first by way of the ladder; the second by a small, grated opening for the stream to freely flow to the river. If the grate was removed, a slender man could fit through.

Miller sat on the bottom rung in ankle deep icy water, his wrists tied to the ladder. Blue lips quivered uncontrollably. Startled by the commotion, he flinched in defense when at a flash of steel. The blade cut the ropes holding his hands to the ladder. A person jumped in the water beside him.

"Phantom?"

"Climb out!"

"My legs are frozen."

"For your life's sake, man, move!" The Phantom pushed a struggling Miller up the ladder. Once out of the springhouse, they saw torches and heard voices. The Phantom urged Miller through the thicket to the tethered cob. "Ride to the Dove Cottage Inn."

"What will you do?"

"Never mind me. Ride like the wind and don't look back." The Phantom slapped the cob's rump then ran toward the river. Henry just waylaid the last soldier. "Miller is away, and we pursued. To horse!"

Henry and the Phantom urged their mounts from the thicket onto the snow-covered glen. The first rays of dawn glistened on the snow, not a good sign to avoid detection. The Phantom and Henry looked back when several shots were harmlessly fired. This served more in warning than seriously aimed at that distance. Four mounted soldiers rode in pursuit.

Once through the glen, they weaved through dense wood and up a steep hill. Recklessly, they drove their horses over the crest. The Phantom grabbed the mane for balance. Henry leaned back when his horse began to skid and shy. Henry tried to steady the animal. When the horse slipped again both tumbled downhill. Flying hooves missed Henry's head by inches. He didn't stop until he reached the bottom where a small river tributary flowed. The fall killed the horse.

"Henry!" The Phantom called.

Shouts came from the hill. Two riders barreled down upon them. The Phantom's well-aimed pistol shot unhorsed one soldier. Before the Phantom could get into position to receive Henry in a jump mount, the second soldier arrived. With drawn sword, the Phantom met the bold attack. The cuts and slashes proved harmless, as both riders tried to steady their mounts on the slippery river bottom. The Phantom managed to avoid a chest high slash by ducking to one side. A rapid riposte struck the soldier in the left shoulder and sent him into the icy water.

"Two more!" Henry warned. With a helping hand, he mounted behind the Phantom. With the weight of two people, the horse could not go as fast as desired. Across the snow-covered meadow stood a stone fence.

"Ready for action?" asked the Phantom.

"Not like at Bardney?"

"Do we have a choice?"

Henry grumbled in the negative. The Phantom's horse left the ground. On the way down, Henry threw himself off. The Phantom completed the landing and made the horse fall.

As the pursuers cleared the fence, the Phantom released the horse and yelled to frighten the animal. The horse quickly rose to its feet directly in the path of the first rider. This was no planned fall. The masked figure stood ready and waiting for the Cavalier to recover. A flash of surprise flashed in the Phantom's eyes when William stood and reached for his sword.

"Don't do it, Captain!" warned the Phantom.

Nathan's horse cleared the fence, which caused a brief distraction that allowed William to draw his sword.

"I begged you not to," the Phantom spoke with reluctance.

"Then yield your sword and we won't fight."

"Impossible!" The Phantom thrust at William.

William jumped back then launched a riposte. The Phantom acted keen in defense.

While the Phantom and William tested each other, Henry unhorsed Nathan shortly after his horse landed. A powerful man, Henry weighed thirty pounds more than Nathan. It became a brawl rather than a duel. Nathan used the sword like a club. Nothing stopped Henry. Finally, Nathan ran out of tricks and Henry's blade pierced him just under the last right rib. A shallow wound but brought him to his knees. A sword point pressed against his throat.

"Yield, Captain! If you want your friend to live," shouted Henry.

William and the Phantom disengaged. William's eyes flashed in fury at seeing Nathan down. "You would butcher him?"

"No. Give me your sword and you both may live," said the Phantom.

William incredulously stared at the black figure. Blue eyes peered out from behind the mask. The sincere expression told of trustworthy person.

"Please, Captain." This time the Phantom held out a receiving hand.

Once William handed over his sword, Henry removed the threat.

"Tell Major Hedgepeth we deal mercifully with honorable men. But if he and I cross paths, the outcome will not be the same for him!"

"I will tell him," William solemnly agreed to the Phantom's request.

"There's a gate a quarter mile east. It will make for an easy ride," said Henry.

William and Nathan exchanged perplexed glances at the generosity, but no comment. Nathan leaned upon William for support.

Henry came beside the Phantom to watch William help Nathan mount then ride off. "Was it wise to let them go? They could recognize me."

"Hedgepeth hasn't seen you since his return. You will be away on family business. Go to the woodman's cottage. If I need you, I will send Tom."

"What of you? It's daylight."

"Brave Henry, you are a worrywart. Have we not built up our network this past year? I shall manage."

Henry walked toward town, while the Phantom rode in the opposite direction.

At Foxglen, William took Nathan to the surgeon before he reported the incident to Hedgepeth. Of the eight soldiers involved in guarding Miller and pursuit, three received wounds and three missing. Irate, Hedgepeth yelled uncontrollably in the study. Household servants and soldiers became fearful of his wrath. He stormed out of the study with Wallace and William on his heels.

"The whole house is awake, but my wife is ill in bed!"

"That is not true, husband." Samantha wore a dressing gown. Ivory combs pulled back the sides of her red hair while the rest fell loosely down her neck and shoulders. She appeared tired about the eyes and her cheeks held the fading pink of a passing flush.

"Then Mistress Cunningham lied to me?"

"No, I was ill with some disagreement from last night's supper. Since the horrid incident, I have been tending to duties. In all this confusion, it is a wonder anything got done."

From behind Hedgepeth, William observed Samantha.

"Well, madam! Do you now see evidence of this Phantom's existence?"

She began to weaken. "Do you think me unfeeling and inhuman? Of course, I do!" Her eyes became moist. "And it happened at Foxglen."

Her emotional reply confounded Hedgepeth. "Come!" he ordered Wallace and William.

Before departing, William caught Samantha's eye. In the brief exchange, he noted a difference in her composure than previously. Several times she shied away or studied him with intense recollection. This time, he saw neither acute shyness nor brazen boldness, merely a steadfast regard. So vivid and compelling were her eyes in their blue gaze that a disarming sense struck him to the core. Compelled by the confounding feelings, he made a respectful bow before he hurried after Hedgepeth.

After calming the chaos, William visited Nathan. The sergeant lay propped up on pillows in the bed of one of a smaller guest room.

"Why he allowed her to marry the major I shall never understand!" William complained under his breath.

"He could hardly refuse to fulfill the marriage contract his father arranged," said Nathan.

"It was a rhetorical question, not one requiring an answer," snapped William. He then sighed and sat on the edge of the bed. "Oh, Nathan, what happened to those carefree days at Oxford?" His stared at some unseen spot on the floor. His brows knitted in curious consideration "Duncan? The Phantom? Impossible. He fights for Parliament. Or as far as I know." He began to pace. "He knew me and spared our lives! The eyes betrayed him. And the way he handled the sword is familiar. It must be Duncan!"

Nathan shifted to get comfortable. "If it is the duke, what will you do?"

William rose. He stared into the hearth. Warmth of the fire bathed his face. "I don't know. We owe him our lives."

"You were forced to yield because of me," chided Nathan.

"Good servants are hard to come by. Not to mention good friends," he said with an encouraging smile.

"You have done me a great honor by calling me friend. So much so I often forget my station. Either way, I fail miserably when you are forced to such debase actions on my behalf."

"Forget it," William snapped, not meaning to. "Forgive me. My mind is divided." He went back to staring at the fire.

"Lady Samantha or Lord Rutherford?"

"The lady at present. She is the sister of a once good friend, to whom I feel indebted, despite what you say." He absentmindedly kicked the hearth.

In the brief silence that followed, Nathan watched his friend and master. He raised a skeptical brow when William turned to from the fire and wore a satisfied grin. "I know that look. It means some risky scheme."

William hurried to the bed. "Maybe with the Phantom's help I can pay my debt to Duncan and deal a blow to Hedgepeth. How have you made on with the pretty gossip of a maid who seems to fancy you?"

"Well enough, why?" he asked with suspicion.

"If she visits you, inquire further about this Phantom Rider of Lincolnshire."

Chapter 15

A WEEK LATER, SAMANTHA RECEIVED A SUMMONS TO BREAKFAST. Since the Royalist arrival, she and Anne took most meals in their rooms to avoid interaction. Anne remained shaken by Hedgepeth's disregard for her father. Samantha felt it safer to conduct estate business in the privacy of her chamber. There were other ways to move about Foxglen without being seen.

Thus far, Hedgepeth kept his distance, and for that, Samantha was grateful. Anne had a legitimate excuse, and he did not question her absence. However, as his wife, she had no reasonable excuse to refuse the summons. Whatever prompted it, she would be prepared.

She hastened to arrive in the dining room before anyone in the hope of forestalling any criticism. She found William already there. With a cordial greeting, he helped her to sit. She noticed his altered manner. His hazel eyes sparkled with a mischievous mirth she found slightly irritating.

Hedgepeth arrived with Wallace. "Good morrow, wife," he spoke in unusually good humor.

This agreeable mood change did not go unnoticed by either Samantha or William. "And you, husband," she carefully replied.

"I hope the events of this Phantom have not disturbed you too greatly."

"I had a bit of trouble at first."

"I am sorry to hear that," he continued in his congenial manner. "Rest assured, I shall catch this *Phantom Rider*, and the knave will be severely dealt with." The first course of sausage pie was served. "Wife, would you thank the Good Lord for his bounty?"

Though wary, Samantha proceeded. "Gracious Lord, we thank Thee for Thy bounty, and pray Thy blessing and protection this day. Amen."

After several moments of eating, Hedgepeth spoke. "Forgive me. In the rush of arrival, I forgot to inquire as to the health of your family."

At this question, Samantha paused in eating to look directly at him. "My family fights a war, sir. You know that."

"Aye. I meant to ask about your brother."

Her instincts never failed her, as she sensed he was getting to the heart of the matter. "To which brother do you refer?"

"The younger," he said with a rakish smile.

He struck the nerve, which made the fork slipped from her hand to the table. "I have not heard from Rory in almost a year."

Hedgepeth feinted sympathy. "Pity. I had taken a fancy to him, and hoped the rumors were not true."

Despite the obvious trap, she bravely asked, "Rumors?"

Hedgepeth cued Wallace to speak.

"Lady Hedgepeth, I fear I bore the sad news to the major and now to you. Your brother was killed in a skirmish at Leicester eight months ago."

Samantha suddenly grew ashen.

Concerned, William impulsively laid hold of her hand. "Lady Samantha?"

His warm, strong touch made her look from his hand to his face. His expression of compassionate concern. A coarse clearing of the throat from Hedgepeth caused her to compose herself. She removed her hand.

"I am well, Captain Hawkins. Thank you." She confronted Hedgepeth. "If you knew this, why did you inquire about his health?"

He smugly reclined and toyed with the ring on his left hand. "Because, my dear, if you had heard from Rory my theory would be proven."

She suspiciously eyed him, as she fought to contain grief and anger. "What theory?"

"The identity of this Phantom Rider." Hedgepeth leaned forward snarling. "Rory."

She could not hide her astonishment. "You cannot believe that."

"Why? Rory has always been a reckless free spirit. What better device than pretend to die and come back as this Phantom Rider."

Piqued, she stood. "I find your disrespect and accusation against my brother deplorable!"

"Oh, aye! The ever-loyal O'Malleys. Losing half your holdings was not enough to be humbled before your King. You take up arms with rebels and pretend it is a righteous cause." When she moved to leave, he commanded, "Sit down, madam!"

Despite the quiver lower lip, Samantha stormed from the room.

At her leaving, William rose to confront Hedgepeth. "Major, was that public display and humiliation of your wife necessary?"

"You question my conduct, Captain Hawkins?"

"I question any man who takes unfair advantage of a woman by thoughtlessly informing her of the death of her brother while joined with a wild accusation—"

Hedgepeth bolted to his feet. "Odds blood! I warned you! This is my house and here I answer to no man." Anger propelled him down the table to stand face-to-face with William. "Any higher influence you had ended the day your transfer was denied."

William's eyes narrowed in suspicion. "No man in the company knew that I requested a transfer. How did you discover it?"

Hedgepeth sneered. "Do you think I would allow my career to be jeopardized by a spoiled brat from the country with overly haughty ideas of war and chivalry? Or Prince Rupert's reputation and generosity to be compromised by such trifles as plundering a few Parliamentarian houses?"

William grew rigid with cold realization. "You stopped my transfer!"

Hedgepeth spoke with hauteur. "One false step, and you will find your career ended, *if* not your life! Now, get out of my sight so I can finish my meal in peace."

William marched from the room.

In her chamber, emotions propelled Samantha to pace. Her eyes wet and cheeks tear stained. "Damn Hedgepeth!"

Anne stunned by the curse. "Samantha!"

"He should be for daring to tarnish Rory's name-!" Overcome, she sank into a chair and wept. "Rory."

Anne knelt beside the chair to offer comfort. "It may not be true. If it were, why has Duncan not written? Surely, he would tell you and not allow the major to take such horrid pleasure."

With a shaky hand, Samantha wiped away tears. "Aye. Duncan would tell me." Some of her composure returned, though anger remained. "He is a heartless monster! First mistreating you, now maligning Rory. Until we know for certain, we must withstand his vicious attacks."

Sound of brisk footsteps in the hall drew their attention. Samantha moved to the door and slowly opened it enough to look out. At first, she feared Hedgepeth. Instead, she saw William. His expression grim and hard. He entered the adjacent room and slammed the door behind him. She carefully closed her door and leaned against it. She chewed on her thumbnail. With sudden purpose, she hastened to the vanity and pulled out a key.

"Unlock the secret door and tell Captain Hawkins I wish to speak with him." When Anne balked, she shoved the key into Anne's hand. "Do it."

William saw the panel slowly opened. He grabbed it and sung it open. When Anne began to scream, he pulled her inside and covered her mouth.

"Promise not to scream and I will release you," he hastily whispered.

"You will release her because I require it, Captain." Samantha appeared in the panel threshold.

"Of course, my lady."

Once released, Anne quickly hid behind Samantha.

"You startled the captain. No harm meant," Samantha reassured Anne.

"Indeed not. I only wanted to prevent discovery." He looked through the short passage to see another bedchamber. "This leads to your chambers?"

"Aye."

"Why have you come to me in such a fashion?"

"That should be obvious. My husband is a vicious man."

"Aye. Only that does not answer my question."

"I thought—" she balked. "You and Duncan were once friends."

William kindly smiled. "If it is any consolation, I have heard nothing to confirm what the major said about Rory."

Samantha sighed with relief. "Thank you, Captain. You confirm my own conclusion. Duncan would not allow such dreadful news to be so wretchedly told to me."

"I am certain he would not."

Samantha closely regarded William. His features serenely confident. "Your belief in my brother is admirable under the circumstances. Despite the memories, you enter a house divided."

"Many houses are divided by this war," he said with unction.

Samantha saw a hidden hurt behind the sympathy of his hazel eyes. "Before, you came to our home as a friend. Now, you come as an enemy."

William winced with regret. "The dilemma is two-sided. I feel great pain when I think of Duncan. Being his sister, and occupying this house, causes me to dwell upon my old friend. Both the good and the bad times we shared."

Samantha became flustered. "I did not mean to say you were unfeeling, Captain. I see you are distressed. On one hand, the memories of an old friend torment you with new complications; while on the other, duty demands your full attention."

He replied with a grin of admiration. "You rightly discern my situation."

She regarded him with sympathy. "Perhaps, if it were another time and place, we too could be friends, Captain Hawkins."

"Friend or enemy, because of the love I bear your brother, I am your servant." He bowed and kissed her hand.

She balked at the bold action and quickly withdrew her hand. She left by way of secret passage. Anne followed and closed the panel.

For several moments, William stared at the wall. If not for the encounter, he would never know it existed. Although he fumed over the major's interference and thwarting of his transfer, he found himself more concerned about the relationship between Hedgepeth and Samantha. True, he visited Rutherford as a friend, but now came as part of an occupying force.

Occupying an enemy's home and commanding his property were part of war. However, since serving under Hedgepeth, those occupations turned into wanton plunder and savage butchery. He consoled himself with the thought that Foxglen was Hedgepeth's home. Surely, he would not degrade this house. Still, he kept close watch on all that transpired at Foxglen. Perhaps, doing so would ease his disturbed spirit on Duncan's behalf. He knew it illogical and unrealistic, but he had to occupy himself in some way or go mad with anger. Anger at himself for losing a friend, anger at Hedgepeth actions, anger at the war for tearing England apart!

William made his way to the servants' quarters where Nathan convalesced. Nathan sat up against the pillows to finish supper.

"How are you feeling?"

"Much better, thank you. I should return to duty in another week." Nathan noticed William's thoughtful demeanor. "You didn't come just to inquire about my health."

William sat on the bed. "Have you learned anything from the maid?"

Nathan placed the empty plate on a nightstand. "Aye. Sadly, it fits the major's character."

During the disturbing retelling of what Nathan learned, William paced. When Nathan concluded, William plopped into a chair by the fire. His face screwed in disgust, his fist clenched, and eyes narrowed. "If he lays a hand on her in my presence, I will kill him!"

"You speak of his wife. The law permits such beating."

William's head snapped around. "Not wanton brutality! If a man cannot keep mastery of his impulses let him find a tavern wench and not abuse his wife!"

"Unfortunately, the major has had numerous liaisons of which he boasts. Even to his wife."

William snarled at the revelation. "Then the man should be castrated for his debauchery!" He pushed himself out of the chair.

Nathan watched with concern. "Keep your wits, Will. War is no time for love."

William pulled to a stop at the warning. "Who spoke of love? I made a vow the day I put in for my transfer, remember?" He lashed out in frustration. "I wish to God I could find a way to stop him, but so far that has not happened. How can I make sense of it all? Why, of all places am I here where memories torment me?"

"A man often asks such questions during a crisis of conscience."

William looked askew to Nathan. "Have you asked those questions?"

"A few times I have inquired of God to what purpose I am here and why we fight. The answer is always the same, to look within myself and examine my heart towards you, others, and God. I suppose it is simpler for me being a servant and accustomed to obeying without question and murmuring."

"I can think of a few times you have done so," snickered William.

Nathan flashed a retiring smile. "Aye, we have a unique relationship. Only never with your father, or any of my betters. I understand my position in relationship to them. For you, relationships are not always clear. To some you are subordinate while to others superior. Find the key to balancing those relationships and you may learn why God has placed you here. Or for that matter, why you fight."

William thoughtfully nodded. "Until then, I must do as my conscience dictates."

"Even if it brings you into conflict with the major on the lady's behalf?"

William became annoyed. He kept his voice to a low rebuke. "She is the sister of a once-dear friend. I can do no less than he and defend her honor."

Nathan frowned. "Hedgepeth already learned of your transfer and intent to report him to the King. If he discovers you meddling with his wife, there is no telling how he would vent his anger. No matter what your conscience says, the law is on his side."

"I cannot leave her to his spleen!"

Nathan made a long futile sigh. "So, you are committed then. God help us both. As I will not leave you face him alone."

William sat on the bed. With a grateful smile, he gripped Nathan's shoulder. "Thank you. However, no more prying out family secrets. Enough has been learned. Concentrate on recovery. And *this* discussion never happened."

"What discussion?" Nathan wryly grinned and settled back against the pillows.

Chapter 16

THE CLOUDY TWILIGHT THREATENED RAIN. HE WORE A DARK brown cloak and matching plumed hat. A long scarf was tied around his face from the bridge of his nose downward. He stood at the edge of the trees to observe the comings and goings in the compound behind the Dove Cottage Inn. When all became clear, he ran to the compound. He used his hands to hop over the four-foot-high gate rather than open it. He flattened himself behind the tack shed to peek out for any sign of activity. Seeing none, he moved closer to the house. Opening of the door made him divert his course to hide behind a corner of the stables.

Carrying two buckets, Duffy crossed to the well. He set down the buckets and reached for the crank when the man snatched him from behind and covered his mouth. Duffy tried to wrestle away, but difficult when dragged backwards. Once safely behind the corner of the stable, he spoke in Duffy's ear.

"Be still, Duffy!"

When released, the innkeeper braced for assault. "Who are you?"

"A friend." He carefully lowered the scarf and pushed back the hat to reveal himself. A young man aged twenty-two with dark russet hair and eyes of robin's egg blue set in a clean-shaven face.

Duffy's surprise recognition came immediately, and he began to speak. He quickly covered Duffy's mouth with a harsh warning, "No names!"

Duffy nodded and was released. "What are you doing here?"

"There has been no word from Howard for months. Then came reports of Royalist occupying Lincolnshire. I came to confirm the rumors and found Royalists are everywhere," he groused the last sentence.

"Aye. They cause nothing but trouble. Including being responsible for the good Reverend's death."

Stunned, he said, "Howard is dead? When? How?"

"There is much to tell. Though I can't be away long, or they might grow suspicious. A group of Royalist are here for supper. Wait in the tack shed. I'll come as soon as I can."

They parted ways, Duffy for the house, he for the shed. He tried to make himself comfortable but learning of Howard's death made resting difficult. Everything about the war brought only death and destruction. Not a single family had been spared from grief. He hoped Duffy would not be long in returning. He needed to find the patience to wait. For the sake of all, he could not act out of impulse. Being dark and rainy, he found a corner to sit. To his surprise, he fell asleep. In fact, Duffy woke him.

"I brought food and drink." Duffy indicated a plate and tankard on a crate.

"What time is it?"

"Past closing. The Royalists are gone."

"What has happened?" he asked with a mouthful.

"Major Hedgepeth returned three weeks ago. Before that, Royalists patrols came and went."

He paused in eating. "That will make going to Foxglen awkward."

"It's not advisable for you to even be in the village."

"Well, I'm here. So, tell me the way of things." He proceeded to eat while he listened to Duffy. "Howard? The Phantom?" He finished the food and sat back to consider all he heard. "Howard didn't mention half of what you told me."

"Probably didn't want to worry you. Not with fighting a war and all."

He shook his head in dismayed wonderment. "We had no idea the depth of the trouble Samantha faced at home."

Duffy grinned in admiration. "She's done right by the people. You should be proud." The smile faded as he continued, "Although, with the major back, the situation is more difficult for her."

"I can imagine. Lawrence is hardly an aimable fellow." His tone turned somber. "The marriage weighs heavy on us." He shook off the melancholy mood to ask, "Can you think of a way for me to meet with her?"

Duffy scratched his chin in thought. "I can send a coded message. It is how we communicate when in need of the Phantom's services." A sly smile appeared in sizing him up. "It should fit you."

"What should?"

Duffy moved to a trunk. "We kept extra clothes hidden. In case the need came while he was in the village. Which he frequently was when visiting people." He continued to speak while removing the Phantom's clothes from the trunk. "This can facilitate a clandestine meeting and help to thwart the major."

It took several moments for a change of clothes. "A bit loose fitting in certain places, but definitely manageable," he said.

The shed door opened and brought in a cascade of light from a lantern. Duffy swiftly pulled Simon inside and slammed the door shut. Confused, Simon balked at the seizure then stunned at sight of him.

Duffy covered his son's mouth. "Say nothing." When Simon muttered in his hand and nodded, Duffy released him. "Is something amiss?"

"Aye. The Phantom is needed. Trouble at the Reynold's forge."

"What kind of trouble?" he asked.

Simon shrugged. "Don't know exactly. Little Bart came running into the village calling for help. He said Royalists are harassing his parents something fierce. Mama is comforting him. Poor lad."

"How old is he now?" he asked.

"Barely seven."

He slyly grinned. "Let's see what can be done about that." He took the mask from Duffy.

"Are you sure about doing this? I meant the disguise just for a meeting."

He tied on the mask. "They always called me impulsive. Why not live up to the reputation?" He stuffed a pistol into the belt and adjusted his sword.

"Where's your horse?" asked Duffy

"Tethered safely in the woods." He donned the hat.

"Better hurry!"

"Turn down the lantern so can I leave unobserved," he instructed Simon.

Leaving the tack shed, he again used his hands to hop the fence then disappeared into the wood. Duffy and Simon watched and waited. They heard a neigh then horse and rider emerged from the trees at a gallop.

Ed desperately tried to stop three Royalist soldiers from destroying his forge. "For pity's sake, stop! I've done nothing, I tell you."

Maggie stood in the forge threshold trying to calm a crying infant and small girl of three. "Why won't they stop?"

"Take the children inside the house," Ed said. At a crash, he again confronted the solider. "You're frightening my family! Please, for the love of God, stop."

"Tell us about the Phantom and we will leave."

"I told you; I don't know who he is. No one around here does. He comes and goes."

A horse loudly neighed and reared just outside the forge. Upon sight of the black figure, the soldier spoke. "It seems he knows you." He shoved Ed aside. "Just the person we wanted to see tonight. Phantom of Lincolnshire, I arrest you in the name of King! Get down off the horse." He pulled out a pistol from his belt.

The Phantom drew his sword and kicked the horse to enter the forge. With a downward slice, he cut the soldier's hand which made him drop the pistol. The other Royalists rushed the Phantom. Using the skills of a calvary officer, he guided his horse in a circle while slashing at the soldiers to keep them at bay. He pulled tight on the reins for the horse to rear. One

Royalist tripped when he backed away to avoid flying hooves. He fell and hit his head. He lay semi-conscious.

Ed used a log to strike another Royalist from behind. He went sprawling. Dizzy from the blow, he tried several times to stand, but unable. The one with the wounded hand reached for his sword. However, being on foot against an experienced mounted solider, the encounter didn't last long. He stumbled aside when deeply wounded in the right shoulder.

The Phantom leveled the sword at the wounded man's face. "Take your men and leave!"

"Hamil. Atworth." He waved with his good hand for the men leave.

The soldiers staggered out, still unsteady from blows to the head.

The leader held his wound to stem the bleeding. "This won't be the end of it. You're a traitor to the crown with a price on your head."

"Let us hope this increases the bounty. Now, go!" He moved the horse to force the last Royalist from the forge. All had difficulty mounting, but eventually rode from the forge.

"Thank you, Phantom," Ed spoke with relief gratitude.

He surveyed the extensive forge damage. "Can the damage be repaired?"

"I don't know yet."

He sheathed his sword and reached into a purse for coins. "Buy what can't be repaired."

Ed's eyes widened at the amount. "Oh, sir! This is too generous. I can't …"

"Keep it. Use what remains to feed your family." He snapped the reins and rode away into the night.

At the Dove Cottage Inn, he tethered his horse behind the tack shed. Rather than unsaddling the animal, he fetched a bucket of water and some hay from the stables. Inside the shed, he found Duffy preparing a cot.

"There is a basin, pitcher with water, and a towel to wash up." Duffy indicated the items.

"Much obliged."

"How are Ed and Maggie?"

"Unscathed, although the forge practically destroyed." He removed the hat, mask, cloak, and gloves to wash his face. He felt the scratch of whiskers. "I could use a razor and soap."

"I'll bring them before dawn. On the crate, is pen, ink, and paper. Write the message."

After drying this face, he wrote a few short lines. He folded the paper and glanced around. "Where is sealing wax?"

"I need to copy it into code first."

He watched Duffy make fewer markings on another piece of paper than what he wrote. "Is that everything?"

"No names. Only time and place." Duffy folded the coded note and stuffed it in his pocket. He then used the candle flame to burn the original handwritten note. "I'll dispatch this before bringing the razor and soap. Sleep well."

Chapter 17

SAMANTHA'S AVOIDANCE OF WILLIAM HAPPENED DUE TO THE feelings he stirred. Having married at age seventeen, she never experienced the receiving of suitors with their flattering salutations and flirtatious conversations. The only masculine attention she ever knew were those occasions her husband forcefully took his marital right. Affection, though a part of her youth, was never a part of her marriage.

The change from a charitable Christian family into a loveless marriage felt like being flung into icy water after a day basking in the sun. A tremendous shock to the system that needed time for the body adjust. Whereas the war weighed heavily upon the country, it kept Lawrence's visits few and far between. She felt grateful that he had thus far not made her to be with child.

Now, a new twist comes along in the form of William Hawkins, once a dear friend of Duncan. Since he lived in Nottingham, he frequently visited Foxglen during the summers between semesters at Oxford. Son of a knighted baron, he possessed all the breeding and mannerism of nobility. Shortly before Anne came to be her companion, Samantha often followed and mimicked her brothers. During William's visits, she found him likeable. His stated memory of her climbing the tree, revived feelings she thought long buried. Not really a girlish infatuation in the romantic sense, more intrigued and fascinated by him. The *spying* infuriated Duncan, who complained to their father. William's intervention convinced them to forget the harmless incident.

After nearly three years of war, William Hawkins remained gallant and kind. He defended her to Lawrence and treated her with the same gentleness as during those carefree days. Alas, he wore the King's uniform. Although unpleasant and loveless, she was married. She could never break her vows. Not for her husband's sake, but to do so would be a sin against God and disgrace her family. Such thoughts prevented her from sleeping. Near dawn, she finally rose from bed to pray at the small table.

"Lord, you know I am married to a beast, a mocking atheist! To obey You and honor my family, I have diligently tried to endure this marriage. Now this!" Her breath caught and her lower lip quivered. "Grant me strength, for my spirit is weak at the appearance of this gallant—my brother's friend."

The hurried sound of footsteps and spurs in the hall drew attention from her prayers. She carefully looked out the door. Wallace and a soldier headed for Lawrence's chamber. The soldier slightly wounded and wet. When they were admitted, she hastened to the chamber door to listen.

"What!" she heard Lawrence shout in demand.

"The Phantom again, major," said the soldier.

"Twice in as many weeks! I will have the rogue's head for this! Take a troop and learn what you can. Wake everyone in the shire if need be."

Samantha swiftly returned to her room. "The Phantom?" she muttered in confusion. For a moment of consideration, she chewed on her thumbnail. Sudden action propelled her to the wardrobe.

In the soft glow of early morning, people gathered outside the constable's home. Henry watched from a shadowy corner at the last village building. He held the reins of his horse. He became defensive when a hand touched his shoulder. His initial reaction turned to surprise upon sight of a black clothed and masked figure. "You?"

The Phantom drew Henry deeper into the darkness. "What happened?"

"You had nothing to do with this?"

"Since when have I acted singularly?"

"Royalists destroyed the forge."

Anxious, The Phantom seized Henry's arm. "Anyone injured?"

"No, just property damage. I also overheard they can't find Miller to arrest him."

"Why Miller?"

Henry shrugged. "Maybe they think he is connected to the incident. Or use him as bait for another trap."

"No trap. A wounded soldier rode to Foxglen to inform Hedgepeth." The Phantom chewed on a gloved finger. "This impostor could cause trouble. Hedgepeth has sworn to have my head."

"Leave immediately and seek asylum in London," he urged.

The Phantom smiled and patted Henry's arm. "What would I do without my faithful worrier? No, there has been too much hardship and loss to abandon this venture. I won't let so precious a sacrifice go unrewarded. Come, there is work to be done, impostor or not."

"Where?" Henry led his horse to follow the Phantom to where a black hunter waited.

"The mill. If his family is safe, they can't use them against him."

As they rode toward the mill, light from the rising sun reflected off the patches of snow. Bare icy tree limbs glistened. They drew rein just short of the mill. The Phantom stood in the stirrups and looked around. The house appeared quiet.

"We may have come in time. Fetch them. I will reinforce you if there is trouble."

Henry dismounted and carefully made his way to the back door. Water cascading over the wheel drowned any noise. Flowing water kept the river from totally freezing. Henry's knock brought Gertie to open the door very slowly. Sight of a large shadowy figure startled her. He grabbed the door to stop her from slamming it shut.

"Easy, Gertie. The Phantom is here to take your family to safety."

She curiously stared at him. She was partially dressed for the day. At Henry's indication, she stepped from the door to spy the Phantom. "Oh, praise be. I'll fetch the boys."

"We must be quick." Henry helped Gertie rouse the boys, ages six and eight.

The boy remained in night clothes, though wrapped in blankets with shoes on their feet. Gertie finished putting on a shift and cloak. Outside, she expressed her gratitude to The Phantom. "Bless you! I've been sick with worry since all this started!"

"Haste is needed. Ride with my companion. I shall take your sons."

The boys stared in awe at the black figure seated on a fine black horse. Henry lifted the youngest on the saddlebow. The oldest climbed behind the Phantom. The added weight of two small boys seemed insignificant to the black hunter. The horse restlessly chewed at the bit and stamped at the snow. When all were ready, they galloped off. The departure came none too soon, as a troop of Royalists arrived at the mill.

From a nearby knoll, a solitary black figure sat upon a black stallion to watch all that transpired at the mill. When the soldiers arrived, he made the horse rear and neigh. As planned, they noticed him and hastened to pursue. The figure waited until certain all the soldiers followed, then galloped in the opposite direction taken by the Phantom, Henry, and the Miller family.

A half-hour later, the Phantom and Henry stopped in the woods behind the Dove Cottage Inn. Henry helped the boys down and gave the reins of his horse to the Phantom. He escorted them to the back door. Woken by persistent knocks, Duffy scratched the thick mop of unkempt hair. Upon recognizing his visitors, the sleep vanished.

"A present for Miller," said Henry. "Keep them safe."

"God bless you, and the Phantom," Gertie said before going inside.

Duffy stepped outside to see where the Phantom waited with the horses. "I have some news—"

"Look!" exclaimed the Phantom and pointed to a black mounted figure. "We must fly!"

Henry ran to his horse.

"That man is why I need to speak with you! The message—" insisted Duffy.

"What if it's the impostor?" Henry asked the same time as Duffy spoke.

"Doesn't matter!" The Phantom and snapped the reins for speed.

"But—!" Duffy protested only to be ignored, as they rode off.

Not far from the inn, a Royalist patrol of five men emerged from the trees onto the road in front of the Phantom and Henry. The Phantom violently drew rein to avoid a collision. "Hawkins!"

Simultaneously, William spotted them. The Phantom and Henry turned their horses into an open field. The patrol followed. Despite the difference in size and weight, the patrol horses were fresher and gained ground. Under the sting of the spur, the Phantom and Henry urged their hunters to give every ounce of effort to escape the advancing pursuit. Alas, the horses already rode hard with extra weight. It became only a matter of time before they were either caught or the horses died from exertion.

A pistol shot wounded the lead Cavalier and halted the pursuit. William wheeled his startled mount around. A black figure astride a black horse appeared on the hill. In confusion, William looked ahead to the fleeing Phantom, the gap between them widening by delay.

"You two, after him!" William indicated the black figure. He and the others continued the original pursuit. Another pistol shot unhorsed a soldier. William saw the black figure chased off by his men.

The soldier who remained with William, aimed his pistol at the fleeing Phantom. The pistol discharged. The Phantom's horse screamed and fell in mid gallop, throwing its rider aside. The hat lost, yet mask remained.

Painfully slow to rise, the Phantom clumsily drew blade. The soldier slashed and cut the Phantom's sword hand, which made the sword fall. Before the soldier made a second swipe, Henry shot him from his horse. Sword in hand, Henry engaged William. He may have been a powerful man, but he faced an experienced cavalry officer. Broad shouldered, and strong, William matched Henry blow for blow.

"Henry, leave off!" the Phantom called. Unfortunately, the shout caused a brief delay in Henry's assault. William sent a slash across Henry's midriff. With a cry of pain and surprise, Henry fell from the saddle.

"No!" the Phantom cried.

William sprang from the saddle, his sword ready to confront the Phantom. "Yield!"

Fretful, the Phantom looked from Henry to William. "I cannot!"

"I beg you, do not provoke me!"

The Phantom proudly prepared for the end. "If you do not kill me now, Hedgepeth will later! I would rather die by your hand than his."

A groan of anguish escaped. "I cannot kill you, Duncan!"

A ripple of surprise crossed the Phantom's face. "Then spare my life as I did yours!"

The plea made William grimace and caused a lowering of his sword.

At the visible anguish, the Phantom took advantage and hastened a retreat. With an angry grumble, William sheathed his sword. In a flying tackle, he brought down the Phantom.

"I spared your life!" The Phantom kneed William aside and scrambled away.

"Curse you, Duncan O'Malley!" William swore. Again, he swiftly leapt upon the Phantom, who fell face first to the ground. "Now will you yield?" He struggled to turn the Phantom over onto the back. He grabbed the mask and yanked it. With a cry of pain, the mask tore away. A long braid of bright red hair tumbled free. "Samantha?"

"Move and I'll blow your brains out!" Henry leveled a pistol at William. Although he held his wound, the pistol remained steady. "Don't be fooled by my wound. I'll kill you if you make a false move. Now away!"

Too stunned and bewildered to object, William moved aside.

Samantha scrambled to her feet. "Henry won't hurt you, but you must be silent! I am lost if you are not."

Conflicting emotions played across William's face. He thrust the mask at her. "Go! I will say nothing."

She took the mask. Moved by impulse she kissed his cheek in gratitude. To her surprise, he grabbed her by the shoulders and kissed her mouth.

"Not so fast!" Wallace and six soldiers encircled them. "A touching scene, Hawkins. Conspiring with a traitor, who happens to be the major's wife. Sergeant, relieve the captain of his sword. Bind them. We shall have some amusement when the major hears of this."

William offered no resistance. Henry reluctantly yielded the pistol.

Chapter 18

IN THE COURTYARD AT FOXGLEN, HEDGEPETH RECEIVED REPORTS from two returning patrols. Wallace appeared leading a wounded Henry Wyatt by rope. Further curiosities came into view. William followed Wallace. He appeared disheveled with hands awkwardly held before him. Bright red locks caught Hedgepeth's attention. Only a moment of confusion before he recognized Samantha mounted on horseback wearing men's clothes.

"What manner of business is this, Captain Wallace?"

"Major, we captured the Phantom. A pretty catch she is too."

"My lady!" shouted Godwin. He and Anne ran from the house, only soldiers stopped their approach.

"You?" Hedgepeth's bluish-gray eyes flared in cold enraged brilliance.

"Aye," she bravely admitted.

"And shall be treated accordingly!" He pulled her down from the horse so roughly that she fell hard to the ground. He knelt and seized her doublet. "Your noble birth will not save you from the justice due a traitor!"

Anne seized Godwin. She stifled a scream by covering her mouth. William stiffened at the abused.

"There is more, Major. Two accomplices."

"I see one. The bailiff Wyatt." Hedgepeth motioned to Henry, who collapsed to his knees after the two-mile trek. "Who is the other?"

"Hawkins. Aiding and abetting the lady's attempted escape."

Enmity boiled, as Hedgepeth advanced upon William. "I knew it was only a matter of time before you acted. But with my wife!"

127

"No, he is innocent! I was making my escape at gun point," Samantha protested.

"Rarely does innocence speak with so passionate a kiss," said Wallace.

"Kiss?" Hedgepeth glared down at Samantha. "You add infidelity to your treason?" He kicked her aside.

"No! The kiss was my folly, not hers," William strenuously objected.

"Silence! I will deal with you later." Hedgepeth jerked Samantha to her feet. "You shall feel my wrath for such disgrace!"

"Major, no!" Godwin stepped forward. The butt of a musket in the midsection sent him back. He doubled over in pain. Anne helped him stand.

"Flog me to appease your anger, but harm not the lady!" shouted William.

Whatever inner turmoil compelled William, Hedgepeth noticed the outward manifestations of a clenched jowls, set chin, and intense eyes leveled at him. Such bold defiance even under desperate circumstance brought a small, twisted grin to Hedgepeth's lips. "I intend to have you punished, Captain."

"I told you William is innocent!" Samantha argued.

"William? Has this been a lengthy affair? Since Oxford, perhaps?"

"There is no affair, Major! Your wife's virtue is intact," said William.

Hedgepeth noticed her distress. "Very well, Hawkins. It will be as you say."

"Lawrence, please! I am the one responsible," Samantha pleaded.

He ignored her. "As for that man," he pointed to Henry. "Hang him! The oak tree on the road to town should serve well. Let all see how we deal with traitors. Lieutenant Hodges."

"No! Henry!" Samantha sobbed.

Though pale, Henry tenderly smiled. "It's all right, miss. I nearly bled my life away. I won't even feel the rope."

"Lord, receive his soul in peace," she prayed as soldiers drug Henry away.

"Corporal, fetch Sergeant Strickland," Hedgepeth ordered. "As for the house," he glared at Godwin and Anne, "Perhaps witnessing the King's justice will curb their insolence. Fetch the servants," he told a nearby soldier. "Wallace." He waved him toward the stables.

With a snap of the reins, William's horse launched forward. He did not reply to Hedgepeth's stinging comments on the short ride to the stables. He purposed in his mind that the least he could do was shield Samantha from harm. *Duncan would do no less*, he told himself.

Upon arrival, Nathan became befuddled. William stripped to the waist, Lady Samantha in men's dress, and Hedgepeth practiced with a whip. By instinct, he advanced a step toward William when a firm hand from Wallace stopped him.

"Strickland. Nice of you to join us for some amusement," the major snickered.

William met Nathan's look of dreadful comprehension. His recklessness had gone too far this time. What pain would Hedgepeth inflict upon his most trusted yet innocent friend because of his folly? He knew whatever the punishment, Nathan would suffer in stalwart silence, the same as when caught in some childhood mischief. This fact caused William great distress. He shied from Nathan's watchful stare. Inadvertently, he caught Samantha's gaze. Her eyes moist with tears. He wondered just how much his lashing would help her.

"I tried, Duncan," he murmured.

Hedgepeth practiced with the whip several more times. Behind him, the men forced the household servants into position to watch the flogging.

Two soldiers shoved William toward a supporting timber of the stable. One held him still while the other fastened his hands above his head. Upon hearing the crack of the whip, William took a deep breath to prepare for the lash. He gritted his teeth in an effort not to give Hedgepeth the satisfaction of hearing him cry out in pain. Alas, not even a moment passed between being secured to the post and feeling the first blow. He held back an outcry to stinging pain by gripping the bounds that held his arms. Straightening the limbs with tight bounds made the beating more painful, as taut flesh bruised and striped more easily.

The sting of the blows soon gave way to sharp pain. The quick, harsh succession of lashes exposed torn flesh. After the tenth lash, William tried to lessen the pain by raising himself on the rope and standing on tiptoes. The last thing he wanted to do was cry out. It became increasingly difficult. His face grew taut, and he perspired profusely in a valiant attempt to remain mute beneath the savage beating. He bit his lower lip so hard to keep silent that it became as bloody as his back. He screwed his eyes shut against the increasing pain. Tears of anguish fell from the corners of his eyes as raw opened flesh felt the whip. He could no longer maintain his raised position. He sagged beneath the vicious onslaught of Hedgepeth's whip. Finally, a savage lash cut into his left shoulder at the base of his neck. William could endure no more, and with a horrific outcry, he fainted.

Samantha seized Hedgepeth. "For mercy's sake stop before you kill him!" she tearfully pleaded.

From behind could be heard the weeping of the female servants.

Hedgepeth chuckled with hauteur. "I won't kill him. Simply gave him a thrashing he will never forget. Such an impression is more effective than death. Do you not agree, dear wife?"

In terror, Samantha drew back. Nathan managed to move directly behind her, so she bumped into him. Her fretful glance at him was met by his reassuring squeeze at her elbow.

"Take him down and throw him in the cellar!"

"Have mercy and let Sergeant Strickland tend his wounds," she urged.

Nathan retained his hold on her until he met Hedgepeth's critical eye. By the pale pallor and beads of sweat on Nathan's brow and upper lip, he too suffered the lashing.

"For pity's sake!" Samantha's voice quivered.

Nathan remained stubbornly resolute beneath Hedgepeth's unwavering gaze. Only a slight movement of his brow displayed defiance as loathsome as William's earlier expression. A sadistic smile appeared on Hedgepeth's mouth.

"Very well." He signaled two soldiers to take William and Nathan away.

"Is it wise to allow Strickland to tend Hawkins?" asked Wallace.

"Strickland is no threat if Hawkins is contained. Have her locked in her room with a foot chained to the bed until I decide how to deal with her." He gave Wallace the whip. "As for the servants, place all under house arrest!"

Several women squealed; others murmured soft prayers. Anne pale, her eyes red and cheeks stained with tears. Godwin snarled in rigid silence.

Down in the cellar, beyond kegs of ale and bottles of wine, were two small rooms with heavy doors. Into one of the rooms, the soldier roughly dropped William. He neither moved nor made a sound. When the door closed, Nathan knelt, anxious for any sign of life. The bloody crisscrossed scars on showed William endured a ruthless beating just shy of lethal.

"Will?" There was a faint groan in response, then stillness.

With his hand on William's bare shoulder, Nathan felt the cool skin. Lying half naked on cold stone floor in a damp cellar could cause more problems. He spied an old pallet in one corner. It would be better than the cold hard floor. Gingerly, he lifted William and laid him on his stomach atop the pallet.

The eyelids blinked then slowly opened. The light very dim. "Nathan?"

"I'm here."

"Where are we?"

"The cellar."

"What of Samantha?"

"I don't know what Hedgepeth is planning. Your whipping only saved her for the moment. From what? I don't know, though I see the painful results. Sixteen vicious stripes. Could have been more if not for the lady."

William shivered from the cold and fought to stay awake to answer. "My patrol happened upon the Phantom. I lost two men in the pursuit, but we caught them. There was a plea for death rather than face Hedgepeth. I couldn't do it. In the struggle, I pull off the mask—! Oh, Nathan, it wasn't Duncan, but Samantha!" He gritted his teeth against the pain and cold.

"Explains her manner of dress. I would give you my coat, but not on your raw back."

William fought unconsciousness to finish the tale. "Before I could think or act clearly, Wallace and his men surrounded us. Oh, wretched man that I am! If I granted her request and not acted on impulse, she would be free now …," His voice weakly trailed off.

Godwin entered and accompanied by a soldier. He carried a tray with a lantern, bowl, bandages, and several small jars. A blanket hung over his arm.

"Put everything on the floor and get out," the solider ordered.

Godwin followed instructions. A careful nod to Nathan was enough to convey the meaning of his visit. When the door closed, Nathan tended William's wounds.

Meanwhile, the soldiers escorted Henry to a sturdy one hundred-year-old oak tree in view of the road leading to the village. Lieutenant Hodges ordered a sign written and nailed to the tree for all to see.

While a soldier lifted Henry onto the cob from which they would hang him, another tossed a rope over a high thick branch. He secured the rope to the trunk with sufficient slack to for the noose.

"Any last words? Make amends to your Maker, perhaps?" asked Hodges.

Henry gritted back pain to sit up in the saddle. "I have served my earthly master and heavenly one to the best of my ability." He lifted his eyes to heaven and spoke in loud voice, "God bless the O'Malleys and have mercy on England!"

A shot struck the soldier before he could place the noose around Henry's neck. Startled by the violence, the cob reared, threw Henry, and galloped off. Hodges turned in the direction of the shot. Ten yards up the road a black figure sat astride a black horse with pistol in hand.

"Impossible!"

Suddenly, Hodges and his men were attacked from behind. One soldier became wounded by pistol shot while the other engaged with a club. The black figure gallop towards Hodges, now with sword in hand. This second Phantom wore the exact same clothes as the first; all black with a silk mask. Only this one sat taller in the saddle, with superior strength and ferocity in combat. Hodges fell unconscious from his horse.

Henry felt hands grab him by the arms. He stiffened with what little resistance he could manage in his injured condition.

"Easy, Henry," said familiar voice.

Through the haze of weariness, Henry saw, "Duffy?"

"Aye, old friend. Lean on Miller and me." Duffy and Miller raised Henry to his feet.

"My mistress!" Henry clamored and bit back pain.

"She will be saved," said a new authoritative voice. The black rider appeared in front of them and lead the cob intended for execution.

Baffled, Henry asked, "Who are you?"

He flashed a winsome smile. "An old friend. Now, no more questions, Henry Wyatt. Gently, lads, lift him into the saddle. Miller, you mount behind and keep him steady."

Thought of rescue, gave Henry a surge of strength. Once Henry was astride with Miller seated behind him for support, they left.

Chapter 19

AFTER THE ROYALIST SMITH FASTENED AN ANKLE FETTER TO Samantha's left leg, he fixed the other end to her bed. Barely enough chain remained to lay upon the bed in a reasonably comfortable manner or reach the vanity.

She felt a cold shiver when the door locked. The furnishings and trappings of her chamber remained the same, yet oddly devoid of comfort she once drew from her favorite manor. Foxglen went from being her dowry, to a place of sanctuary from her husband, now to a prison. Overcome with emotion, she wept. She cursed the day Lawrence was born. His abuse drove her to the point of utter despair and hopelessness time and time again. When war came, her first inclination was to wish him dead, a victim of the bloody civil war. A stray musket ball or sword would free her from Lawrence Hedgepeth and his private tyranny. In God's mercy, his absence from Foxglen became the respite her soul needed, while the war provided focus and direction for her energies.

The unfortunate aspect in all this, was the sporadic communication with her brothers. Any letters she received spoke of deep regrets for England and hopes for her well-being. Since they fought so valiantly to keep the country from being overrun by a tyrant, how could she add to their burden by complaining of her marriage? In the face of anarchy, a troubled marriage was a trifle matter. She knew Duncan would move heaven and earth if she needed, but duty and honor demanded she accept the current situation. Thus, she endured, and with God's help, protected all Rutherford holdings within her charge.

Her mettle became sorely tested each time Lawrence unexpectedly returned. The old terror and despair that had been her close companions for so long came crashing back upon first sight of him. She couldn't give in to those named devils! She would not! Too many people depended upon her. They would suffer his wrath if she faltered. Despite the onslaught of the haunting memories and surging feelings, she pressed on—until she pushed too far. Now she was in chains, her household punished, and— *Oh, William!* Duncan's old friend received the violent lashing meant for her. With silent courage, he endured the vicious beating.

"Why, William? Why did you do it?"

She touched her lips in remembrance of his kiss. Tears began anew. She fervently prayed. "Dear Lord, mine heart and mind are confused and discouraged. Once more that monster heaps his wickedness upon this house. More wretchedly, with him comes a gallant, a man of strength and courage, with tenderness of heart toward my family. Oh, Lord!" she cried. "I do not want to sin, but my heart stirs with affection for a man who is not my husband. I beseech You, Almighty Father, keep my heart safe. Somehow remove the wickedness from this house. As for William's stripes, show grace and mercy, ease his pain and suffering on my behalf! Amen."

Downstairs, a messenger arrived. He wore the coat and colors of Prince Rupert's Personal Regiment. He requested urgent admittance to Hedgepeth. The stout grizzled man handed a letter to Hedgepeth.

After scrutinizing the messenger's appearance, Hedgepeth read. "Rupert commands me to Pontefract Castle for a meeting of all commanders in three days."

"Perhaps the King has decided upon a course of action," said Wallace.

Hedgepeth glanced outside to see the sun passed its apex. "Too late to start today. Have my platoon ready at dawn." He turned to the messenger. "Give my regards to the Prince. Tell him, I will see him shortly."

"My orders take me to Colonel Fleming from here not back to Pontefract."

Hedgepeth nodded acknowledgement. "Go to the kitchen and refresh yourself before departure."

"Thank you."

In the kitchen, he spied Godwin. The steward's eyes grew wide as he quickly approached.

"Duf—!" Godwin began, yet quickly silenced by a hand.

Duffy carefully withdrew a small letter from inside his doublet and gave it to Godwin. "Read and destroy," he whispered then turned to Cookie, who did not know him. "I need refreshment and food." He sat at the table.

Cookie scowled but went to fetch the food.

Godwin turned aside to read the coded message. A faint smile appeared. He made a nod of understanding to Duffy. He moved to Cookie. She ladled soup into a bowl from a kettle over the fire.

"That should be sufficient," he said.

"Aye, Royalists have gotten fat on my food."

"Gently, Cookie." Godwin ushered her away. In doing so, he let the crumpled note fall into the fire. He watched it burn before leaving the hearth.

Samantha heard the horseman arrive then depart. She wondered *why?* Her curiosity turned to fear at the door opening. Her stomach churned to the point of upheaval when Lawrence entered. His cold bluish-gray eyes sent a dreadful chill to the core. When he deliberately locked the door, her knees grew weak in understanding of the action. She grabbed the bedpost in support lest she fall from fright.

He flashed a haughty smile. "You know your punishment, wife."

"I would rather you kill me." She managed to speak in forced response.

"And deprive me of the enjoyment?" He seized her. "It is my kiss you will remember far longer than his."

She knew the futility of struggle. In the end he would have his way, and once more leave her to deal with the humiliation of violence forced upon her. No punishment could be more effective.

All the months of regaining her strength taken away in one night. It felt as if he never left Foxglen, when, he and his platoon left at dawn. She heard rather than saw the departure, as she listlessly sat in bed. Even Anne's words of encouragement spoken when she brought food, gave no hope or strength. For the entire day, Samantha wished, prayed, and sobbed for Lawrence never to return. Finally, with great fatigue of body and soul, she fell into a fitful sleep around midnight.

She awoke with a start when one hand covered her mouth, and another restrained her body. Her eyes snapped opened in sheer terror. Did Lawrence play a cruel trick? A shadowy figure loomed over her, back lit by a candle. Her heart raced when the dark face moved closer. She wanted to scream, but the hand over her mouth prevented her. His weight pressed down on her. A small squeal escaped.

"Softly!" he whispered. "I mean you no harm. I have come to take you from here," he spoke with a soothing tone. He showed her a key.

With uncertainty, she searched his masked face, or rather his eyes as seen by candlelight. The friendliness in his gaze increased when he smiled with reassurance.

"You need not fear me. Promise not to scream and I will release you."

When she nodded, he removed his hand from her mouth. "Who are you?"

"A friend." He undid her fetter.

She sat up to rub her ankle once the cumbersome weight was removed.

"Come," he beckoned.

His outstretched hand hopeful, but she hesitated.

"If you wish freedom from your husband, then come."

Again, his voice friendly in prompting. It may prove folly, but anything was better than being a prisoner in her own home. She grabbed his hand.

They proceeded into the hall without the candle. Dim moonlight shown through a few small windows in the hall. Wall sconces lit the way near certain rooms. This provided enough light to navigate, yet not for clear facial recognition.

Upon hearing a noise, he halted at the corner and pressed back against the wall to avoid detection. She did the same. She clenched his hand when he peeked around the corner. The sound came from a soldier, who fell asleep on duty and stirred to get comfortable. They continued down the back stairs. Whoever her rescuer was, he knew the house.

When they reached the kitchen, Samantha saw Nathan and Miller bring William up from the cellar. He wore a shirt and cloak about his bandages. "William?"

"Shh!" the black clothed man commanded. "Time for reunion later."

Silently, yet slowly with the wounded William, they made their way to the stables. Duffy waited with six horses.

"Master Duffy—" Samantha began only silenced by a hand of her rescuer.

Miller and Nathan helped William to mount. He swayed in pain, wobbly in movement.

"Steady, Captain." The man braced William. "Your wounds will soon be tended. For the present, you must be strong for the gallop."

William gritted back the pain and straightened in the saddle. "Lead on."

Samantha found each new revelation increasing her curiosity concerning the black dressed individual. True, he offered freedom from Lawrence and aid for William, but who was he? Why were Miller and Duffy helping him? Did they know him that they obeyed without question? Once they were safely away, she would learn the reason. At present, freedom called, freedom that brought her hope and courage to ride from Foxglen in the dead of night.

Chapter 20

AT FOXGLEN, WALLACE WOKE. HIS HEAD ACHED, HE FELT DIZZY, and sickness in the pit of his stomach. He staggered to the door where he struggled to open it. In the hall, he noticed the guard at the lady's door lay slumped against the wall. He staggered to the guard and nearly fell when he knelt to examine him. His eyes glossy and unresponsive.

"Captain!" Hodges wobbled over with a hand on the wall to remain standing.

Wallace supported himself on the door handle to rise. "You too?"

"And Morris."

"This was no accident! Someone drugged dinner." At a sudden thought, Wallace burst into the lady's chambers. He let out a phrase of Scottish curses upon finding the room empty. "To the cellar!"

Hodges tripped and nearly tumbled in his rush to follow Wallace. The captain appeared to regain his senses by the way he moved. Hodges barely reached the cellar when a tremendous roar came from Wallace.

"Gone!" He pushed passed Hodges to quickly climb the stairs. By the time they returned to the kitchen, even Hodges' head cleared. They noticed a doped Godwin trying to get about.

"Steward!" snapped Wallace.

Godwin could barely stand much less move. "Captain?"

"He's been drugged too. Maybe the whole house," said Hodges.

"I found this on the table." Godwin handed a paper to Wallace.

He snatched it to read aloud. "'*They ate the stew and then did sleep, while under their noses the Phantom did creep!*' We've been duped!"

"It must be the one I told you about yesterday," Hodges said.

"Two Phantoms?"

Godwin fought a smile when Wallace and Hodges left the kitchen.

A soldier met them in the hallway. "Captain, the major is back!"

The soldier no sooner spoke when a very agitated Hedgepeth arrived.

"We've been played for fools! The message was a ruse. This is an actual letter from the Rupert!" Hedgepeth pulled out a wrinkled piece of paper. "If I had not met Lieutenant Gilmore on the highway, I would have ridden all the way to Pontefract Castle on a wild goose chase!"

"He laid a clever trap. Your discovery only saved a journey. It did not prevent the intended," said Wallace.

"What do you mean?"

"Remember the man Lieutenant Hodges reported? The one who rescued the bailiff?"

"What about him?"

Wallace gathered his courage to make the unsavory report. "While you were being led on a wild goose chase, everyone, household and soldiers, were drugged at dinner—"

Hedgepeth did not wait for Wallace to finish and raced up to Samantha's chambers. The expletives he uttered far exceeded those of Wallace.

"Hawkins and Strickland are gone also. This was left." Wallace handed over the note.

After reading it, Hedgepeth tore the paper. "What have you done?"

"I was in the process of ascertaining the situation when you returned."

"Send out patrols immediately!" He went to Anne's chamber.

Anne gasped in fright when Hedgepeth entered followed by Wallace and Hodges. She wore a dressing gown and sat on the edge of her bed. Pale and groggy, she stared at him with dread.

"What do you know of this?" he demanded.

"Know of what?" she stammered with fearful uncertainty.

"Don't play the fool with me!" He seized her and jerked her to her feet.

She screamed and said, "I know nothing! I awoke feeling sick!"

"Sick indeed!"

"Major!" Wallace said before Hedgepeth could strike Anne. "She speaks the truth. Witness her condition. If she were involved, why is she still here?"

Hedgepeth snarled. "This was done on purpose, so I would be convinced of her innocence in plotting the escape!"

"She was never alone with the lady. Either Lieutenant Hodges or I accompanied her when bringing food or anything else. Nothing transpired between them that we did not hear or see," said Wallace.

Anne trembled and shook her head. "I don't know what you're talking about. Has something happened to Samantha?"

Hedgepeth roughly released her. She fell to the floor against the bed. "She won't elude me for long. Confiscate whatever is needed to equip and satisfy the men."

"Destroy this house and the duke-" Anne bravely began.

"Will what? Save you? I could crush the arrogant Duncan O'Malley with one hand!" He waved a clenched fist in her face then stormed out of the room. "Due to Hawkins' condition, they cannot travel far. Tear the village apart if you must but find them!" he ordered Wallace and Hodges.

By the time they arrived at Walcott's farm, William was in intolerable pain. He nearly fainted when dismounting. Nathan and Miller caught him.

"Miller, Duffy, leave once you have helped the captain get situated," he said.

"Aye, sir," they spoke in near unison.

"They will tend him. Come with me," the masked man assured her.

Samantha hesitated to search his face and see beyond the mask. Most certainly the impostor since he wore an identical costume. His benevolent gaze confused her.

"Sir, you are my rescuer and I thank you. Yet, I cannot help but wonder who you are. You command my servants and know my habits. This is unnerving and perplexing."

He smiled, large and gregarious. "Come, and I shall explain." When held out his hand, she drew back, skeptical. "I have brought you safe this far why distrust me now?"

With a defiant scowl, she waved at him. "Lead on."

She followed him upstairs from the lower barn to a large dormitory room with three cots, stove for heating, chairs, and small table. By lantern light, she saw Henry laid on one cot. His torso bandaged, but alive!

"Henry!" Tears swelled as she hurried to the cot.

"There now, miss. Henry Wyatt is not so easy to kill."

"But your wound?"

"With rest and food, I am better. The wound is a nuisance."

"How -?" She turned to her rescuer. She gaped at seeing the hat and mask were off. "Rory?" She embraced her brother with tears of joy. "Rory!" She held his face. "Lawrence told me you were killed in battle!"

"Happily, no. Although, I nearly lost both legs from wounds. It took many months to recover and walk again. I am whole and hardy once more."

Through tears she examined him. He shaved off his mustache to reveal a gentle face accustomed to mirth. His generous mouth smiled in his winsome manner. There was no mistaking the energetic gleam of his bright eyes. "Your upper lip must get cold."

"The mask kept it warm." He affectionately kissed her hand.

"How did you come to be dressed in such a fashion? And to rescue me? Or Henry?"

"One question at a time." Rory drew her to the table to sit. "With Royalists everywhere, I covertly arrived in Lincolnshire a few days ago and spoke to Duffy. He told me all that has happened these last few years. About Howard's death, and Lawrence's return. Imagine learning that my little sister was the Phantom Rider engaging Royalists in deadly escapades."

"Anne still grieves for Howard," she lamented then quickly: "Oh, dear! What of Anne? Why was she not rescued as well?"

"I first went to her chamber. Alas, she must have received a bowl of drugged stew by mistake. I could not wake her."

"Drugged stew?"

"I sent Duffy in the disguise of a Royal messenger to draw Lawrence away from Foxglen. While there, he delivered a coded message to Godwin with instructions for rescue. This included employing Cookie's talents for medicine. To mix a sleeping draught into the stew that all would to eat, except, you and Anne. What happened with Anne, I don't know. I had no choice but to leave her to rescue you and Hawkins."

Samantha fretfully chewed on her thumbnail and muttered; "Lord only knows what Lawrence will do to her once he finds us gone. He swore to have my head or rather the Phantom's."

"There is nothing to be done without greater risk. We must leave her in God's hands."

Samantha fought back a wave of regretful tears. "How did you know about William? He received the lash after my capture. You couldn't have known that. And why wasn't he or Nathan drugged?"

"Duffy heard about him while at Foxglen. As for not being drugged, prisoners usually eat bread and water."

Hearing movement on the outer stairs, Rory drew his sword. He waved Samantha to stand back when the door opened. Henry pushed aside the covers to rise. He grabbed the pistol on the nightstand and took up position in front of Samantha. Walcott balked at sight of a blade and pistol pointed at him.

"You should give a warning before entering," Rory chided. He sheathed his sword.

"Too dangerous. Royalist are swarming the countryside. Apparently, the major returned earlier than expected and arrested everyone at Foxglen. You cannot stay here."

"We can't leave William. If they find him, Lawrence will kill him," she said to Rory.

"My task is to get you safely to London."

"Rory, he took the lash meant for me! I will not leave him," she declared.

"We can take him to the woodman's cottage," said Henry.

"Aye," she heartily agreed. "We," she motioned to Henry, "have used it before."

"You must move quickly before discovery," Walcott advised.

"Very well," said Rory.

With Rory once more disguised at the Phantom, and Henry fully dressed, they left the upper room to fetch Nathan and William. With cloak and shirt off, William sat on the edge of the cot. Nathan rewrapped the bandage around William's torso.

"There is a change of plan," began Rory. "Hedgepeth returned sooner than expected. Patrols search for us. We must continue to a safer location."

Samantha sat beside William; gravely concern. "Can you manage?"

"God willing." He reached for Nathan. "Help me dress."

"We need another horse for Henry," Rory told Walcott.

"I'll saddle one while he makes ready," he spoke in regard of William.

Again, William needed help to mount. Nathan rode beside him. Henry took the lead. Samantha rode behind Henry, with Rory as rear guard.

Henry kept the trek as slow and steady as possible while avoiding main roads and well-trodden paths. His wound painful, but tolerable. Despite the numerous Royalist patrols, they arrived safely at the woodman's cottage. A sturdy stone structure with a wood tiled roof, and small windows. The roof pitch showed tall enough for a loft. Moss and vines grew on the tiles and stone signs of age and lack of maintenance.

Behind the cottage, stood a small pen suitable for horses. Henry dismounted to open the gate for entry. He ignored the pain. Once inside the corral, Nathan aided William to dismount. William's face pale from obvious pain. A cry escaped when his knees threatened to give way once on foot. Nathan caught him.

"Steady, Captain. You can rest undisturbed once inside," said Rory.

Samantha came along the other side of William to aid Nathan. The bottom floor consisted of a middle room with a table, four old chairs, and a hearth. A door at the north end led to a bedroom. A ladder rose to the loft. They took William to the bedroom and gently lowered him to sit on the edge of the bed.

Nathan removed the satchel he wore. At Samantha's inquisitive gaze he explained. "Godwin brought this when he first went into the cellar. Some ointment and bandages."

She simply nodded. "I will let you tend him." She moved to leave when Rory entered.

"I shall just be a moment," he told her and shut the door. "Doubtless you wonder who I am," he said to William.

"The question did cross my mind," William spoke between clenched teeth and Nathan removed the shirt. He exhaled with relief once the shirt off. He gingerly lifted his arms for Nathan to unwrap the bandage.

"It has been years, but I may look familiar." Rory removed his mask.

William made a lopsided smile of recognition. "I thought the Phantom was Duncan. It appears I was wrong twice. First Samantha, now you."

"Duncan is a bit too busy for such a task." With the bandage completely gone, Rory moved to view William's back. He uttered a low impulsive gasp.

"I can assure you; it feels as painful as it looks," William groused.

"Take care of him, Sergeant." Rory left.

Henry built a fire while Samantha searched the store of food.

"I can make porridge, but William will need meat for strength," she told Rory.

"Tomorrow may be safe enough to hunt or set a trap. By then, the search should be less intense. As for accommodations, Henry will stay down here, while we take the loft." He ushered her up the ladder.

The loft also showed signs of occupation. Two cots were complete with bedding along with a small table containing a pitcher and basin. "You obviously made use of the cottage," Rory said.

"It served multiple purposes. Howard used it as meeting place for those employed in the Phantom's network. When necessary, we hid Parliament sympathizers here. Even some of our own people ..." Her voice cracked, as she sat on the cot.

Curious, he asked, "Who?"

She sniffled back emotions to answer. "Do you remember Jack Bannon? I played with his sister Penny when father took us to visit the farmers."

"I remember Jack."

"He lost an eye when forced into service for the King! Pat Sully lost an arm, other men of the village maimed or killed." She paused when the words stuck in her throat. "Jack and Sully deserted when a Royalist captain threatened their family for not continuing to fight. How could they?" Passion made her rise. "Jack's vision nearly gone and Sully with one arm. They came to me for help. I did so … only … they were found …" She screwed her eyes shut against tears.

Sympathetic, Rory held her. At his touch, her eyes opened. She tenderly smiled at him.

"I thank God you are alive. Lawrence's cruelty …" she couldn't finish, rather chewed on her thumbnail as a sudden wave of tears rose.

When she hesitated, he tilted her head to look at her. "Tell me."

"He meant the lash for me!" She abruptly moved away silenced by tormented memories. She gathered her arms about her in hopes of rubbing away cold terror. When he gripped on her arm, her whole body stiffened, and she withdrew further from him.

The reaction disturbed him. "This was not the first whipping, was it?"

She lowered her head. She could not let fear ruin the reunion.

At her silence, he spoke with dismay. "I have witnessed Lawrence's vehemence toward Duncan and myself. I never thought he would harm you. Hawkins' back shows otherwise."

She opened her eyes to speak, though did not face him. "I discovered an unfinished letter father addressed to me, though strangely sealed with the family signet. He directed me to read grandfather's journals, where I learned about a scandal involving the Duke of Buckingham, Lord Kyle, and grandfather. Along with names of two estates. Foxhill and Foxmeath."

The abrupt change in subject surprised him, but more so the revelation of their father's letter. "Good heavens! Why didn't you tell us?"

"I never knew where you were. What exactly would I say since father arranged the marriage to satisfy Lord Kyle's ambition?"

He shifted a bit awkward at the rebuff. "You should have fled to London for safety."

Pricked by the statement, she grew defensive. "I am the duke's sister and have duties to protect our family's legacy. Too many have suffered. Howard, Jimmy Oswell, Jack, and others died at the hands of Royalists. Many had their homes ransacked. William whipped instead of me!"

"I meant no offense. You have always been a brave girl. The thought of anyone harming you-" his voice choked. "Well, it is over now. Lawrence won't touch you again. Once Duncan learns of this, he will have marriage dissolved."

"Father said the same in his letter." Her brows knitted in anger. "Lord Kyle used this scandal against father to force the marriage contract."

Rory scowled at her persistence of the subject. "This is not the time for such a discussion. There will be, I promise," he said to forestall her objections. "On the morrow I will take you to London. The army has been recalled by Parliament so Duncan will be there."

"What of William? We can't leave him. Not in his injured condition."

"He is safe here."

"No. We stay until William regains his strength. Then we all proceed to London."

Rory pursed his lips with annoyance. "You're being stubborn."

She urgently seized his hand. "Rory, those stripes were meant for me as punishment for my taking up the Phantom's mantle. I cannot abandon William. I will not!"

His argument waned. "I saw those stripes. It can take weeks to heal."

"I owe him my life. What are a few weeks?"

Rory scratched his chin in thought. "Very well. Duffy mentioned you and Howard as the Phantom, yet not *why*?"

Samantha explained the whole sequence of events from the origin of the Phantom, various escapades, Howard's death, and her subsequent actions. In conclusion she said, "After what happen to Jack and the others, I could not deny Howard's dying request. The Phantom became the people's hero, their hope, a reason to persevere. I needed a reason …" her voice faded.

"What?" he asked, not hearing her last statement.

Samantha righted herself and continued. "Armed with Henry's strength, and our underground network, I assumed the role."

Rory grinned. "You never ceased to amaze me, little sister. Now rest."

Chapter 21

DUFFY BECAME THE SOURCE OF SUPPLIES AND INFORMATION. Several times he implored Rory to lend his aid when the Royalists became too harsh. Hedgepeth mercilessly turned the countryside upside down searching for Samantha, William, and the man who engineered their escape. Although Rory originally donned the disguise to rescue Samantha, he took advantage of the situation to thwart Hedgepeth and confuse the search until William sufficiently recovered to travel. He rode four times as the Phantom during their month of hiding.

One time when Rory returned, Nathan stood at the table mixing a paste in a wooden bowl. He saw no one else in the room. "Where are Samantha and Henry?"

"Setting traps. They will return before nightfall."

"How is he?" Rory motioned to the bedroom.

"Much better. This may be the last salve needed."

"Wait here. I would speak with him." Rory removed his hat and mask before he entered the bedchamber. William sat up in bed. "Nathan says you are doing better."

"Aye. I should be ready to leave in few days."

"Good." Rory shut the door. He pulled the chair up the bed. "Samantha is setting traps with Henry, so we can speak freely. I would hear your intentions toward my sister."

"Save protecting her from the major, I have no intentions."

Rory shook his head. "Do not try to fool me. I have watched you both for weeks."

149

"My intentions are honorable. Past that, I can say no more."

Rory scrutinized William. "Why do it? Take the lash."

William closed his eyes with a heavy sigh. "I have seen enough death and destruction to last many lifetimes. This war has turned peaceful men into wanton beasts. Hedgepeth is among the worst. Especially after his father became crippled by cannonade. He plunders without mercy." He stared at the far wall. His voice thick with disgust, as he continued. "Although, he is not alone. Rupert cares not a whit for the people. Old, infirmed, women, children. His only desire is to keep his uncle on the throne. His determination to do so is as equal in ferocity as Hedgepeth's desire for revenge." He glanced at Rory. "I'm certain you have experienced similar on Parliament's side."

Rory slowly nodded. "Some are overzealous, though more in reaction to reports of Royalist atrocities. Not that I excuse it," he hastily added. "You knew Samantha's identity."

"Aye. However, before we arrived at Foxglen, I had no personal connection to the other places ransacked. As we grew increasingly disturbed by events, Nathan and I participated as little as possible. Even so, I will never forget the faces of horror. Knowing Samantha's identity, I could scarcely believe he would be cruel to his own wife. The sister of a once dear friend," he murmured mostly to himself. "Such debase men should find a tavern wench or brothel." He swore. "It might have been impulsive, yet I could no longer tolerate his cruelty. Or this war's atrocities."

Rory's brows deeply furrowed in concerned curiosity. "You make her situation sound barbaric."

"Aye!" William declared. However, when he saw Rory's guarded expression, he asked, "Has she not told you about Hedgepeth?"

"She deflects any conversation about him. By your condition, I surmised she suffered past whippings. However, your words suggest more." Rory noticed vacillation, so he pressed William. "Tell me what you know."

"It is a very sensitive issue. One she may feel great shame, thus unwilling to speak."

"What shame?" Rory insisted. "Wait! Have you and she ..."

"No! Hedgepeth." At Rory's gaze of insistence, he spoke with discretion. "In a word, violent marital rape. Savage beatings if she refused, which resulted in numerous injuries."

Enraged, Rory bolted up. In agitated steps he circled the room. Several times, he began to speak to William only stopped. The third time he resumed his seat to ask, "How did you discover this?"

Empathy filled the response. "A scullery maid took a fancy to Nathan, and free with information that is common knowledge among the servants."

"Bribed?"

"No! After witnessing his cruel and brutish behavior towards her, I sought to learn *why*. I directed Nathan to ask questions." He paused to gather his words. "I am the oldest of eight with three sisters. Thought of anyone harming them, especially wanton brutality by a husband … When the Phantom's identity was discovered, he ordered a public whipping-"

"And you took her place," Rory concluded.

William nodded. He again focused on the far wall. "As I said, I witnessed too many heinous acts committed by debauched men."

"*That* type of behavior is not tolerated by Parliament. Some men hanged for daring to touch a woman not their wife. Cromwell is particularly strict when it comes to discipline. Fairfax too. Others maybe lax." Rory grew a touch melancholy. His voice barely above a whisper. "As Puritans, we believe marriage should be between two people in love and the bed an honorable estate before God." He sniffed back distress.

"I believe the same. Even being raised Anglican." William sneered, as he said, "Though the law views it differently between men and women. Men dominate and women chattel."

Just *one* of the many points of contention between us, the King, and royal law. We believe the Scriptures call for men and women to be treated equally before God with the same rights. Only different in function and responsibility. Do you treat your sisters differently because of their sex?"

"No. Which is why I said what I did about harming them."

"Then even as an Anglican, you believe the law to be wrong."

William nodded. "Aye." A small wry smile appeared. "We used to argue law and politics at Oxford. Though Duncan more astute in such matter. Still, we found common ground." The smile faded at hearing voices.

"Sounds like they have returned," said Rory. "Say nothing of this discussion," he spoke in hasty voice to William. He emerged from the bedroom. Samantha and Henry placed two rabbits and a small sack on the table. "Success, I see.

"I dug up some tubers and wild onions. Should make for a good stew," said Henry.

"How is William?" she asked Rory.

"Much better. This should help strengthen him for departure."

"Oh," said Henry with thought. He pulled out a piece of paper. "Duffy sends this."

Rory snatched it to read. "The ploy didn't work. I must return."

"I can help. My wound is completely healed," said Henry.

Rory clapped Henry's shoulder. "Once they have left for London. For now, remain here. Save me some stew." He donned the disguise to depart.

William heard Henry, Nathan, and Samantha in the main room. By the sounds of conversation and smell, they prepared dinner. Since arriving at the woodman's cottage, she fed him the evening meal and they talked. When Rory was present, William kept the conversations from dwelling on sensitive subjects. During the times of Rory's absence, he noticed shyness from Samantha not seen before. She always acted so self-assured. Indeed, she proved to be a capable and resourceful woman. Having gained knowledge of her past, he knew it would take time to overcome inhibition from the brutalizing.

Speaking on casual topics, she proved bright and intelligent. Their conversations ranged from God, childhood, the war, to their hopes for the future of England, and peace. In matters of religion, his background limited to what he heard in Anglican sermons. His belief in God tempered by years of war.

After his discussion with Rory, William determined to be bolder. He might not get another chance. He needed to wait for the right moment, perhaps when finished with the stew. He sat on the bed on top of the covers fully dressed, but without boots. He smiled when she arrived.

"Are you well enough to join us in the main room?" she asked.

"And miss our private discussions?" His smile widened. "Though I am well enough to feed myself." He took the bowl. "This is quite good."

"Henry calls it a secret family recipe."

"What about you?" he asked with a mouthful.

"I already ate."

"Did I hear Rory leave?"

"Aye. Apparently, Duffy sent word the task is not done."

A few moments of silence passed as he ate. He placed the bowl aside when finished. "I appreciate the risk you and Rory take to remain here. My back is well enough that we can leave for London whenever you like."

"I'm sure Rory will be glad to hear that," she murmured.

"And you?" he asked at her forlorn reaction.

"Do not misunderstand, I am pleased. I sorely regret every lash you received."

William gallantly smiled. "Thank you for your concern, but the stripes on my back mean nothing compared to helping a friend by rescuing his sister." He kissed her hand.

She quickly withdrew her hand. "Please, I am a married woman!"

"To that beast? You owe him no allegiance!"

"I owe it to God and my family not to disgrace them. Neither has our situation ended. We must go to London and Duncan for protection."

"What makes you think Duncan will receive me?"

"When he learns what you did, I am certain he will," she said confidently. "The least he can do is offer you protection until Lawrence can be dealt with. Perhaps, a broken friendship can be mended."

"I hope so," he droned with great melancholy.

She became sympathetic at his discomposure. "What happened between you and him?"

"Duncan never told you?"

"I have not seen him in three years. The few letters were casual in tone, nothing of great depth. Rory says he is well, only neck deep in politics and war to the point of distraction."

William screwed his lips. "Yet you are confident he will receive me?"

"I know my brother. Despite his occasional temper and bellowing, he is a fair man. Often, he speaks rashly in the heat of passion and later regrets it. Your actions, on my behalf, speak of a deep affection and remorse words could not express. I believe Duncan will discern that for himself."

"I can only hope," he murmured. "In the years since, I pushed the incident from my mind. Until I met you again. As for what happened, I am not entirely certain. It was a chance meeting. I noticed his upset, thus approached him." His furrowed his brow in remembrance. "In reflection, I believe he purposely provoked a fight. Why? I don't know. He behaved more edgy and testy, even for Duncan's temperament."

"When was this?"

"Spring of forty-two. I arrived in London to report for duty with the major's regiment and surprised to see Duncan in town. I heard the unfortunate news about the duke. I made my condolences and offered to buy him ale, but he refused. He even went so far as to accuse me of being sent by Major Hedgepeth to spy on him. I denied it, but he did not believe me, rather threatened me if I ever went near his family again. When he seized me, I tried to break free. In doing so, I struck and bruised his jaw and split his lip. That is when he drew his sword."

A small cry escaped when Samantha bit her thumbnail.

William briefly looked up at her reaction. "Before we could do each other harm, Nathan intervened. Upon recognizing Duncan, he broke off. At that moment, Duncan denounced our friendship," he spoke with great lament. "If only I had not acted so impulsively and kept my temper!" He clenched his right fist.

"You cannot blame yourself."

By her distracted look, he saw she only half meant what she said. "I knew Duncan was upset. Accidental, aye, but I struck him in anger!" he said with a heartfelt groan. "I would have given my life for him if he asked."

Greatly moved by his confession of devotion, she tried to comfort him. "If it is any consolation, you were not the object of Duncan's anger."

"You know what upset him?" he asked, confused.

She slowly nodded. "At least I can give a possible reason, for I believe the severance in friendship and my troubled marriage are linked by a single incident."

"How so?" he asked, his interest piqued.

Spurred by his prompting gaze, she forced herself to speak. "Since you served under Lawrence you know his father, Lord Kyle. When the trouble with the King began, my father struggled to keep peace in Parliament and between our families. Naturally, Lord Kyle claimed for the King. I am unfamiliar with all the particulars," her voice grew reticent, "only a past incident involving my grandfather gave rise to the marriage contract. Lord Kyle used it to force father's agreement."

"Blackmail," chided William.

She nodded. "Father unexpectedly died that spring, a few months before the wedding." She swallowed back some discomposure to continue. "Lord Kyle arrived at our London home a week after the funeral. We were in middle of making preparation for departure to Foxmoor where father would be laid to rest in the family crypt. He did not come to express condolences," bitterness crept into her voice, "rather impress upon Duncan the importance of fulfilling the contract. They had a terrible row. Lord Kyle claimed Duncan struck him …"

"Duncan would not act so base!" William emphatically said.

"So, said Rory and me. However, his lordship insisted."

"Did you witness this assault?"

"No. We waited in the hall listening to loud voices from the study. However, Lord Kyle did hold a handkerchief to his head when he emerged. According to Duncan, he tripped and bumped his head on the hearth. Nothing too severe, a small cut."

"Was the major present during this argument?"

"No. Lord Kyle came alone. After his lordship left, we pressed Duncan for answers, but he refused to speak. In fact, he stormed from the house, very upset. From what you described; I believe you encountered him after the argument. Being his friend, you know Duncan. He has an occasional temper and can be verbose, but violence is not his way."

"No, it is not," said William, thoughtful in as to the explanation.

"Sadly, you became the scapegoat for his grief and rage. Fortunately, he realized his anger for what it was, thus left you and Nathan intact."

William gave a sardonic snort. "Why not seek me to make amends?"

Samantha raised her chin when replying. "My brother is a proud man. He may have been the antagonist, but you admitted to striking him. The responsibility is not Duncan's alone. Besides, how would it appear for a duke to humble himself to a Captain of Horse, and an enemy? No, Will. If Duncan's honor is to be restored, it must be in private, and by you. I believe you know that."

He uncomfortably scratched the back of his neck. "What of you?"

Her voice hoarse and tight in reply. "My situation is not so easily resolved. Due to the *supposed* assault, Lawrence became consumed with the bitterness and enmity one develops for a hated enemy. He changed from the aloof person I married into a monster. War increased his animosity—" She lowered her head. Her lips quivered.

The answer confused and disturbed William. "Then ... you love him?"

Her head quickly rose at the question. "No! He is my husband and I strive to follow Scripture and publicly show respect." Her voice faded.

Her increasing distress pricked him. He took her hands. "Forgive my earlier thoughtlessness. You need not speak of his indiscretions and debased treatment of you."

Fearful, she studied his compassionate expression. "You know?"

"I learned a few facts at Foxglen," he sheepishly admitted.

Aghast, she immediately grew pale and withdrew from him.

"It does not change my concern for you. Nor my growing affection."

She gasped at the declaration. "Affection? Have you forgotten the power my husband commands? Each stripe on your back is testimony to a hopeless situation!"

He rose to comfort her. "It is not hopeless. You are free from him, and Duncan will petition to have the marriage dissolved."

"But to speak of affection—" she stammered, her eyes woeful and wet. "Despite my husband's sins, it is before God, I am bound by my vows! Until that can be rectified, I dare not even entertain thoughts of affection from another man. Though, God forgive me, my mind and heart have been weakened these past weeks!"

Her words were a hard blow to him. "I never meant to compromise you. My sole purpose was to help you for Duncan's sake. These feelings are new and recent. Forgive my folly to speak of them." He bowed.

"I do not make light of your feelings. I, too, have them," she weakly admitted. "I cannot! And you must help me."

He stared in befuddlement. "Deny my feelings for you?"

"Aye," she barely whispered, to which he painfully grimaced. "Perhaps not in your heart. That would be cruel to ask. Howbeit, in your words and actions it must be done. If not—" She could not finish.

She didn't have to. He knew what she was about to say. Heaven help! For speaking such things moved his heart with tenderness. She stood before him helpless and confused. At that moment, a strong impulse to kiss her soft inviting lips and feel her in his arms threatened to overtake him. However, the pleading look in her misty blue eyes stopped his impulse to charge passionately ahead. He drew a steadying breath before speaking.

"I have no choice. Although I have questioned God's mercy and compassion on occasion, my actions shall not cause you to be compromised."

She folded her hands in prayerful relief. "Thank you."

He grew firm in speech and posture. "Despite my agreement, I swear before God, Hedgepeth will pay for his wanton acts even if it is after Duncan has the marriage dissolved."

She tearfully nodded, muted by her emotions.

An abrupt clearing of the throat surprised them. William stepped in front of Samantha ready for defense. Rory leaned against the threshold, still cloaked and masked. "We didn't hear a horse approach."

"It's a wonder you heard anything." Rory tossed his sister a surly glance. "The poor beast was shot out from under me." He motioned for them to follow him into the main room.

"Are you hurt?" she asked.

"A few scrapes and bruises." Rory flashed a glance to William, as he continued. "It is too dangerous to remain here. The three of you are leaving for London immediately."

"What about you?"

"I still have work to do. Henry will remain with me." Rory poured himself some ale.

She grew annoyed by his cool behavior. "You can't be serious?"

"Very much so." Rory drank.

"If you wanted to fight why not re-enlist?" she sharply said.

Rory paused in his drinking at her provoking tone. "While the armies fight each other, poor folk are left at the mercy of men like Hedgepeth! You should understand, little sister."

"I also know a fool when I see one!" she hotly returned.

"Fool?" Rory slammed the tankard on the table. Some ale spilled.

"Aye! The odds increase tenfold each time you ride. I am not a coward, but I used discretion, and did not bear-bait a company of Royalists."

When Rory took an angry step towards Samantha, William intervened. "She is your sister."

"Sister or no, I will not be spoken to in such a fashion!"

"I will not have a brother killed twice!" Her voice cracked.

Rory suddenly understood her argument thus tempered his words. "Having been away fighting, I thought of home as a place of refuge. Until Lawrence is gone and Foxglen restored, I cannot leave. I'm sure *you* understand."

"Of course. Have you been successful in contacting Godwin or Anne?"

"No. With all imprisoned, news is scant."

"I can do so," Henry assured Samantha with a smile and wink.

"This is my fault," began William. "I have seen Hedgepeth use any means to take *royal revenge* during occupation." At Rory's quizzical glance, he added, "*Royal revenge* is term coined by Rupert to justify such actions."

"It is not your fault," Samantha tried to assure William.

"Indeed. Hedgepeth has been waiting for any opportunity to vent his spleen on our family," spat Rory.

"Samantha told me what happened between Duncan and Lord Kyle. How it connects to the deterioration of her marriage and the severance of our friendship."

Rory grew skeptical glanced shifted between Samantha and William. "Duncan said you struck him."

"Inadvertently!" insisted William. "He accused me of spying on him for Hedgepeth. I denied it. When I try to get loose from his grasp, my fist connected with his jaw. He cursed the day we ever met!"

Samantha said to Rory, "This happened immediately after Duncan left the house very upset."

Rory folded his arms, as he thoughtfully regarded William. "Let us hope what you did for Samantha will make up for an accidental blow. We leave at first light." He saw the '*we*' did not escape her notice, but added: "Henry and I ride with you as far as Grantham."

Chapter 22

HAVING SEPARATED FROM RORY AT GRANTHAM, SAMANTHA, William, and Nathan drew near to the city of Leicester. The odor of smoke made them stop.

"Do you smell that? An army camp perhaps?" asked Samantha.

"Too thick and pungent. See the horizon?" William pointed to the ridge gently rising ahead of them. "The mix of light and dark gray smoke. No black clouds to indicate current fire. More than likely the aftermath. We should find the answer over the rise."

Leicester, the pride of the midlands, lay in smoldering ruin. In stunned silence, they rode amongst the carnage. Not a home, shop, stable, barn, or storehouse left untouched. The scene ranged from broken windows and minor mischief to destruction by fire. Several unfortunate souls vanished upon sight of riders. Cries of bitter wailing occasionally disturbed the devastating silence. Dead and wounded lay where they fell. An overwhelming scent of burnt timber mingled with a pungent sour smell.

"What is that horrid stench?" Samantha's face ashen with a sickly cast of a nausea.

William and Nathan exchanged wary knowing the answer; burnt flesh. Whether human or animal was unknown. Nathan moved his horse next to Samantha in case emotions overcame her when spying the source. William came along the other side to block some of the ghastlier sights.

"Look neither right nor left," William hastily told her.

She fought to keep her focus straight ahead. Her lips tightly pressed together to hold back bile. When the smell intensified, she clapped a firm hand over her mouth and nose.

All abruptly halted when a clod of dirt struck Nathan in the shoulder and splattered on his neck and face.

"Begone, villains!" shouted a man. His clothes scorched and face covered in blood mingled with ash.

Nathan threw up his arms, hands opened. "We mean you no harm! Only strangers passing through."

"Aye." William mimicked Nathan's non-aggressive action.

Samantha's gaze fixed on the man. His wretch condition threatening the bile to erupt. Both hands now covered her mouth while her eyes showed the effort needed to resist sickness.

"What happened?" asked William.

"The damned Royalists!" the man cursed. "The savages massacred half the city and took everything they could get their filthy hands on."

"Had you no garrison for defense?"

"Aye," the man solemnly said. "The brave lads rode to meet them, but that cursed foreign Prince outnumbered them. All six hundred killed."

"Rupert. Hedgepeth could be close by," Nathan said lowly to William.

Unfortunately, he had not spoken low enough. Hearing his name, Samantha set spurs to horse. She whipped the animal with the reins to race from Leicester. Wind blew the tears from her eyes and blurred her vision. She constantly wiped her eyes clear. She didn't hear William call for her to stop. The echoing of Hedgepeth's name connected with the savagery of Leicester is all she knew. Not until the poor beast collapsed from exhaustion miles from the city, did William and Nathan catch her. Samantha sat on the ground beside the wretched horse. Its head touched the ground. Blood flowed from its nostrils.

William's horse wobbled when he leapt off the animal. Nathan quickly dismounted to take the reins of both horses to keep them on their feet. The loss of one was trouble enough. Losing all three would be disastrous.

William knelt beside her. She lost her hat, hair disheveled, and patches of turf on her cloak and clothes. She buried her head in her hands. "Are you hurt?" he asked, to which she shook her head. "I know how difficult this is for you, but 'twas foolish to ride off like that."

"His name reeks with heinous cruelty. I want no part of it!"

From behind, Nathan heard horses. "Will! Riders."

William rose to see an approaching troop.

Samantha watched the horse rolled over and die. "What have I done?"

"Quick! Cover your hair." William snatched up the hat to give her. She stood and hastily stuffed the fallen braid underneath. A few bright red strands remained exposed.

"Roundheads," said Nathan.

As precaution, the Roundhead patrol readied their pistols. The lieutenant halted near enough for conversation yet maintained a proper distance for defense. "What have we here?"

Samantha stepped out from behind William. "Sir. We wish no harm. Only to find the Duke of Rutherford."

"Now what would you be wanting with the duke?"

"I am Sam—"

"Servants," William swiftly interrupted. "We have been dispatched by His Grace's sister on urgent business."

The officer's skeptical gaze shifted between the trio. "I am Lieutenant Brandon of His Grace's command. Yield your swords and you may travel with us to Oxford."

"Ox—" Samantha began to speak when William carefully gripped her arm for silence.

"We are arrested?" William asked with uneasiness.

"Precaution. If you truly are his servants, you will comply."

"Sir, we do not refuse. However, it is a dangerous time for an armed person, deadly if unarmed."

"I have ten stout men all armed to the teeth. You will be safe enough. Now, your swords," he said with more authority than politeness.

After yielding their weapons, William inquired, "Sir, we have killed one horse in our duty and the rest can barely stand. How shall we travel?"

"There is a post house a mile hence. Take the walk at your leisure. We shall follow."

A warning look from William stopped Samantha's protest. He and Nathan led the tired horses while Samantha walked between them.

"Why did you not want me to tell him I am Duncan's sister?" she cautiously asked William.

"He might not believe you. And we could still run into an enemy patrol. It is best to remain incognito until we reach Duncan."

"Do you call the Royalists your enemy?"

"Aye," he grimly admitted. "This is not the first time Rupert has allowed wanton greed to overcome his men. I have seen it more times than I care to remember. Anyone who allows such butchery is no God-fearing man or able commander."

"My view of war has been limited to my husband and shire. I thought all Royalists were like him. I have since learned they are not."

"I witnessed many things over the years to change my views." He looked earnestly along his shoulder at her. "Nothing as significant as meeting you again, and the memories connected to a more pleasant past."

She did not reply, simply looked ahead. Silence fell between them.

Nathan listened to the conversation. He carefully glanced back to the patrol. The Roundheads seemed ignorant of what was spoken. Upon facing forward, he spoke out of the side of his mouth. "If Oxford has fallen to Parliament—" he stopped at a harsh glare from William.

Chapter 23

GENERAL FAIRFAX'S ARMY CAME WITHIN TWO MILES OF OXFORD with the intent to siege the city. When news of Leicester reached him, he halted his advance in the town of Botley to consider a response. Rupert split his forces. Lord Goring took his command to Bath. Fairfax acted quickly, dispatching Duncan and his company to join Cromwell and pursue Goring.

Road dusty from the short campaign, Duncan returned to his quarters in Botley. Senior officers occupied homes in the town while five thousand men camped on the common. Now, twenty-five, he was among Parliament's youngest commanders. Years of war tamed handsome youthful suppleness into the firm strength of manhood. Pale blue eyes shown forth with steely confidence. Like most Puritans, he kept his face clean-shaven, while dark copper hair shoulder length. He found Brandon waiting for him in his quarters.

"Ah, Brandon. Leicester has been avenged. Neither Goring nor Rupert will soon recover from the smarting we gave them at Bath! God be thanked, at least some dignity and goods can be restored those unfortunate souls."

"That is good news, Your Grace. However, there is another matter. During our northern patrol, we came upon three travelers claiming to be your servants."

"Really?" Duncan glanced passed Brandon. "Where are they?"

"In custody, Your Grace. I took the liberty since I do not believe them." He quickly continued the explanation when Duncan's raised a brow of reprimand. "There is a pretty boy whose manner of speech, bearing, and dress are of nobility. The other two also appeared out of character, dressed in pieces of uniforms. Maybe spies using your name as very poor cover."

Duncan scowled with annoyance. "Describe this pretty boy."

"A head shorter than Your Grace, yet red hair and clear blue eyes. Now that I think about it, very similar in feature to you."

"Red hair and blue eyes? Does this servant call himself Rory?"

"No. He identified himself by the name of Sam—"

Duncan straightened in surprise. "Take me to the prisoners at once!"

Even at quick march, Brandon found it difficult to keep pace with Duncan as they made for a tent in the center of the commons. Guards snapped to attention at the duke's brisk approach. Duncan pushed aside the tent flap. His features flushed by effort and sharp expectation as he spied her. The blustery entrance momentary stunned the occupants.

"Duncan!" Samantha ran to embrace him.

Quizzical, he held her at arms-length. The face was his sister, though marred by hard traveling, hair disheveled, and complexion reddened and dirty. *Gad! She wears sheaths for sword and dagger!* "In heaven's name what are you doing here like that?"

"You know this lad, Your Grace?" asked Brandon, baffled.

"This is my sister!" Duncan snapped. "Forgive me. You could not have known. Thank you, Brandon. See to your men."

With a last curious look at Samantha, Brandon withdrew.

"Good heavens, Samantha. What has caused this?" He again looked her up and down.

"There is much to explain."

He caught some movement out of the corner of his eye. "Hawkins?"

William and Nathan bowed.

Surprise at seeing his sister in such a manner was one thing, but this most unexpected sight brought a wave of anger to the surface. "What are you doing in the company of this Royalist?" he asked tight-lipped, eyes heavy on William.

"Friend," she corrected.

Duncan gave her a brief look before he returned to William. "What have you done to my sister?"

"Nothing, save bring her to you."

"Liar!"

Samantha seized Duncan to stop him. "William speaks the truth! He and Nathan risked their lives to bring me to you. A mission Rory entrusted them with."

"What business would Rory conduct with him?"

"Please, Duncan! There is much to tell. Save judgment until then."

Duncan fought anger at the request, yet one look her state and he yielded. "Come."

As briskly as he made his way to camp, Duncan returned to his quarters with Samantha. William's surprise appearance opened a floodgate of memories he thought buried beneath the weight of war. The instant return of anger and bitterness showed how close to the surface the emotions lay. This disturbed him along with the memories that came flooding back.

Duncan attempted to curb his agitation and focus on Samantha's tale. He did all he could to keep listening and not allow his mind wander to William, university, or the ugly incident with Lord Kyle. An involuntary smile appeared at Rory's decision to remain in Lincolnshire.

"So, the rascal plays hero. But you, Samantha?"

"Do I not have the same O'Malley blood and spirit as you and Rory?"

"Aye." Even in her present condition, she had grown into a woman, and not the teenager he last saw. "Your discovery as the Phantom prompted flight. Where does Hawkins fit into this?"

With great deliberation and purpose, she retold her story.

"Dear God, Anne must be heartbroken," he lamented.

"Aye, she still grieves." She continued the narrative yet grew tentative in describing the aftermath of her discovery as the Phantom.

"How dare he lay a hand on you! His fight is with me!" He struck his chest in anger.

She ignored his outburst to keep the course lest she breakdown. Duncan slightly flinched when she told how William received the lash for her. She spoke of their rescue by Rory before she concluded with all at Foxglen being placed under arrest.

"He could not fetch Anne away?" asked Duncan with great concern.

"Unable to wake her due to the drug. Lord only knows what Lawrence has done to her since—" She fought back tears.

"Harming her will only add to his crimes. Crimes I promise he will pay for!" Duncan swore.

She swallowed back emotions to find her voice again. "I came to you for asylum. As duke you can petition to have this marriage dissolved. Same as father told me he would do in his letter."

To this statement, Duncan grew wary. "What letter?"

"The letter hidden in his journal. The one addressed to me."

"You found it? I thought I sealed it and hid it well."

"Why hide it?"

"To protect you until I could find the evidence needed to dissolve the marriage. They already threatened me and father. I never thought he would harm you." He gently wiped the tears from her face. "Alas, I failed. I'm sorry."

"His name is marred with shame, and I want no more of it! As if Foxglen is not enough, what they did at Leicester …" She swallowed back a wave of bile in remembrance.

He held her as she wept. "How do you know of it?"

"We rode through the city on our way to find you."

"I fear with the war raging, a divorce will be a trivial matter to the courts. It may not be decided upon until the fighting is over."

"I don't care how long it takes! I want never to see his face again." She wiped away the tears. "What of William and Nathan?"

"I don't know." A hard-edge creeping into his voice.

"Duncan, William has changed. The Royalists are as much his enemies as ours. With much regret he told me what happened between you."

Her statement renewed his earlier anger. He visibly snarled.

"You doubt me?" she asked at his reaction.

"I doubt him. Impulsive hothead."

"Sounds like yourself."

"Mind your tongue! My dishonoring is a shame I bear as heavy as any title."

The rebuke stymied her. His rigid posture, taunt features, and title reference reminded her she spoke not solely to her brother, but also the Duke of Rutherford. "Aye, Your Grace," she timidly answered. "Please, do not ask me to hate a man who risked his life to save me. I cannot."

Duncan softened at her submission. "I would not make such a request. You have borne enough ill because of the past. I shall have my orderly draw you a bath. As for clothes." He screwed his lips regarding her soiled attire. "Maybe the quartermaster can manage something. If not from camp followers, maybe dressmaker or women of the town." He made certain she was comfortable before he left.

William and Nathan snapped to attention when Duncan arrived. For a moment William and Duncan locked eyes like two stags measuring each other for the ultimate encounter. William noticed Duncan's once gay and vivacious spark of youth had grown hard and serious.

"Be seated, gentlemen." Duncan indicated the table. "My sister gave an impressive account of you both." He skeptically eyed them.

"Yet, Your Grace is not pleased," said William.

"Would you be pleased with what has befallen your sister, Captain Hawkins?" His cool regard never left them, as he walked the length of the table. "What was the motive behind this gallantry, Captain?" He slapped William's back when passing behind him.

William winced in anger at the action. "If you seek proof, I can show you the scars."

Duncan took a seat opposite William. With heavy scrutiny, he asked, "What made you defy your commander?"

William returned the stare. He hoped to see beyond the new hardness in Duncan's eyes. Unfortunately, the intense gaze only confirmed a new severity that deeply concerned him. Whereas affection for his friend drove him to action, it became obvious such a motive would not be believed. When he found himself at a strange loss for words, he glanced to Nathan.

"Injustice, Your Grace," said Nathan.

"One of Parliament's reasons for this war," Duncan dryly commented.

"I do not understand politics, Your Grace. My place is with Captain Hawkins. Always has been. Always will be."

Duncan snickered sardonically. "Which is the more fool, the fool who leads or the fool who follows?"

"I'm no fool, Your Grace. If a King's officer can turn upon his men, why not a King upon his people? My loyalty to the Crown ended the day Captain Hawkins received the lash for your sister. Enemy though she be."

"Nathan!" scolded William.

Duncan jowls tightened. "You always had as impudent a tongue as your master." He jerked a thumb at Nathan while asking William, "Do you subscribe to this motive of injustice?"

"Aye. And to amend the dishonoring of an old friend."

"Do not use my sister to satisfy that which can only be done in one way."

Offended, William bolt upright. "The shedding of my blood is no game! If you want it all, draw your sword and take it!" He struck his left breast.

Duncan also stood. War had matured William's features, but the face remained open and honest in expression. The light hazel eyes incapable of hiding what passion stirred within. "I fear there is another reason. One I find very distasteful at present."

William met the cross gaze with stubborn determination. "If to think it is so distasteful, then to speak it would not make it otherwise."

"I may be able to bring myself to accept what you did to save Samantha, but not this! Consider your price to forget such folly."

William's eyes flashed with outrage. "Do you think I would suffer what I have if all I craved was money? Your bloody honor be hanged! Withdraw the insult or defend it!"

Duncan slyly smiled. "*This* is the Will Hawkins I remember; bold and cavalier."

Realizing he fell for the bait; William took a deep breath to regain his composure. "I'm sorry you are not the Duncan O'Malley I remember, sprightly and gallant. My dear friend."

"Yet never without a sharp bite when needed! Enough of this childish reminiscing. I asked you for a price."

"I said I would not give one! I shall ask a reward instead."

"Reward?" Duncan said incredulous at the audacity.

"To wear Parliament's uniform."

Duncan burst out in laughter. "You haven't lost your sense of humor."

"I'm not joking, Duncan," William said in earnest.

"Desert your Royal commission?" Duncan asked, skeptical.

"I did that when I helped your sister."

During the inspection, they tried to read the other's thoughts beyond the stern expressions. Upon meeting only determination and sincerity in William, Duncan broke eye contact to speak. "Unfortunately, that is not within my power. Tomorrow you will be brought before General Fairfax and General Cromwell. They shall decide your fate."

William squared his shoulders. "I am a prisoner, then?"

Duncan casually shrugged. "You are a Royal Captain of Horse. Your change of heart is up for scrutiny. However, since you performed acts of bravery on behalf of my sister, I disqualify myself from judging you."

William bowed to the offer. "That is gracious of Your Grace."

Duncan's brow rumpled at the contrition. "Good-day, gentlemen.

Chapter 24

PROMPTLY AFTER BREAKFAST, DUNCAN PRESENTED WILLIAM AND Nathan to Fairfax and Cromwell. The generals sat behind a large table. In appearance, they showed a dramatic contrast. Sir Thomas Fairfax, the younger at age thirty-two, handsome in feature with tawny complexion. Black hair fell about his shoulders. The fashionable mustache and small beard added to his dark appearance which earned him the nickname "Black Tom." Natural dark complexion tended to make one appear foreboding and ill-tempered. Fairfax was quite the opposite. A man of mild disposition, even tempered, and few words. His battlefield expertise nearly unrivaled in Parliament's army due to his participation in the Dutch Wars. When he did speak, many elders found such insight surprising for his age.

At age forty-five, Oliver Cromwell suffered a terrible case of smallpox, thus his face badly scarred about the jowls and chin. He had no delusion about his rough appearance so grew no facial hair while his brown hairline began to recede. He took what looks God gave him and dealt with it. He also differed from Fairfax in temperament. Strong in opinion and discipline in judgement joined with a shrewd political mind made for a forceful individual. Together, they made a formidable team.

Also present was David Leslie, a brawny Scotsman. Every inch a seasoned veteran in total command of his subordinates. Where Duncan became a shadow of his commander Tom Fairfax, Leslie was Cromwell's favorite junior officer. An orderly sat at the end of the table with pen and paper to record the meeting. Two guards flanked Fairfax and Cromwell.

"Gentlemen, this is an inquest, not a trial. That shall be determined by your conduct," began Fairfax. "Captain Hawkins, your father is Sir Herbert Hawkins of Nottinghamshire. He inherited his land and title from your great-grandfather, who was knighted by King James I for helping save His Majesty from Lord Bothwell."

"Aye, General."

"Sergeant Strickland?"

"My family has served as bailiff to the Hawkins since James I."

The orderly furiously wrote. Fairfax deferred to Cromwell to begin the questioning. "Captain Hawkins, when was the last time you were with Major Hedgepeth?"

"Five weeks ago."

"Do you know of Leicester?" asked Cromwell with a disdain.

William swallowed hard. "I assure you, General, neither I nor Sergeant Strickland were at Leicester." He caught a glimpse of Duncan. The firm expression on his old friend caused great distress and foreboding. William forced himself to continue when Cromwell cleared his throat. "On our journey here, we learned of the unfortunate city."

For a long silent moment, William endured the scrutinizing eyes of Cromwell and Fairfax. He sensed Nathan shared his anxiety but dare not look to his faithful servant. Neither would he chance another glance at Duncan. No solace would come from his former friend no matter what motive was behind his actions. *Lord, help us! You know we are innocent,* his mind prayed. *A single word from these powerful men will decide our fate.*

"You escorted the lady for reasons of safety from her husband, Captain?" asked Fairfax.

William's mouth went dry. "Aye, General. Major Hedgepeth intended cruel harm due to her sympathies with Parliament," he discreetly answered. The inquest proved taxing enough. To speak boldly of what he knew concerning Samantha and Hedgepeth in front of Duncan could be his undoing.

Fairfax pursed his lips in consideration while Cromwell leaned forward to speak. "Captain Hawkins, this is all confusing. You are a Captain of

Horse under Major Hedgepeth's command. Yet, you claim to save the duke's sister from your commander because of her sympathies to Parliament. You expect us to believe your story?"

William's palms sweated. He clenched his fists until the knuckles turned white. "I realize it sounds unbelievable, General. However, as God is my witness, it is true. I am sure the lady will confirm our story."

"No need to bring Samantha into this," Duncan protested.

Fairfax raised a stern hand, which forced Duncan to resume his silent observance.

"Your gallantry in this matter is unquestioned since the lady is safe and unharmed. What intrigues us is your motive," said Fairfax.

William cast a quick glance to Duncan, whose expression remained unaltered. "For reasons of friendship with her brother. We were classmates at Oxford."

Both Fairfax and Cromwell glanced quizzically to Duncan. The younger duke gripped the hilt of his sword. His firm facial facade cracked into a pricked frown.

"Thus, when she was in danger, for the memories of an old friend, you saved her. Is that the whole story, Captain Hawkins?" asked Fairfax.

"In summation, aye."

Duncan's grip on his hilt tightened. He remained stubbornly silent to Fairfax's second admonishing glance.

"What did you hope to gain by this action?" asked Cromwell.

"Nothing, save the lady's liberty."

"You desert your Royal Commission on a heroic whim? A convoluted story, Captain," And, under the circumstance, difficult to believe."

Nathan nervously swallowed hard. He had yet to speak or make a move. With all appearing bleak, his nervousness manifested itself in an impulsive cough.

Cromwell noticed Nathan's apprehension. "What of you, Sergeant Strickland? Do you subscribe to this gallant motive?"

"I have been Captain Hawkins' servant since childhood, General. It is not my place to question or dispute my master."

"Your life could depend upon your answer, Sergeant."

"If it pleases the general and Lord Fairfax, I have given my answer."

"A noble answer, Sergeant," said Fairfax.

This was too much for William. If not for himself then for Nathan, he must speak. "Pardon, sir, but I request our mettle be tested before you pronounce judgment. If proven false, you may do with us as you wish. If otherwise, we join your ranks."

Duncan straightened with mute surprise.

"You are a bold for speaking such!" said Cromwell in rebuke.

William could not withdraw and recklessly proceeded. "I have been told that before, General. Yet brashness is best utilized when one's life is at stake. The Bible says that God judges good and evil, truth and falsehood. Let God judge us."

Before an irate Cromwell could reply, Fairfax took hold of his arm and rose. "You should not take too much stock in your boldness as to invoke the Lord's judgment, Captain Hawkins!"

"Solomon petitioned the Lord for wisdom to judge in righteousness and truth. I only ask the same be done now as two innocent souls stand before you!" William urged.

Cromwell's wrath tempered by Fairfax's restraining hold. Fairfax keenly studied William. "As you aptly referred to Solomon's wisdom, we find ourselves with a situation worthy of him. You are the enemy. Howbeit, with lady's welfare the issue, this inquest was a test of your mettle. You made bold argument. Enough to allow further consideration about your dispensation. Colonel!" He motioned Duncan to take charge of the prisoners.

"Thank you, sir." William made a deep bow of respect. Nathan mimicked the action.

The tent flap barely closed on their departure when Duncan heard an irate Cromwell speak. "Tom, what of Duncan not telling us their history?"

Duncan waved the escort to proceed and continued to listen. "I will deal with Duncan," Tom firmly said. "As for the prisoners—"

"What happened?"

Startled by the question from a voice right beside him, Duncan bolted a step backwards. Samantha. He noticed the escort was out of sight. "They spoke their piece. Now it is up to Fairfax and Cromwell."

"Did you speak for them?"

"It would have been useless. They are prisoners of war."

"We shall see about that!" Samantha briskly entered the tent, which briefly startled Fairfax and Cromwell. "My lords, forgive me." Correctly attired and hair properly groomed, she appeared every inch a noblewoman.

"Sirs, a moment and I will have her gone," Duncan apologized. He reached to take her arm. She jerked away from him.

"No! I wish to speak on behalf of the prisoners."

"Duncan!" scolded Fairfax. With a kind smile at Samantha, he motioned to a chair. "Please, have a seat, my dear."

"I prefer to stand, if it is all the same to you."

"Of course. We are at your disposal."

"I do not know all that transpired, so pray, indulge me if I repeat facts, you already know. It was from my husband that Captain Hawkins and Sergeant Strickland rescued me, and in doing so, placed their lives in peril. Upon his back, Captain Hawkins voluntarily bears the scars of a lashing meant for me by my husband because of my sympathies with Parliament."

"He raised a whip to you?" Taken back by the news, Fairfax sent a harsh glare to Duncan. The latter became rigid.

"Aye," she said with a choked voice. "Despite being Royalists, they dealt kindly with me," she continued after finding her voice. "Call it mutiny, insubordination, or what you will, they have risked much without it being asked! Have they not earned the right to be treated with the mercy and kindness they have shown?"

Fairfax grinned with admiration. "I see you are not the only one with a persuasive tongue, Duncan. If your sister were a man, she would make an excellent lawyer."

Duncan stiffly bowed to what he took as rebuke and not a compliment.

Fairfax continued. "My dear, because of you, we have already agreed to allow Captain Hawkins and Sergeant Strickland to live. Whether they wear Parliament's uniform or remain prisoners of war has yet to be determined."

"General Fairfax!" A road-dusty officer entered. "We captured a Royalist courier with a dispatch from the King to Rupert. They are to meet at Naseby in two weeks."

Fairfax took the dispatch to read. "What do you say, Oliver?"

"We shall be there to greet them."

"Exactly." Fairfax returned to the officer. "Thank you."

"Tom," Cromwell began with a nod toward Samantha. "About the prisoners proving themselves."

"In battle?"

"What better way to prove or disprove a traitor than by setting him against his own?"

The implication disturbed her. "General, is not my rescue enough?"

"My lady, this is war. What was done for friendship's sake, can easily be undone for loyalty's sake. Captain Hawkins and Sergeant Strickland swore an oath to the King. The question we must ask is will they be loyal to Parliament or are they only interested in saving their necks? We have not the luxury of acting upon our emotions toward an individual. We must be guided by cold logic for the security of England."

Subdued, she meekly replied, "Then I am compelled to leave the matter to your hands, General. Good day."

As Duncan moved to follow his sister, Fairfax sternly addressed him. "Colonel O'Malley! Once you have informed the prisoners of their good fortune, report to my private quarters."

"Aye, General," Duncan replied in a husky voice of restraint.

Outside, a whirlwind of emotions propelled Duncan after Samantha. His grasp of her arm was harder than intended. He kept his course despite her short cry of painful surprise. "Well, my cunning vixen! Let us hope Hawkins proves as brave, gallant, and unselfish as you make him sound!"

"I would be dead if not for William! Which seems to mean nothing to you." She jerked away and stormed off.

"I would grieve terribly," he insisted. He caught her arm again, only more gently. "Among all this chaos, thoughts of home are all I have to bring me some measure of comfort."

"Then believe me! William and Nathan are not your enemies. I once thought the same and hated all Royalists. Some I still do. I cannot hate someone who saved my life by risking his own. Duncan, Lawrence nearly killed him! A lashing I felt as if it had been done it to me as intended!"

"If he had, Lawrence would be as good as dead!" Duncan swore.

"Yet you feel nothing but hatred for the man who used to be your friend and now bears scars that should have been mine? You have changed, Duncan," she sadly pronounced.

"War changes people."

"Alas, for the worse." Her eyes filled with tears of lament.

Pricked, he lashed out, "I am only doing what I think best!"

"Now only for yourself. It used to be for others." Upset, she ran inside.

He followed her while he insisted, "It is for your sake, Samantha!"

She reached the stairs and turned to confront him. "No! If it were, you would listen to me. Yet there is a hardness and vindictiveness that now drives you. I no longer see the brother I love and respect, but a vicious stranger!" Overcome, she raced up stairs.

Her words stunned him to the core. So much happened that he did not have time to reflect, only press on in an impossible and desperate situation. Life became a matter of survival. Until Samantha arrived with William, he gave no thought to himself or his character. Had he become the vicious monster she said? There was only one way to find out.

Chapter 25

WHEN THE TENT FLAP OPENED, WILLIAM AND NATHAN ROSE from the table where they sat conversing. Both stiffened with apprehension at sight of Duncan. The duke's harsh expression unchanged from earlier. William swallowed back a lump at the thought of learning their fate.

"Be easy, gentlemen. I bring good news," Duncan began. "A situation has arisen in which you will be given the chance to prove your mettle."

"How so, Your Grace?" William asked suspiciously

"Battle of course. We intercepted a message from the King to Rupert. It instructs him to meet at Naseby in two weeks. Since we are closer, we shall give them a warm reception."

"Why tell us this?"

Duncan casually shrugged. "What better way to either prove or disprove a traitor?" he quoted Cromwell. "If Rupert learns of our coming, we shall know who the traitors are."

William squared his shoulders at the challenge. "The gauntlet is accepted, Your Grace."

"See it is returned favorably or a lady's honor, one greatly extended on your behalf to grant this chance, will be compromised. If that happens, arm yourself, Hawkins! We leave in the morning." Duncan turned upon his heels and stormed out.

"What say you to that?" Nathan asked.

William shook his head, as he pondered the exchange. "Uncertain. Duncan is clever. Samantha's involvement is what concerns me."

"She is a formidable woman."

"Her honor will be defended." With level brow of disconcertion, William sat.

Nathan resumed his seat to ask, "Do you fear facing Rupert?"

"No. Simply struck by the cost of my actions. Not in stripes. Rather dragging you into this, and what my father will think when he hears of it. His eldest son and heir branded a deserter."

"You followed your conscience. As for me," Nathan cocked a small grin, "fret not. In this, I wholeheartedly agree. Serving under Hedgepeth became untenable. Leicester, inexcusable brutality! At Naseby, we will learn if Parliament is any better."

On Duncan's part, he paused to look back at the tent. Inside, he fought to conduct himself with civility, and in doing so, learned the truth. His heart twanged with remorse at the memories of the man he just left. *Alas, memories do not change the facts or alter the present.*

Drawing a deep breath, he braced for what he hoped would be the final onslaught of the day. He admired and respected Tom Fairfax. *Perhaps he will deal kindly when he learns the truth and hears the explanation.*

Arriving in Fairfax's private quarters, he noticed the emotional struggle on Fairfax's face.

"My deepest apologies for offending you, Tom."

"It goes beyond offense. Aye, you were untruthful and that caused me grief, but humiliation was also suffered."

"I never meant that."

"Then what did you mean?" Fairfax's temper exploded when Duncan hesitated. "By God, Duncan! Where is your head? It was a military inquest not some comical play staged by Shakespeare! And Samantha. He threatened to raise a whip to her. What would Patrick say to your callous treatment of your sister?"

"If you let me explain—"

"That is precisely what you will do! I want the whole truth. I will settle for—No—I deserve nothing less."

Duncan searched for the words to begin. He pushed what happened between he and William aside for more important matters. Or so he thought, until he saw Prince Rupert's Standard, or caught a glimpse of William on the battlefield, then memories came crashing back. Although he brooded about William and the blow, this would be the first time he discussed the incident with anyone besides Rory.

"Will Hawkins and I knew each other when studying at Oxford. More than that," Duncan slowly admitted. "We roomed together for three years and became very close friends." He uncomfortably paused to gather his thoughts. "It is common practice to place a junior classman with a senior. Although William was hardly a senior, he arrived six months before me. The headmaster thought it would be a good pairing. It was. We got on smartly and did practically everything together. He became a frequent visitor to Foxglen during the summer whenever we came to the manor. As for Strickland, I brought my own servant, but he proved more of a nuisance. I dismissed him after a month and Strickland waited upon both of us. All went well for two young and carefree youths. Until the war," he droned. "We had a terrible quarrel in which a blow struck, and swords drawn—" his voice trailed off. The anger he felt for so long now accompanied by a twinge of remorse.

"The war caused many severances in friendships and between families."

"I must digress to what happened with Lord Kyle for explanation and clarification."

"You mean the marriage contract."

The question surprised Duncan. "Aye. What do you know of it?"

Fairfax wryly grinned. "Have forgotten my friendship with Patrick? Whereas I often sought his counsel, he too came to me for advice."

"Of course, I haven't forgotten. Simply unaware he spoke with you on the matter. Though, in retrospect, I can understand why." Duncan proceeded to tell Samantha's tale since the war started. "I had no idea of her predicament until yesterday. It is the first time I have seen her since the war began. Naturally, we corresponded, but no mention of such bitter disregard nor the dire straits at Foxglen. All she suffered was because of my temper," he spoke to himself then continued aloud after a brief pause since Fairfax closely watched him. "Now Lawrence has confiscated Foxglen! Foxhill and Foxmeath weren't enough! Alas, there is little I can do other than file to have the marriage dissolved by divorce."

"Aye, she should suffer no more humiliation. Patrick would do the same. In fact, he yearned to find a way and free her from Kyle's influence." Fairfax sympathetically regarded Duncan. "So, Captain Hawkins did save her life to make amends."

Duncan heaved an uncomfortable shrug. "I suppose."

"You sound unconvinced."

"An angry blow is hard to forget."

"An angry blow you provoked."

Duncan's jowls tightened. A change noticed by Fairfax.

"I understand the past is painful. What I fail to understand is why you did not tell me all this before the inquest. You know of my friendship with Patrick, and you. Not to mention, I know well Kyle's temper. It is on constant display in Parliament." Fairfax watched Duncan's visible struggle, thus asked, "Did you fear I would reward Captain Hawkins' gallantry and negate the satisfaction of your honor upon him?"

Duncan's shoulders sagged.

Fairfax groaned in annoyance. "Bold and inciteful though it was, I thank God for his brashness and Samantha's intervention. Your foolishness could have gotten him hanged!" When Duncan shied away, he became concerned. "Is that what you wanted? To see your old friend hanged?"

"I don't know what I wanted!" Duncan snapped in frustration. "I just learned the horrible truth from Samantha. Then, to see her with the man who—" Anger prevented him from finishing.

"So, you defend your honor with injustice?"

Duncan gripped the hilt of his sword against warring emotions.

Fairfax took firm hold of Duncan. "Pull yourself together, man. As soldiers we cannot allow ourselves to wallow in or rejoice over situations.

You must clear your mind and come to terms with the past. Not solely for your sake and that of your sister, but mine as well. I need you! You are a good fighter and one of my more able and trusted commanders. Not to mention, a dear friend." He took Duncan by both shoulders to look him squarely in the eyes. "Before God, laying all malice aside to answer me. Are we doing right by being merciful to Hawkins and Strickland?"

The day had taken Duncan through the darkest recesses of his heart and mind. A journey no one is ever willing to take, and with it learn a hard truth. A truth more difficult to overcome than the initial falling out. Yet in that moment, when faced with such a question, he felt compelled to answer with what he knew deep in the recesses of his heart. "Aye."

Fairfax gave Duncan a hearty embrace. "Go. Rest before tomorrow."

Feeling some measure of relief, Duncan made his way back to his quarters. He knew he must make amends with Samantha. Avoiding the inevitable would only prolong the discord. Although, she rushed upstairs earlier, he found her in the parlor reading. A moment of awkward silence hung between them. She stood and held up the book, a leather Bible.

"I hope you don't mind. I found this among your belongings. I needed to read the Scriptures."

"No, I don't mind." When she shied, he spoke with regret. "The war has produced circumstances I never envisioned. To be so discomposed with my sister, whom I have greatly disappointed."

"I don't know what I expected. Only recently have I seen the true ravages of war."

"I'm afraid you shall see more. The army moves to Naseby to meet the King and Rupert on the field of battle. There is no time to secure your safe passage to London. I'm sorry."

She placed the Bible on a side table to bite her thumbnail.

Duncan took a step toward her, uncertain and remorseful. "Samantha, I wish I could make you understand. It is not by choice I have changed, more circumstances and necessity. I hate this war! What it has done to England, to you, to our family. Alas, the more I see, the more I am convinced of the necessity. The King would have ruined this country if allowed to continue his selfish reign. In his army, men like Lawrence are the rule not the exception. They would rather rape, plunder, and pillage every Parliament house to viciously subdue the people than reasonably listen to their representatives!"

In confusion, shook her head. "I am not schooled in war or politics. Alas, what I see in you goes beyond those things. Where is the brother I remember? The one, who despite sometimes being too serious, was optimistic and gay? God gave you a gift to see clearly both sides of an issue and the good in each situation."

"That person was an inexperienced youth," he tried to say with levity.

"Please, do not make light of it, Duncan. Whereas in the past you had an occasional temper, you were reasonable. Now, you are consumed with an anger that blinds your reasoning." When he painful scowled and turned away, she offered a challenge. "Look at me and tell me you do not hate William Hawkins."

"Hate?" Duncan painfully echoed. A term placed to his emotion he never considered. "I suppose I did hate him," he slowly admitted.

"Have your feelings changed?"

"My feelings are confused. I detest what happened, but he saved your life." He touched her cheek to which she embraced him. "I shall do whatever I can to win back your love and respect."

"You have not lost my love."

"I severely wounded it and lessened myself in your eyes." He stopped her from speaking. "You may use kind words of protest, yet I see your heart. As for God's gift." He gave a short sardonic chuckle. "It and He have not been a consistent part of my life of late."

"Then make Him so again."

Duncan smirked. "If it were that easy."

"Why? Faith is what I reply upon to see me through difficult times."

He affectionately regarded her. "You are the more sensitive of us in spiritual matters. If your prayers have sustained you, perhaps they will for me."

"Of course, I pray for you. Always. The question is will you pray?"

"One step at a time."

"Perhaps you can begin by forgiving past transgressions?"

To this he became rigid. "It is a matter of honor and must be dealt with as I deem satisfactory!" His rebuff made her recoil. "You would have me remain dishonored?"

"No, you are the Duke of Rutherford. Your dishonor is a family matter. I only ask it to be done in as painless a way as possible." She shied away from his regard.

Her reaction made him ask, "Are you in love with Will Hawkins?"

"I cannot deny feelings of gratitude and fondness. He suffered so unselfishly on my behalf. Yet I assure you, I have not acted improperly. I am still a married woman!" she said with a crackle of pain in her voice.

"Your virtue is without question. However, you ask a great deal about Hawkins."

"I shall not hold you to a promise you are unable to keep," she droned.

"Oh! Words to wound the heart," he groaned. "I will try. Now, rest. It will be a long march." With a kiss on her forehead, he sent her upstairs.

Once she was out of sight, his gaze became drawn to the Bible. He picked it up and sat in chair she occupied. His father used to retire to the study at night for Scripture reading and prayer. Over the years, Duncan tried to develop the same habit, only difficult to maintain during war. In hindsight, he always made excuses. What Samantha said about God giving him the ability to see clearly both sides of an issue, disturbed him. She accused him of being unreasonable and blinded by anger.

He began to see the truth when confronting William yet grasped its depth in speaking with Fairfax. *Is that what you wanted? To see your old friend hanged?* Fairfax's questions echoed in his mind.

Duncan randomly opened the Bible to Proverbs 29:22. *-An angry man stirreth up strife, and a furious man aboundeth in transgression.* He slammed the Bible closed. "Is that what I have done, caused strife for those I love?"

"Wilt thou be angry forever?" a male voice spoke from behind.

"Tom! I didn't hear you come in."

With a soft smile, Fairfax sat opposite Duncan. "Trying to mimic Patrick's habit?"

"Trying. Not succeeding." He stared at the Bible.

"How is Samantha?"

"She said I have changed. Become cruel," he painfully admitted.

"War does not bring out the best in men. I witnessed many who were endowed with great wisdom, fortitude, and courage, crumble beneath the weight of war and turn into helpless simpletons. Others became consumed with rage beyond reason."

"She also said my reason has become clouded by hatred." Emotions filled his voice. "I never thought of it as hate."

"What do you call condemning a man when all he did was good for someone you love?"

Duncan screwed his eyes shut and shook his head.

"Since our discussion, I strolled the camp trying to decide how to approach you and encourage to turn you back from the path which consumed other men." Fairfax grinned and indicated the Bible. "I am pleased to see God prompted you. His Word has a way of putting everything in perspective. Of giving hope where there seems to be none."

"I'm glad you do not consider me hopeless."

"Where there is life, there is hope. Where there is forgiveness, there is peace." Fairfax gripped Duncan's arms and smiled. "Now, I can retire contented. Good night."

Chapter 26

THE DAWN OF JUNE 14TH, 1645 BEGAN AS A PLACID SUMMER'S DAY. Just beyond Naseby from Mill Hill in the south to Dust Hill in the north, a gently rolling pasture stretched for a mile. The road to Market Harborough ran through the pasture, while a hedgerow marked the western border. Rupert arrived before the Parliamentary forces and positioned his troops along Market Harborough Road.

On the hill overlooking the broad open field, Prince Rupert patiently watched the Parliamentary army scramble into position. He steadied his horse when several mounted officers joined him, including Hedgepeth.

Rupert waved a hand toward the Parliamentary line. "What a day for easy victory! They are already retreating." He then spoke to his orderly, "Is His Majesty's foot and cannon in place?"

"They should be shortly, Highness."

"Tell the King we will strike to keep enemy occupied." When the orderly left, he told his commanders, "Gentlemen, the enemy is at hand. Let us move to take that ridge opposite." He pointed to Dust Hill.

On Parliament's left flank, Ireton deployed his troops. Colonel Okey positioned his Dragoons behind a hedgerow to cover Ireton's movement.

A distant trumpet alerted Ireton to Rupert's charge. "Odds blood! That cursed black renegade will doom us all!" He pointed to the Royalists and shouted, "Colonel Okey! Rupert!"

Okey waved his sword in acknowledgement. He issued immediate orders to the Dragoons. "Fire at will! Keep them from our forces until we are ready!"

The sounds of muskets fired in unison echoed over the field. It did little to stop the Royalists. Ireton had no choice but to meet the charge.

"Give it to them!" He led his troops against Rupert.

A shot killed Ireton's horse and sent him tumbling from the saddle. He no sooner recovered than a Royalist pike pierced his thigh. Wounded and unable to move, he watched the left flank begin to crumble.

"God's teeth! Stop them! Don't let them reach the baggage train," he shouted when the Cavaliers broke ranks. He pushed himself to his feet. Ignoring the massive wound in his thigh, he called, "Regroup!"

Cromwell assigned William and Nathan to his most formidable commander, David Leslie. They waited on the right flank and listened to the sounds of battle grow nearer. William stirred in the saddle, as he wondered about his mettle. Not for lack of courage, rather, could he fulfill all those expectations in one day? The weight on his heart and mind made him grimace. He sensed a presence watching him. Nathan. So, faithfully did Nathan serve, that even when brought to this fierce battle by his master's passion, he went without question. William saw concern in those unflinching eyes. Such loyalty and devotion brought a small involuntary smile to William's lips.

"Let us quit ourselves as men and leave the outcome in God's hands." He drew his sword in readiness.

"Aye." Nathan's mimicked William in preparation.

"Prepare to advance!" Leslie shouted.

William glanced heavenward. "Lord, although I acknowledge my neglect of You, I see Your handiwork in the events leading me to this day. Take pity on this wretched soldier and do not abandon us."

"Charge!" Leslie shouted.

The words rang in William's ears with grave anticipation. Duty called. He entered the fray with Leslie's troop.

Nathan followed William. At the sound of a familiar trumpet, he drew his horse to a hard halt. He stood in the stirrups to determine the direction of trumpet call. Hedgepeth's standard! He remained standing to look for William, who was nowhere nearby.

"Strickland!"

The harsh calling alerted Nathan in time to deflect Wallace's attack. Like a madman Wallace slashed at him. The blows came with such ferocity that Nathan did all he could to defend himself. He tried to maneuver his horse and avoid another attack, only miscalculated. Cold steel sliced his right shoulder. A tingling sensation radiated down his arm, momentarily paralyzing the limb. The sword fell from his grasp, as he slumped over the saddlebow in pain.

"Nathan!"

Wallace recognized William an instant before the horses slammed together. The clash threw the riders off balance and nullified any exchange. Furious, Wallace lashed at William, who managed a block and riposte. William aimed his next attack at the flank of Wallace's mount. The injured horse shrieked and skidded out of control. William seized the opportunity to rush the injured and frightened animal with his horse. Wallace's horse fell and pinned him. Impact with the ground rendered Wallace unconscious.

William moved beside his friend. "How bad?"

Nathan gritted back the pain to reply. "I can feel my fingers and move my hand again."

"What is this?" Leslie arrived. The dark Scotsman soiled from battle.

"Sergeant Strickland is wounded, and the foe put down." William motioned to the unconscious Wallace.

"Can you still fight?" asked Leslie.

"I can—"

"He cannot," William spoke over Nathan's beginning reply. "The wound made his hands and fingers too numb to hold a sword."

"Aye." Nathan tried to make a fist but winced in pain.

"Withdraw and tend to your wound, Sergeant. Captain, take your men and steer Rupert toward that hedgerow of Dragoons. We must hold the flank!"

In the center, Fairfax, Duncan, and Lambert's horse rode in support of the infantry and musketeers. During the heat of battle, there was no time to think only to react. However, this time was different. Duncan recalled Samantha's concern before the call to assemble. To have his sister present proved unnerving. He shook his head clear of such thoughts. Sight of another charge caught Duncan's attention.

"Tom!" he shouted.

In respond to the call, Fairfax wrestled his agitated horse to a halt.

Duncan used his bloody sword to point. "Rupert is charging the left flank again."

"They won't survive." Fairfax whipped his horse to head for the flank.

Hearing a familiar hissing, Duncan urged his horse to follow. "Tom! Cannonade!"

The cannon shot landed a few yards in front of Fairfax. The concussion separated Fairfax from his horse. The explosion frightened Duncan's horse. It reared and bucked. Duncan managed to steady the animal enough to dismount and make his way to Fairfax.

"Tom? How badly are you hurt?"

Fairfax scrambled to his feet yet swayed. Duncan caught him in support. Fairfax took a moment to assess his state. He lost his hat, and something dripped into his eyes. He discovered blood from a cut on his forehead. "At least I'm standing."

Duncan examined the gash. "Appears superficial. Any other injury?"

"Merciful heaven!" Fairfax cursed. "Ireton is being overrun!"

"We can recall the men."

Fairfax angrily spoke, "Why is Okey not defending the baggage train?"

Duncan seized Fairfax's sleeve when he began to move toward the flank. "We must fetch your horse to find out."

"Hold your fire!" Colonel Okey ordered. He curiously watched the approaching figure. At that distance the only distinguishing feature were long black locks blowing in the wind. "I wonder what Fairfax wants?" he mumbled. Suddenly, he recognized the standard. "Rupert! Open fire!"

A hail of musket fire stunned the Cavaliers. The initial volley caused disarray among Rupert's ranks. Some Cavaliers managed to reach the baggage train while others appeared undecided. A second hail of musket fire brought more confusion to the Cavaliers.

Hearing the Dragoon's fire, Ireton called his men to regroup. His wound hastily bandaged, he found another horse and brought his cavalry to outflank the Royalists.

For the Cavaliers, all appeared so easy at first. Reality sunk in, as pursuit of baggage train plunder resulted in being caught between a thousand Dragoons and a full regiment of Parliamentary horse. The fight for Rupert's men became desperate.

Fairfax's cavalry rejoined the battle with vigor to aid the Dragoons. Musketeers and Pikemen rallied to support the cavalry. Duncan and Lambert's companies charged together and drove a wedge in the center of the battlefield. Confusion swept through the Royalist ranks.

When Parliament gained the upper hand, Rupert and his battered men reappeared from their skirmish at the baggage train. Their arrival reinforced the Royalists against a resurgent Parliament.

Cromwell snarled with disgust at the ebb and flow of the battle. His flank experienced some fighting, but the rest of Parliament's forces fared far worse. Ireton valiantly tried to regroup while Fairfax became hotly engaged in the center. He witnessed Fairfax unhorsed and became greatly concerned when Rupert's calvary returned.

"Colonel Leslie!" he shouted. "Ready your men, gentlemen."

When Leslie repeated the order, all officers, including William, assumed position with their company.

Cromwell shouted, "Charge!"

With all the Royal forces committed to battle, the reserve cavalry under Sir Langdale met Cromwell's charge. Not accustomed to being forced into action, they barely escaped Cromwell's men.

"Shall we pursue them?" Leslie asked Cromwell.

"No. It is time to show our true mettle. Regroup!" At Cromwell's signal, a trumpet sounded above the battlefield.

Cromwell's entire horse regiment assembled. At a second trumpet, they advanced in perfect unison. So, calm, and confident in their movements that the Royalists found themselves captivated by the military precision. With uncanny control, all Parliamentary forces joined the second offensive. From his position, Okey shouted for fire. A thunderous sound shook heaven and earth when a thousand Roundhead Dragoons simultaneously opened fire upon the confused Royalists.

William drew his horse hard to rein. He stared in amazement after the fleeing Royalists. The banners of Hedgepeth, Rupert, and others sagged in a rush to leave the field.

Leslie drew rein alongside William. "Captain Hawkins."

It took a moment for William to reply. "They are retreating."

Fairfax's horse reared when he and Cromwell arrived. Together they viewed the disarray of the Royal army.

"General!" Duncan pushed his horse to catch up with Fairfax. "The King is leaving!"

Fairfax stood in the stirrups to where Duncan pointed. Cromwell, Leslie, and William also turned their attention to the sight. The proud royal standard disappeared beyond the horizon.

"Pursue them, Colonel! Give no quarter. Capture the Royal baggage train!" Fairfax ordered.

Duncan saluted and rode off to comply.

As he turned to leave with Fairfax, Cromwell paused his horse beside William. "A difficult sight for you, Captain?" He motioned toward the disappearing Cavaliers.

"I cannot deny it is surprising. Yet, I also have never been a part of so precise a military advance as under your command, General." William focused back on the horizon. "Nor is it something they are accustomed to witnessing from us."

"Us?"

William met Cromwell's curious regard. "Us," he boldly repeated. "At least that is my hope after today."

Cromwell looked to Leslie. The Scotsman nodded. "It is a good day for *us*. Attend to your men, Captain Hawkins." He rode off after Fairfax.

After a long and hard battle, William led his weary horse toward the field hospital. To his horror, the baggage train suffered heavy damage. The tent housing Samantha lay trampled. He pushed aside a stake to lift various parts of the canvass in a quick search. Nothing! He ran to the field hospital. His heart pounded with anxiety, as his eyes scanned the rows of wounded.

"Samantha?"

"William," replied a soft female voice from behind.

Samantha wore a linen cap to cover her hair. A blood-smeared apron over her dress. She appeared unharmed. In two strides, he caught her in his arms and kissed her. She mewed, as he held her close.

"When I saw your tent destroyed, I feared the worse." He held her face between his hands. "Dearest Samantha, nothing is turning out as I expected! Not the war, us. Am I insane to feel the way I do?" He searched her eyes for an answer.

"If so, then I too am insane," she said then fled in tears.

"When all this is over, I will come for you. Despite your husband and brothers, if need be," he spoke under his breath as watched her departure.

He took a moment to compose himself. Samantha touched his heart and soul with a deep desire he never felt before. Alas, he stood to lose too much, Samantha included, if he pressed the matter. The cry of a nearby wounded man brought him back to reality. Sitting beneath an elm tree, he found Nathan with his right shoulder bandaged and arm in a sling.

Relieved, William knelt and smiled. "It doesn't look too bad."

"No." Nathan flashed a cocky smile, which quickly faded, replaced by confusion. "What happened? I thought Rupert would sweep the field. I heard talk they fled."

Confounded, William sat beside Nathan. "In all my years as a soldier, I have never seen a man command like Cromwell did this day. Military precision during battle, the likes of which even the King's army has not achieved. They fled like frightened cadets."

Duncan approached. "Sergeant Strickland. How is your shoulder?"

"A clean wound and should heal quickly, Your Grace."

William stood, rigid in anticipation.

Viewing the braced posture, Duncan spoke in all sincerity. "Today, your actions on the battlefield saved one honor and restored another. For that, I am grateful—Will."

William's rigidity turned to surprise at hearing his Christian name spoken for the first time in years. A touched smile appeared. "That pleases me more than I can say."

Duncan too smiled. "Rest while you can. With capture of the Royal baggage train, we will be moving soon."

"All of it captured?"

"Aye, including a chest full of the King's correspondence." Duncan grew reflective and hopeful. "Perhaps from what is learned, we can end this bloody war." He flashed another smile. "Good-night, gentlemen."

For Charles, capture of the baggage train placed him in a foul mood. Slightly wounded, battle-worn, and disheveled, Rupert became the object of his uncle's wrath. All other commanders vacated the room, leaving uncle and nephew alone.

"My God, what happened?" Passion curbed Charles' usual stammer and brought forth the Scottish accent inherited from his father. "Where were you when I needed you?"

"We were fighting for our very lives! We rode after Ireton's broken horse only to be confronted by a thousand Dragoons. We rejoined the battle as quickly as possible."

Charles slammed a fist on the table. "I could not believe those men fighting were under my banner! Professional soldiers outdone by mere militia. By God, they will never defeat me."

"You need not be defeated. Neither should you defeat the people of your country so sorely."

"Do you mock your King, sir?"

"No, Sire. After years of battle, I believe it prudent to retain something than to lose all."

"Speaking either as a soldier or statesman, I must say there is no probability of my ruin! Yet as a Christian, I tell you this. God will not suffer rebels and traitors to prosper nor this cause to be overthrown; and whatever punishment it shall please Him to inflict upon me must not make me repine, much less give us a quarrel," Charles spoke with kingly pride.

Rupert deeply sighed. If his uncle was bent on self-destruction there may be little he could say or do to change his kinsman's mind.

"We must reorganize. I have only Bristol, Chester, and Sherborne Castle left." Charles drummed his fingers on the table. "Bristol must be held at all costs!"

In humility, Rupert knelt before his uncle. "Sire, I pray you at least retain me in your service. To ask return to your favor would be folly. Noble Uncle, I beseech you, allow me to hold Bristol for Your Majesty."

Bitter and angry though he was at the loss of Naseby, Charles pitifully gazed upon the youth kneeling before him. He tugged on Rupert's shoulder. "Arise, Rupert. You are still my kinsman."

"Thank you, Most Noble Lord."

"Remember, Bristol must be held at all costs!"

"On my oath, I shall hold it at least four months!" With a deep bow, he withdrew.

Outside, Rupert rejoined his officers just as a courier arrived. He dismissed the man to read the message.

"Highness, have we orders from the King?" one asked.

Rupert told them about Bristol. "To your commands, gentlemen. We leave in two days. Hedgepeth," he said when the officers made to leave. He waited to speak again when alone with Hedgepeth. "I have a specific task for you, Major." He held up the dispatch. "Parliamentary troops are moving south from Naseby. Sherborne Castle lies in that direction. To protect our supply lines and support, we must protect what remains! Immediately take your company and determine if it is a scouting party or entire regiment. If a regiment, which one and what is the intention. When you have learned the necessary information, make haste to join us in Bristol. And Hedgepeth!" His brows became dark and foreboding. "Nothing is to interfere with this assignment. Our lives depend upon this mission succeeding."

Hedgepeth proudly lifted his chin. "I shan't fail, my Prince."

"If you do, you shall answer to the King with your head!"

Hedgepeth saluted and took leave.

Chapter 27

THE HARROWING BATTLE OF NASEBY PROMPTED DUNCAN TO move Samantha to safety. Since the army would leave the next day, he needed to act quickly. He arranged an escort of ten volunteers with a trusted junior officer from his personal staff to take her to London. Once again, she donned her manly disguise.

Samantha hugged Duncan. "Take care. I could not bear to lose you."

"Fret not. I'm too ornery to die so young. I promise to write. Aye, more often," he said forestall her dispute. He held the stirrup for her to mount. "Take care of her, Lewis. Once she is safe in London head for Bath."

Despite the lump in her throat, Samantha moved off with the escort. Riding through camp, she caught sight Nathan. He touched his hat and kindly smiled. She smiled in return then forced to compose herself when a sudden wave of emotion overcame her. She did not have a chance to say good-bye to William. Perhaps it was best. Duncan mentioned the possibility of a restored friendship. However, witnessing the death and destruction of war made her uneasy about their safety.

The first night, they slept in the barn of a Parliament sympathizer known by Duncan and his company. To venture into an unknown inn or hostel brought the risked of her identity being discovered. For safety's sake, they exercised discretion.

The next morning, they reached the main road: "Royalists!"

"Ride on, miss!" Lewis drew his sword and pulled back. "Corporal Faintree, see to the lady," he ordered before being unhorsed by pistol shot.

Faintree rode hard after Samantha, who was already a quarter mile ahead. Soon they were overtaken. Faintree fought yet fell when wounded by Wallace. A company of Cavaliers surrounded them. Faintree remained on the ground and pretended to be unconscious to listen.

A soldiers grabbed the reins of Samantha's horse. She reached for her sword when another soldier stopped her. The horror of her fate became apparent when Hedgepeth arrived.

"Well, well. Look who we have here."

She swallowed back fear. "Release me, lest my brother, the duke—"

His haughty laughter rang in her ears. "The duke be hanged! You made a fool of me and shall answer for it. Captain Wallace, call the men to order. We continue to Bristol."

Samantha could not hold back the tears. The brief freedom she experienced gone in a single moment. Her situation infinitely worse than before. *Lord, grant me the courage to face what awaits.* Even prayer seemed hollow in the face of what she knew would be outcome of her capture.

The longer they rode, the more time she had to gather her courage. She also considered various scenarios, none of which ended well. Her courage ebbed and flowed between frightening thoughts and desperate prayers. Finally, they reached a small village where Hedgepeth ordered food and lodging from the populace.

Since escape impossible, her hands were not bound. Being in a public house helped to curb his attitude. At least, he launched no personal attacks of her. However, his hostility evident even toward the locals.

"What rooms have you?" he demanded of pub owner.

"We only have two rooms upstairs. We don't get many visitors."

"That will serve for me and my officers. Captain Wallace, see the villagers accommodate the troops. Come." Hedgepeth shoved Samantha to ascend the stairs before him.

When he shut the door, her emotion reached a boiling point. "What more do you want from me? Is it not enough that you succeeded to add Foxglen to your fortune by blackmail? Must you torment me?"

"*Blackmail.* An interesting word."

She clenched her fists. "Do you deny it?"

"I deny nothing. More to the point, how did you learn of it?"

"Does it matter?" she hastily brushed the question aside. "Your scheme is known. My brother will not tolerate it."

He moved threateningly close. "Your brother already knew when he agreed to fulfill the marriage contract. What say you to that, madam?"

Stung by the news, her lower quivered. "I do not believe you."

His scornful gazed at her. "Women are pawns in the fortunes of men. Be they pauper or queen. You were used by your father and brother to satisfy an old debt they owed my father. If not for him interceding with the King *twice*, Rutherford would be no more. First with your grandfather then your scheming father!"

"No, they were not schemers," her voice trembled in a weaker protest.

"Reality distresses you. That is natural since women know as little of politics as they do war." He removed his hat and gloves.

Despite growing distress, she forced herself to speak. "God's law …"

"Ha!" he huffed with bitterness. "A typical Puritan tactic to evade the truth." He again stood before her. "Your father went against the Crown's generous offer of marriage to the Earl of Strafford's son to promise you to some Irish pig of a lord! You should be grateful my father stepped into to keep you on English soil."

She shook her head unable to speak at the stunning revelation.

He cocked a scoffing grin. "You pretend ignorance yet speaking of *blackmail* tells me you know the truth. You simply refuse to accept it."

She closed her eyes and swallowed back emotions enough to ask, "What more do you want from me?"

"Everything and nothing."

Her brows knitted in confusion. "What?"

"From you, the woman, nothing. From you, the sister, everything."

Her eyes grew wide with understanding. "Rutherford. That means my brothers—Murderer!" She went to strike him, but he caught her arm.

"Not murder. Many are killed in battle. For now, I keep you alive should the worse happen to Duncan. It already has to Rory."

His statement spoke of his ignorance regarding the identity of the latest Phantom. She also did not need to fear death. At least for the present.

He jerked her by the arm to sit on the edge of the bed. "Cooperate, and I can be reasonable. You know what happens when you cross me."

Her courage immediately fled, replaced by terror.

"To show you I speak truth, I shall leave you to sleep *alone.* I will not accost you. Rather make myself comfortable in the chair."

For several moments she warily watched him arrange the chair with an ottoman for his feet. She removed her boots to carefully slip under the covers. She remained fully dressed. Even after he extinguished the candle, she kept her eyes opened. Shortly, she heard his light snore of sleep.

She lay awake to ponder all he said. His insistence of being used by her father and Duncan contradicted her father's letter, entries in her grandfather's journal, and conversations with Duncan. All of them expressed regret concerning the past and her current state. However, reality showed he spoke the truth of how she became a pawn. Family regrets confirmed it. Silent painful tears fell. She never thought to be used in such a fashion by her family. Under the circumstances, who could she trust if not her brothers? Lawrence already proved an untrustworthy cad.

"William," she whispered. She screwed her eyes shut against the thought. *Why? How could my father . . .* She recalled a line from his letter, *God willing, if I survive this war, I shall seek forgiveness in person and speedily remedy that which has been forced upon us.* She blinked back new tears. He didn't survive. Even Duncan said the courts would not be willing to hear her case while war rages. *God, please help me.*

Chapter 28

THREE DAYS LATER, PARLIAMENT'S ARMY REACHED BATH. Summoned to Fairfax's quarters, William suspected something amiss. His suspicious became confirmed upon entrance. Nathan stood at attention, Fairfax displeased, David Leslie stoic, and Duncan scowled. A surgeon escorted a wounded Corporal Faintree from the room just after William entered.

"Captain Hawkins reporting, General." He saluted Fairfax.

"Grave news has come to our attention, Captain. It may or may not be coincidental to you and Sergeant Strickland's involvement with Lady Hedgepeth."

Perplexed, William darted a glance to Nathan. The latter avoided eye contact, which increased his befuddlement. "You have me at a disadvantage, General."

"Did you know the lady left under escort for London four days ago?"

"No, sir."

"Interesting," said Fairfax to Duncan.

"Sergeant Strickland, did you know of my sister's departure?" Duncan bitterly inquired.

Nathan assumed a position of attention to answer. "I saw her leave."

William's jowls tightened at the answer.

"You could have relayed this information to Major Hedgepeth."

"Hedgepeth?" William could not contain his surprise.

"Obviously, the captain knew nothing of this," said Leslie.

"Sergeant, what is this all about?" William ignored Leslie's comment.

Nathan could not look at William. Instead, he spoke to Fairfax. "It is true, I knew of the lady's departure. But I did not relay such information to Major Hedgepeth. The man is a fiend! Soothe, we risked our lives to steal her from him. Why would I give her back?"

"You knew and didn't tell me?" demanded William.

"What purpose would it serve?"

"I gather there is more here than a soldier's interest in a lady's well-being?" said Fairfax.

William composed himself. "Forgive my outburst, General."

"Tom, I cannot believe this is sheer coincidence," chided Duncan.

"Why not?" began Leslie. "Stranger things have happened. Besides, these men proved themselves at Naseby. I believe Sergeant Strickland."

"Your view of them is colored by your association as their commander!" Duncan lashed out in frustration.

"And yours by prejudice!"

Duncan stared at Leslie, stunned by the rebuff.

"Enough!" Fairfax scolded. A disapproving eye passed between the officers coming to rest on Duncan. "I understand your concern, yet I agree with David. Captain Hawkins knew nothing of Samantha's departure, while Sergeant Strickland has proven to be a model soldier."

"What of my sister?"

Fairfax winced at the question. "Duncan," he slowly began. "Harsh as this may sound, I cannot desert the field of battle to rescue one woman."

"I can!" Duncan began to storm out when William stopped him.

"You will lose more than your sister if you walk out."

Leslie moved to help William persuade Duncan. "Desertion is punishable by death and confiscation of your lands. Will you lose everything in a moment of haste?"

Duncan jerked away from them. "What of Samantha? You defend them but condemn my sister!" When Leslie failed to reply he turned to Fairfax. "Tom!"

Fairfax grimaced with painful sympathy, as he wrestled with the plea.

"Let us go, General," William said of he and Nathan. "By joining Parliament, we already forfeited everything. We have nothing else to lose."

Fairfax turned to Duncan. "What say you?"

Duncan studied William. The latter's staunch features determined. "Do I have a choice? My sister's life at stake. I dare not refuse."

"With all that is in me, I swear, I will not fail," William pledged.

Duncan stoutly nodded. "Go swiftly. Perhaps you can catch them before they reach Bristol."

"General." William and Nathan saluted and left. They just rounded the corner of the building when William seized Nathan. "I would have an explanation, Nathan Strickland!"

The force of William's anger briefly silenced Nathan. When he did speak, his words halting. "Men in love act impulsively. I knew you would not take her departure well."

"So, you made it your business not to tell me?"

"The business we speak of is Lord Rutherford's and Major Hedgepeth's concern only." Unexpectedly, William struck Nathan. The force of the blow sent Nathan back a few steps before he regained his balance. His mouth open, and eyes wide in disbelief. He felt the sting on his face and a swell of rising emotion. He looked to his feet to compose himself.

William clenched his fists against the rage. Without a word, he marched off.

Nathan hesitated to follow. The blow kindled the most intense feelings of anger toward William he ever experienced. Over the years, he received the occasional tongue-lashing, but never violence. He also knew he fared better than most servants with privileged treatment and intimacy few knew. This time he went too far in meddling in his master's affairs.

"Nathan!" William bellowed from a close distance. "We have work to do!"

With a quick wipe of tears, Nathan obediently complied.

Several days later, William and Nathan arrived in Swindon, a town directly on the road to Bristol. To facilitate the task of gathering

information, both stripped their uniforms of identifying marks and appeared as dusty travelers.

After dismounting, Nathan recognized, "Hodges!" he warned.

Hodges would pass very close to them in the direction he walked. Nathan pretended to check his horse's girth. William leaned down to fix his boot. After Hodges passed, William carefully began to follow.

Oblivious to his new shadow, Hodges made his way to the inn. William disappeared into a doorway when Hodges entered the building. He nearly jumped at Nathan's touch.

"I discovered more signs of the company," whispered Nathan.

"Then Hedgepeth maybe in there with Samantha."

An elderly man in a large floppy hat and old cloak casually walked nearby.

Nathan said, "Go around back. I have an idea for going in front."

Before William could reply, Nathan approached the old man, spoke a few words, and gave him coins in exchange for the cloak and hat. Nathan made certain the cloak covered his sword. He pulled the large floppy hat low. He hunched over and faked limp in his gate to enter the building. He looked for a secluded place to wait. Footsteps came down the hall. He glared out from under the hat. Wallace came towards him. Nathan turned and further slouched his shoulders to appear bent and ailing.

"Keep to one side, old man!" Wallace shoved Nathan. There came a ring of spurs when the old man took a step. Upon closer examination, Wallace saw not only the boots and spurs, but also the end of sheath hung below the shawl. "Old man, have you traveled far? Or do you always wear spurs?"

Nathan's heart skipped a beat. He carefully reached for his sword.

"Let's have a look at you!" When Wallace grabbed the hat, Nathan sprang forward, and drew his sword. The sudden action sent Wallace to the floor. Nathan turned for the door, but two Royalists appeared in the threshold. The only avenue of escape was down the hall where Wallace had come. To avoid capture, he knocked over a table with a burning oil lamp on top.

"Strickland!" Wallace shouted and scrambled to his feet.

At back of the building, Nathan slammed into the rear door. It didn't budge. "Will!" He frantically tried the doorknob. Locked. "Will!"

"Nathan?" he heard William from the outside of the door.

"Wallace! The door won't open."

"I'm coming!"

Wallace raced towards him. Nathan burst into the closest room, tripped, and tumbled to the floor. The sudden force of entry sent Hodges backward off the chair when the door hit him.

Nathan rose and readied his sword. "Get behind me, miss!" he told a stunned Samantha.

Wallace stood in doorway with sword drawn. "Caught like a rat!"

"Rats bite hardest when cornered!"

"Do you smell smoke?" Wallace mocked. "The building is on fire from the lamp you knocked over. There is no escape, Strickland."

Hodges coughed and looked out the door. "We must flee!"

"Drop your sword.! Unless you want the lady to perish?" said Wallace.

Smoke filled the room. Samantha hid her face in Nathan's back to stifle a cough. With great disdain, he dropped his sword.

Hodges threw open the window. He climbed out then helped Samantha. Using sword point, Wallace forced Nathan back to the window. When Nathan reluctantly turned, Wallace used the hilt of his sword to render Nathan unconscious. He fell limp out the window.

William balked at the sight of flames coming from the front of the building. Two soldiers and other men rushed to try and put out the fire. A female screamed. "Samantha?"

A soldier spotted him. William drew his sword in defense. Sound of horses came from behind. He dared not look back.

"Hawkins!" someone called. Still, he didn't turn, as the soldier he fought sent him back against a building. Not liking the idea of being cornered, he shouted and lunged.

Three men on horseback surrounded them. Pistols aimed at the soldiers. William recognized Rory, Miller, and Henry.

"Yield and live!" Rory commanded.

Reluctant, the soldiers dropped their swords. Henry and Miller dismounted to bind them.

William's relief cut short by the sound of crashing timbers. "Nathan! Samantha!"

He rushed to the building now totally consumed with fire. He sheathed his sword and shielded his face to enter. Unfortunately, the intense heat forced him back. He tried again. The front doorway caved in. A burning timber knocked William down and grazed his left shoulder with searing pain of fire. Rory kicked aside the timber and dragged William away.

"Master Rory!" called Miller. He pointed toward the edge of town.

Now mounted, Wallace had Samantha while Hodges held the reins of a horse with a body slung over it.

"After them!" William tried to stand. He had not realized he twisted an ankle and fell to his knees.

Rory knelt beside William. "Without a plan, we are no match for a company of soldiers. Nor are you in any condition to fight. Henry, see where they are taking her. We're going to join the army." He helped William stand.

"What are you doing here?" William painfully limped to the horses. "I thought you remained at Foxglen."

"Hedgepeth left and I got bored," Rory casually replied.

William huffed a chuckle. "Was this chance or did Duncan send you?"

"Purely chance at finding you. Although Duncan sent word about Samantha's capture."

Now that the shock had worn off, William felt the throbbing pain of his burned shoulder. Another mark his body would bear from dealing with Hedgepeth.

"Come, you need a surgeon," said Rory.

Upon sight of the Royalist camp a few miles outside of Swindon, Henry veered off from following Hodges to hide in a thicket. He dismounted and positioned himself to hear and observe all that transpired.

Hodges and his companion continued, unaware of being followed. "Roundheads!" shouted Hodges in warning.

Hedgepeth emerged from his tent to confront the arrival. "Where?"

"In town. May be advanced scout. We lost Atherton and Murphy."

"The trap is sprung." Wallace motioned to a man slung over the horse. "Strickland. Hawkins won't be far behind."

"Neither are the Roundheads," Hodges said.

"Aye. Break camp. We ride to Bristol!" Hedgepeth ordered.

"What of Hawkins?" asked Wallace.

"He will come. He now has two reasons," replied Hedgepeth.

Nathan stirred. He opened his eyes and saw only dirt and grass. Feeling the saddle under his stomach, he knew his predicament. His hands where bound but not his feet. His head and neck ached. Slowly he turned his head to gauge his surroundings. He heard commotion, only difficult to move or see anything in his position.

Hedgepeth noticed Nathan's movement. "Good, you're awake. You can ride astride. I want you unharmed. At least until we reach Bristol." He ordered two soldiers to help Nathan mount. "Make sure his hands are secure. I don't want him to slip and fall from the saddle."

Samantha remained silent atop the horse during the entire scene.

Hedgepeth grabbed the bridle to get her attention. "Your presence could prove troublesome once we reach Bristol."

"More so now, since my capture is known," she said.

Hedgepeth snarled. "You are not to speak unless you want Sergeant Strickland to meet with an untimely death!"

Nathan's eyes narrowed in anger at the threat. He felt Samantha's gaze upon him and changed his focus from Hedgepeth. Her pale despondent countenance showed the major would follow through with what he said. Nathan witnessed the major's brutality long before arriving at Foxglen. His attention became abruptly drawn back to his own situation when they tied his hands to the saddle and drew the rope tight.

"Well?" demanded Hedgepeth.

"Aye," she meekly responded.

"Wisely done. Hodges, find a uniform for our new recruit. That way she can pass unobserved. I don't want any trouble with the Prince over our little deviation from duty."

Hedgepeth waited until Hodges left with Samantha before speaking to Nathan. "I may not have the pleasure of personal satisfaction. The Prince will be interested in your arrest as a traitor and deserter from his regiment. Either way, your days are numbered, and so are Hawkins'!"

Cavaliers proved very efficient in breaking camp for quick departures. By the time Samantha was dressed in a Royal Harquebusiers uniform, the company moved out. So, did Henry, riding in the opposite direction.

Chapter 29

WILLIAM AND RORY REACHED THE MAIN PARLIAMENTARY ARMY in a town south of Bristol. Rory left William in the capable hands of a surgeon and went in search of Duncan. The duke secured his own private quarters.

"You rascal! You look well. Legs all healed," Duncan said after a long hearty embrace. "How goes everything at Foxglen? What news of Anne?"

"Very shaken by the whole incident, yet unharmed. Thank God, the damage to Foxglen is not substantial or permanent. I left Godwin happily setting everything to right. Naturally, I left as soon as I got your letter about Samantha. Henry insisted on coming with me. Miller also. He feels indebted to Samantha for being rescued twice by her."

"Who is running the estate?"

"Tom." Rory reached into the pocket of his doublet. "Anne wrote letters for you and Samantha." He gave Duncan the one addressed to him. He carefully watched for reaction. A small, discernable smile of affection passed Duncan's lip. Just as he suspected. "When are you going to tell Anne how you feel about her?

Duncan balked, like a child caught in mischief. "Now is not the time for expressing such sentiment."

"On the contrary! Every time I tried to ascertain her state of mind, she diverted attention to you. Asking after your welfare and involvement in the war. According to Godwin, she felt terrible about not being able to prevent Lawrence from ransacking Foxglen."

"She is not responsible for his base actions."

"And I told her so. A letter from you would do much good."

Duncan smiled. "Aye." He put the letter in the inner pocket of his doublet. "As for Samantha, Will is hunting for her."

"Not anymore," droned Rory. He helped himself to ale and sat at the table. "I happened upon him in Swindon. His left shoulder burned trying to rescue Samantha and Strickland from a burning building."

"Dear God! Samantha?" Duncan quick to join Rory at the table.

"Alive, only still with Lawrence. He laid a clever trap. Will is fortunate I happened by, or he could have been killed. He's with the surgeon now. They captured Strickland. I had Henry follow them far enough to ascertain the plan. They ride here—to Bristol."

"To join Rupert. Fortunately, we are here to rescue her."

"If she survives his debauchery again. Wanton beast should be castrated." Rory swore and took a drink.

"What are you talking about?"

Rory looked over the tankard at Duncan as he drank. Duncan's probing gaze made him ask, "Did Samantha not tell you? No, she is too ashamed. She could not even speak to me about it," he answered his own question before Duncan replied.

"What could Samantha be ashamed of?" Duncan grew angry with a disturbing thought. "Hawkins said her virtue is intact. Did he lie?"

"No! Not Will. Lawrence." When Duncan appeared confused, Rory said, "He committed the worse violation a man can to control a woman. Marital rape and savage beatings."

Stunned, Duncan sat. "Good Lord. She said nothing."

"She became defensive when I reached for her from behind. A frightened look in her eyes I never seen before. I thought nothing of the action at first. Even contributed it to her being The Phantom. After learning the horrid truth, I realized the action was survival instinct."

"She acted skittish with me also," said Duncan in sober recollection. "How did you discover it?"

"Will learned the details from a maid at Foxglen. Apparently, the abuse is common knowledge among the servants. *That* is why he acted. To protect her." Rory's voice turned bitter. "This war has made beasts of even the most reasonable men. Although, Lawrence was hardly reasonable to start." Emboldened with passion, he demanded, "When will you end this travesty of a marriage?"

"Take care, brother!" Duncan warned.

Enraged, Rory slammed down the tankard and began to leave when Duncan stopped him. His own temper at fever pitch.

"You think me unfeeling? That I want to leave her in such a state? I wish to God father had never made the contract!"

"When you became duke, you could have annulled it!"

Duncan somberly shook his head. "It is not so simple." He drew Rory back to the table. He refilled Rory's tankard before resuming his seat. Although, in the privacy of his quarters, Duncan lowered his voice. "Three letters from Kyle to the King were discovered among the King's personal correspondences in the captured royal baggage from Naseby. Tom gave them to me in hopes of uncovering the truth behind the marriage contact. However, the letters only posed more questions than answers."

"How so?"

"The tone and wording of the letters suggest Kyle is not the author of the contract. Rather a go-between to protect the original author. From comments in his letters, this individual proposed the Earl of Strafford's son. A means to control Rutherford, should the hostility between Parliament and the King erupt into armed conflict."

"Who was the original author?"

Duncan shrugged. "There are several possibilities. You know our heritage dates to King Henry the seventh. Since there is royal blood in our family, an ancient law states that all marriages of royal family members must be approved by the Crown."

"You mean the Ki—" Duncan seizing his arm stopped Rory.

"Kyle is careful not to use any formal title. It could be Archbishop Laud. Or the Earl of Strafford. Even the Queen. Many official letters of correspondence were found in the baggage. At this point, I cannot confirm which one."

"You said the Crown must approve any marriages."

"Aye. However, getting the King's approval does not necessarily mean he is the author. Remember, the Archbishop, Strafford, and the Queen all goaded Charles into action. Parliament dealt with Strafford and the Queen, but Laud remains a thorny problem. Father could not deal with all of them due to grandfather's past. Although rarely enforced, that law became a pressing point Kyle constantly used against father. He would later *remind* me of the fact," he groused.

"So, Kyle saw an opportunity to profit at the expense of our family." Rory swore.

"Aye. Father found himself cornered with a choice between Strafford's son or Lawrence. He dared not refuse or we all lose our heads."

Rory sat back to digest the news. After a long moment of heavy silence, he said, "You must tell Samantha."

"Not yet ..."

"She has suffered enough! At least she should understand *why*," Rory passionately interrupted

"I agree. However," Duncan sternly stressed to prevent further interruption. "Nullifying the marriage is dependent upon the outcome of the war. If Parliament wins, I will have the authority by law to break the contract via *divortium a vinculo maritnoii*."

Rory complained at the use of Latin. "What does that mean in plain English?"

"Royal and noble divorces can only be granted by a petition to Parliament. At present, the war consumes Parliament's resources. Until then, I tread lightly. When possible, I will fetch the journals from Foxglen for comparison to Kyle's letter. Perhaps, I can determine *who* is the actual author, thus have all the necessary evidence to bring the petition. For now, Bristol requires our undivided attention."

"What about Bristol?" William entered. His left arm hung in a sling. He cleaned up his appearance, yet nothing helped the pale weariness on his face.

The injury and fatigue startled Duncan. "How is your shoulder?

William pensively frowned. "Well enough. The pain draught has helped." He darted a questioning glance to Rory.

"I told him," replied Rory.

"I'm sorry I failed, Duncan," droned William, the best emotion he could manage.

"No apology. You did your best. I could ask for nothing more."

"Generous of you to say so."

"Generous of you to appear in your condition. Please, sit." Duncan pulled out a chair at the table.

William cradled his arm as he gingerly sat. Duncan fetched him a cup of ale. He accepted the gesture in silence. Whether pain or the fatigue, William was incommoded.

"What is the latest news?" Rory asked when Duncan resumed his seat.

"We captured Bridgewater and Sherborne Castle. The district is ours. Bristol will be under siege by week's end. Hedgepeth won't elude us for long."

"If Bristol falls, the King will have no refuge left," William spoke in a listless voice.

"Aye. Cromwell estimates the war could be over by the end of the year, if not shortly after New Year's."

"That would be nice." Rory refilled William's cup then his own.

"What will Cromwell do to the King when all is over?" chided William.

Duncan raised a questioning brow at the sour tone. "That is for Parliament to decide not the general. We have fought for equality in the law, whether he be king or pauper."

"A bit idealistic," William murmured in his cup as he drank.

Duncan sighed in weary frustration. "Are you to vex me on all accounts or just those important to me?"

"Not so! The idealistic person inspires change. I understand and embrace those ideals. It is the cost I am opposed to."

"You just said it inspires change. Do you contradict yourself?"

"No, but did Parliament count the cost before pursuing them? Or for that matter, the King when he abolished Parliament? If you could gaze into the future and see the loss your family would suffer, would you still have engaged in this battle?"

"Hindsight and foresight are not for men, but God," began Duncan. "We can only act upon what we know. If I knew the same as I did before, aye. As I am certain you would have responded to the King in the same manner. The armies will meet at Bristol. Only God knows for how long, and the outcome. Hedgepeth has a whole city to hide them. We must wait until an opportunity arises."

"I hate to think what he will do to Samantha if the battle lingers," Rory gloomily said.

"He may do her injury, but he won't kill her. Nathan is in immediate peril. He will protect her with his life," William spoke with catch in his voice. "I need rest." He groaned upon standing as movement caused pain.

"I will help you back to your quarters," said Rory.

"A moment, Will." Duncan crossed to a desk and pulled out a sealed piece of paper. "A gift from one old friend to another."

William read the paper. "A promotion to major and second-in-command of the Dragoons?"

Duncan grinned. "When Okey lost Gibson at Bridgewater, he needed an able replacement. I suggested you and Tom agreed."

William looked at the paper. "I'm overwhelmed. Does David know I am to leave him?"

Duncan heartily laughed. "He fought like a tiger to keep you. You can report to Okey tomorrow. Until then, rest."

For a long moment, Duncan stood in the threshold until they were out of sight. Only a man in love would suffer what William had on Samantha's behalf. *Or a woman.*

He closed the door and pulled out Anne's letter. He crossed to the window for more light, broke the seal, and read. She wrote of the dismal situation at Foxglen. Rather reluctantly, in his estimation. She acknowledged that Rory would inform him so she said she would prepare a full accounting for his review. She mentioned great sorrow at Howard's death, yet pride at his attempt to aid Samantha and the people of the shire as the original Phantom. She inquired after Duncan's health and wished him the best and God's blessing.

The portion of the letter he found most disturbing was her reference to Hedgepeth's malice toward Samantha. She insisted he would not allow such treatment to go unanswered. At that statement, he smiled at her certainty. Not once did she mention her imprisonment nor Hedgepeth's attitude toward her.

By the end of the letter, Duncan agreed with Rory's assessment. In the past, Anne and he easily conversed on all subjects. However, the letter sounded different, disjointed, switching topics ever few sentences. "Dear Anne, what did that monster do to you?"

He went to the desk. It took a moment to consider a response. She may not have written about herself, but he wanted to know her heart and mind. He began by inquiring after her health and thanking her for such diligence in managing Foxglen. He praised Howard for his faithfulness to Scripture and to his family, while complimenting her quiet and stalwart character.

In conclusion, please do not equate the infrequency of correspondence with lack of affectionate thoughts or deep concern for your welfare. It is quite the opposite. In the chaos of war, finding time to write is rare while thoughts of home and loved ones are all I have to keep me sane. So, I beg you, my dearest Anne, write me often and help my sanity.

Yours always and faithfully,
Duncan.

He just sealed the letter when someone knocked and entered. "Tom."

"I saw Rory leave with Captain Hawkins. Any word about Samantha?"

Duncan scowled with disgust. "Still in Hedgepeth's clutches. Although William suffered great injury trying to free her."

"That explains why he walked with such a halting gait." Fairfax noticed the sealed document on the desk. "By your smile, I would say this is written to the charming Miss Cunningham you have spoken so often about."

"That obvious?"

Fairfax laughed. He clapped Duncan's shoulder. "Take my advice, marry her as soon as possible. It has been of great help and comfort to have my *Anne* with me these many months."

Duncan slightly flushed. "Speaking of letters. Those you gave me. Kyle mentioned something about Strafford's son. I don't recall father mentioning him. Yet, according to Kyle, a choice had to be made between the earl's son and Lawrence."

Fairfax made a long exhale. An obvious stalling tactic.

"Tom?" Duncan pressed.

"The *choice* was made when Strafford discovered Patrick used your family's Irish connection to help thwart the earl's plan to bring the Irish army against Parliament."

"I remember. I participated in the dispatch of letters between London and Liverpool. Father wouldn't trust anyone else. I simply didn't know about the earl's son." Duncan picked up Kyle's letters. "Though it explains *why* Kyle quickly stepped in." He waved one letter. "A shame father died so soon after," he lamented. He placed the letters on the desk.

"Aye," Fairfax groused. His features hard and brows leveled.

The sour tone and brooding countenance made Duncan curious. "Why say it like that?"

For a moment, Fairfax regarded Duncan before replying. "Anything that involved Strafford caused great skepticism and mistrust. Patrick acted in the best interest of England but loathed placing himself at odds with Strafford and the King because it once more left Rutherford vulnerable."

"And why he agreed to the marriage to protect the family."

Fairfax drew close to speak in a near whisper. "Patrick suddenly dying of a mysterious illness is cause for great suspicion."

Duncan stared at Fairfax in dread. "Are you suggesting father was murdered?" He could barely speak the word *murdered*.

"I said *great suspicion*." Fairfax gazed shifted to Kyle's letters and back to Duncan. "These are just a few of the correspondence recovered at Naseby between the King, his advisors, and commanders. However," he stressed to forestall Duncan's speech, "it will take time to discern."

"But *you* believe it!"

Fairfax's expression showed agreement, though he made no verbal response. Seeing Duncan's anger kindled, Fairfax grabbed him by the shoulders. "Steady! Suspicion is not proof."

Duncan's jowls flexed. "When can I get access to the rest of them?"

"Not until Bristol is secure. Even then, it may be difficult with everything in the custody of Parliament." At Duncan's visible resolution, Fairfax added, "I will make arrangements as soon as possible. Until then, we must concern ourselves with the siege, and with it, the recovery of *your sister*. Agreed, Colonel?" he sternly used Duncan's military rank.

"Aye, General."

Chapter 30

AUGUST 21ST, 1645, THE SIEGE OF BRISTOL BEGAN. FOR TWO weeks, Parliamentary reinforcements arrived. Trade to the city was halted by blockades.

During this time, Rory renewed his commission under Duncan's command. He joined William and Duncan in strategy meetings to coordinate efforts between the Dragoons and Cavalry. The differences that separated William and Duncan for years, melted away the more time they spent together. A spark of the old friendship resurfaced. Still, war matured and tempered their personalities. Duncan acted more serious and not as easily amused. At least he did not become quickly offended by William's opposing comments or ideas. Or more rightly, Fairfax, Cromwell, or Rory would point out that having an ex-Royalist's view proved helpful in planning. Thus, Duncan accepted William's opinion. On several occasions, he specifically asked William to evaluate a plan.

On William's part, he experienced an unusual melancholy. Especially, when he dwelt too much upon effects of a siege on those inside Bristol. He experienced difficult speaking about Nathan, which puzzled Duncan and Rory. Any conversation concerning Samantha and Hedgepeth came laced with frustration. He purposed in his mind not to deny his feelings for her. However, since neither brother asked, he did not verbalize them.

One morning, in his bedchamber, William gingerly removed his nightshirt to wash and shave at the basin. His shoulder remained tender from the searing at Swindon. For a moment he stared at the mirror. He touched his shoulder. One more mark on his body from dealing with

Hedgepeth. After pouring the water into the basin, he splashed his face. Upon straightening, he saw Rory's reflection in the mirror. This made him turn to face Rory.

"The scars have improved since Foxglen," said Rory.

William put his shirt back on without comment.

"To think. Those scars could have been on Samantha. I can never thank you enough."

"Gratitude was not the reason for my actions." He returned to the basin to shave.

Duncan arrived to hear William's last statement. "Then what compelled you to act?"

William glanced at Duncan in the mirror. He flashed a wry smirk. "Impulse. Something you should recall from our days at Oxford." He applied the lather to his jaw and chin, careful to avoid his mustache.

Duncan snorted a chuckle. "A trait that plagues us both."

William tried not to laugh while shaving. He flinched slightly when he nicked his chin.

"Another scar?" teased Rory.

William blotted the cut with a small towel. He spoke again to Duncan's reflection. "What brings you here? I thought you were posting today's duty assignments."

"I was, until Tom stopped me. He believes Rupert is stalling to answer the demand for surrender. Hopes for reinforcements from the King. Tom will not give any more time and summons his senior officers to plan the assault."

William paused in his shaving to face Duncan. "Now?"

"Aye. You best report quickly to Okey." Duncan motioned for Rory to leave with him.

Shaved and fully dressed, William rode to the Dragoon position. Drawing near, he witnessed a company of Royalist horse attack the Dragoons. The unexpected move caused disarray among the ranks. He took command to organize resistance. By the time the rest of the camp came to help, ten were killed, fifteen wounded, and the Cavaliers retreated.

Cromwell abruptly stopped his horse to demand of William, "Where are the sentries?"

Before William could answer, Fairfax shouted, "Major Hawkins!" He reined in his horse. "Colonel Okey has been captured."

"God's Teeth! I shall have those sentries up on charges for this," Cromwell exclaimed.

"They are dead, General," William solemnly said.

Fairfax swore. "If this is the way Rupert wants to conduct this siege so, be it! General Cromwell, alert all commanders we launch an immediate counterattack. Major Hawkins, you are now the Dragoon commander. Assemble your men for battle."

Within a half an hour, Fairfax dispatched the Dragoons in an assault on the fort guarding the south entrance to Bristol. William galloped along the front line and violently drew rein before one of his commanders. "What news, Captain Winston?"

"The fort is manned by a company with artillery. Ten cannons in all. One demiculverin on the west side. The rest are sakers. In all, eight hundred yards effective range and five thousand maximum."

William stood in the stirrups to observe Winston's report. "If we knock out their largest cannon, we can cut their maximum range by more than half. Tell Colonel MacIntosh to concentrate his artillery on the west end of the fort." He took out a spyglass to watch his order carried out. The wait proved short between his order and execution.

The Parliamentary artillery conducted a vicious bombardment. Before the Royalists realized the target, it proved too late. The west side of the fort became breached, and the largest cannon destroyed.

Parliamentary musketeers opened fire. Every shot rained havoc on the already stricken Royalists defenders. When Cromwell and Fairfax's forces charged the weakened fort, the Royalists retreated before being totally wiped out. Luckily for the wounded and fleeing Royalists, a fierce storm prevented further pursuit. The road became a bog, impossible to transport artillery. Horses sank into the mud up to their fetlocks.

Despite the stalled pursuit, the following week of rain proved profitable for Parliament. Further reinforcements arrived by sea, which allowed troops to encircled both sides of the river Avon. They built a bridge across the river for easy of supply access and communication between troops.

Whereas the rains of September did not prove a hindrance for Parliament, the outlook turned bleak for Rupert. A weather-related plague killed three hundred men within a week. With trade to the city halted, food and ammunition became desperately low. Unrest grew among the citizens while moral problems stirred in the ranks.

When news of the city's predicament reached Fairfax, he wrote Rupert to again request the surrender of Bristol. The days slipped by. Fairfax stood at the window of his billet to look toward Bristol. His senior officers gathered at the table behind him.

"He's stalling again, Tom," said Cromwell.

"If the King comes, we cannot allow ourselves to be attacked from behind," said Leslie.

"So far, there is no sign of the Royal Standard," said Duncan.

William shook his head. "Since, we have total command of this region, I doubt the King would risk such a venture."

"Bristol is his only seaport," Leslie argued.

"Aye, but it could mean his capture along with Rupert. We had standing orders to prevent the capture of both Rupert and the King, either separately or together. Everyone else is expendable," William countered.

"Gentlemen." Fairfax turned from the window. "We could debate until dawn but are pressed for time. Although I appreciate your candor, Major Hawkins, the longer we wait, the stronger the possibility of the King joining Rupert. It may be a gamble, but at the risk of losing everything, he may take such a chance. We have worked too hard to gamble on that chance. Rupert has until tomorrow to surrender, or we attack!"

With no word from Rupert after his declared deadline, Fairfax ordered the Dragoons to take the Prior's Hill fort. After twenty minutes of bombardment, return fire from the Royalists ceased. Once a large breach appeared in the wall, William ordered his troops to take the fort.

The Royalists valiantly fought, but within an hour all were killed. William wiped some blood from his mouth. He suffered a small cut to his cheek. As he surveyed the dead, each soldier reminded him of Nathan. What had become of him? Since failure at Swindon, images of striking Nathan plagued him. He deeply regretted the physical assault upon learning Nathan knew of Samantha's departure and didn't tell him. He could only hope such irrational behavior would not be the last moments he and Nathan shared on this earth.

"Lord, let him be alive so we can be reconciled. Yet, if not, and harm comes to either him or Samantha, let my hand be the instrument of your justice!"

"Major Hawkins." A soldier ran to him and saluted. "General Fairfax requests a report."

"Tell the general, the fort is ours. He may begin the battle to take the Citadel."

Chapter 31

FOR SAMANTHA, THE DREARY WEEKS OF CAPTIVITY PASSED SLOWLY in isolation. Immediately upon arrival, she and Nathan were separated. Under the circumstances, she feared for him. Many hours she spent in prayer. At times she felt God's presence and peace in her spirit. Alas, those times became less frequent as the situation lingered. Her spirit waned. She barely ate what little food the guard brought. She grew horribly thin.

She thought of her brothers, Anne, and Foxglen. Duncan changed so much that thought of him burdened her soul. Rory appeared to be handling the war well, and that concerned her. When dwelling upon William, she no longer denied her feelings and constantly confessed them in prayer. She consoled herself with the thought that she would die knowing she was worthy of a man's love and respect.

She managed to piece together scant pieces of news she overheard from the guards. Parliament blockaded all routes into the city, which caused supplies to become dangerously low. Of course, the greatest complaints dealt with caring for her. Only twice did she endure Lawrence's presence and goading. Apparently, he had more important business. With Parliament threatening the city, his energies were needed elsewhere.

She fell into a fitful slumber when loud bangs woke her. Her heart raced. It took a moment to realize the sound came from cannons. A solitary window allowed light and air into the cramped room. One could climb out the window, however, the sixty-foot drop prevented thoughts of escape.

Upon opening the window, the cannonade sounded fearsome and deadly. Did Parliament bombard the city or were Royal cannons attempting the thwart an invasion? Would the city fall, and she be saved, or the attack repelled? She did not fear death for it would bring her closer to her Lord, but she feared for her brothers and William.

The door burst open. Startled, she hastened from the window. Two soldiers threw Nathan into the room. He fell to the floor with a groan. One eye black and puffy while both cheeks badly bruised with dry blood from his mouth and nose.

Samantha knelt beside him. "Nathan?"

"I'm alive, miss." He painfully rose on his left elbow. He bit back an outcry while holding his right side.

"How badly are you hurt?"

"A few broken ribs," he replied between deep breaths to stem the pain.

She supported him in a semi-reclining position. She gently brushed the matted hair from his face. Throughout their ordeal at Foxglen, in the woodsman's cottage, and now at Bristol, he remained stalwart in loyalty and duty. To see such a kind and courageous soul abused grieved her. "I'm sorry for what my husband has done—!" she wept.

Nathan grew awkward. "Don't cry for me."

The door opened again. Wallace entered.

Pain notwithstanding, Nathan rose to one knee to shield Samantha. "What more do you want?"

Wallace glared at Nathan. "I have not the time to deal with you personally, so you will be hanged and done with! I only regret Hawkins won't hang as well."

Embittered by the beating and threat, Nathan lunged at Wallace. The Scotsman easily knocked him aside.

"Nathan!" Samantha stepped forward. Wallace shoved her back.

A soldier's arrival prevented Wallace from inflicting further injury to Nathan. "Captain, the Roundheads approach. The Prince commands all to his aid!"

Wallace snarled. "Bind him and take her to the major!" He left.

Nathan backed down when the soldier appeared. Once jerked to his feet, he sprang into action. A sudden fist to the face sent the soldier to the floor unconscious. Ignoring the pain of his injuries, he quickly drew the soldier's sword.

"Flee before Hedgepeth comes!" he told Samantha. He staggered toward the door.

She grabbed him. "You are in no condition to fight! He will kill you."

"Where Wallace is, Hedgepeth is not far. I will draw them off while you flee." He tried to remove her hand, but she held fast.

"What will I tell William if something happens to you?"

Nathan gallantly grinned. "Tell him all is well. Now, go!" He pushed her away before dashing out the door.

"Blast you, Nathan Strickland, for the gallant you are!" She stepped into the hall unaware of someone nearby—that was until seized.

"Come, wench!" Hedgepeth pulled so hard that Samantha fell forward with a cry. He cursed and shoved her against the wall. Already soiled from fighting, he unfastened the battered cuirass and angrily hurled it aside. "Useless piece of metal!"

Despite being briefly stunned by his appearance and aroused state, she tried to creep aside while he stripped his cuirass. He intercepted her.

"No. You are coming with me." He pulled on her arm and hurried from the Citadel.

She struggled under the crushing grip that held her wrist. Her fingers numb from lack of blood and shoulder hurt from constant pulling. In her weakened state, she breathed heavy from physical exertion.

Outside, they descended a flight of stairs. Suddenly, he halted. Exhausted, she slipped and fell on the step next to him. He glared down the final steps. Her eyes widened in surprise. At the bottom stood a battle-hardened and determined Duncan.

"Release my sister!"

Hedgepeth snarled with hate. "I have waited a long time for this." He drew his sword and charged down at Duncan.

The momentum from the height advantage, made Duncan retreat. The first blow sent a shockwave through Duncan's arm due to the added force of elevation. Once on even footing, Duncan repelled the attack, and launched a counterattack. For several moments they engaged on equal footing. As the duel progressed, Hedgepeth's rage seemed to enhance his strength. With a feint to one side, Hedgepeth lunged and caught Duncan high and deep in the left shoulder. Duncan lost his balance and fell backwards into a building. He struck his head and sat dazed against the wall.

"Duncan!" Samantha screamed. To protect her brother, she leapt on Hedgepeth's back and locked her arms about his throat. He let out a monstrous growl at the thwarting. Despite her physical weakness, a surge of adrenaline helped her act. However, he was stronger. He ripped her off his back and threw her to the street. When she rose to her knees, he lunged. The blade pierced through her abdomen. She collapsed to the street.

Hearing her warning call, Duncan fought dizziness to stand. Seeing her wounded, he shouted, "Villain!"

With staunch resolution, Duncan went on the offensive. His blade sliced at Hedgepeth and sent him back. The swords clanged and scraped, as the blades came together at the hilt. Duncan clenched his teeth against the painful wound and head blow. He brought his knee up into Hedgepeth's groin and shoved him back. Hedgepeth staggered to regain his footing. He remained bent at the waist to regain his breath at the lower assault.

"Standfast!" came a shout. Six Roundhead calvary surrounded them. Fairfax leveled a pistol at Hedgepeth. "One move and I shoot to kill." When Hedgepeth snarled in defiance, Fairfax cocked the pistol. "Drop your sword!"

In disgust, Hedgepeth threw down his weapon.

"Lieutenant, take Major Hedgepeth into custody." Fairfax kept the pistol cocked and ready until Hedgepeth secured and taken away.

"Samantha!" Duncan dropped to his knees beside her to gather her in his arms. She was unconscious while the front of her doublet covered in blood. "I must get you to the surgeon," he told Fairfax.

"God, no!" Rory violently drew his horse to a halt and leapt from the saddle. Henry and Miller rode close behind him.

"Give her to me. I'll take her to the field hospital," said Henry.

Being wounded, Duncan could not help Rory lifted Samantha, so Miller dismounted. Together, they handed her up to Henry. Samantha groaned; her eyes lids flicked at movement.

"Easy, miss. I got you," Henry soothed. She once more fell unconscious.

"Help him mount your horse. He too needs tending," Fairfax told Rory about Duncan.

"I can manage," Duncan painfully groused. On the second attempt to mount, Rory gave him a leg up. He mounted behind Duncan.

Nathan stumbled along the courtyard wall. He knew he was no shape to fight but could not let Wallace escape. He looked from side-to-side before he cautiously stepped out into the open. A figure jumped him from the shadows. They tumbled to the ground. He managed to get on top but easily thrown off.

Wallace stood with sword ready. "Looking for me?"

Nathan awkwardly defended himself from one knee. Taking the hilt in both hands, he slashed at Wallace and forced the Scotsman back. When he managed to stand, Wallace made him retreat. His ribs ached and a sharp pain shot through his chest with each breath. He gritted his teeth to fight off the pain as the duel continued.

Wallace's frenzy of attacks caused Nathan to trip and fall on his back. This time, too weak to stand and no chance to defend. Wallace's blade penetrated deep into his left side of his chest. Another glint of steel blocked Wallace' second downward lunge. Through fading vision, Nathan recognized William.

The swords came together at the hilt. Although equal in strength, the Scotsman shoved William back. A brilliant parry and repose by William dealt Wallace wound to the left arm. At the sight of his own blood, any form of sanity left Wallace. A fearsome attack sent William retreating until he hit a building's wall near a window. On the sill sat an empty flowerpot. Using cat-like speed, William pushed the flowerpot at Wallace. In defense, Wallace broke the pot with the hilt of his sword. The ploy worked. William moved from the building into the open.

William knocked aside Wallace's riposte and lunged before the Scotsman recovered. Wallace's eyes widened in surprise when the sword penetrated his abdomen just below the cuirass. He sank to the ground, seriously wounded.

William hastened to Nathan. He looked from Nathan's bruised and battered face to wounds. His lower lip quivered as he felt for a pulse. None. He gathered in his arms and bitterly wept. "Forgive me," he begged.

His grief spent; William carried Nathan to the field hospital. He gently laid Nathan on the ground. A sudden hand grip on his shoulder.

"Is he ...?" Rory stopped when William nodded. "I'm sorry. I came to find you. Samantha and Duncan are wounded. Samantha the most serious."

"Where is she?"

"Come."

Samantha lay on a cot. Her eyes closed and terribly pale. The blankets pulled up to her waist. She wore a shirt over a bandage wrapped around her torso. Duncan sat beside her. His head and left shoulder bandaged, and arm in sling. Henry and Miller waited nearby.

Duncan grimaced, as he rose to reassure William. "She only sleeps."

"How?" William barely had voice to speak. His focus on Samantha.

"Hedgepeth. Both of us. But he is captured," Duncan added at William's intense anger.

William knelt next to the cot and took hold of Samantha's hand. He gently stroked her forehead. Tears swelled. "She is so thin and pale."

"Malnutrition from the siege. The wound goes completely through her abdomen, yet, God be thanked, missed the vital organs," Duncan spoke through grunts of pain.

Rory coaxed Duncan to sit. He leaned close to say, "Nathan is dead."

"Oh, no," lamented Duncan.

Fairfax arrived. "Her color seems better," he said to Duncan.

"Aye. The surgeon stopped the bleeding, and she sleeps."

"Your shoulder?"

"A clean wound."

"Gentlemen, the day is won. There is still work to do. With you incommode, Rory will assume temporary command of your company to secure the region," Fairfax said to Duncan. "Send word when she wakes." He nudged Rory's arm to leave.

"Stay with them," Rory quietly told Henry. "Miller, with me."

"General." William pursued Fairfax. "What of Major Hedgepeth?"

"He will be held prisoner to await the outcome of the war and Parliament's pleasure."

William flashed a reticent glance to Duncan before speaking further. "His crimes go beyond Foxglen. He ruthlessly plundered and destroyed wherever he went."

"Can you bear witness to this?"

"Aye."

Fairfax's glance passed from William to Duncan then back to William. "I shall summon you when in need of testimony. For now, duty calls."

With a sympathetic glance back at Samantha then Duncan, William left with Rory, Miller, and Fairfax.

An hour after sunset, Rory returned to the hospital to learn of Samantha's condition. She lay awake. Duncan sat in a chair with his feet up on a crate, his eyes closed in sleep. Henry sat on another crate to watch over them.

"It's good to see you awake," said Rory.

Duncan woke to voices "Ah. Samantha. How do you feel?"

She managed a small smile. "Very weak. Where is Will? Is he well?"

"Unscathed, though grieving."

"Grieving?"

Rory looked quizzically to Duncan. "Did you not tell her?"

"Tell me what?" She tried to sit up but fell back in great pain.

"Stay." Rory hurried to help her get comfortable. "You should not move for several days." He took her hand. "Nathan is dead."

She gasped at the news. "No. Oh, God, no." She began to weep.

"Please, don't get upset."

"He tried to protect me and create a diversion so I could flee. Only Lawrence …" She screwed her eyes shut, both from pain and grief.

"As he should," began Duncan with sympathy. To her hurtful look, he explained, "Nathan had a threefold duty. No, hear me," he forestalled her objection. "First, as a soldier in enemy hands, duty required he take up arms in support of his advancing comrades. Secondly, he aided his friend in the best way he could—protecting you. Thirdly, he was a servant. A servant's paramount duty is the welfare of his master or mistress. Grieve you may, but Nathan could do no less than what he did and be loyal to all accounts."

"His Grace is correct," agreed Henry.

"Being a servant doesn't lessen the sacrifice." She took Henry's hand. "I feared for you."

"It does explain his actions," said Duncan. "Remember, Nathan served Will and *me* during our days at Oxford."

"Where is Will now?"

"Making arrangements for Nathan's dispensation," replied Rory. He pulled the covers over Samantha. "Now, rest." He stroked her head until she closed her eyes. He drew Duncan aside. "With Bristol taken, the army leaves tomorrow to secure the region."

"Then I best get ready."

"No. You also must heal. Tom gave me temporary command." He flashed a rakish smile that quickly faded. "Also remember, she found father's letter. She needs your protection, and an explanation."

Duncan looked back at Samantha, who appeared to sleep. "I shall accompany you to the quartermaster to make arrangements for our transport to London when she is able to travel."

Although her eyes closed, Samantha overheard the conversation. Her mind too disturbed at the news of Nathan's death to sleep. Lying in bed, all she could do was pray. For the better part of an hour, she poured her heart out to God. Freedom from Lawrence came at a higher price than she ever imagined. Silent tears fell from the corners of her eyes at the thought of Nathan's unselfish sacrifice. Then William. She grieved for his sorrow. Finally, she came to her brothers. She felt a measure of relief concerning Rory, for he truly handled himself well amidst the chaos. Alas, Duncan. A greater responsibility fell to him than she realized. His words came back to mind when he gave reason for his change, to survive. True, he once harbored anger and bitterness toward William, but the war played a larger part in his dark change. A war she now witnessed firsthand. Death and destruction far beyond Foxglen. Whole cities leveled in wanton greed. Starvation and desperation drove people to appalling acts to survive. Wounded soldiers valiant in battle to defend comrades. Her prayer went so deep, she became startled at someone beside her.

"I did not mean to wake you," Duncan apologized.

"I was not asleep. Rather praying."

"I too prayed. God answered me when you woke. Yet, night is for rest." He reached for the blanket when she grabbed his hand. He saw fear in her eyes. "I am not leaving. I will be here when you wake." She closed her eyes yet continued to hold his hand.

Chapter 32

ALTHOUGH THE SWORD THRUST MISSED INTERNAL ORGANS, the depth of Samantha's wound made the move from Bristol to London very difficult. The normal four-day journey by carriage took a week, as she could only tolerate the jostling for ten miles before the pain became too great. By the time they reach London, infection set in.

Samantha teetered on the brink of death. Fever threatened to consume her. Fits of delirium ravished her already fevered mind. Not until seven weeks after arriving in London, did she sleep peacefully.

Lingering between dreaming and wakefulness, she felt something cool and wet on her forehead. She tried to shake her head to dislodge it. A hand placed pressure on her forehead, and she heard a voice; the light tone of a female. Her eyes blinked to open. It took a moment to focus on the face hovering above her. Her lips moved, but words choked. The face left momentarily then returned. A hand lifted her head and placed a cup to her lips. She took a few sips. When gently laid back on the pillow, her focus grew clearer.

"Anne?"

"Aye." She warmly smiled. She removed the wet cloth from Samantha's head. "You gave us quite a fright."

"Where am I?"

"London. Where you have been for nearly two months."

"How did you get here?"

Anne rinsed out the cloth to again place on Samantha's head. "Duncan sent for me when you became seriously ill with infection."

Samantha tried to move to get comfortable only collapsed back onto the pillows. "I have not the strength to move."

"You will once we get food in you. Start with some broth and bread." She removed the cloth. "I shall leave for a few moments to fetch the broth. Duncan will be pleased to hear you are awake." She barely reached the door when Duncan entered.

"Samantha." He hurried to the bed. "Thank God."

"Stay while I fetch her some food."

He nodded to Anne's comment, more focused on Samantha. He sat on the edge of the bed to hold her hand. "I cannot begin to tell you how frightened we were that you would not wake."

Samantha managed a smile. "How are you feeling?"

"Completely healed. It has been almost two months." He moved his left arm and shoulder.

"So, Anne said. Any news?"

"Rory and Will remain unscathed. The army is putting down Royalist hold-outs. Fret not for them. You must rest and regain your strength."

Her face showed distress. "I had terrible nightmares. Some regarding them and war. Horrible visions …"

"Hush." He placed a finger on her lips. "The result of delirium. Nothing more."

She squeezed his hand. Her face and voice fearful with anxiety. "What of Lawrence?"

"Arrested."

"When?" Her voice grew weary.

"No more questions. Talking is taxing the energy you need to heal. Rest until Anne returns. There shall be time for discussion when you are stronger." He stroked her forehead.

She barely nodded before closing her eyes.

Over the course of the next three months, Anne diligently tended to Samantha. With food and rest, her strength gradually returned. With Anne as escort, Samantha took to walking the upper hallways for exercise. On the evenings Duncan was home and not tending to Parliament duties, Mistress Hortence, the housekeeper, stayed with Samantha while Anne took supper with Duncan. This night, he noticed she picked at her food.

"Anne. What troubles you?"

She placed down the fork. "I have never seen Samantha so frail."

"With your good nursing, she is recovering," he spoke with encouragement.

"I do not mean physically. She insisted upon telling me her dreams."

His good humor faded slightly. "I told her they were brought on by delirium."

Anne vacillated in what to say. "Perhaps. Yet, I sense a profound impact upon her spirit. The war ..." Her voice faded as tears swelled.

Concerned, he moved from seat at the head of the table to sit beside her. "Anne?"

His action prompted her to continue in hurried, anxious words. "The war harmed so many." She buried her face in her hands and wept.

He held her, fearful of her meaning. "Dear Anne. What did that beast do to you?" She shook her head. He removed her hands from her face. "Please, tell me."

She swallowed back the tears. "He did not abuse me like Samantha. Yet, his men. Women in the village and at Foxglen." She wept anew.

He kissed her forehead. "You are safe now. No one shall ever come near you again. Not Lawrence. Not any man." He tilted her head up. "No man would dare accost my wife. If you would do me the honor."

Her smiled quivered at the sudden proposal. "Oh, aye." They kissed.

"Well, this is pleasant sight."

The female voice stopped their embrace. "Samantha!" Anne squealed.

Samantha stood in the threshold wearing a dressing gown. She laughed. "I beg forgiveness for the intrusion."

"For heaven's sake, what are you doing down here?" Duncan helped her sit at the table beside Anne.

233

"I grew tired of staying in my room. Or maybe I should have remained upstairs," she teased Anne. The latter blushed through a girlish smile.

"Did Mistress Hortence help you?" he asked, in a half-scolding tone.

"No. I managed fine by myself," Samantha said. "Now, what are you eating for supper? I want something other chicken broth or portage with bites of beef."

Duncan laughed. He pulled the bell cord for Cowan. "Supper for Lady Samantha."

Cowan widely grinned. "At once, Your Grace."

Duncan resumed his place at the head of the table. He winked at Anne though he spoke to Samantha. "There is news."

"William and Rory?" she asked with excitement.

"No. A bit closer to home." He again winked at Anne, who giggled.

"You mean the kiss just now? Did he finally propose? Did you?" she asked Anne then Duncan in quick succession.

"Aye. You are dining with the future Duchess of Rutherford."

Samantha made a squeal of delight. "At last! It took you long enough," she playfully scolded Duncan. "When is the wedding?"

"Well, there are matters at Parliament I must attend. Once those are done, we can journey to Foxmoor. Perhaps, a month to six weeks."

Elated, Samantha reached for Anne's hand. "I shall be strong enough to travel by then."

Cowan returned along with another male servant. The man brought food for Samantha while Cowan handed Duncan a letter.

"This just arrived, Your Grace."

"Thank you." He turned it over to look at the seal. "It's from Rory."

"Please, Lord, let it be good news," Samantha prayed.

At first a faint smile appeared, followed by a cheer. Duncan announced, "The best news! The King surrendered. The war is over, and the army returns to London."

Both Samantha and Anne shed tears of relief.

"This is day for double celebration," began Samantha. "A happy engagement, and the war over!"

"Aye. Cowan!" Duncan shouted. When the steward returned, he said, "Break out grandfather's special bottles. The war is over!" He waved the letter. "Let everyone celebrate."

"Aye, Your Grace," Cowan cheered.

In wonderous relief, Duncan sat back. "Five bloody years," he thoughtfully muttered. Misty tears filled his eyes as he looked at the letter. "Oh, father, I kept my promise."

"Duncan?" Samantha asked, not having understood what he said.

He smiled. Unashamed of his tears. "I promised father we would survive, and we have."

"Not totally unscathed. Much has been destroyed," she droned.

"Buildings can be raised again. We are alive, and that is what matters."

"I also speak of lives." Samantha glanced to Anne.

"My father would rejoice at this news," Anne graciously in response to the glance. She smiled at Duncan. "And about us. So, let us not dwell on past sorrows. With the war over, our future lies ahead." She took hold of Samantha's hand. "We shall be sisters. Think on that."

"I always thought of you as a sister. I'm glad my brother will finally make it official." She giggled.

Cowan returned. He carried a tray with four glasses and a bottle and placed them on the table. Duncan uncorked the special whiskey to pour. Cowan gave glasses to Anne and Samantha. Duncan stood and handed one glass to Cowan then raised his glass.

"To peace!" Duncan declared. All repeated the salute and drank.

Chapter 33

THE NEW MODEL ARMY RETURNED TRIUMPHANTLY TO LONDON. A happy reunion took place at the O'Malley home in Kensington. Anticipation of the upcoming wedding between Anne and Duncan aided in Samantha's recovery. Overjoyed, she watched her brothers and William take turns making toasts. Anne graciously accepted the congratulations of Rory and William. Samantha kept her drinking of ale to a minimum, yet soon began to tire.

"If you gentlemen will excuse me, it is late," she sweetly said.

"Oh?" Duncan questioned. The mantle clock in the drawing room struck midnight. "So, it is. Good night, dear sister. Sleep well." He kissed her cheek. Rory did the same.

William made a sweeping bow to kiss Samantha's hand. His gesture showed signs of drinking. "Goodnight, sweet lady."

"I too shall retire and leave you gentlemen to continue the celebration." Anne accompanied Samantha.

"I should return to my house. Or maybe not," William thought aloud. "My father might be there. No, he probably returned to Nottingham after Parliament's victory."

"You shall stay here tonight. You have an interview in the morning," said Duncan.

"I do?"

"The Committee of Both Kingdoms is preparing to bring charges against the King's officers. This includes Hedgepeth. Remember, what you told Tom about giving testimony."

William briefly frowned at the reminder. "They intend to move swiftly?"

"Stability requires quick action."

"Who is on this Committee?"

"Aside from myself, there is Manchester and Essex from the House of Lords. For the Commons, Cromwell, Sir Anthony Haselrig, Sir William Waller, and eleven others, and the Scots. A total of twenty-five members."

William's brows leveled as he looked down to consider.

Keen to the uneasiness, Duncan clapped William's shoulder. "Fear not. They are favorable to all who seek justice."

William slowly lifted his head. "Then I must do as I have said."

First thing in the morning, Duncan, Rory, and William arrived at Parliament. Duncan led them upstairs to a private room to meet Fairfax.

Fairfax smiled at their blurry-eyed appearance. "I take it celebration continued late into the night."

"As did most of London, I'm certain," replied Duncan with a chuckle.

"Indeed. However, serious matters call for attention." Fairfax turned to William. "The Committee appreciates your willingness to testify, Major."

"Circumstances being what they are, I feel compelled." William made a quick survey of the room. No one else was present. "I see no Committee or clerk to transcribe my testimony."

"Circumstances what they are," Fairfax quoted, "We believe it best for witnesses to write their testimony for inclusion in the official records. Some details may be too personal for certain ears, shall we say. Lord Kyle more directly."

William shot Duncan an irate glare, as he left out the name last night.

Duncan answered the silent rebuke. "It is enough I must deal with him almost daily. Although, I have recused myself in the matter of his son. He would not take kindly to your public participation."

Fairfax picked up the explanation. "Thus, we considered by writing in private, you avoid an unpleasant encounter while providing much needed first-hand testimony."

William's gaze shifted from Duncan to Fairfax. "I am grateful for the consideration, General."

Fairfax indicated a table upon which sat ink, paper, a candle, sealing wax, and seal. "We shall leave you to compose. Take what time you need. When finished, use Parliament's stamp to seal it, and leave it on the desk. We shall be in the Members' dining room."

William made himself comfortable. It took several moments to consider where to begin. Once he took up the pen, words flowed. However, when it came to recounting the events at Foxglen, he paused. He relived many emotions already during the composition. Now, it involved his heart. Images flashed across his mind's eye. Nathan wounded by Henry; pulling off the mask to reveal Samantha; and the sting of the lash. He paced to regain his composure. For the course of justice to proceed, he must finish the account. Taking a deep breath of determination, he sat to write. Twice, he wiped his eyes clear of rising tears. Not tears for himself, rather Samantha and Duncan. To a lesser degree Rory, but he too figured into the outcome. Thoughts of Nathan most painful in the writing. When finished, he folded the paper.

"Lord, may justice be done," he prayed. He sealed his testimony.

William made his way to the Members' dining room. When he was stopped by a guard, Duncan called him over. The guard stepped aside to permit entry. He joined Duncan and Rory at a table. A servant promptly brought him a tankard of ale.

"Finally finished?" asked Duncan.

"Aye." William took a drink. "Where is General Fairfax?"

"Called away for a meeting. We left you two hours ago."

William paused in drinking to regard Duncan. "Two hours? I didn't notice the time. Sorry for the delay." He frowned in thought, as he stared into the tankard.

Duncan gripped William's shoulder. "Will." He made a gentle nudge to get attention. Once he did, Duncan said, "We truly appreciate your help." He grew concerned at the forlorn expression. "Do you regret it?"

"No," William replied, though his gaze returned to the tankard. "I relived every word I wrote." He took a long drink.

Duncan waved to a servant and indicated William. The man brought another tankard of ale. William shoved the empty tankard aside to drink the second. To this action, Duncan said, "Every man involved must deal with events of the past few years. Some episodes we wish could be changed. Alas, that is impossible. All we can do is move forward."

"Easier said than done," grumbled William.

"You have already started."

"How does your lawyer mind reckon that?"

Duncan wore a partial smile of remembrance. "My father once told me: *confession is good for the soul.* By facing our past, we acknowledge the deeds, both good and bad. With such action, we can move beyond the pain to grow. Take you and me for example. A year ago, did you believe we would be sitting here together like old times? I confess, I did not." Again, he held William's shoulder. "Writing the testimony is your cathartic moment. The opportunity to move beyond those painful events. To heal, grow, and move on."

For a long moment, William regarded Duncan. "There is much truth in what you say. Yet many obstacles remain."

"One step at a time. The important part is you have started."

"We all have started," said Rory. "It may be Will's testimony, but it involves Lawrence and Lord Kyle."

Duncan scoffed and picked up his tankard. "No need to remind. The old man is more cantankerous since his injuries. He takes no thought of using his canes as weapons on anyone within range. Nasty things, heavy oak with large silver tops to bear his weight."

"Have you encountered him since Lawrence's arrest?" asked Rory, concerned.

Duncan nodded since he drank. "Fortunately, Tom, Cromwell, and Essex have kept him in check during the Committee meetings. Otherwise, I would have been a victim of his canes." He turned to William, "Hence, why you—"

"Wrote my testimony," William finished the sentence. He grew worried with sudden thought. "Wait! Is my father still on the Committee?"

"No. While we waited for you, Tom told us that he *did* retire to Nottingham."

"Which is what you thought last night," Rory added. "So, you can safely go to your family's townhouse. Or come, return with us to Kensington," he added upon receiving a scowl from Duncan.

"It is best I go home. To avoid one of the *obstacles*," William pointedly said to Duncan. "Good day." He grabbed his hat and left.

"I take it he means Samantha," Rory said.

Duncan watched William leave. "It is for the best."

"I'm not sure she will see it that way."

Duncan seized Rory's arm to stop him from taking a drink. "Mind your tongue in public!" He cautiously glanced around before he leaned closer to speak under his breath. "A broken body does not lessen Kyle's influence. If anything, it embitters his resolve. I have distanced myself from any dealings with Lawrence. However, Will is vulnerable. So, is Samantha. There can be no hint of scandal."

Rory mimicked the cautionary tone. "You are not without influence."

"Aye. Only I must use it judiciously. Whoever the original author is, wields much power." He removed the tankard from Rory's hand. "Come. We should return, for *she* will be curious."

240

Chapter 34

THE JOY OF PEACE AND REUNION OF FRIENDS AND FAMILY IN London, rejuvenated Samantha's spirit. The upcoming wedding provided focus for her energies. During the months of her recovery, Anne took over responsibility of running the Kensington household. After all, she would shortly become Duchess of Rutherford. All the servants already knew Anne, so the transition not too difficult. However, Samantha insisted on planning the wedding, to which Anne agreed.

Samantha sat at a small writing table in the drawing room. She reviewed details they discussed before Anne was called away for household duties. Loud male voices came from the hall. She jerked in surprise when something pounded on the door.

"Open this bloody door!"

"Aye, my lord."

She covered her mouth in dreadful recognition of the first voice. The second was Cowan. Thus far she avoided her father-in-law. In fact, she had not seen him since the start of the war when he cursed her family and all those who opposed the King. However, when other Royalists chose to abandon London due to the King's surrender, Lord Kyle stubbornly remained. According to Duncan, he stayed to act as a thorn in any plan launched by Parliament. Now, it became her turn to deal with him. Her lips moved in silent prayer to prepare for the unpleasant encounter.

At age sixty-three, Kyle was nearly bald, thus wore a dark brown wig that starkly contrasted his gray beard, mustache, and pale countenance. His clothes befitted his lofty station. Since his injuries, he used two canes made

241

from oak topped with large ornate silver grips for stability. He moved in an uneven gait where he practically dragged his right leg. Extra weight aggravated his condition. The same scowl and contemptuous gleam in the eyes showed the similarity between father and son. A reality that chilled Samantha to the core.

She remained seated. "My lord. To what do I owe this visit?"

"You know well my purpose! You received my correspondences."

She shook her head at the revelation. "I have received none."

Kyle snarled. "Your brother must have kept them from you. Which I suspected, and why I came. Ugh. A chair, you fool!" he scolded Cowan. The pain of standing obvious.

At a nod from Samantha, Cowan moved a chair for Kyle to sit. The chair rocked when he practically fell on to it. He huffed and grunted.

"Comfortable, my lord?" Biting sarcasm crept into her voice.

"Do not take that tone with me, woman! You and your brothers are responsible. Do not deny it."

"Deny what?" she cautiously asked. She played this dueling game with him before the war. A time she hoped never to endure again.

Angry, Kyle ponded the canes on the floor. "Lawrence's arrest!"

Now she understood why Duncan intercepted the letters. As calmly as possible, she spoke. "My lord, I suffered a near fatal wound. Thus, unaware of how it transpired …"

Kyle again pounded one cane and used the other to point at her. "You lie, madam."

Despite being initially startled by the pounding action, her temper flared at the accusation. She bolted up. "Lawrence tried to kill me!" The sudden flush of passion drained her energy. She swayed and caught herself on the desk to sit.

"Samantha?" Anne rushed to assist her.

"Stay out of this, woman. Remember your place," Kyle roughly brushed off Anne.

"Sir. I am affianced to the Duke of Rutherford!"

"Oh! So, you are the wench," he spoke with disdain.

"Sir!" Anne huffed.

Samantha gripped Anne's arm to rise again and confront Kyle. "My lord, what do you want?"

"For you to stand by your husband, as is your duty."

"A husband who tried to kill me?" Her voice rose and fell with fervor.

"No more than you deserve after your treasonous escapades in manly disguise. Enough of this!" He waved a cane. "You will accompany me to visit Lawrence, where you shall beg his forgiveness, and assume your rightful place in our household."

His callous command and cold eyes made Samantha visibly tremble. The surge of emotions threatened to overtake her.

Sight of weakening, Kyle launched the final volley. "You shall do so immediately, or your family will suffer consequences worse than previous."

Samantha covered her mouth to stifle a sob of fear at the threat. She collapsed into the chair weeping.

Deeply concerned, Anne knelt beside Samantha. Her own anger piqued. When she turned to confront Kyle, she saw him in the threshold. Rory and Cowan behind him. "Duncan!"

"What is going on here?" Duncan demanded of Kyle.

"Rory! Brandy," Anne hastily instructed in reference to Samantha.

While Anne and Rory tended to Samantha, Duncan confronted Kyle. "I asked a question. Be good enough to answer, sir." When Kyle sat in stubborn refusal, Duncan told Cowan. "Fetch some men and have Lord Kyle forcibly removed!"

"What?" thundered Kyle.

"You come into my home uninvited, bring my sister to tears, and upset my betrothed. For that, sir, you will leave at once."

"Do not threaten me."

"I made no threat. I am merely protecting my family from an unwelcomed guest. That is the right of any man be he common, or in my case, *duke* of the realm."

Cowan quickly returned with two male servants.

Duncan flashed a caustic smile. "Ah, here is your escort, my lord."

Kyle had difficulty standing. Once on his feet, he leaned heavily on his canes to glare at Duncan. "*Your Grace* does realize that in the eyes of the law, she is married to my son thus legally under my domain as daughter-in-law."

Duncan stood firm. "*Your lordship* does realize that in the eyes of the law, attempted murder is a crime even for a husband. A crime I witnessed. As my sister, she will remain under my protection."

Kyle's contemptuous sneer deepened when his eyes narrowed. Again, Duncan boldly withstood the supposed intimidation.

Duncan's gaze only briefly left Kyle to say, "Cowan."

When the men grew near, Kyle roughly jerked them off. He sent a last withering glare to Samantha. She buried her head in Rory's shoulder to avoid eye contact.

Duncan moved to the threshold to make certain Kyle left. He then hastened to the desk. "What did he say to you?"

Rory encouraged Samantha to take another sip of brandy. When she showed an unwillingness to answer, Anne spoke.

"He said her wounding was deserved. More heinous, he wanted her to go with him to beg forgiveness from Lawrence and made vile threats against us if she did not comply," Anne's voice cracked with angry emotion.

Duncan turned red-faced with rage. "Fiend!"

When Samantha wept anew, Duncan knelt. He held her hand. "No one will force you to do anything. You will remain under my protection until everything is resolved." He took the glass from Rory to encourage her to finish the brandy. "Now, go upstairs with Anne." He helped her stand and gave her in Anne's charge.

Rory angrily sneered yet did not give voice to his wrath until Samantha left. "Beg Lawrence's forgiveness! Bah! It is he who should beg for mercy."

"Steady," Duncan warned. "The ordeal has weakened her in a way I have never seen."

"I thought she was healed."

"Physically. But in here." Duncan motioned to the left side of his chest. "Her heart and spirit languish. Our little sister is a shadow of her former self. It is only by God's grace she lives."

"I knew the wound serious, but you speak as if near fatal."

"Infection and fever kept her on the brink of death for nearly two months. It became a daily struggle to contain the fever as she fought delirium. Many times, we wondered if she would survive."

Rory's dismay at the news turned to anger. "Why did you not tell us?"

"For the same reason she did not contact us, unsure of location. By the time I received the first letter from you, the worst had passed. The fever broke and she awoke. Because of her diminished strength, I kept Kyle's letters from her. To protect from such upset as you witnessed." He tossed a sneering glance at the door. "Alas, he acted boldly in coming here."

"You rebuffed him."

"For now. Unfortunately, he will find another way to get at her. At us, until all this is rectified."

An hour later, Duncan called upon Samantha. She sat in a chair by the window. The room occupied looked out over the back garden. She wore a dressing gown with her hair down. Anne waited nearby yet allowed Samantha privacy. He spoke a soft word to Anne, who quietly left. He joined Samantha at the window.

"Are you feeling better?"

She smiled, although it didn't reach her eyes. "I want to apologize for my weakness ..." She stopped he spoke.

"You have no reason to apologize. To me or *anyone else,*" he emphasized. He took her face in his hands. "I promise to use all avenues within my power, so you never again have to deal with Kyle or Lawrence. It has pained me as much as it did father."

"Why?" came her breathy distressed question. "Please! Do not put me off again." She insisted. At his hesitation, she added, "I know it deals with grandfather's past. Along with father and the Earl of Strafford's son."

Surprised by the mention of Strafford, Duncan hastily asked, "How do you know that?"

"Lawrence told me. He thought to torment me with horrible accusations that father promised me to an Irish lord instead of the earl's son. How his father intervened to *save* me by marriage to him."

Annoyed, Duncan rose. "The cad!"

Concerned by his reaction, she ventured to ask, "Is it true? Did father promise me to an Irish lord?"

Duncan leaned on the back of the chair. "The answer is not a simple one. The complexities and machinations are not easy to unravel without great harm, even ruin. Soothe, I am still contemplating the depths of what occurred. Or even *why?*"

She grew annoyed. "I am the daughter and sister of a duke, so politics are involved. I am not so ignorant. Although Lawrence considers women as pawns. Is that what I am? A pawn?"

"I never said that. Nor would I—or father—use you as a pawn," he firmly refuted.

"Then what happened for Lawrence to say so?"

He resumed his seat and took hold of her hands. "Please, understand, there are shades of legality and hierarchy of power that make it difficult to explain in short detail."

Offended, she tried to withdraw her hands, but he held fast. With sudden dismay, she said, "You don't trust me."

"Not for trust's sake, rather the safety of our family." He lifted her chin when she turned away. Her eyes misty with tears. "Dear sister, I am trying to protect you. This is a burden that I, as duke and head of our family, must bear alone. No one else can secure a remedy but me. As such, I must keep what I know private until all is put right and I can speak freely." He gently brushed her tears away. "I did not come to talk politics or even our unwanted visitor. I came to tell you about this morning and Will."

"Oh," she said eagerly, then gasped in disturbance. "Was it his testimony that brought Lord Kyle here?"

"He did not testify before the Committee rather privately wrote a detailed report. We, Tom and I, thought it best to avoid revealing his identity as long as possible."

She relaxed with a smile. "Why did William not return with you?"

"He had other business. Enough talk," he continued to forestall her protest. "Rest knowing all is well with him. And you are safe." He kissed her forehead, but before he could leave, she seized his hand. Earnest eyes looked up at him.

"You are wrong about one thing. It is not you alone who can secure a remedy. God must help you."

Duncan softly smiled. "Aye. Continue to pray for me in that end."

Chapter 35

AFTER TWO WEEKS OF GATHERING TESTIMONY, THE COMMITTEE of Both Kingdoms and Parliament assembled for the trial of Royal officers arrested during the course of the war. Speaker Lenthall presided. At the front of the Hall, sat the Committee members, five from the House of Lords, ten from the House of Commons, and three of the Scottish representatives.

Gallery of the House of Commons overflowed with spectators. The crowd buzzed with anticipation. Dressed completely in black with cloak, black wig, and Venetian mask, Duncan stood at the furthest extent of the gallery to observe. He excused himself from rendering judgment due to his relationship to Lawrence. He recalled Kyle's vehement refusal to take his place among the Committee in what he called a *usurping of military authority*. A rather puzzling argument since the vast majority of Committee Members were army commanders. No one tried to persuade Kyle to change his mind, rather allowed him a moment to bellow.

Despite his choice not to sit with the Committee, Duncan spied Kyle on the front row of the Lords' side. No doubt as a bold reminder to his fellow Committee Members of his station. *So like him to say one thing and do another. All to intimidate,* Duncan thought.

When Kyle occasioned to glance up at the gallery, Duncan drew back. Though doubtful of recognition since the wig hid his dark copper hair, precaution dictated wariness.

Lenthall called for order and those in the gallery grew quiet. He gave stern warning about interruptions during the proceedings. In total, thirty-five officers would be arraigned.

How long it would take before dealing with Lawrence was unknown. Yet with each officer, Duncan grew anxious. Most of the junior officers accepted the punishment, which ranged from confiscation of lands, hefty fines, or imprisonment. A few senior officers protested and declared unwavering allegiance to the King. So far, two committed similar crimes to Lawrence, that of wanton pillaging, rape, and murder. Due to evidence of their involvement, the highest penalty was rendered, death by hanging.

During inquisition of those officers, Duncan kept keen watch of Kyle. The old man's face severely screwed in disgust. Several times the gallery erupted in jeers at the worst reported crimes. Lenthall called for *silence*. One man needed to be escorted from the gallery by guards. His passionate outburst cursed the officer and accused him of killing his family! His removal forced Duncan to step aside. He became knocked back into the wall where his hat and wig became askew. He righted himself before being noticed. He just resumed his position when Lenthall commanded the guards.

"Bring forth Major Lawrence Hedgepeth!"

At this announcement, Duncan noticed Kyle stirred as if to rise. A quick restraining hand by the Earl of Manchester, kept Kyle seated. The Earl also spoke. No doubt a warning since the corners of Kyle's lips turned in the deepest sneer yet.

Chains on his wrists and ankle fetters notwithstanding, Lawrence Hedgepeth proudly entered with arrogance unabated. He held his head high and eyes fixed on the Speaker. If he made a glance to his father, his head did not turn. The guards roughly drew him to a halt at the bench.

"Clerk," Lenthall spoke.

Like the two dozen officers before him, the clerk read the charges. "Major Lawrence Hedgepeth, you are hereby charged with high crimes against Parliament and the people of England. You did wantonly and without mercy pillage numerous homes and villages resulting in the ravaging of women, death of some said women, making orphans of children. Participated in ransacking of Parliament storehouses, unlawful imprisonment of House Members families. Sedition against Parliament and people of England. Attempted murder of Lady Hedgepeth. How do you plead?"

"I offer no plea. I fulfilled my sacred duty to my liege King."

"If you offer no plea, then by law, it shall be considered an admission of guilt."

"Ha! Guilt. You have no proof rather hearsay by traitors to the Crown."

The clerk picked up a stack of paper. "We have sworn testimony from numerous witnesses of your crimes. Including men under your command. Not to mention the physician who treated Lady Hedgepeth of the near fatal wound you inflicted. So, again, I ask, how do you plead?"

Duncan froze. His eyes in rapt attention on the clerk when he mentioned *sworn testimony* and *men under your command*. He slightly relaxed when the clerk withheld names.

"Traitors all," scoffed Hedgepeth.

The clerk turned to Lenthall. "Mister Speaker, I request the record show the defendant refused to offer a plea. Therefore, by law, he is considered guilty."

"So, shall the record show," agreed Lenthall.

"Thank you, Mister Speaker." The clerk again addressed Lawrence. "Being these are high crimes of willful attempted murder, issuing orders that acted as an accessory to numerous murders, sedition against Parliament and people, the sentence is death by hanging."

Duncan grimaced and turned aside at the announcement. He believed he considered the ramifications of either imprisonment or death, yet woefully unprepared for the mixture of emotions at hearing the death sentence pronounced. His attention drawn back to the floor when Kyle vehemently protested.

Canes banged loudly as Kyle stood. "This is an outrageous miscarriage of justice! He is a commissioned officer in His Majesty's army and my son."

"My lord Hedgepeth," Lenthall sternly spoke. "You will confine your comments until after the proceedings."

"Mister Speaker," began the clerk. "His lordship had ample opportunity to present defense witnesses on behalf of the Major. I, myself, visited his lordship several times during the months since the Major's arrest. Howbeit, his lordship refused to present counterevidence."

To this startling revelation, Lawrence questioned his father, "Sir?"

Kyle turned from Lawrence to the Lenthall. "It is my intent to bring this matter directly to His Majesty rather than condescend to this assembly."

"That shall be rather difficult considering His Majesty is also a prisoner. By the will of the people, this Parliament assembles, with all right therein," rebuffed Lenthall.

Several in the gallery shouted agreement with Lenthall.

"Silence!" warned the Speaker. "Guards, escort the prisoner to the executioner."

"What?" Lawrence questioned, a tremor of fear in his voice. "Sir!"

Kyle's expression shifted between grief and anger, unable to watch his son's removal.

In contrast, Duncan could not keep his eyes off Lawrence until the door closed upon departure. His breathing slightly labored at the reality of the sentence and immediate execution. He pushed past people to leave.

Outside, Duncan hurried into a nearby alcove. The wig made him sweat, so he removed it and tossed it aside. He pocketed the mask. He leaned against the building with his eyes closed. He took a deep breath followed by a slow exhale as he silently prayed.

Lord, your justice be done. Thank you for keeping our hands innocent in this. Yet may this lead to vindication of our family. For now, give me the words to tell Samantha, and strengthen her spirit to hear the news.

"Duncan."

His eyes snapped open. His heart raced in surprise. "Tom."

Fairfax drew near for a private discussion. He withdrew a folded paper from a doublet pocket. "I managed to retrieve this from among the evidence collected."

"Evidence? Against Lawrence?"

251

"No." Fairfax lowered his voice to a whisper. "Found among the King's personal letters. Although sealed, it is addressed to someone of great personal interest." He turned it over for Duncan to see.

His eyes widened in recognition but did not speak when Fairfax gave his shoulder a warning squeeze.

He gave it to Duncan yet held the younger man's hand. "There is more. The dreaded possibility we spoke of in Bristol is confirmed reality."

Duncan grew pale. "Father—?" But Fairfax's nod and jerk of his arm, stopped further words. "How? Who?" he demanded in breathy insistence.

"Poisoned by one of Strafford's servants in an act of revenge. A confession found among the legal documents along with the judgement of death by hanging." He reached into his doublet pocket for another piece of paper. "This is a copy of his confession. A staunch Royalist, fiercely loyal to Strafford and loathed anyone opposed the earl or King."

Duncan blinked back tears of grief when accepting the second paper.

Fairfax held Duncan the entire time. "If I had known sooner, I would have told you."

Duncan simply nodded, unable to reply.

"If asked, you came these at Naseby. I had no part in it."

"Understood. Thank you," Duncan replied in a husky voice.

For a moment, he watched Fairfax shrink into the shadows. Duncan pocketed both papers then made his way to the family's Kensington home. He took the journey at a deliberately slow pace. He needed to compose himself. The shock of his father's untimely death enough to deal when it happened. Now, to learn it was a murder of revenge, made the situation more tenuous. Perhaps, in time, he could tell his siblings. For now, he had to inform Samantha about the outcome of her husband's trial.

In the drawing room, he found Anne, Rory, and William with Samantha. She sat on a sofa to work on a needlepoint. She placed the hoop aside when he sat next to her.

"It is done. Lawrence shall never again trouble you."

She barely uttered, "How?"

Duncan glanced to William then back to Samantha to answer. "As of today, you are *permanently* free to follow your heart."

She gasped and paled at the dreadful meaning. William knelt beside the sofa. She pushed away from them and ran from the room.

"Samantha!" William bolted up only Duncan intercepted him.

"No. She must come to terms with Lawrence's fate."

"Have you come to terms with it? Or me? I testified against him," William rebuffed.

"You knew the sentence of death a possibility. No!" Duncan hastily added when William went to object. "Names of witnesses were not mentioned. The charges were enough."

"What were the charges that brought the death penalty?" asked Rory.

"Sedition against Parliament and the people. Willful orders of violence that lead to the murder of women. Attempted murder of his wife." Duncan turned from Rory to William. "When Kyle objected, the clerk said his lordship refused to present counterevidence even when given multiple opportunities. This made the naming of witnesses unnecessary."

William's brows rose in astonishment. "He would not defend his son?"

"It is difficult to defend against the truth." Duncan held William's shoulder. "God kept our hands clean in this affair. We bear no reproach while justice served, both earthly and divine. The past is done. I would warmly welcome you as a second brother."

William regarded Duncan. "What a turn of events God has rendered."

"Aye," agreed Duncan with low chuckle.

William glanced to the ceiling. "Samantha needs to hear what you just divulged." When Duncan again tried to prevent him, he removed Duncan's hand. "For the sake of our future, she *must* be told I had no part in the sentencing. There can be no shadow of this between us."

Upstairs, Samantha lay on the bed weeping. All the emotions that became her close companions for years spilled forth in tears of grief, sorrow, anger, bitterness, and fear. The beast of a man, she called *husband* punished for his crimes. Crimes far beyond herself. Consumed by distress, she did not hear the knock, nor realize someone sat beside her until a hand touched her shoulder. She sat up in fright. William.

"No, please, leave."

She went to lay down again when he embraced her. She grew rigid, so he tightened his hold. Her instinct to fight rose, but he refused to release her. He made the *shhh* hush sound and spoke "Easy". His voice reassuring. No anger or bitterness. He used his hand to gently hold her head against his chest. She heard his heartbeat. An embrace of comfort. She began to grow calm. Soon, the tears gave way to relief, and she relaxed.

Feeling her tension ease, he lifted her head. "Duncan told us something you must hear. Now, do not distress," he soothed when she began to stiffen again. "No names were revealed of those who gave testimony."

"How could there be a conviction without witnesses?"

He reached for her again, but drew back, so he held her hand. "This is what Duncan said occurred. The crimes were so grievous, including your attempted murder, that even his father presented no evidence for defense when given multiple opportunities before the trial."

Thunderstruck, she gaped at him. "He did not defend his son?"

"It is difficult to defend against the truth," William quoted Duncan.

Her expression turned to anger. "He said my wound was justified and wanted me to ask Lawrence forgiveness."

"You are free from them. By God's mercy, *we* are free to be together."

Thunderstruck, she murmured, "Free." Her arms crossed herself, as if warding off a chill.

William again embraced her. He held her until she fell asleep.

Chapter 36

DETERMINED TO PUT THE RECENT EVENTS BEHIND THEM, Duncan arranged for departure from London. For the siblings, thoughts of home warmed their hearts. William simply smiled at their excitement. Duncan, Rory, and William took turns riding in the carriage with Samantha and Anne or mounted escort.

Once at Foxglen, Henry presented his report to Duncan. The bailiff resumed his duties after informing Anne of Duncan's desire for her to come speedily to London. With Henry's help, Duncan reassured the servants and villagers of his commitment to restore order. Major Hedgepeth's death brought a sense of relief. The announcement of the duke's wedding to Anne met with a joy not seen in years. However, Samantha's betrothal to Major Hawkins was met with mixed feelings. Despite his pleasant demeanor and bravery on their mistress' behalf, occupation and imprisonment by the Royalists remained fresh on their minds.

After three weeks, they set off for Foxmoor. Before departure, Duncan privately placed the journals among his personal belongings. He would not divulge anything unless he discovered an answer by comparing the journals to the letters found in the King's baggage.

Once through a thick patch of wood, the majestic walls of Foxmoor came into view. A quarter mile further, in a vast clearing and slightly elevated, the twin-turreted gatehouse that guarded the entrance harkened back to the day of knights and crude warfare. Built from local gray stone, the battlements ran the length of the front wall to half-rounded turrets at the corners. The front wall strictly for defense and void of windows or housing. Even with present artillery, the house could withstand a considerable onslaught. A few pox marks of cannonade appeared upon the turrets.

Duncan sent his horse into a gallop. Once passed the main gain, he entered the large gravel and grass courtyard separating the massive main house from the front battlement. Also on horseback, Rory arrived shortly after Duncan. The carriage a few moments behind Rory.

The once properly maintained central fountain showed neglect. The stable occupied the west wall of the manor-castle while on the east wall was the family chapel and servants' quarters. The lawn rough and overgrown in places marred by deep ruts. The grand garden once contained some of the most beautiful roses in Staffordshire. The back lawn continued for a hundred yards beyond the garden where it fell sharply down to the river Trent. A small three-foot terrace wall kept out unwanted varmints as the sharp incline and river provided natural protection for the rear of the manor.

Duncan vaulted from the saddle. The joy of being home seen is his wide smile. "It seems to have weathered the war well enough. Let's see about inside."

"You go first. I will wait for the carriage."

Duncan moved to the front door. The lock and handle had been battered off, so he pushed it open. Damage and neglect starkly visible upon entrance. Some of fine pottery and valuable statues smashed, paintings gouged or missing. Curtains torn down and furniture destroyed or missing. He fought to contain his temper. Five years of war left their mark. He rushed to the study. To his relief, portraits of his father, mother, and grandparents remained untouched.

"Oh, Duncan!" Samantha muttered in distress.

He took a deep breath to regain his composure. Anne quietly moved beside him in support. "It would be unrealistic to think we emerged unscathed by this madness."

"What business have you here?" A tall man slightly bent at the shoulders appeared in the threshold. He held a pistol ready.

Duncan stepped forward. "Wadsworth?"

"Your Grace?" Wadsworth sniffled back emotions. "I dare not hope. Your lordship. My lady," he said in recognition of Rory and Samantha. Bashful, he indicated the pistol. "It is not loaded. I use it to scare off vagrants who come looting."

Duncan grinned and patted the steward's arm. "How many remain?"

"Only four of us, Your Grace. Myself, my wife, our son Jim, and Nick the old groom." He leaned closer to Duncan to say, "Alas, Nick is no longer right in the head. Cracked skull from Royalists. He still believes there are horses in the stables and pretends to care for them."

"There shall be horses again. The ones we rode and those of the carriage."

Wadsworth smiled. "Aye. I don't know if there much in larder, but I shall have my wife prepare what she can for a homecoming." He turned in the threshold. "Oh, I hid a few bottles of your grandfather's favorite whiskey."

"Whiskey?" said William, intrigued.

"Irish whiskey," Duncan clarified then to Wadsworth, "Bring a bottle now. We shall drink to being home."

"If there are any glasses left," Rory groused. He walked about inspecting the room.

"Then we shall pass the bottle." Duncan slapped Rory's arm. He spoke to the others. "There is enough time to determine the extent of damage and loss. For now, let us drink to home, friends, and family. After all, we have two weddings to celebrate."

Despite difficulty of dealing with the destruction and vandalism to Foxmoor and surrounding hamlets, Duncan relished the planning of a double wedding. A poignant moment came when choosing a minister to perform the ceremony. Anne bore up well, yet he knew the sorrow she felt at Howard's absence.

With Lawrence dead, there was no need for a decree of divorce nor require Samantha to pass the normal time of a mourning widow. Still, Duncan spent very late nights in his bedchamber reading and re-reading the journals for clues regarding the marriage contract. He compared the journals, Kyle's letters, and King's letter recovered at Naseby. The letters ranged in dates from the time Kyle approached Patrick through a year after the wedding.

In the first letter, Kyle wrote in detail about *persuading* Patrick, then Duncan. The second letter told of the wedding and reassurance that the hold of Rutherford was now secured. The third letter was dated eighteen months into the war. Of course, battle started shortly after the wedding, so Kyle and Lawrence were serving in the King's army. This letter mentioned his wounds and the difficulty of recovery. However, he gave reassurance that his incommode would not diminish his efforts to *contain Rutherford.* He wrote how Lawrence managed *the sister well enough,* but that he would make certain *Lord Rutherford* knew his place. Duncan's jowls clenched in an angry sneer. He tossed it aside to snatch up the King's letter.

Although sealed, being among the baggage told it not been dispatched before battle. Which is odd considering the dates, so there must have been something between the last letter and this response. Whereas Kyle's letter contained no new information the King's letter did! Charles addressed it directly to Kyle and referred to details contained in Kyle's previous letters. He unequivocally stated his *fervent desire* of dealing with Rutherford.

Stupefied by what he read; Duncan sat back to consider the revelation. He snatched up the King's letter to read again. Could Charles have ordered the servant to kill a duke of royal blood? True, Henry VII was a Tudor, and Charles a Stuart, but such a bold move as to—*No!* his mind refuted. *Charles listened to base counsel. Strafford among them.*

The thought of Strafford made him recall Fairfax's words about the murderer. *A staunch Royalist, fiercely devoted to Strafford and loathed anyone opposed to the earl or King."* Duncan took up the man's confession to compare with the King's letter.

"Aye, that would make sense. Being Strafford's man, he might have known the King's sentiments," he muttered in consideration. He jerked in shock at hearing a voice. "Rory!" He hurried to gather the documents.

"No need to hide them. That is why I came. Although you didn't hear me when I knocked."

Duncan regarded Rory, as his mind warred at what to tell his brother.

"I take it by your expression, you discovered something."

"Aye. Sit." Duncan waited a moment for Rory to become comfortable at the small table. With discretion, he proceeded. "Kyle's letters confirm everything we already know about his personal profiting at our expense. But the scope." He picked up another letter yet held it in such a way as to hide the wax seal. "This solves the mystery of the contract author along with the motive." He looked firmly as Rory to say, "Brace yourself." He removed his hand so Rory could examine the seal.

"Good heavens! It was the king!" Rory exclaimed.

"*Shhhh*," Duncan warned. "I compared all the letters to grandfather's journal. The scope is disturbing. He," Duncan held up the King's letter, "never forgave grandfather for what he saw as *betrayal* of Buckingham."

"How *betrayal?*"

Duncan shrugged. "Unsure. Even grandfather wondered. He supposed, that in Charles' mind, anything short of full and unconditional support for Buckingham was *betrayal*. Like his stance against Parliament in first wanting to raise taxes for Strafford's Irish army then dissolving us when we refused the money." His voice cracked and words stuttered in speaking of *Strafford* and the *Irish army*.

Rory noticed the incommode. "Duncan?" When his older brother didn't immediately answer, he asked, "Where does the marriage contract fit into this?"

The momentary pause gave Duncan time to gather his composure "A plan of revenge by Charles to destroy Rutherford for said *betrayal*. Confiscation of Foxhill and Foxmeath were just the beginning. The estates have been held in trust for a single purpose." With intense earnestness, Duncan regarded Rory. "Upon Samantha's death, Lawrence would not only inherit Foxglen, but the Crown would bequeath him Foxhill and Foxmeath. Lawrence's efforts were meant to break her. If she died in bed, he could claim natural causes. At Bristol, he could use the war as a legitimate excuse of her death."

Dumbfounded, Rory shook his head to comprehend. "*You* are the duke, while I am next in line. She would not inherit the title."

"Either, or both, of us could easily be killed in battle like so many others. In fact, Charles boldly states," Duncan read, "*it is my fervent desire for a speedy end to these betrayers of us and our dear friend.* He goes on to mention the bequeathing of Foxhill and Foxmeath as a reward. However, if by chance I survived, Rutherford is reduced by three quarters. Robbed of my sister, wealth, and influence, it would simply be a matter of time before I became the target marked for death or utter ruin." His voice choked again only this time with a sudden rising of tears. "This king's machinations include destroying individuals by any means while tearing this country apart to maintain his tyrannical grip. Even murder!"

"Murder?" repeated a stunned Rory. "What do you mean?"

Duncan scowled at his indiscrete slip of the tongue. "There has been murder since the beginning of the war. You know the men call him *The Bloody King*. A nickname the pamphlets have circulated."

"No, you discovered something else," said Rory with certainty.

Duncan avoided eye contact to shift through the papers.

Rory seized Duncan's hand to get attention. "What?"

Duncan tried to remove his hand, but Rory wouldn't yield. "To give you the answer." When released, he handed Rory the man's confession.

All the color drained from Rory's face as the paper slipped from his hand back onto the desk. "Father," he shaky voice barely above a whisper.

"This king means our death," Duncan harshly whispered.

Rory swallowed to regain his voice. "You should tell Samantha—"

"No!" snapped Duncan. "She needs to heal and regain her fortitude before learning of anything of this dreadful magnitude."

"Then Will."

"No. He might tell Samantha."

"I thought you trusted him?" said Rory, a bit confused.

"I trust him to keep confidences from others. However, he already told her about situations with Lawrence that I would not. Like his testimony."

"Well," said Rory judiciously. "I agree with him. There should be no issue between them. I fail to see how keeping her ignorant is helpful."

Duncan fought to restrain his temper. "Neither of you were present those seven long weeks Anne and I feared she would die! Physically she may appear recovered, but you witnessed her weakness in London against Kyle. She needs to regain her strength of heart, and peace of mind. These," he held up the King's letter and man's confession, "go beyond what *we* could imagine, and difficult for us to comprehend so diabolical a plan. I fear it would be a devastating blow to her at present."

"Aye, for Samantha," Rory agreed. "You should not keep Will ignorant for long."

"I take great risk in allowing her to remarry."

"Why?"

"As widow of a court favorite, she must obtain royal consent to remarry. Same as the original contract due to our station." Duncan put up a hand to stop further argument. "Hopefully, Parliament can bring a sense of normalcy and all of this relegated to the past."

"If Parliament cannot? What course of action then?"

"When I return to London for the next session, I shall speak with Tom. Father confided in him, so he is familiar with the situation. For now," Duncan smiled in a change of attitude, "we have a double wedding to plan."

261

Chapter 37

FOLLOWING FAMILY TRADITION, THE DOUBLE WEDDING WOULD be held in the family chapel at Foxmoor on the first Saturday in September. What better way to revitalize a family and household after years of suffering than with a joyous event?

Samantha sat at the vanity in her room fiddling with her hair. For a moment, she paused to gaze at herself in the mirror. The last time she prepared for a wedding, she was a naïve girl of seventeen. Now, age twenty-two, her face matured. So much turmoil happened the past five years, she almost felt unrecognizable from the carefree girl of yesteryear. The weight of war and abuse aged her and dampened her spirit. She attempted to counter the dreary thoughts with recent events: the war over, happy family reunion, return home, and William. Her smile at the thought of him faded at the realization of marriage. She flinched at a knock on the door and returned to fixing her hair. Rory entered. She saw his reflection in the mirror yet avoided eye contact. She blinked back tears to clear her vision.

"Samantha?"

She turned aside to brush her hair. He wouldn't be put off and took the brush from her.

"Something troubles you. What is it?"

"I don't know." She paused with reluctance. At his insistent gaze, she admitted, "I am suddenly scared."

"Of what?" When tears rose, he escorted her to the settee where they sat together. "Tell me your fears."

"It is not easy to discuss. Like … at the barn."

"Ah." He understood. "Hear what I say. After a year of observing Will Hawkins, I am convinced of his honorable character. Remember, Duncan knew him before the war. If there were the slightly hint of anything inappropriate, he never would have agreed to the marriage."

"Of that I am certain. Yet … the past is difficult to forget. His scars."

"Will loves you dearly. He has proven that repeatedly. As Christ borne stripes for us as a demonstration of unselfish love, Will borne them for you. Do not let memories of Lawrence rob you of happiness. Leave the past buried with him. Look to a future full of happiness with a man who loves you. And, I assume, you love him." He curbed a smile at the last sentence to watch her reaction.

She smiled and gently wiped her eyes. "I do love him. Something I never felt for the *other* or thought possible for any man. Except my brothers, of course." She hugged him. "Thank you."

He kissed her cheek. "Now, I go to look in on the nervous grooms." He widely grinned, a mischievous twinkle in his eyes. "Jolly fun playing the groomsman."

A short time later, Duncan and William stood before chapel altar. Rory waited behind Duncan. Only the household servants were in attendance. A Puritan minister from a neighboring village agreed to preside. At Samantha's request, Henry came to serve as escort for her and Anne.

"Relax, gentlemen," Rory teased.

"I shall remind you of that on your wedding day," Duncan bantered.

"I hope to see more people at my wedding."

Duncan sent a hard jab into Rory's side. Rory frowned in apology. Although, curious to the exchange, William made no comment. In fact, he became distracted when the door opened. Samantha and Anne wore the best gowns available among the remaining wardrobe along with veils over their faces. Henry stood between the women, one on each arm.

At the minister's signal, Henry escorted Samantha and Anne to the altar. He handed each woman to their respective grooms, bowed, and joined the servants. Both couples knelt. Samantha reverently folded her hands. The words were spoken when and where they should as the minister addressed each couple individually.

"According to the grace of God, and by your declared love for Him and each other, I pronounce you husband and wife," he said first to Duncan and Anne then repeated the charge to William and Samantha. "Go and rejoice in what God has brought together."

When they turned to exit the chapel, servants cheered and threw petals of dried flowers. Outside, villagers gathered to congratulate the happy couples. Duncan and William expressed thanks and ushered their brides toward the main house.

Anne hesitated. "Let them celebrate on the courtyard lawn," she said to Duncan. When he frowned with indecision, she whispered, "Another way to let them know the duke considers their well-fair."

Duncan kissed her cheek before he said, "Enjoy the day on the lawn." He motioned to Henry and spoke in private. "Keep an eye on things." He delayed Henry's departure. "Perhaps you can stay until I find a new bailiff."

"Of course, Your Grace."

While the villagers held their own celebration outside, Mistress Wadsworth managed to find enough food to make a small feast. With the fine tableware gone, pewter and wood served for dishes and cups. Wadsworth's son, Jim, played the fiddle while old groom Nick, the flute. Lively dancing tunes. Anne told Wadsworth to open the windows so the villagers could hear the music. The joy of laughter came as the villagers danced the same steps as those inside.

Out of breath from dancing and laughing, Duncan grabbed refreshment for him and Anne. She giggled and sat to catch her breath. After Duncan gave Anne a tankard, Rory approached.

"Why did you poke me in the chapel? I commented about more people at my wedding."

Duncan hid a scowl by taking another drink. "An inappropriate time for such a comment considering the circumstances."

Rory looked confused. "How inappropriate to celebrate a wedding? Come to think of it, you didn't look pleased about the villagers. Although Anne convinced you to let them celebrate."

"I would hardly disappoint my bride on her wedding day." Duncan turned his back as if refilling his tankard from a pitcher. He lowered his voice. "I told you the risk I took in allowing them to marry."

"I still don't agree. Lawrence is dead."

"His father lives, as does the *original author*."

"What can they do now? The war is over."

"Hopefully nothing. I pray that the matter has been put to rest. Only time will tell."

"Duncan," Anne hailed him.

He smiled. Out of the corner of his mouth he told Rory, "Not a word of this discussion."

William arrived to partake of refreshment. Samantha stood beside the sofa where Duncan now sat with Anne. "You look rather serious. Is something wrong?" he asked Rory.

"A touch of melancholy. Celebration during rebuilding from war."

William nodded with understanding as he drank. Hearing laughter from the women, he nudged Rory. "Dance with your sister. My feet need a rest. Jim, play a jig."

That evening, William entered the bedchamber wearing a dressing gown and slippers. Samantha sat before a hearth in her dressing gown. The fire glowed on her profile as she stared into the flames. She bit her thumbnail, a habit when nervous or uncertain. She became startled at his approached. He knelt, and gently took her hands, which were cool and trembling.

"There is nothing to be afraid of," he softly said.

"I know." She shyly looked away.

With a light touch, he encouraged her to face him. "I want to show you something."

He stood and undid his dressing gown to reveal his bare chest. Years of war made his torso lean of fat and muscular. His left shoulder scarred. Not a large scar, but different in color with a rough, wrinkled texture. She grew fearful at the sight, so he quickly knelt again.

"What do you see? Another scar from the past?"

"Aye. Caused by my husband-"

"*I am* your husband," he tenderly insisted. "What I see is you. My love. Marred flesh is nothing compared to your life and safety. These scars became my hope and dream for a future with you. One filled with happiness, laughter, children." He widely smiled. "That is what I want you to see. Not the past. Rather the man who loves you, and desires to make the rest of your life the happiest and most blessed life it can be."

They kissed.

Chapter 38

THE REST OF SEPTEMBER SAW A CHANGE IN EVERYONE. WILLIAM grew more relaxed while his relationship to Duncan gave no hint of trouble. A friendship restored and a new bride. By late October, William thought best to leave for Foxglen before winter. He sent Henry on ahead to prepare for their arrival.

The sweet smell of freshly cut hay hung on the soft breeze. Few leaves remained on the trees. As they neared Foxglen, Samantha rode side-by-side with William. Emerging from the wood, he drew rein to observe the manor. Some repairs had been made. Smoke rose from the rear kitchen chimney. She noticed his apprehensive.

"We could have remained at Foxmoor through the winter," she said.

William jerked, as if awoken from a trance. "No!" he piped, then sighed over his harshness. "I have never shrunk from a challenge. What of you?"

Samantha grinned. "You forget. Foxglen is my favorite. Many of my happiest memories are here. The *other* an apparition. This house has withstood more than war. Look around, Will. In spring, the meadow and trees come alive with sweet fragrances. The blooms of summer roses grace the garden. Duncan fancies Foxmoor because of its strength and history. I love Foxglen for its beauty and tranquility."

William smiled. "You are an amazing woman, Samantha Hawkins."

"Samantha Hawkins," she happily repeated. "I like that name very much."

He chuckled. "I hope so! You shall have it for the rest of your life." When he looked at Foxglen again, a ripple furrowed his brow. "They look upon me as enemy."

Samantha held his hand. "Remember how Henry spoke favorable for you last time."

"A guest is one thing. Master is another."

"I am certain Henry has kept speaking well of you."

"Henry Wyatt is as good and loyal a servant and friend to you as Nathan was to me." His eyes averted to one side when Samantha studied him too closely for his liking.

"Thought of Nathan still pains you," she said with unction.

William didn't respond. His face remained turned aside.

"Oh, Will, I am sorry," she began apologetic. "I should have told you sooner, yet afraid to speak of Nathan and how it would make you feel."

"Told me what?" He partially turned though not meeting her gaze.

"In Bristol, I became concerned of him. Terribly beaten, as I'm sure you saw." She swallowed back disturbance of the memory to continue. "The day the city fell, Nathan rendered the guard unconscious and took his sword. He bid me flee as he would create a diversion. Being in no condition to fight, I tried to stop him! I knew you would be very cross if anything happened to him, and I told him so. He simply smiled and told me to tell you *all is well* before he ran off."

William sat perched on his saddle to listen. "He truly said '*all is well*'?"

"Aye. And you know Nathan's smile, generous and kind. I thought he was just being stubbornly gallant. I went to pursue him, only Lawrence arrived. The rest you know."

"Aye," said William with a distracted smile. "*All is well*," he repeated. He lifted his eyes heavenward. "Thank you, Lord!" He loudly laughed.

"Will?" she inquired, baffled.

"Sweet wife, you have been the instrument by which God has graciously answered my prayer," he said, much to her pleasure though not to her clarification. "Nathan saying '*all is well'* has more meaning than I can begin to explain."

"It must. Again, I apologize for my slothfulness in telling you."

"No, my dear," he said generously. "I clearly see God's timing. I first needed to come to grips with Nathan's death. If you had told me at Bristol, I would not have heard, for I was not ready. I blamed myself severely."

"His death is not your fault."

William expression showed forbearance. "I know. However, earlier circumstances were. This evening I shall explain. For now, you have renewed my spirits! Let us enter our home with boldness."

For the next few months, William and Samantha led a carefree existence. No curfews, rules, regulation, or commanding officers. Not that William neglected his new duties as Lord Hawkins. He had to win over the household. There was a natural hesitation from past experiences with Hedgepeth, and the war, to fully embrace the new master. Henry held great influence, and eventually, with the bailiff's help, attitudes changed. Even with initial reservations, William proved more agreeable than Hedgepeth.

Before anyone realized it, Christmas arrived. This prompted a visit from Duncan, Anne, and Rory. Although many Puritans refused to celebrate what they considered a Popish holiday, others kept private observances. A morning chapel service and prayer followed by a specially prepared meal. No decorations or gifts, rather focus on Christ's birth and enjoying the warmth of family. Such was the manner with the Hawkins and O'Malleys. Childhood stories and reminiscences of university life dominated the conversations.

Anne became more talkative and animated under Duncan's soothing influence. They would remain until early February when Duncan felt the need to return to Foxmoor for planting the first spring crop in years.

In April, William hired less fortunate farmers to help with planting. For wages they received money, seeds, food, and cloth. By the end of the planting *The New Major* was warmly embraced by the local folk.

Six weeks later, William spoke to Henry from atop his horse to discuss the barley crop. They noticed a rider approach at full gallop.

"Rory?" asked William, concerned by Rory's grim countenance.

"I dare not trust a courier with such bad tidings. To the house!"

Before William could inquire further, Rory again rode at the gallop. William snapped the reins to follow. Rory vaulted from the saddle. In bounding strides, he entered the house. William hot on Rory's heels.

Samantha oversaw repairs in the family salon. She became overjoyed at seeing Rory. "This a pleasant surprise."

"Something to drink. Stronger than water," he replied in a curt tone.

Samantha tossed William a puzzled look, for rarely did Rory speak so harshly. He heaved an uncertain shrug. He made a slight inclination of the head. Thus, she left to comply.

"Has something happened to Duncan and Anne?" William asked.

"No. They are well. Duncan sent me to fetch you. Those fools at Parliament have disbanded the army! They refuse arrears pay, pension to retiring officers, or any payment to widows."

The news astonished William. "This is incredible. What says Fairfax?"

"He is outraged and sent for Cromwell."

"What harm is there in the army being disbanded?" Samantha asked upon returning. "The war is over."

"Where are the drinks?" Rory demanded, annoyed at her quick return.

"Godwin is bringing them. Now, what about the army?"

"Parliament has taken on the tyrannical role once held by the King and threatens to bring anarchy by disbanding the army," Rory harshly complained. "The problem is preventing a mutiny against Parliament! Cromwell maybe the only man in England who can persuade the army to hold off while he acts as mediator."

Samantha stared in disturbance at Rory. "Has the world gone mad? First war with the King and now mutiny against Parliament?"

"It does not mean there will be more fighting," William soothed.

Godwin entered with ale and tankards. Rory poured himself a drink. "Fairfax has ordered all officers recalled to London. That is why I'm here."

"No!" Samantha seized William.

"Until my commission expires, I must follow orders," he said.

In fearful anger, she lashed out. "Go then! I curse the army and those who would make widows of brides!" She ran from the room.

William stopped Rory from following. "We can't leave her like this!" insisted Rory.

"What did you expect? A warm greeting and friendly good-bye as her brothers and husband again go off to possible war?" When the question stymied Rory, William said, "I shall be ready to leave within the hour."

In their chamber, William found Samantha lay on the bed weeping. He sat next to her and gently stroked her hair. "My dearest love, you know I am duty bound."

Samantha pushed herself off the bed. "A pox on duty! It has brought nothing but destruction and chaos! This Parliament would have more of it, using you as their pawn."

"I go to prevent bloodshed. If the army mutinies, the Royalists would seize the opportunity to rally again. If that happens, there shall be destruction the likes of which England has not seen before."

Desperate, she grabbed him. "Let us flee to France until this is over!"

"No!" William rebuffed. "I fled once before from those named devils and lost my family and a beloved friend. The price was too high then. I will not pay that price again!"

In tears, Samantha ran to the family study where a small altar was used for private devotions. The room faced the front of the house. She fell to her knees, her hands prayerfully clenching. She hoped it was all over! No more war, bloodshed, and pain! *Oh, God, how much more must we endure? Protect Will and my brothers. Let no more scars mar his body.*

Uncertain how long she prayed and wept, she heard horses outside. She moved to the window. Once again, William wore his uniform. He caught sight of her in the window. He touched his hat in salute before he rode off with Rory.

Chapter 39

IN ESSEX, FAIRFAX QUELLED A DEADLY MUTINY. ALAS, MORE UPRISINGS threatened after hearing the Scottish Presbyterians negotiated with the King against the Army. Then the King was captured by Colonel Joyce. This caused further unrest. Cromwell had yet to respond, which puzzled Fairfax. He moved swiftly to appoint David Leslie in Cromwell's stead. In turn Leslie, depended heavily upon his second-in-command, Major Hawkins. For Fairfax, Duncan became his right-hand man.

Finally, Cromwell arrived. During a meeting of the Army Council to discuss the King's seizure, Fairfax kept a keen eye on Cromwell. The latter sat unaffected by the reports. When the last officer concluded, Fairfax gave voice to Cromwell's strange silence.

"Oliver, what do you know Colonel Joyce's actions?"

"Everything. I authorized it," Cromwell calmly answered.

Briefly dumbstruck, Fairfax clamored, "What? For God's sake, Oliver, how could you?"

"Surely, you realize the only way to keep unity and order, is to restore the King to the throne! We now have him." Cromwell made a grasping fist. "Let us not waste this opportunity to rid ourselves of the Presbyterians and their heretical ways. They would bring the Scottish system down upon us and send the army on its merry way while securing their hold on Parliament. Without regret before God, something had to be done and I did it! With the King, we can bargain for religious tolerance and political voice. If the army did nothing, then all who fought, died, and shed their blood, would have done so in vain!"

Fairfax shook his head, astonished by the bold action. "I declare, Oliver, you are a clever man. I wish I had some of your genius in politics. My mind is boggled by all these factions."

"Be strong, Tom," Cromwell encouraged. "God has given us the advantage. In fact, I want Colonel O'Malley to accompany me to the negotiations with the King."

Duncan sat upright in the chair; a bit taken back. "Me?"

"Aye. Your involvement can bolster our cause in the House of Lords." To Cromwell's statement some of the Council grumbled. "Aye, aye, Essex and Manchester are also helpful. Yet among the younger generation, Rutherford can be more persuasive."

Duncan shot a prompting glance to Fairfax. The Lord General's brows lightly furrowed before he nodded in understanding that Duncan wanted to speak privately.

Unaware of the visual exchange between Fairfax and Duncan, Cromwell spoke. "Once we have the points for negotiation, we can decide upon who will treat with the King."

When others agreed with Cromwell, Fairfax said, "Gentlemen, until our next meeting, let us pray for guidance on how to proceed further with General Cromwell's suggestion."

Duncan hung back, as the Council members filed out.

"You would do well, Duncan. I am certain of that," Cromwell said before departing.

Fairfax shut the door. "I take it there is a reason you would rather not participate?"

"No. Quite the contrary."

"Really? You appeared taken aback by the suggestion," said Fairfax, slightly confused. He sat at the table beside Duncan.

"True, the thought had not occurred to me. Yet, it may serve well. My reason for speaking privately is tell you that the letters proved very helpful—only in a much disturbing way," he emphasized the word *disturbing.* "In fact, it is germane to the negotiations. On a personal level."

He proceeded to inform Fairfax of the discovery involving the King and the Hedgepeths. "Now, you see why I wanted to speak privately."

Fairfax blinked, astonished. "Good Lord! A fiendish murder plot."

"One that succeeded with my father," groused Duncan.

Fairfax hastened to say, "I assure you; Patrick spoke of no suspicion regarding such a heinous plan. Any inkling, and he would never have agreed to the marriage."

"I know. He felt trapped. As did I. Not any longer!" declared Duncan.

Fairfax rose to pace. Something he did when presented a new problem. "It would not be wise to bring this matter into the negotiations."

"That is not my intent. Being a prisoner, I wish to determine his mindset. Is he still bent on stubborn resistance, or more yielding? I have allowed Samantha to remarry. Will Hawkins."

Fairfax smiled with understanding. "You wish is to protect them should the King's attitude not be altered."

"Exactly. Because of what I just told you, I took a great risk in allowing her to remarry without royal consent."

Fairfax's smile remained. "God will bless their union." He resumed his seat. "Only mind your temper and keep this discovery as an option for later use. I fear, the King may not be so easily swayed by his confinement."

"General Cromwell believes so."

"Oliver is more astute in politics than I. Put me on a battlefield, and I will win the day. In Parliament, I find their remonstrances and debates puzzling."

"You hold your own against others. I have witnessed it."

Fairfax flashed a tolerant smile. "Perhaps at times. You too have more political acumen. I shall depend upon it in the days ahead." He rose to escort Duncan to the door.

With the points of negotiations refined, Cromwell and Duncan rode to Hampton Court to treat with the King. Charles sat impassively before a hearth. A small fire reflected on his face. At forty-seven, war aged Charles beyond his years. Gray invaded his hair, mustache, and beard. Despite the relaxed jowls and bags under his eyes, royal dignity remained in the steely gaze and firm tone.

"Gentlemen," Charles greeted them.

"Sir, we come with a proposal which we believe is more agreeable to both parties than previous," Cromwell formally spoke.

"If you will leave the papers with Sir John, I shall consider the proposal later." Charles regally returned his attention to the flickering flames.

Duncan keenly watched the King. "Sire, we ask you consider these terms now."

Charles deliberately scrutinized Duncan. "Be warned, Lord Rutherford, the O'Malley boldness cost your family much in the past. Do not repeat the same mistake."

Duncan clenched his fists in anger at the threat. His voice strained, yet formal. "Sire, we are here for the good of all England, not individual personal gain or loss."

Cromwell spoke to divert the King's marked attention of Duncan. "It is our earnest hope to negotiate for the betterment of all."

The intervention only marginally succeeded, as Charles' gaze flashed to Cromwell before he returned to Duncan. "Be careful in the company you keep. Since the death of Lord Kyle's son, it is best you tread lightly."

Duncan visibly snarled. Before his temper could ignite, Cromwell forcefully spoke. "Sir, the Army has been trifled with long enough and we desire a swift end!"

"So, has Our Royal Personage been trifled with, sir! None desire a swifter end to this than I," Charles warmly rebuffed. "Leave the papers with Sir John. If this request is not complied with then neither shall the terms."

Cromwell laid hold of Duncan to prevent further discussion. Cromwell stiffly bowed and gave the papers to Sir John. Duncan turned upon his heels without paying respect to the King. They emerged from the building to mount their horses.

"That was ill-timed," Cromwell angrily chided.

"Was I to remain quiet when he threatened my family?" Duncan rebuffed.

"No. You handled it well. I meant his personal threat ill-timed. Even as a prisoner, he continues to bully rather than deal forthrightly."

"General Cromwell!" A rider brought his horse to a skidding stop. He thrust a letter out to Cromwell.

"Odds blood!" Cromwell swore after he read. "Put spurs to horse. We are needed immediately."

Meanwhile, in Parliament, Fairfax ordered William to post ten armed men in the Hall and a score of calvary outside under the command of Rory. This debate could prove violent since it concerned the fate of the King. Dressed in his full uniform with cuirass and helmet, William positioned himself inside the door. Passion among the Members rose to fever pitch.

No wonder Fairfax is puzzled by them! William thought. Although the heated debate dealt with the King, the session only made politics more confusing. When the door opened, he quickly moved to see who entered. Dusty and weary, Cromwell and Duncan arrived. Cromwell joined Fairfax.

The loud arguing almost deafening, so Duncan leaned close to William to ask, "What has happened?"

"The King signed a treaty with the Scots for troops."

Duncan's anger immediately rose. "Another war? The man's duplicity knows no bounds!" He made his way to Fairfax and Cromwell.

"This is bold evidence the King is not to be trusted!" shouted a Member.

"Aye!" yelled another. "More Scottish troops to begin the war anew!"

"What is this?" Cromwell asked Fairfax.

"After you left, we learned that he signed a treaty with the Scots for aid against Parliament."

"No doubt, he believes his ends justified the means," chided Duncan.

"Keep your wits from making this personal," Cromwell warned.

"Has it not been personal for everyone here?"

To the counter question, Cromwell nodded. "However, his threat to you is still fresh."

"Threat?" asked Fairfax.

Duncan looked directly at Fairfax to say, "He mentioned the past, and boldly warned about consequences concerning my former in-law. The *option* may be the only means of defense."

Before Fairfax could reply, the voice of Henry Ireton shouted.

"By this treaty, he has once again betrayed the trust reposed in him. To raise new war and enslave the nation! He continually violates his oaths and tramples underfoot our laws! We desire that impartial and speedy justice be done. If found guilty, the same punishment whether that person is King, Lord, or the poorest commoner!"

Some Members agreed while others loudly dissented.

"Sirs!" Duncan stood. "If what General Ireton say is true, how can we sit idle in this great House? A House that has stood for hundreds of years as a symbol of the freedom and rights we as Englishmen hold dear! Many a king, nobleman, and commoner alike have tried to prevail against this House and all it stands for. Yet Magna Carta, and the laws made in this great House have remained undaunted by such onslaughts. Can we truly allow this warmonger of a King to commit such heinous crimes against this nation and its laws just to be set free? I beseech you, good Sirs of this Great House, in memory of those valiant men lost and our loved ones still with us, let us agree to what has been proposed by General Ireton. For if this King be above the law, then the law is for naught, and this mighty House is brought to ruin!"

Canes banged on the floor in a call for attention. "What know you of law and justice?" demanded Kyle. "The King is our divinely appointed ruler to be judge by God alone. Not by some popping-jay who wishes to settle family disputes."

"Sir, withdraw that insult!" Duncan rebuffed.

"I will not withdraw as my son lies rotting in the grave because of you."

Fairfax quickly rose to Duncan's defense. "His Grace had no part in it. *I* arrested Major Hedgepeth. *I* brought the charges."

Lenthall pounded the gavel. "Order! Order! This is not the time nor place for personal disputes. The fate of England is at issue. Be seated, gentlemen."

Fairfax needed a firm arm to make Duncan sit. The sting of humiliation in public clearly seen on the young duke's face. The brief debate that followed the terse exchange between Duncan and Kyle ended in agreement there would be no further negotiation with the King. Duncan brusquely left the Hall the moment Lenthall adjourned the meeting. He brushed passed William without a word.

Duncan rode to Kensington. He paused short of the house. He did not want to upset Anne. Then he remembered Lady Fairfax planned to call upon Anne. Tom's wife took it upon herself to help the new duchess. Once dismounted, Duncan tossed the rein to the groom. His horse covered in sweat from the day's journey. He threw his hat and gloves on a chair in the foyer. In his trek to the study, he ignored Cowan. He plopped in a chair before the hearth and stared into the emptiness. As if the King's threat was not enough, Kyle publicly humiliated him!

Lord Rutherford, the O'Malley boldness cost your family much in the past. ... Since the death of Lord Kyle's son, it is best to tread lightly, the King's voice echoed in his mind. Followed closely by Kyle's declaration, *I will not withdraw as my son lies rotting in the grave because of you.*

Of course, Tom spoke rightly in his defense. He took no part in Lawrence's arrest nor the trial. All the same, the plot against Rutherford failed. Or had it? Hard to keep Samantha's new marriage a secret. Did Kyle know about William's testimony?

"No, Will volunteered his testimony at Bristol. I did not request it," he spoke to himself. What more could they do to Rutherford? Would making the diabolic plan public knowledge protect his family? Perhaps the threat of trial will make the King more willing to listen and negotiate. Or maybe incite him further? For several hours, Duncan sat contemplating various scenarios. He did not realize Anne's presence until she spoke his name and touched his shoulder.

He forced a grin. "How was your day with Lady Fairfax?"

"Very pleasant. Sharing the same name is not all we have in common." She moved to sit on the footstool. "I told Cowan to prepare the drawing room for after dinner to find you sitting here in the dark staring into an empty hearth. Why?"

Duncan noticed darkness outside and the room lit by candles. "Problems at Parliament, what else?" He tried to laugh it off.

"That does not sound too convincing." She touched his arm.

"Chaos abounds." He took her hand to kiss the knuckles. "Nothing to cause you worry."

"I worry for you. Aye, and for England also."

He held her hand against his chest, as he again stared into the hearth.

"Duncan, I have kept many secrets over the years. For example, the fact you *secretly* took the journals from Foxglen and placed them in your baggage believing no one suspected." At his surprise she added, "I know the marriage contract has plagued you. Please, do not shut me out. Anne Fairfax is Tom's confidant. Let me be yours."

He pulled her to sit on his lap and held her close. "Your offer means more to me than I can say. The tale will be a long one."

"I'm not going anywhere."

For several moments he stared at the hearth before speaking. "What is happening in Parliament goes beyond the marriage contract. It goes to heart of England and our way of government."

"A topic of great discussion today."

Duncan raised a surprised brow. "Between women?"

Anne lightly scoffed a laugh. "You think us ignorant?"

"No, of course not." He grinned. "I suppose I have been preoccupied."

"Which is why I made the offer." She moved from his lap to sit on the footstool and look him in the face. "Our outing today shows a city divided on the possibility of a trial."

"Aye," he groused. "Daily arguments in Parliament nearly come to blows. Yet the King's latest duplicity calls for action."

"Years ago, father used an illustration about David and Saul. Even though David was appointed king, and hunted by Saul, he never wanted to harm Saul. In fact, when presented the opportunity to kill Saul and take his rightful place as king, David only cut off a piece of Saul's garment."

"I remember the story well. But—"

"Let me finish. Father told us how Sir Patrick wanted to emulate David and bring the King into alignment with Parliament. He wanted to protect, not dethrone."

"I was there for *that* discussion. My father never wanted war. Alas, it happened, and we must deal with the aftermath. My hope is the mere mention of a trial, will help him see that honest negotiations is the best way to resolve this." His face grew grim yet pained. "However, his personal threats towards me, joined with Kyle's public accusations may make it impossible."

Greatly concerned, she touched his face to make him look directly at her. "Tell me everything."

Chapter 40

IN A NOVEMBER SESSION OF THE ARMY COUNCIL, FAIRFAX RECEIVED a new remonstrance. One that severely challenged his mind and heart as he listened to Ireton's passionate reading.

"Whereas it is notorious that Charles Stuart, King of England, not content with the many encroachments his predecessors made upon the rights and freedoms of people, wickedly design to subvert the ancient and fundamental laws and liberties of this nation. And in their place would introduce an arbitrary and tyrannical government. Besides all other evil ways and means to bring his design to pass, he prosecuted it with fire and sword. He levied and maintained a cruel war against the Parliament and Kingdom. Whereby the country was miserably wasted, the Treasury exhausted, trade decayed, thousands of people murdered, and infinite other mischiefs committed.

"Whereas the Parliament, hoping that after it had pleased God to deliver him into their hands, would have quieted the distempers of the Kingdom. It was then decided to proceed judicially against him. However, such remises only encouraged him and his accomplices in the continuance of their evil practices. This was done by raising a new commotion, rebellion, and invasion to traitorously and maliciously enslave this nation. It is therefore demanded that Charles I be put on trial for his life before a special Court consisting of a hundred and fifty members presided over by two Chief Justices." When he concluded, Ireton sat.

The profound ramification rendered Fairfax silent. Had they gone so far as to place the King on trial? In discomposure, he observed the heated debate that followed. Most favored the remonstrance, while those opposed vehement in their arguments. Finally, he spoke. "We shall bring this remonstrance before the House of Commons and let them decide."

As all took leave of the Lord General, Fairfax signaled Duncan to remain. When alone, he paced. "In battle my mind is clear and precise. No doubts cloud my judgment. Here in London, with all its factions and remonstrances, I find myself wondering just what role I am to play." He paused to ask Duncan, "What do you think of this latest remonstrance? What says your legal mind?"

During a moment of heavy silence, Duncan considered the question. "Legally, I believe there is a precedent for a trial as stated in the Magna Carta. He violated many clauses such as 14 when issuing constant taxes without Parliament consent for twelve years. Unlawful seizure of properties and imprisonments during those years, and numerous other violations.

"Then you agree with Ireton?" ask Fairfax, concerned.

With due solemnity, Duncan replied. "Chapter 61 of Magna Carta states that if the king violates any point of the charter, Parliament has the authority to seize the king and his property by military force until he complies." He paused with somber reflection. "You know my father tried to bring agreement between the King and Parliament to avoid conflict. His efforts cost our family greatly. Now, after years of war, numerous failed negotiations, and double-dealing by the King, I agree with acting within the parameters granted us."

The weight of possibility visible on Fairfax's countenance. "Personally, I pray it does not come a trial. But we will let the House decide." He motioned for Duncan to leave.

Duncan donned his gloves before he stepped out into the cold. Bright sunshine began the day, now a threat of snow hung in the air. Perhaps, he should have taken the carriage. The weather seemed to mimic the mood in Parliament; pleasant one moment, dismal the next. He signaled a nearby groom for his horse. At home, he found Rory and William in the drawing room warming themselves by the fire.

"Well, this is a surprise. I thought both of you went with Cromwell to Pontefract."

"We just returned." Rory blew on his hands then held them out near the flames.

"Cowan, warm cider and food."

"Aye, Your Grace."

"Apparently, there is some crisis with the Army Council." William sat on a foot stool in front of the fire to pull off his wet boots to warm his feet.

"Ireton's remonstrance against the King," said Duncan. Rory appeared perplexed while William frustrated, thus Duncan proceeded. "I'm not surprised you heard something, as rumors have been circulating for weeks. He finally presented it this morning. Most of the Council agreed, so it will be presented to the Commons for a vote."

"What exactly does this remonstrance want with the king?" William massaged each foot to encourage circulation.

Duncan took the return of Cowan with cider as a moment to consider the answer. He gave a tankard to Rory. When it came to William, he paused to look directly at his brother-in-law to reply. "To bring the King to trial." He left William to fetch his own tankard.

"Trial?" echoed William, astonished. "On what charge?"

Duncan sat and took a drink before he replied. "A traitor to the people of England and their murderer. The remonstrance demands he answers these charges."

"But he is the King!" William insisted

Duncan shook his head. "Will, no one is above the law. If the king breaks the law and is not held accountable what will become of the law? The common man can claim if the King is not made to respect the law why should he. In the sight of God, all men are equal. Why should the law be different for kings and commoners?"

With a tilt of his head, William glanced to Rory. The latter avoided eye contact to drink.

"Will, you were at Parliament during the debates when it was discovered he turned to the Presbyterians for military aid. Soothe, you just returned from battle because of that duplicitous agreement. This decision should not be a surprise," Duncan argued.

"If a jury is by one's peers, then how shall the King be judged fairly?" asked William.

"By the law itself, which the Magna Carta established by the people in Parliament, and the King swore to uphold."

"The King shall be brought to trial by his own people against whom the crimes have been committed," Rory wearily surmised.

"Exactly," said Duncan. "We fought to preserve the laws of this country, as the right of free men. God set up the law for all men to live by, not misuse. Those who have done so shall be judged. We are not the first country to take a stand against a tyrant. Neither shall we be the last. Kings rise and fall as it suits God's purpose. If they prosper, then they are blessed. If they sin, they shall be judged. God did not spare David after he sinned with Bathsheba. I believe God has shown what He thinks of our King and judged him already. We are but the instruments in levying His justice."

"You make a valid argument. However, I'm not of the same mind. I once sworn allegiance to him. Although for various reasons, I renounced that allegiance. Still, my mind cannot comprehend much less concur with the idea of prosecuting the King," William argued.

"The trial will be a reality. It is the outcome I fear," Rory said dolefully.

"The outcome will be as the law decrees," Duncan stated.

"What if the law decrees death? Are you prepared for that?" William crossly challenged.

Duncan sternly answered, "I am prepared for whatever God wills. The same as with Lawrence."

William winced at the reference. "Will you recuse yourself in this also?

Duncan jowl's tightened to contain his temper. "The jury will be chosen by lot. Howbeit, if it falls to me, as God is my witness, I shall judge according to the law."

"That will be a sorry day for England since your family holds a grudge against him."

Insulted, Duncan bolted to his feet, which brought William to stand.

Rory quickly stood between them. "Before you two come to blows bear this in mind! The one who kills the other will have to tell Samantha and Anne. I shall not be the bearer of such miserable tidings! So, Duncan, will you tell our sister you killed her husband? Or you, tell Anne?" he challenged them in turn. "By God, has not enough blood been split by this damnable war? If this is what the King has caused, then let him be hanged in answer for the bloodshed of kinsmen!"

Rory's forceful rebuff hit a nerve. Uttering a disgruntled murmur, William sat.

"I'm sorry, Will. I truly did not mean to let my temper interfere. I understand the difficult situation this presents for you," Duncan apologized.

"Not unlike Samantha at Foxglen during the war," Rory added pointedly to William.

This made William look up. His expression struck by the comparison. "Indeed."

Duncan resumed his seat. "Will, you once said this King would do whatever is necessary to take back his throne. Do you recant?"

"No. Simply confounded by the staggering possibility of such a trial. I too apologize for my temper."

Duncan grinned and lifted his tankard. "Accepted." After taking a drink, he said, "Since this situation is poised to move forward, Parliament needs good honest men with level heads to keep control. For surely, such action can ignite a powder keg."

"We scarcely kept level heads just now," William wryly said.

"True," said Duncan with a chuckle. He sat forward, his expression earnest. "I am asking, not only as your brother-in-law, but also as the Duke of Rutherford, and Member of Parliament, help support me in the effort to bring about justice. Whichever way it is decided. Can you do that? Can you help *our* family?"

"Well, this a wonderful sight," said Anne. She was not alone.

"Samantha!" William happily met his wife. "What brings you to London?"

"News the army was returning."

"How did you know so quickly?"

Anne lightly laughed, which made William curious.

Duncan answered William's silent inquiry. "Anne has become great friends with Lady Fairfax. No doubt, the information came from her."

"Indeed," Anne confirmed. "Once I knew, I sent word to Samantha."

Samantha leaned against William with a sigh. "Are you ill?" he asked.

"Fatigued from the journey."

"We shall retire until supper." He escorted her upstairs.

Once in the chamber, Samantha was out of breath and sat on the settee.

"You are ill. You should not have come," he lightly scolded her.

She widely smiled and reached for him to join her. "Dear husband, I am not ill in the way you think." Her smile grew tender, her eyes misty with excitement. "Anne sent for me because she knows there is news, I have longed to tell but impossible until now. Do I not seem a bit plump to you?"

His curiosity increased as he examined her. "Your face is slightly rounded and—" Her bodice looser than normal with a slight rise. "A child?"

"Come early spring we shall be parents."

"Precious love!" He embraced her. "Have you told Duncan and Rory?

"It is not proper until the father knows."

"Come! No, wait. You rest. Maybe at supper." His words came fast and a bit discombobulated, which made her laugh. "Oh, I must sound out of my mind. Which, I am. Happy, that is." His face fell with thought of the conversation with Duncan and Rory. Of turmoil and chaos. Of hope and peace. Of the present and future.

"Will?"

In poignant regard, his eyes moved from her face to her belly. "Our child."

"Aye." She placed his hand on her belly, though curious of his change.

"My darling Samantha." He kissed her. When they parted, he said, "Rest. I will return shortly."

"Will ..."

He grinned with reassurance. "I'm just going downstairs. I shall only be a few moments."

When he entered the drawing room, Duncan and Rory were alone. "Where is Anne?"

"Seeing to supper. I thought you went to rest," replied Duncan.

"Some news has altered my view from earlier. News that will please you, in more ways than one." William crossed to a sideboard and poured three glasses of port to distribute.

"What is this for?" asked Rory.

"A toast. To a blessing from God expected by spring, and the uncles-to-be."

With a cheer, Rory and Duncan eagerly drank and offered congratulations.

"What of the *other* pleasing way?" asked Duncan when he refilled the glasses with port.

William's attitude grew sober. "I do not want my child enduring such calamity as has befallen us. I shall help protect the future of *our* family whichever way it is decided."

Chapter 41

LATER THAT WEEK, DUNCAN JOINED CROMWELL AND FAIRFAX in a meeting of the Committee of Both Kingdoms. All twenty-five Members present along with John Cook, a barrister of Gray's Inn, who served as legal advisor.

"Gentlemen, these charges are good. However, in a court of law witnesses are required. A few brave souls from Leicester have sworn affidavits along with citizens from Bristol. We need more. People who have witnessed the King in battle and planning strategy. Thus far only two soldiers have given testimony. Both of lower rank," said Cook. He shuffled through papers to pull out a single sheet. "There is one officer whose prior testimony could prove very helpful. Major William Hawkins."

Duncan shifted in his seat. Both Cromwell and Fairfax noticed his discomfort. Fairfax inquired of Cook, "He already provided testimony for a previous trial. How can it be helpful against the King?"

Cook read the paper. "As a junior officer of Major Hedgepeth, Hawkins served in Prince Rupert's regiment from Edgehill until he joined Parliament just prior to Naseby. It is common knowledge that Rupert's regiment worked closely with the King. Surely, in his position, Major Hawkins participated in strategy meetings and saw the King in battle."

"If he already offered testimony what more do you need from him?" asked Ireton.

"Simply a few questions to clarify some minor points from earlier."

Duncan shrank back in his seat to avoid eye contact with anyone. That was until Cromwell asked, "What says, Your Grace? Can you persuade Major Hawkins to offer further testimony?"

"Your lordship is familiar with the major?" asked Cook.

"Aye. We are well acquainted."

"Then fetch him so we can move forward," said Ireton.

"It is not so simple, Henry," Fairfax said.

"Why not? If Hawkins can help to protect the future of England, it is his duty to do so."

Duncan sat up when Ireton used the words *help protect the future.*

"Gerald, issue a subpoena for Major Hawkins," Cook told a clerk.

"No!" Duncan objected, which caught everyone's attention. Ireton firm and expectant, as were most of the others. Only Fairfax's expression held a hint of sympathy. Duncan tempered his words. "Allow me." He nodded to Fairfax and left.

Duncan purposefully made his way to Army Headquarters at Whitehall Place across from the Royal Banqueting House. He thought of how to approach William. Even though he did not agree with the trial, his words *protect the future of our family* echoed the sentiments expressed by Ireton in similar words. Taking a deep breath, Duncan entered the office. William stood at a window reading some papers.

"Afternoon."

"Duncan," William greeted, distracted. "I thought you would be at Parliament all day." His focus shifted back to the papers he held.

"A personal matter has arisen, which concerns your involvement with the King's Army." Duncan quickly proceeded before William replied. He had to or lose his nerve. "There are questions that need clarification. The Committee of Both Kingdoms wishes to speak with you. I tried to assure them that you would not cause trouble, but they command your immediate presence." He inwardly scowled at William's displeasure, but for justice's sake and family honor it had to be done.

"Why am I not surprised?" William groused, as he tossed the papers onto a desk to fetch his hat and cloak. "Written testimony again?" He asked once outside Whitehall Place.

"No. John Cook is a lawyer, and a good one. I became acquainted with his reputation at Oxford. He asks strange questions, almost contradictory to what we might think useful or necessary. He issued a subpoena for your appearance, but I thought best to find you first and give you warning." Duncan stopped in the foyer of Parliament. "I'm sorry," he apologized.

William cocked a wry grin. "I won't hold Cook against you."

Duncan tried to smile at the humor as they climbed the stairs to the meeting room. Once inside, he made the introduction, "Major William Hawkins." He stepped back.

"Major Hawkins, I am sure you are aware we are preparing to bring the King to trial on charges of High Treason against the people of England," Fairfax began.

"Aye, General."

"Some matters have come to light that require your participation. Mister Cook," Fairfax indicated the small wiry middle-aged man, "Our legal counsel can more effectively explain and ask the necessary questions."

"Thank you, General Fairfax." Standing, Cook barely reached William's chin. He held some papers as he moved from behind the table. "Major Hawkins, Mister Marten will be writing everything said during this interview, so please speak clearly. To begin, your father is Sir Herbert Hawkins of Nottinghamshire." He read off the paper. "A stout Royalist from what I hear." He strode about the room as he spoke. William did not answer for it was more a statement than a question. "When the King came to Nottingham in the summer of 1642, were you there also? And is that when you enlisted in the King's Army?"

"Aye. To both questions."

"Did the King stay at your family home for the duration?"

"No, His Majesty stayed at Nottingham Castle. Prince Rupert was our guest for several weeks."

"Did the King ever come to your father's house?"

"Once, for a banquet given in His Majesty's honor."

"Were there any military discussions at this time?"

"Aye. The King and his staff spoke of battle plans."

"Before the war began?" the lawyer quickly asked.

"Aye." William sent a quick glance to Duncan, who heaved a shrug.

"Were you privy to this?"

The question brought William's attention back to Cook. "As son of the host, I heard a few comments. Although, it was through the chain of command I received my orders like any other junior officer." William watched Marten furiously write.

"In your time of service to the King, did you know of, or participate in any unseemly military behavior ordered by His Majesty?" Cook pressed.

William visibly swallowed at the disturbing question.

Duncan felt a wave of immense guilt at seeing William's distress. Alas, interference would be folly thus he remained silent. Instead, Fairfax spoke.

"I believe those details are contained in the Major's prior testimony."

Cook picked up a paper to read. "'*During the later course of the first part of the war, supplies for the Royal Army were terribly short. By order of His Majesty, all horse regiments were sent to find whatever means of sustenance we could. Unfortunately, that did not always come from Royalist sympathizers. In those times, food and supplies were, if necessary, forcibly taken from wherever it could be found.*' Are those your words, Major Hawkins?"

William kept his eyes straight ahead, focused on a spot above the heads of the men gathered. "Aye, sir."

"So, innocent people were murdered, and homes sacked to feed an army of mercenaries!" Bradshaw exclaimed.

William remained at rigid attention, not daring to look at anyone.

"Well, Major Hawkins?" Bradshaw caustically demanded.

"Aye," came William's low and painful response.

Duncan could tolerate no more. "Sirs! This is an interview not a trial. Nor is Major Hawkins the defendant. He came here of his own freewill to offer testimony. Do not berate him, as he is not responsible for the orders of the King! Besides, he has long since vindicated himself with distinguished service in our army."

Cromwell spoke in agreement to Bradshaw. "It is true, John. Major Hawkins' service is to be commended. Save your zeal and outrage for the King."

"Your pardon, Major Hawkins," Bradshaw formally apologized.

William simply nodded to Bradshaw then asked Fairfax, "Are there any further questions, General?"

"Mister Cook, are you finished with the major?"

"One more question. Have you ever seen the King in armor?"

William quizzically drew his brows. "Aye. He prepared for battle like any other soldier."

Cook scribbled on a sheet of paper. "Since this is a formal inquest, your signature is required on the amended transcript." He held out a quill pen.

Duncan caught William's uncertain glance and nodded for compliance. William dutifully signed his name. Duncan inwardly shivered with each stroke of the pen.

"Thank you, Major Hawkins. That is all," said Cook graciously.

After William saluted his superiors, Duncan opened the door and briefly stepped into the hall with him. "Thank you for submitting to this," he sincerely said.

William shrugged. "It had to happen sooner or later. Until tonight."

Duncan watched William walk off. "I'm sorry, Will. Perhaps someday you can understand," he dolefully whispered before returning inside.

When Duncan returned home to Kensington, he heard voices in the drawing room, Samantha and William. Rory dined at a nearby tavern with fellows from his company while Anne due to return any moment. Since sharing the house with family, they chose to give each couple privacy one night a week. This evening, he and Anne agreed to dine out. He carefully drew near the door. He heard exasperation in William's response.

"I don't know. Some strange questions dealing with the King."

"I thought this madness would end with war. The King on trial is almost unimaginable," she said.

"Aye. A dangerous and unknown venture is about to be undertaken. One that could change the course of England's history. Sadly, I am part of it all," William complained.

Duncan shrunk back from the door, struck by the bitterness in William's last sentence. He heard a noise. Anne arrived. Before she could speak, he hurried to greet her. "Ready for our evening out? No need to remove your cloak and hat."

"I suppose," she said somewhat surprised by the suddenness.

He fetched his hat and cloak then ushered her back outside to the awaiting carriage. "The Swan and Harp, James," he told the driver.

"Duncan. I see you are flustered. More upset at Parliament?"

He tightly held her hand. "Remember our discussion about David and Saul?" When she nodded, he said. "Sometimes the means of defense is not always to our liking, but necessary. It is what I did today which troubles me more than Parliament. I fear that cut off piece of garment will come back to haunt me."

She moved closer to him. "Tell me before we dine, so you do not spend the evening fretting."

Chapter 42

ON JANUARY 20TH, 1649, THE TRIAL OF CHARLES STUART, KING of England began. By order of the Lord General, Pikeman and Parliamentary Guards were stationed within the Hall. A company of horse remained outside, commanded by Rory.

Rory held the reins of his horse, as he glanced about the crowd gathering outside Parliament. He wore his breastplate, sash, gloves and plumed hat, symbols of his rank. He stood beside William as he spoke. "These are the ones who could not fit in the gallery."

"Hard work this day if the crowd becomes rowdy," said William.

"Any suggestions on how to control them?"

William flashed a wry grin. "Pray and rely on your experience." He grew serious at Rory's frown. "Irving is inside while the Army waits in reserve at Whitehall. Send for Irving first, reserves *only* if necessary. We don't want to provoke a riot with an excessive show of force."

"I hope it doesn't come to that."

"Keep a sharp eye. I go to join the women. *If* there is a seat near them."

For the proceedings, the Committee of Both Kingdoms believed it imperative the President be of Parliament and not the Army, so they chose John Bradshaw. The Commissioners waited inside the Painted Chamber to be summoned by the President. All wore black suits for the somber occasion.

Duncan nervously flexed his fingers. He peeked out the chamber door. At one end of the Hall, stood a section constructed for the Commissioners. In front of the Commissioners' stand, a single elevated chair from which the President would preside. On either side, and slightly lower, would sit the two barristers who advised Bradshaw along with the court clerk, Andrew Broughton. The barristers were William Say and John Lisle. These three gentlemen dressed in black barrister's robes.

John Cook acted for the prosecution. This would be the greatest trial of his life. Cook and his associates, Mister Aske and Mister Dorislaus, occupied a table in front of the President. At the center of the room, on a platform, sat a red velvet armchair for the King.

Duncan turned his attention to the upper gallery. The seats occupied. To the left and near the rear, sat Anne with Samantha and William. With a heavy sigh, Duncan ducked back into the chamber. If Cook used names, William would discover the truth about his amended testimony. Upon learning of Major Hawkins participation, other soldiers offered testimony. Would it be worth his brother-in-law's wrath? He tried to console himself with the thought that if it protects Rutherford, and brings peace, William would understand and approve.

At the summons for Commissioners, Duncan braced himself to enter with his fellows. Bradshaw issued a stern warning, that on penalty of arrest, there was to be no disruption in the Hall during the trial. Cook and his colleagues conferred in hushed voices.

Bradshaw called for the prisoner. Preceded and followed by soldiers, the King appeared from the rear of Westminster Hall. Although royally dressed, the misery that had befallen Charles evident in his countenance. His beard now speckled with gray. The cheeks sagged, and skin pale. Deep pouches formed underneath the eyes from sleepless nights. Still, he looked every bit his station wearing his blue ribbon and jeweled George about his neck. On his black cloak was the great silver star of the Garter. Charles walked with a cane. His eyes never looked right or left. His face held no hint of fear or appall as took his seat.

Bradshaw spoke. "Charles Stuart, King of England, the Commons of England, assembled in Parliament, being sensible of the great calamities brought upon this nation, and of the innocent blood that has been shed in this nation, which are referred to you as the author of it. According to that duty which they own to God, to the Nation, and to themselves, and according to that power and fundamental trust that is reposed in them by the people, have constituted this High Court of Justice before which you are now brought. You are to hear your charge upon which the Court will proceed."

When Bradshaw, finished Cook rose. "My Lord, on behalf of the Commons of England, I do accuse," he swung upon the prisoner. "Charles Stuart, here present, of high treason and high misdemeanors. In the name of the Commons of England desire the charge be read unto him!" He picked up a scroll.

"Hold a little," said the King. Cook ignored him and unrolled the scroll. Charles used his cane to tap Cook upon the arm for attention. The barrister did not respond. On a second tap, the head of the cane fell. There came a momentary pause, as the King glanced about then down to the fallen cane head. No one moved to retrieve the fallen object. With dignity, Charles stooped to pick it up.

"Sir," Bradshaw began after Charles resumed his seat. "The Court commands the charge to be read. If you have anything to say afterwards, you may be heard."

Cook proceeded to read. "Charles Stuart, trusted with a limited power to govern by and according to the laws of the land, and not otherwise, created a wicked design to erect and uphold in himself an unlimited and tyrannical power to rule according to his Will. To overthrow the Rights and Liberties of the People. In this pursuit he traitorously and maliciously levied war against the present Parliament and the people therein represented. Charles Stuart also devised the invasion from foreign parts to renew the said war against the Parliament and good people of this nation in this present year. These wars were solely used in upholding a personal interest of Will, power, and pretended prerogative to himself and his family. It was against the public interest, common right, liberty, justice, and peace of the people of this nation. Being so, he is held responsible for all treasons, murders, rapings, burnings, spoils, desolations, damages, and mischiefs to this nation, acted and committed in the said wars or occasioned thereby. It is on behalf of the people of England that Charles Stuart is a Tyrant, Traitor and Murderer, and a public Enemy to the Commonwealth of England!"

During the reading, Charles carefully scanned the Commissioners and the crowded gallery so intent upon seeing their King brought to trial. Never was there a more emotionless face than the one Duncan saw as the King looked about. *It was unnatural!* he thought.

Charles arrogantly laughed at the absurd words, *Tyrant, Traitor and Murderer.*

"Sir, you have heard your charge. The Court expects an answer," said Bradshaw.

Haughtily the King glared at the Court, his eyes coming to rest on the President. "I would know by what power I am called hither. I would know by what authority, I mean lawful." He scornfully emphasized the last word. "For there are many unlawful authorities in the world, thieves, and robbers by the highway. Remember I am your King, your lawful King. What sins you bring upon your heads, and the judgment of God upon this land; think well upon it. I say, think well upon it, before you go from one sin to a greater. I have a trust committed to me by God, and by old and lawful descent. I will not betray it to answer a new unlawful authority. Therefore, resolve me that, and you shall hear more of me."

Cromwell, Ireton, and many of the Commissioners sat unaffected. For Duncan, it caused reflection. That was until Cook spoke.

"In the name of the people of England, of which you are elected King!"

Charles gave a short haughty laugh. "England was never an elective Kingdom, but a hereditary Kingdom for near these thousand years. I do stand more for the liberty of my people, than any here that come to be my pretended judges."

Duncan shifted in his seat to stare at the King.

Angered by the blatant disregard, Bradshaw chided Charles. "Your way of answer is to interrogate the Court, which you are in no condition to do. You have been told twice. Do good enough to answer."

Charles grew annoyed. "I do not come here submitting to the Court. I will stand as much for the privilege for the House of Commons, rightly understood, as any man here whatsoever. I see no House of Lords here that may constitute a Parliament, though I see familiar faces. Let me see a legal authority warranted by the Word of God, the Scriptures, or warranted by the constitution of the Kingdom and I will answer."

Bradshaw fumed. "Remove the prisoner!"

At Bradshaw's declaration the in the gallery erupted with a cry: "Justice! Justice!"

The outcry momentarily startled Charles, but as his bearing decreed, he quickly recovered. "Let me tell you it is not a slight thing you are about! I am sworn to keep the peace, by that duty I owe to God and my country, and I will do it to the last breath of my body. Therefore, you shall do well to satisfy my request."

"Sir," Bradshaw bravely countered. "As done according to the law, if you refuse to plead then it shall be accepted as an admission of guilt. Think well upon that!" He waved for the prisoner to be removed.

Without further statement, the soldiers escorted Charles from the Hall.

"We are adjourned until Monday. Keep the Sabbath by praying for wisdom," Bradshaw dismissed the court.

After leaving the gallery, William paused outside Parliament to signal for the carriage. The driver hopped down to open the door.

"Take them straight home, James," he said.

"Aye, sir."

William's instruction made Samantha pause in entering the carriage after Anne. "What about you?"

"I rode remember." When she appeared unconvinced, he added, "I want to wait for Duncan and Rory. Now, go." He gently urged her inside.

He stepped a bit further out into the street to observe Rory and company move the crowd. All seemed to cooperate without complaint.

William turned at hearing discussion. Some of the Commissioners exited Westminster. He caught sight of Duncan. Nothing was said as they regarded each other. The grimness of the situation too heavy for words. Duncan made his way to where the horses were kept. William followed. Again, no words spoken as they mounted.

Rory drew his horse to rein. "That went better than expected." His comment met with stone-faced silence. "Well, outside at least."

"Tell the men they resume the duty on Monday. See you at home for supper." William rode off with Duncan.

Chapter 43

ONDAY AFTERNOON DUNCAN RETURNED TO THE COMMISSIONERS stand along with seventy other Members; half those of Saturday. He curiously glanced about the empty places. Fairfax had not presented himself at either session, which distressed Duncan. There had not been time to call upon Tom. Cromwell and the other Commissioners sat stone-faced. Anne, William, and Samantha resumed their seats. Rory again commanded the calvary posted outside Parliament.

Bradshaw began with warning of arrest for any disruption. The gallery grew silent. He then called for the prisoner. Charles entered the Hall. He appeared well rested with royal dignity on full display in countenance and bearing. Again, he wore all the trappings of his royal estate.

After a moment of conferring with his counterparts, Cook said, "May it please your lordship, Lord President. I did at the last Court on behalf of the Commons of England exhibit and give to this Court a charge of High Treason and other High Crimes against the prisoner at the bar. My Lord, he was not then pleased to give an answer, but instead of answering did dispute the authority of the High Court. My humble motion is that the prisoner be directed to make a positive answer by way of confession or negation. If he shall refuse to do, then the matter of the charge be taken *pro confesso*, and the Court may proceed according to justice."

Charles coolly spoke in response. "If it were only my own particular case, I would have satisfied myself with the protestations I made last time against the legality of the Court. A King cannot be tried by any superior jurisdiction on earth. But it is not my case alone; it is the freedom and the liberty of the people of England. Pretend what you will, I stand more for their liberties. If power without law may make law, may alter the fundamental laws of the Kingdom, I do not know what subject he is in England, that can be sure—"

"Sir," Bradshaw interrupted. "The Court will hear no more arguments. You are hereby commanded to make a punctual and direct answer."

Charles raised a regal and reprimanding brow at Bradshaw's interruption. "Sir, by your favor, I do not know the forms of law, but I know as much law and reason as any gentleman in England. Therefore, under favor, I do plead for the liberties of the people of England more than you. If I should impose a belief upon any man, without reasons given for it, it were unreasonable."

Momentarily angered by the rebuke, Bradshaw struggled to find his voice. "Sir, you speak of law and reason; and it is fit, both are against you!"

Duncan fidgeted in his seat. True, the King was being tried for abuses of the law in raising an army against all reason, but what if the King continued to refuse to answer? Duncan became increasingly uncomfortable as the trial progressed.

"Sir," Bradshaw continued. "You are not to dispute our authority. It will be noted that you stand in contempt of the Court, and your contempt will be recorded."

"Why should he be charged with contempt when he is already accused of treason and murder?" Ireton whispered the absurdity of Bradshaw's threat to Cromwell, who curtly nodded.

"I do not know how a King can be a delinquent," Charles coolly proceeded. "Every man may be allowed to be demur if he can show just reason for questioning the capacity of the Court."

A visible stroke for the King. Bradshaw sat dumfounded at this unexpected attack. Hearing grumbling from the Commissioner's stand, Bradshaw righted himself and forcefully spoke.

"No one shall be permitted to question the capacity of this Court! They sit here by the authority of the Commons of England, and all your predecessors and you are responsible to them."

"Show me one precedent," came the King's simple but devastating request.

Incensed, Bradshaw thoughtlessly spoke. "Sir, you ought not to interrupt while the Court is speaking!"

"The Commons of England was never a Court of Judicature. I would know how it became so," said the King firmly.

A precise hit! Though Parliament was a Court, not so the House of Commons alone. By now a desperate Bradshaw called to the clerk, Andrew Broughton, to call the prisoner to answer the charge. This strategy proved futile, and the King remained stubborn.

"I will answer when I know by what authority you do this."

Exasperated, Bradshaw ordered, "Remove the prisoner!"

Charles would have none of it. "I do require that I may give my reasons why I do not answer and give me time for that."

"It is not for the prisoner to require!" Bradshaw quickly reproved him.

"Sir, I am no ordinary prisoner," the King firmly said.

This statement brought disruption to the Hall. Those against the King became incensed by his audacity. Soldiers surrounded the King to prevent any thought of violence, though some soldiers were among those angered. Charles approved the disturbance and pressed on with his challenge.

"Show me that jurisdiction where reason is not to be heard!"

Bradshaw's temper exhausted, he said, "We show it here, the Commons of England!"

Cromwell visibly winced at the blunder while Ireton groaned. Duncan's brows furrowed with concern. Other Commissioners made various reactions of annoyance. Bradshaw's inexperience made a fiasco of the trial.

Bradshaw realized his folly and quickly added. "Sir, be warned the next session shall be the last. Do well to prepare your defense."

Charles remained seated. "Well, sir, remember that the King is not suffered to give his reasons for the liberty and freedom of all his subjects."

Bradshaw saw an opportunity for redemption and boldly said, "How great a friend you have been to the laws and liberties of the people, let all England and the world judge!"

For the first time during either proceeding, Charles looked visibly shaken by the stunning retort. Not only Bradshaw's words, but the closing in of the guards. Charles glanced about. His discomfort reflected in his affected speech.

"Sir, under favor, it was the liberty, freedom, and laws of the subject, that ever I took up—defended myself with arms. I never took up arms against the people, but for the laws."

Duncan chewed on his lower lip at the King's startling admission. He bit so hard he, had to stifle an outcry.

"Guards!" Bradshaw waved the prisoner to be removed. He appeared quite pleased to end on a more secure note than a few moments earlier.

However, Cromwell, Ireton, and others were not pleased. They confronted Bradshaw when the Commissioners retired to the Painted Chamber.

"This must end tomorrow!" Ireton urged Bradshaw

"Aye! He must be made to answer the charges," insisted Cromwell.

"Should this be rushed?" Duncan asked.

"There is no defense he can rightly offer to dispute the charges," Cromwell answered Duncan in a reasonable tone. However, with Bradshaw, his tone returned to irritated. "Be more forceful. He does not feel threatened save with your last sentence. He believes we shall not pursue justice to its fullest extent. He reckons if he debates long enough, we shall turn coward."

"We have proof enough! Cook need only to read the list of witnesses. Let the outcome be on his head," said Ireton.

Duncan flinched at mention of *witnesses* while Bradshaw silently nodded his agreement.

Cromwell escorted Duncan from the Painted Chamber. He spoke in a confidential tone as they left the building. "I know Tom gave you *certain documents*. Say nothing in either denial or confirmation. Those alone, should be enough to convince you that speediness is needed to end this situation. The longer it delays, the more unrest grows in demands of justice."

"What about Tom?" Duncan asked.

"Tom Fairfax is not man to be pushed. That is why he remains incognito, to quell the rumors."

"What rumors?"

"That he would take the King's place. Or storm Parliament and establish a new government." Cromwell scoffed to add a terse comment, "Some of these dunderheads in Parliament need a good thrashing." He sneered in looking back at Westminster.

"Tom never had such ambition. It is absurd to think he would make himself king."

"Aye, which is why he remains absent. His presence, as Lord General, could confirm those rumors. Now, we must prepare for tomorrow. Good day."

Rory arrived as Cromwell departed. He dismounted. "How goes it inside? Any better than Saturday?"

Duncan simply scowled as he stared in the direction Cromwell left. "This is a convoluted business."

"The trial or what Cromwell just said to you?"

"Both." Duncan continued to stare.

Rory put a guiding arm around his older brother's shoulder. "How about a pint before we head home?"

Duncan balked slightly, as if woken from sleep. "Are the streets cleared already?"

"I am quite efficient in duty, even if I do say so myself. Let's fetch your horse."

Chapter 44

THE CROWD GATHERED FOR THE NEXT TRIAL SESSION. DUNCAN helped Anne alight from the carriage. He hesitated a moment to gaze at the entrance to Parliament. Many thoughts flashed through his mind: his conversation with Cromwell about Fairfax; Bradshaw's mishandling of the trial, and Ireton's urging of witnesses. Would today be another fiasco or would Bradshaw rise to the occasion? Would Cook read the names? If he did, what about the outcome?

Anne gently tugged on Duncan's arm to draw him aside and avoid those arriving. "This day troubles you."

He turned his back to the door to speak privately. "The King is tearing apart the Court with his arguments while rumors of Tom's absence disturb me."

"Tom is well."

The statement made him curious. "How? Ah, his wife." He leaned closer to say, "Cook has been urged to name witnesses." He saw the flash of dreaded understanding in her eyes. "I regret not taking your advice to tell Will. Although, I am glad Samantha chose to remain home."

"Two days here has taxed her energies."

"If only Will stayed with her."

"He comes," Anne spoke in quick warning.

William dismounted and gave the reins to a soldier. "Another day."

Duncan simply nodded. "How was Samantha when you left?"

"Sleeping. She tires more easily these days." He grinned.

"Duncan." Cromwell hailed him. "Time for the Commissioners to enter."

"Courage, husband. Let God be the judge."

He kissed her cheek. "Take care of her in this crowd," he told William before joining Cromwell.

Rory arrived, once more in uniform and mounted. "Any new orders for the day?" he asked William.

"No. Simply secure the perimeter like before."

"Shouldn't be a problem. The crowd lessens as the trial drags on."

"Shall we." William offered his arm to Anne. Inside, he helped her navigate the way to the gallery. Sight of the duchess made men politely move aside. A soldier made two scruffy looking men leave to provide seats for them.

The third session opened no differently from the previous two. A stern warning against disruption followed by a calling of the Commissioners by name either present or absent. When it came to Fairfax, a woman in a venetian mask shouted, "He had more wit than to be here!"

"I warned against disruption. Away with the woman!" Bradshaw instructed the guards.

"That makes two who would rather not be here," groused William.

Anne laid a firm hand on his arm. "Gently. We are here to support Duncan." When he made a reluctant frown, she added, "For the good of our family." He still visibly vacillated. "Please, Will. If you have any love for me, or Samantha, endure this one more day."

He huffed an ironic chuckle. "You masterly employ the art of womanly endearment."

Once the masked woman was gone, Bradshaw again issued the warning. Facing forward, Anne caught sight of Duncan looking up at them. She tenderly smiled with encouragement.

"Bring forth the prisoner!" Bradshaw said.

The King barely sat when Cook rose. He reiterated the charges brought against the King and demanded a plea. He then spoke upon the subject of the King's refusal.

"According to the known laws of the land, a prisoner who does not put in a plea of guilty or not guilty should be regarded as having pleaded guilty by implication. There was, anyhow, no possibility of doubt as to his guilt. The House of Commons, the supreme authority and jurisdiction of the Kingdom, have declared, that it is notorious, that the matter of the charge is true. If the Court, be not satisfied there are witnesses." Cook cast an angry sideways glance at the King. "I have in my possession thirty-three accounts of eyewitnesses to the King's involvement." He shuffled through many papers. "These statements range from poor unfortunate widows in Leicester to an impressive one of soldiers once under the King's command and now in the service of Parliament." He picked up pieces of paper and began to read off names. "Sergeant James Harris, Lieutenant Mark Winston, Captain Wayne Mitchell, Commander Lloyd Martin and Major William Hawkins to name a few."

William stared in amazement when Cook spoke his name. Anne noticed his shock and touched his arm with concern. The shock turned to anger, as his eyes shifted from Cook to the Commissioners stand. Duncan lied! There was no court of inquest to clear up misconceptions of his past testimony, rather on behalf of Parliament against the King. He signed an affidavit!

"Will?" Anne whispered.

With a sharply raised brow and stern look, he stifled any further words before turning back to the Commissioners' stand. Hearing his name opened a floodgate of hurtful memories; memories of the hostile relationship between him and Duncan a few years ago. He grimaced upon remembering the utter contempt with which Duncan first held him, then the transition to agreeability, and finally marriage to Samantha. As he brooded over the deception, suspicion was cast upon Duncan for past actions that could well have been innocent. Now, he began to think differently. While he thought thus, his conscience listed Duncan's merits. What did Duncan say about being a Commissioner at the King's trial? *Conscience! Ha!* he caustically laughed to himself. *Revenge is more like it! With me as your pawn.*

"Sir," began Bradshaw, "repeatedly the Court affirmed their jurisdiction. It is not for you, or any other man, to dispute the jurisdiction of the supreme and highest authority in England. This Court is not to be trifled with. However, we shall allow you another chance to give your positive and final answer in plain English, whether you be guilty or not guilty of these treasons laid to your charge." As Bradshaw concluded there was a profound silence.

Charles spoke with more care and thought than during the previous sessions. "When I was here yesterday, I did desire to speak for the liberties of the people of England; I was interrupted. I desire to know yet whether I may speak freely or not."

"Make the best defense you can but give a positive answer concerning the matter that is charged upon you only," said Bradshaw.

Arrogantly the King brushed aside the condition. "For the charge, I value it not a rush. It is the liberty of the people of England that I stand for. For me to acknowledge a new Court that I never heard of before, I that am your King, should be an example to all the people of England. You spoke very well the first day I came here of the obligations laid upon me by God to maintain the liberties of my people. The same obligation you spoke of, I do acknowledge to God that I owe Him, and to my people. That is to defend, as much as in me lies, the ancient laws of the Kingdom. Therefore, until I may know that this is not against the fundamental laws of the Kingdom, by your favor, I can put in no particular charge."

At the slip of the tongue, Cromwell and Ireton exchanged hopeful glances. The King thus far refused to admit there was a *charge* to answer.

When Bradshaw went to interrupt, Charles continued. "By your favor, you ought not to interrupt me. How I came here I know not; there is no law to make your King your prisoner."

"Clerk, do your duty!" Bradshaw heard enough.

"Duty, Sir!" the King scornfully exclaimed.

Undaunted Broughton read the charge again.

Bradshaw spoke before the King could utter a word. "How far you have preserved the privileges of the people your actions have spoken it. Truly, Sir, men's intentions ought to be known by their actions. You have written your meaning in bloody characters throughout the Kingdom. Sir, you have heard the pleasure of the Court, and you are before a court of justice."

"I see I am before a power," Charles said dryly. "For, sir, I care not a straw for you!"

The Hall erupted with a cry of outrage when the King stepped down. The guards immediately surrounded him and escorted out.

Embittered, William made his way to find Duncan. Anne followed as fast as the crowds allowed. When William reached the Painted Chamber, Duncan was nowhere to be found.

"Will?" Anne asked.

He roughly pulled her aside. His voice thick and angry. "I have been deceived by your husband! I did not give my testimony against the King. According to Duncan I was commanded to appear before the Committee of Both Kingdoms to answer charges brought against *me* for actions done while I was in the King's uniform. If I had known the true nature of that inquiry I never would have agreed, and he knew that when he brought me forth under a false pretense!" With an angry grunt, he departed.

Anne forced her way through the crowd in pursuit. She grabbed his arm. "Will, please! There is a reason. One that presents a very great danger to all of us. Let us return home so I can explain."

William's jowls flexed with anger and indecision at her plea.

"So! My son's death is not enough for you." Kyle's angry raised voice made them turn.

"Come." William took Anne's arm to draw her away from Kyle.

"I am speaking to you, cur!"

William stopped. His face flushed with renewed anger. Anne tugged on his arm in warning. They continued to the carriage, which waited nearby. His horse tethered to the rear.

"Insufferable wretch!" Kyle hobbled in approach. "I will not tolerate being ignored by a cowardly turncoat and common trollop."

William went to open the door when Kyle used his cane to strike Anne's arm. She cried out in startled pain. Before William could react, Rory arrived and leapt from his horse.

"Back off!" he shouted at Kyle. He drew Anne away from Kyle. "Take her home," he told William, his back turned to Kyle.

With terrible force, Kyle stuck Rory with the silver head of a cane. The first blow glanced against Rory's right ear and impacted his shoulder. He staggered to avoid injury. The second blow quickly followed and landed hard on the back of Rory's head, striking the hat from his head. He swayed before he collapsed. Anne screamed.

William snatched away the cane to stop a third blow. Thrown off-balance by the seizure, Kyle fell sideways into the building and clumsily sat on the ground.

William tossed the cane away. "James!" he called to the driver. He knelt beside Rory. Anne already cradled Rory's head. "He bleeds terribly."

"Get him into the carriage," William instructed James. He noticed Kyle remained seated on the pavement. He jerked Kyle to his feet and shouted, "Captain Irving!"

"Unhand me!"

William caught the other cane Kyle tried to swing at him. "Do not press me!" he warned in a harsh, lethal tone.

Irving raced over. "Major."

"Take Lord Kyle into custody. He assaulted the Duchess of Rutherford and struck down Lord Wiltshire, a Parliamentary officer."

"How dare you?" Kyle jerked away from William, only unsteady for having only one cane. Irving caught him.

"There are numerous witnesses to the assault." William stepped threatening close to Kyle. "If he dies, it will be murder."

Kyle's sneer turned into concern at the statement.

"Will!" Anne called. Her voice fretful.

"Go," William told Irving before he hastened to the carriage. Inside, Anne held an unconscious Rory, his face pale. She used a handkerchief to hold over his wound, yet already stained with blood. "I'll fetch the doctor and find Duncan." He then told James, "As quick as you can, get them home."

Chapter 45

DUNCAN MADE HIS WAY TO A NEARBY TAVERN, HOPING TO FIND some place to think. He may have believed himself prepared for Cook to use William's testimony, but hearing the name read aloud caused a stab of guilt that far exceeded anything he anticipated. He never doubted the King's guilt, but Bradshaw's inept handling made the trial a disaster! It was one thing to be associated with such a fiasco, but an entirely different matter to compromise his family's honor in the process.

Duncan barely had a moment to catch his breath when he saw William in the threshold. By the determined look there was no reasoning with him. He thought best to hasten quietly out the back. Alas, William spotted him. In a panic, Duncan left.

William pursued. When he emerged from the tavern into an alley, he yelled, "Duncan, wait! Rory is injured."

Duncan pulled to a halt. "What did you say?"

"Rory is seriously injured. Anne also."

"Anne? When?"

"Just now, outside Parliament. I had James take them home and sent the doctor to Kensington before coming to find you."

Duncan left the alley to fetch his horse, William at his heels. "How?"

William stopped Duncan from mounting. "Kyle. He confronted Anne and me about the trial. We tried to ignore him, but he struck her on the arm with a cane. Before I could act, Rory intervened. He suffered two blows, with worst on the back of the head."

Duncan vaulted into the saddle. He snapped the reins for his horse to launch into a gallop. People jumped out of the way of speeding horses. They weaved around carriages and wagons to reach Kensington. Duncan jumped down before the horse fully stopped. He burst into the house and took the stairs in leaping bounds.

In the bedchamber, the doctor, Anne, Samantha, and Mistress Hortence gathered about the bed. Rory remained unconscious, his face pale, almost ashen, while his head bandaged. Anne's arm hung in a sling.

"Duncan!" Samantha fought crying.

He gave her a quick embrace before handing her to William and proceeded to Anne. "Is your arm broken?"

"No, badly bruised but will mend. Rory ..." She couldn't finish due to upset.

Duncan crossed to the bed. "Dr Bannon. How is he?"

"Quite serious, Your Grace. The blow cracked his skull." Bannon used his hand to demonstrate the location.

"Will he survive?"

Bannon hesitated. "I cannot say for certain, Your Grace. The next day or two is critical."

Anne came along side Duncan. He held her. His expression shifted between anger and distress.

"He needs quiet. I shall remain," said Bannon.

Duncan motioned to William. Together they took the women to the upstairs salon. Anne and Samantha sat side-by-side on the sofa. The men fetched them brandy.

Intense bitterness filled Samantha's voice. "He is as horrid as his son! I wish to God I never heard their names or knew of their existence."

Anne embraced Samantha with her good arm, both in need of solace.

William discreetly spoke to Duncan. "Anne said there is an explanation for the use of *witnesses*." His gaze pointed and prompting.

"Aye," Duncan wearily admitted. "Once they are settled, I shall tell you everything."

After a time of prayer for Rory, Mistress Hortence brought calming draughts for Anne and Samantha. Once the women retired to Anne's chamber, Duncan took William downstairs to the study.

"First, I apologize for not telling you sooner. However, when you learn the darker aspects of this, perhaps you will understand *why* I had to keep silent for so long." Duncan's countenance grew stern as he began the explanation. "With this latest outrage, I shall act swiftly and decisively. They have caused harm to my family for too long. This will end!"

"How can I help with that?"

Touched by the question, Duncan sniffled. "You already did by saving Samantha. Pray, sit." He indicated the desk chair. Once William became situated, Duncan pulled out the journals, four letters, and the confession. "All these hold the answers. I have a ribbon in each place where my grandfather's journals correspond with the letters. These three are written by Kyle. This," he picked up the King's letter, "is the key to everything. Observe the seal."

"The King? How did you come by these?"

"Found among the royal baggage captured at Naseby. I retrieved my grandfather's journals when we paused at Foxglen enroute to Foxmoor. It was during my examination all the pieces fell together. That I discovered what you are about to. I shall give you time to read and compare." He withdrew to the other side of the room. He held on to the confession.

For an hour, Duncan watched and waited as William read letters, re-read the letters, flipped through the journals, used the letters for comparison of the journal then finally sat back. A look of shock as his gaze shifted to Duncan.

"I am at a loss for words. The implications—"

Duncan pulled up a chair to sit in front of the desk. "Not *implications*, solid facts boldly stated with deadly intensions."

"Aye," William somberly agreed.

"Now, do you understand, why I could neither say nor do anything until I uncovered the true motive?"

William again regarded the items before him. He nodded. "Have you told Samantha?

"No. With all that has happened to her, I fear such news too difficult a blow for her to comprehend. I vacillated about tell you. Dreading—"

"I would inform her."

Duncan nodded at the conclusion. "I have come to appreciate not having secrets between husband and wife. Yet, *my* motive is to protect my sister from a shock that may do more harm. And this," he removed the confession from his doublet pocket, "can do just that, if she ever learns of it. For *this* far exceeds anything you have yet read."

"What is it?"

Duncan's face grew harsh. "I need your most solemn pledge *never* to reveal this to Samantha. Of the marriage contract, she has knowledge. But *this* is something even Rory and I are hard pressed to accept. Learning of this, could break whatever is left of her spirit." When William appeared to vacillate, Duncan insisted, "Your solemn pledge to protect your wife."

"On that, I so pledge." Once William read the confession, his eyes grew wide and face pale. "Good Lord," he murmured in distress. "Your father—" The paper slipped from his hand as he sat back stunned to rising tears. "What your family has suffered is beyond words."

"*Our* family now."

William fought to compose himself after reading the murder confession. "Where does my testimony fit into this? Why deceive me?" A hint of anger crept into his voice.

"No deception meant. Nor was it my idea to further question you. I stated the truth when I said Cook issued a subpoena for you to be brought before Committee. Instead, I volunteered to fetch you. Only after the questioning did Cook suggest including your expanded testimony in the King's trial. I strenuously objected, but the Committee voted for inclusion."

"Why not tell me?"

"What would you have done if I had? Accuse me of falsehood, like now?" At William's dismayed reaction, Duncan added, "Remember, you offered to testify against Lawrence. No one coerced anything out of you."

"I never expected it to be used against the King."

"Nor did I!"

"Then why did you speak so passionately at Parliament for the trial?"

"You saw our hasty return from Hampton Court. When we tried to convince him to read the proposal, he repeatedly threatened me. Threatened *our* family." Seeing William's visible battle, he continued, "Before you lay the evidence of his duplicity and desire for personal revenge." He picked up the confession. "He acted not solely for Strafford, but also admittedly for the *Crown.* Charles may not have physically put the poison in father's food or lifted a hand against Samantha, but he clearly made his desire known. In truth, everything that has happened to us was for the expressed purpose of wiping out an entire family. The family into which, your child shall be born."

William snatched up the King's letter. He read aloud, "*it is my fervent desire for a speedy downfall to these betrayers of us and our dear friend.* He means Buckingham," he said to which Duncan nodded. William continued reading, "*To bequeath upon you all Rutherford's holding as a reward to faithful loyalty.*" He sneered in regard of the paper. "Truly a death warrant, and partly fulfilled." He indicated the confession.

"Aye. All those times Lawrence abused Samantha—"

"He meant to kill her," William spoke with rancor.

"He nearly succeeded at Bristol. Sadly, they did with father." Duncan took a deep breath to calm down.

William's brows leveled in thoughtful regard of the journals and letters. "Do Cromwell and Fairfax know about this?"

"Tom knows all. Cromwell suspects. Yet none of this has been entered into evidence for the trial, if that is your line of thinking."

"You could have done so. Why didn't you?"

Duncan took a deep steadying breath before replying. "Impassioned though I was that day, and despite all these," his hand swept over the evidence, "as God is my witness, I hoped the threat of a trial would help him see reason and seek to engage in honest negotiations. To do what my father made me pledge before he died; protect our family and employ my skill to reconcile the King and Parliament. God knows I tried." His voice tampered off with sobriety. He swallowed back emotion to say, "Now, you are fully informed. I pray you do not think ill of me, for I admit, I have not always acted wisely. My only desire was to protect our family."

William's gaze swept over the journals and papers on the desk. He somberly shook his head. "How can I think ill of you when I don't even know how I would react under the same circumstances?" Again, he regarded the King's letter. "What more can we do?"

"Nothing where the King is concerned. The trial shall determine his outcome. As for Kyle." Duncan rose and collected the letters. "Time for his reckoning."

"I ordered him held for the assault, so Irving took him to the Tower."

In the hall, Duncan told Cowan, "If my wife inquires, tell her we left on Parliament business."

They rode to the Tower of London. After passing through the Middle Tower and Byward Tower, they were escorted to the Governor's office.

"Your Grace. How may I be of service?"

"We wish to interrogate Lord Kyle Hedgepeth. Is he here?"

"Aye, Your Grace. Although, I am ignorant of charges."

"Assault upon my wife and brother! Both of whom suffered injury."

"Oh," said the governor, astonished.

"I ordered his lordship taken into custody," said William.

"Your name, sir?"

"Major Hawkins, Commander of Parliament's Dragoons."

"My brother-in-law. Also, a witness to the assault."

Governor nodded acknowledgement. "Please, follow me." He led them across the compound to a room in the Beauchamp Tower.

Kyle sat before a hearth. A small fire helped to keep him warm on the frosty January day. He snarled at his visitors but made no comment.

When the governor turned to leave, Duncan said, "Stay. I want a witness for this interview."

A long moment passed before anyone spoke again. A time in which Duncan and William stared at Kyle. The arrogant lord's focus remained on the fire. His feet stretched out toward the flames. Finally, Kyle, broke the heavy silence.

"I know what brings you here," his voice sharp and unrepentant.

Duncan moved to stand between Kyle and the fire. "My wife is only slightly injured while my brother alive. Yet, that is *not* why I am here."

"What other reason could there be?"

Duncan pulled out the King's letter. He held it up with the seal visible. "Do you recognize this?"

"A letter. What of it?"

Duncan reached down to seize Kyle by the doublet. "Do not play games with me. This letter, along with three in your hand were captured at Naseby. The entire scope of your foul plan laid bare. Confiscation of Rutherford lands. The marriage contract. All revealed in the odious scope of revenge, by which *you* hoped to profit!"

Kyle's face changed from arrogance to dread. Duncan shoved him back in the chair when released.

"I see you understand. The tables have turned."

Kyle sought to regain himself. "If you came to persuade me to give evidence against the King, you have sadly misjudged my mettle."

"No. These letters speak well enough to that end. What I want is the name of the servant you ordered to use enough poison to kill my father!"

Stunned, Kyle said, "Poison Patrick? What nonsense is this?"

"You deny any knowledge of the act?"

"This is the first I have heard of it." Kyle sneered, as he focus shifted to William then back to Duncan. "What ridiculous nonsense has this traitor put in your head to make such a claim?"

"William has nothing to with it. It is the King's own words to you." He read, "*it is my fervent desire for a speedy downfall to these betrayers of us and our dear friend … To bequeath upon you all Rutherford's holding as a reward to faithful loyalty.*"

Outraged, Kyle clumsily pushed himself out of the chair. "That is not what the King meant."

"I thought you would not turn evidence against him?"

"I won't!" Kyle insisted. "However, your accusation of murder is unfounded. Those words do not connect me to what you claim about Patrick."

"You capitalized on the situation when Strafford withdrew his son for consideration."

"That is what the King meant. To keep her from marrying …" Kyle suddenly clamped his mouth. His face worried.

"From marrying whom?"

"Strafford's son, of course."

Duncan took a step toward Kyle, which forced the crippled lord to take an awkward step back. He bumped into the chair. "What do you know of the Irish army?"

Kyle made a feeble rebuttal. "Only that Strafford desired to bring them here to subdue Parliament."

Duncan took quick note of William, whose posture stiffened with anger at Kyle's statement. Thus, he spoke to Kyle. "You confirm the truth of what Parliament suspected. And what my father tried to avoid – war! At the cost of his life." Duncan glanced to the governor. "You heard all?"

"Aye, Your Grace."

Another step forward by Duncan, and Kyle fell back into the chair. "Take heed. *If* you survive the charges of assault, stay clear of my family." He leaned his face close to Kyle. "And *if* I learn you had any connection with my father's death, as God is my witness, I will crush you." He straightened. By Kyle's flinching reaction, he made his point. Duncan motioned to the governor for departure.

He left the Tower with William at his heels. Neither spoke until they were mounted and headed back.

"Do you believe his denial of involvement?" William asked.

"It is said that a frightened man speaks the truth. Besides, he already gained marriage for Lawrence along with all it entails. Killing father would not provide further enrichment."

"Then the servant indeed acted alone as he confessed."

"Aye." Duncan drew rein to look at the Tower. He blinked away tears.

Seeing emotions, William asked, "Duncan?"

"He and Lawrence plagued our family. They hounded my grandfather, coerced my father and me, and used my sister as a pawn. Until now, nothing stopped them." He wiped his eyes and took a deep breath. "I feel a weight has finally been lifted from us."

"Let us hope that is followed by good news of Rory."

Chapter 46

ON JANUARY 27TH, 1649, THE FINAL SESSION BEGAN. DUE TO Rory's grave condition, Duncan chose to remain in Kensington and not return to Parliament. William took direct command of security rather than delegate to a junior officer. He drew extra soldiers from Cromwell's personal regiment to reinforce his men. He placed Captain Irving in charge of the horse outside Parliament, while he assumed position inside the Hall doors. He intensely listened to the Court proceedings.

The clerk reiterated that according to the law, any lack of a plea meant guilty by implication. The charges and authority were valid, but Bradshaw's inconsistency threw doubt upon the Court. Fortunately, Charles made several errors in his defense and when Bradshaw took command, thwarted the King.

Bradshaw spoke. "The Court has fully considered this case. The prisoner, having refused to plead, will be regarded as having confessed. Furthermore, since the charges are of a notorious nature a sentence of severity has been agreed upon. Clerk."

Broughton stood. "Charles Stuart, as a Tyrant, Traitor, Murderer and a public enemy, shall be put to death by the severing of his head from his body." At the conclusion of the reading the Commissioners rose to their feet in agreement.

The pronouncement stunned Charles. "Will you hear me a word, sir?"

"A prisoner is not to be heard after sentence is pronounced," said Bradshaw.

Charles appeared astonished. His last chance gone. History would show him a traitor guilty and condemned to death. "By your favor, sir! I may speak after the sentence!" He spoke as the guards approached and lay hold on him. "By your favor hold!"

"Sir, if you be familiar with the law, as you so claim, then you should know that a prisoner condemned to death is already considered dead and cannot speak to the court! Remove the prisoner," Bradshaw ordered.

"I am not suffered to speak save what justice other people will have!" Charles shouted when forcibly escorted from the hall.

William watched the Commissioners. All stone-faced. Once the King was out of sight, the Commissioners left the Hall. Those in the gallery filed out. Some pleased by the verdict, others remorseful.

For several moments, William stood alone with his thoughts. The King had just been condemned to death! How can one fathom such an inglorious end?

"Major Hawkins."

William snapped out of his dreary pondering to see Cromwell. "General?"

"I'm glad you have not left yet. How is Rory?"

"Still unconscious."

Cromwell frowned in sympathy. "I am truly sorry to hear that. It is a shame Duncan has not been here the past two sessions."

"He does not wish to leave his brother until certain of his fate."

"Understandable. However, Parliament could have used his signature on the warrant."

William made no comment to the statement. "Is there anything else, General?"

"Aye. Since we need trustworthy men, you are to command the calvary for the King's execution at the Royal Banqueting House three days hence."

William stiffened at the unexpected order. "Aye, sir."

Cromwell left when summoned by Ireton and Manchester.

In Kensington, Anne, Duncan, and Samantha sat in solemn silence at news of King's fate. When William spoke of his forthcoming duty, Samantha comforted him. For several moments, they remained in an embrace.

"Your Grace." Doctor Bannon entered. He wore a small smile. "Your brother is awake."

"Thank God!" Duncan and the others made their way upstairs. Upon entrance, he noticed Rory's eyes closed. He accosted Bannon. "You said he was awake."

Groaning and mumbling came from Rory as opened his eyes and tried to speak. With great fear, he looked at Duncan.

"What is wrong with him?" Duncan demanded.

"Easy, my lord," Bannon soothed Rory. "There is swelling on your brain. It should pass with more rest, and your speech return."

"Follow instructions." Duncan placed a hand on Rory's cheek. "Rest and recover." Rory barely managed a grin, before he closed his eyes.

"Then he shall live?" asked Samantha, anxious.

"Waking up is a start. Though, the swelling needs to reduce," Bannon cautiously said.

"If it doesn't?"

"I shall deal with it." He gently smiled at Samantha. "Know the odds of survival improve with each passing day."

Samantha sat in a chair beside the bed. "I shall wait to still any further upset when he wakes."

"When he does, encourage him to eat. Broth to start," said Bannon.

"I will have the cook prepare some," said Anne.

Duncan motioned for William to accompany him in leaving. He spoke once in the hallway. "The assignment distresses you."

"Aye," droned William. He walked off without further discussion.

Duncan went to pursue when Anne stopped him. "I thought you went to the kitchen?"

"I paused at the corner when I heard you and Will speak. He must deal with this himself. Same as you did about your involvement in the trial."

His focus went back to the direction William walked. "It will be a somber three days."

Over the next three days, Rory woke multiple times. His speech remained elusive. Through grunts and gestures, they understood his head hurt. Each day, Samantha fed him broth. He never completed an entire bowl before falling back asleep. According to Doctor Bannon, whatever Rory managed to eat would aid in recovery.

After supper on the third day, Cowan entered the study where Duncan and William reviewed reports from Foxmoor and Foxglen. "Your Grace, Captain Irving and Master Cook are here."

"Ah. Send them in."

Irving and Cook paid their respects to Duncan. "Forgive the lateness of the hour, Your Grace," began Cook. "Only this afternoon did I become aware of Lord Hedgepeth's arrest."

William's piqued glance made Irving speak. "I filed the report immediately, Major."

"Captain Irving acted promptly. The King's trial consumed my time. Otherwise, I would have come sooner to interview the major, her ladyship, and Lord Wiltshire," Cook told Duncan.

"I also provided Master Cook with testimony from other eyewitnesses," said Irving.

"Naturally, I shall answer all your questions," began William. "Lord Wiltshire's recovery is touch and go. Doubtful, he would remember much of the assault."

"All the same, if I may at least see his condition for myself—"

"Out of the question!" Duncan hastily rebuffed. He raised a hand to stop Cook's protest. "Doctor Bannon can provide you a complete medical report. My brother is not to be upset."

"That will suffice, Your Grace. May I proceed with the interview of Major Hawkins and her ladyship?"

"My study is at your disposal. I shall speak with my wife while you interview Major Hawkins."

For the next hour, Cook asked William questions. Between each question, he wrote copious notes. When finished, he interviewed Anne. She insisted William and Duncan remain during the questioning. Cook made a sketch of the injury on Anne's arm. After two hours, Cook and Irving departed.

"I pray I do not have to endure the ordeal of testifying," Anne murmured.

"No. Your written affidavit is enough," Duncan assured her. "Both of you," he added to William.

"It is late. Duty requires an early rise. Good night." William took his leave.

Chapter 47

DAWN, JANUARY 30, 1649. DRESSED IN HIS FULL UNIFORM, William prepared to leave Kensington to assemble his company for the necessary task at hand. He found Duncan waiting in the foyer. He wore a dressing gown. For a moment they soberly regarded each other. Duncan broke the silence.

"A wretched cold day for such work."

"Aye." William pulled on his gloves. "Do you plan to attend?"

"No." Duncan nervously pursed his lips to contain rising emotions. "For days I have longed to speak with you about the outcome but did not wish to impose upon your solemnity. Although, I wanted justice for our family, this end is not what I envisioned when agreeing to the trial."

"I know. My *solemnity* was time spent in great personal reflection upon the course of events that brings us to this day. Being in the army, I witnessed the human cost of war while observing Parliament made bold display of the convoluted politics involved. The outcome is a culmination of the two. Howbeit, made poignant after the evidence you shared and the interview in Lord Kyle. I needed time to prepare for what must be done."

Duncan appeared relieved yet spoke with sincerity. "God strengthen you and watch over you today." He embraced William.

A large crowd of people gathered around the platform outside the Royal Banqueting House; the platform draped in black material. William's horse regiment denied access to nearer than twenty feet. He placed cavalry at either end of the street while he commanded the troop in front of the platform. Between his horse and crowd, stood pikemen. The faces of the people showed a mixture of emotions. Some cried while others smiled and jeered. The soldiers in his command, silently went to their assignments. He sensed their respect for the solemn duty of the day, and sober determination to keep order.

The Royal Banqueting House had been built twenty years earlier at the request of the King. A massive stone facade constructed in the classic Italian style. A few large windows were blocked by boards and masonry for defensive reasons when secured by the Parliamentary Army. The usually bright and naturally lit hallway dark thus the beautifully painted Rubens ceiling barely visible. Charles requested the ceiling display the triumph of wisdom and justice over rebellion and falsehood. A poignant place for his own execution.

Colonel Hacker escorted the King for the final walk. Bishop Jaxon also accompanied Charles. The King calmly went through the widened window, enlarged for access to the platform. In the center, stood a small executioner's block. Near the block, three staples had been driven into the wood should Charles refuse to submit and needed to be bound. On the platform itself stood the High Executioner, his assistant, and Colonel Tomilson; the journalist John Harris also present to record the event. The executioner and his assistant were heavily disguised in thick close-fitting coats, false wigs, and beards. When Charles saw the troop of horse he frowned.

"I shall be little heard of anybody here. I shall speak to you, Bishop."

William heard. He became rigid in the saddle. He stared straight ahead and clenched the reins tighter when the King proceeded.

"Indeed, I could hold my peace, but I think it is my duty, to God first, and to my country, to clear myself as an honest man, a good king, and a good Christian. I think it is not very needful for me to insist long upon this, for all the world knows that I never did begin a war first with the two Houses of Parliament."

William cringed at the falsehood. He heard the King and his officers planning strategy before the first cannon fired at Edgehill.

"God forbid I should lay it on the two Houses of Parliament. I do believe that ill instruments between them and I have been the chief cause of this bloodshed. Yet, as your King, I deny the justice done upon this sentence passed. As a Christian my judgment comes from God and the unjust sentence that I suffered to take effect, is punished now by an unjust sentence upon me. Those in particular that have been the chief causers of my death, God knows, I do not desire to know. I pray God forgive them."

William swallowed hard at the statement concerning those who caused his death. His mind recalled Cook reading his name. He also thought of what Duncan said earlier, and the evidence of wrong against the family.

Charles went on: "I die a Christian according to the profession of the Church of England, as I found it left me by my father. I have a good Cause and a gracious God. I will say no more." He turned to the executioner. "I would pray before the ax is struck." The man simply nodded. He allowed Juxon to help arrange the proud Stuart hair so that not a single strand was severed.

"I go from a corruptible to an incorruptible Crown, where no disturbance can be, no disturbance in the world," he spoke lowly to Juxon. With great resolution Charles removed his George and handed it to sniffling Juxon. "Remember."

Taking off his doublet Charles paused a moment, raised his hand and eyes to heaven in silent prayer. The executor prepared his ax as Charles knelt. "Stay for the sign," he said, thinking the man was about to strike.

William swallowed hard, as he watched the crowd ahead of him. There came a profound silence that preceded the King's last statement. He knew most could not hear, rather saw their sovereign submit to the headsman. A swoosh and deadly blow made him flinch in the saddle.

It took one blow to sever the head from the body. "Behold the head of a traitor!" the executor said, as he displayed Charles' head.

The crowd reacted, some cursed, others wailed. Women swooned.

"Major Hawkins!" Colonel Hacker shouted at the crowd's rising fervor.

William waved for the horse at either end of the street to move in to clear the crowd. It took half an hour to remove all the people from the area. Despite the high emotions there were no protests or ugly incidents.

On his way home, William's emotions shifted between relief at the end of a taxing ordeal, and distraught at his sovereign's death. Someone called to him from the shadows of a nearby doorway. He cautiously drew rein when the man stepped out. Fairfax.

"Is it over?" he asked in a harsh whisper.

"Aye, General," replied William guardedly.

Fairfax became grim and thoughtful. "Did he make any mention of reconsidering or compromise?"

"No, sir."

Fairfax slapped the horse's neck in frustration. William steadied the animal at the strike. He curiously watched Fairfax disappear around the corner. He heard the rumors of Fairfax being king but doubted the validity. He served under the brave unassuming man. Lurking in shadows and speaking in hushed tones confirmed his belief of false rumors.

Once in Kensington, William paused going inside the house. Not for fear, rather a moment of solace after witnessing such a dreadful event. In the foyer, Cowan silently greeted him. The steward aided William in the removal of his cuirass, helmet, and sword.

Cowan spoke in a near whisper. "They wait in family salon."

When William entered, Samantha immediately went to embrace him.

"What of the King?" Duncan asked at length.

"Regal to the last," replied William with distraction. "What of Rory?"

Samantha became distressed in reply. "He suffered fits. The doctor attributes it to swelling. I fear for him!" She clung to William, weeping.

"All we can do is pray and wait," Duncan said.

Chapter 48

TWO WEEKS AFTER THE KING'S EXECUTION, DUNCAN RECEIVED A note from Fairfax requesting his presence for an Army Council meeting. Duncan promptly arrived, yet to his surprise only Fairfax occupied the meeting room.

"You sent for me, Tom?"

Fairfax warmly smiled. "This is a joy I thought unthinkable. One I wish Patrick were here to receive."

"Indeed?" asked Duncan, curious, yet smiled due to Fairfax's delight.

Fairfax held out a sealed scroll. "Open it," he eagerly encouraged.

Duncan's eyes grew wide, his mouth first gaped then turned into a rapturous smile. "We are restored Foxhill and Foxmeath!" He hugged Fairfax. "I don't know what to say! This is … unbelievably wonderful!"

"Parliament is determined to make right what can be. Others also had property and goods restored. It is the least that can be done to aid in recovery. There is other news."

The change in Fairfax's tone to serious, startled Duncan. "Oh?"

"Lord Kyle's trial. Since Rory is recovering, the sentence is five years in the Tower for assault. Unless you want to submit new evidence?" Fairfax asked in a probing tone.

After a moment of consideration, during which he regarded the deeds, Duncan said, "No. Five years is sufficient. If in the future, it becomes necessary …"

"Understood." Fairfax steered Duncan to the door. "Now, celebrate your good fortune."

With a joyous heart, Duncan rode home. He bounded up the stairs. During Rory's recovery, they gathered in the upstairs salon to keep him company. "Anne! Samantha! Will! Rory!"

Anne stepped back when the door opened. "Duncan. What is all the shouting about ...?" Her question interrupted when he picked her up, laughed, and kissed her.

"This is not a common reaction when returning from Parliament," William made the droll comment to Rory, who reclined on the sofa.

Duncan laughed and slapped William's arm when he passed to sit in the armchair beside the sofa. "Dear brother, this will speed your recovery."

"Wh—what ... will?" Rory's words stuttered, but clear. Curious, he unrolled the scroll Duncan gave him. He loudly gasped. Tears swelled. "This ...?"

Fearful, Samantha hurried to Rory. "What is wrong?"

"Noth ... ing." He smiled, laughed, and gave her the scroll.

"Rutherford is fully restored. The title Lord Wiltshire once more complete with his heritance of Foxmeath," Duncan declared.

Overcome with joy, Samantha's knees gave way and she sat at Rory's feet.

"This calls for celebration." William poured and distributed brandy. "To Rutherford. To Wiltshire," he offered as a toast.

"When ... can we ... go?" Rory asked Duncan. He indicated the deeds.

"You must wait until you are completely recovered to make such a journey. However, Will and I shall venture out once the weather clears."

The mid-March temperatures moderated, but rainy weather made travel difficult. Duncan and William kept a westerly course from London to north Wiltshire. Foxmeath sat in a plain near the River Thames close to the border of Oxfordshire.

Duncan stopped his horse at the bend in the road. "Do you remember the last time we rode this way?"

"Aye. A month after your grandfather's death, we snuck away from Oxford because you wanted to see Foxmeath."

"I dread seeing it now. Fearful of what I might find."

"Would you rather Rory be the first to visit?"

Duncan scoffed a negative and gathered the reins to continue.

Around the bend, the grand sprawling manor came into view. Built from the local yellow stone, it consisted of three wings, all gabled windows with steeples and statues at the apex. The lawn destroyed by ruts and gouges. Numerous windows broken or missing. Parts of the slate roof caved in and the hexagon turrets at the corners reduced by half.

"The damage doesn't appear too severe," commented William.

They dismounted and walked the length of the front façade. The front door was missing. "Doubtful anyone lives here," observed Duncan. He went inside.

Empty! Every room on the first floor bare of furniture, window covers, décor, all gone. Upstairs, they found the same emptiness. However, where the roof was missing, weather ruined floors and walls. With each discovery, Duncan's painful expression deepened.

"Worse than Foxmoor," he bitterly complained.

"But not beyond repair." William tried to sound hopeful.

"*If* there are funds to do so. The crops and livestock barely bring enough income for Foxmoor's repairs and expenses."

"It is better than lying in ruins," William continued his attempt of encouragement.

"At least there is that to tell Rory." Duncan hopped on his horse and rode from Foxmeath.

William spurred his horse. "With the family heritage restored, we shall find the means."

"Keep telling me that. This makes me fearful of what we shall find at Foxhill."

Several days later, Duncan and William just crossed into Warwickshire when a fierce storm struck. One of the worst storms in recent weeks. Blinded by driving rain and buffeted by the howling winds, they became separated. Continuous lightning followed by deafening thunder drowned any attempt to call for the other. A tremendous crash from a nearby lightning strike created a concussion that sent William from the saddle and into a ditch where he lay senseless.

William awoke. As he gathered his senses, he realized he lay nestled under old worn blankets. He smelled food. A kettle hung over a hearth fire where an old man stirred the contents. He wore a patch over his left eye. The face peppered with gray whiskers. He wore a pleasant generous smile. He walked with a limp to approach the bed.

"You're awake," he said.

"Who are you? Where am I?"

"I'm Jake Crosby and this is my home. Humble as it is. And you?"

"Will—*ouch!*" He reached his head to find it bandaged.

"You took quite a tumble. Nasty bump on the head and few scrapes and bruises."

"How long have I been here?"

"A couple of hours. I medicined you with what I had."

"My companion. Any sign of him?"

"I saw no one else."

William sat up yet grimaced in pain. "I need to find him."

"In the morning. You'll feel better after rest and food. The good Lord blessed me with a rabbit just before the storm started. Coming home is when I found you. Rather, I found your horse first. She grazed a few yards away from you. Stew is hot and ready."

"I would not trouble you."

"No trouble. I don't get many visitors." Jake lightly chuckled.

William glanced around at the cottage. The furniture old and sparse, the walls damaged, and roof rotting. It certainly seen better days. "Do you live here by yourself?"

"Aye," said Jake a somber tone. "My misses died of fever while I was off to war. I lost my eye and got my limp while fighting for the King." He spat.

The statement and attitude made William wary. "You are a Royalist?"

Jake scoffed. "Pressed into service. My sympathies side with the people. You?"

"In many ways, we were all pressed into service."

"You need have no fear to speak your mind with me, Will. I've lived long enough and seen enough not to judge any man. When the King sent word of needing men, the first place his generals came were Royal lands. Any stout man or youth forced to enlist."

"I did not realize I crossed onto Royal property."

"Such as it is. With the King is dead, who knows what will happen to Foxhill. Parliament probably gained control of all Royal property."

Williams started at the name. "Foxhill?"

"The name of the estate you're on. A proud estate it once was. I served as bailiff in its heyday. That was over thirty years ago. Before you were born."

"Aye. I'm not yet thirty. Though the fall makes me feel much older." He flinched at hearing thunder. Rain beat down upon the roof.

Jake hurried to seal off any leaks. "If this keeps up, the ground will be a muddy mess by tomorrow," he complained.

"Muddy or not, I must search for my friend. Hopefully he found shelter. Perhaps at Foxhill?" William purposely spoke. He watched Jake's reaction.

The old veteran shook his head since his mouth was full of stew. "Doubtful. It's been deserted for decades. Those who lived nearby were displaced by the war and destruction."

"The house was razed?"

"Not totally. One wing remains solidly standing, but no one has lived in the manor since the O'Malleys." He paused, a look of fond recollection upon his brow. "Lord Thomas was a good man and fair master. I grieved his death. Growing up, Foxhill was the favorite estate of his son, Lord Patrick. A good shot who loved to hunt. Could chase a stag all day."

The neigh of a horse came from outside followed a bang on the door. "Anyone home?"

"Duncan," William said in recognition. To Jake's curiosity, he clarified. "My friend."

Jake unlatched the door. Soaked to the skin, Duncan entered.

"Much obliged," he said to Jake. He noticed William sitting up in bed. "Will! Thank God. This wretched weather kept me from making a proper search."

"Master Crosby found me and tended my wounds. He makes a good rabbit stew."

Duncan removed his hat and cloak. He pushed the wet part hair from his forehead. The strains under his hat somewhat dry thus the normal color. "Master Crosby, my heartfelt thanks for helping my brother-in-law. I would have been sore pressed to tell my sister of him missing."

"You're welcome, sir." Jake stared at Duncan.

Duncan sat on the stool beside the bed. "How badly are you injured?"

"A few bruises and a bump on the head. Nothing too serious."

Duncan grew perplexed at Jake's studious regard. "Why do you stare?"

"Your hair? It looks red at the roots." Jake reached for Duncan's hair, which made Duncan slap away his hand.

"Explain yourself, man."

"Easy, Duncan," said William. "Master Crosby was the bailiff at *Foxhill*."

"Foxhill?" Duncan repeated. He rose to confront Jake. "You served my grandfather?"

"I knew you were an O'Malley! That is why I stared. These old eyes were not deceived when I saw Lord Patrick in your face."

"My father. I am Duncan O'Malley. Duke of Rutherford."

Moved by excitement, Jake seized Duncan by the arms. "Have you come to reclaim Foxhill?" He clasped his hand in prayer and looked up. "Oh, Lord, thank ye. This is a blessed day. Well, maybe not once you see it. But a house can be rebuilt. Oh, aye, it can be thriving again." He happily rambled. "Now, where did I put the mead? Ah!" He went to a trunk and tossed items from it to pull a dark bottle from the bottom. He chuckled in his search for various things for drinking. In the end, he used a cup and two bowls for the mead.

Amused, Duncan and William watched Jake.

"To Foxhill!" Jake said. "I shall take you there in the morning."

The rain stopped after supper, thus the morning clear and bright. William felt better after a good night's sleep. He still wore the bandage on his head. Fortunately, his hat fit over it without pain. Jake rode an old pony. Two miles later, Jake stopped on the crest of a knoll. Blooming trees blocked a complete view of Foxhill

"You can see the part still intact," said Jake.

"I have never been here before," said Duncan with a tremor of anxiety.

"A grand house in its day," said Jake, proudly.

Duncan snapped the reins. The slope proved slippery from the previous day's rain. Once around the edge of the trees stood Foxhill. A large level yard led to a gatehouse, not fortified, rather wrought iron and decorative. Gaping holes along the fence from cannon. The stone E-shaped Elizabethan house sustained a good deal of damage. One side completely leveled, while the other wing moderately damaged with broken windows, gutters, and chimneys. The middle section remained intact. A building on the east side, now rubble, could have been a stable or chapel. Difficult to tell.

Duncan passed through the broken gates. A lump rose in his throat. He dismounted and forced himself to continue into the main house. In somber silence, William and Jake followed.

Aside from war damage, years of decay and neglect were starkly evident. The lump tightened and Duncan's eyes grew moist. He wiped them clear to see. Even beneath the dust, cobwebs, and broken timbers, were evidence of a once fine house. Two elaborately carved wooden staircases led from the foyer to the second level. Two large hearths flanked the stairs. Windows that remained intact, contained a special beveling that incorporated the O'Malley coat of arms above each pane.

Overcome by emotions, Duncan's knees gave way. He clumsily sat on the bottom step. "This great house laid to waste for what? Pride of a king?" His loud lament echoed in the foyer.

Sympathetic, William sat beside Duncan. "I'm sorry."

Jake fondly gazed around the room. "Things may look bad on the surface, Your Grace, but God answered my prayer the moment you walked into the cottage. To see Foxhill restored. Now, I know it *will* be."

"I hardly think of myself as an answer to prayer." Duncan used his hands to wipe the tears from his face

"Do any of us?" asked William.

Jake widely grinned, a sly twinkle in his eye. "When the King sent men to confiscate Foxhill, I secretly took estate records along with what gold, jewels, and valuable I could find. They remain hidden to this day."

"You kept everything safe for thirty years?" asked Duncan, surprised.

"I was there when Lord Thomas had a row with Buckingham. His Grace made me promise to keep the family holdings safe should the situation good badly for him as Buckingham swore it would. I have kept that promise."

Duncan clapped Jake's shoulder in a gesture of gratitude. "Then it appears we are both an answer to prayer. To even begin restoration, I need past records and funds."

Chapter 49

DUNCAN AND WILLIAM'S JOURNEY TO FOXMEATH AND FOXHILL took three weeks. By the time they returned to Kensington, April buds dotted the trees. Rory's health improved during their absence. His stutter barely noticeable, and he partook in light daily exercise. Now seven months along in pregnancy, Samantha's condition obvious in wearing of dresses with no bodice or corset.

After dinner, they retired to the family salon and listened to Duncan and William report on the state of Foxhill and Foxmeath.

Rory spoke after Duncan concluded. "I have a home to call my own. I'm only sorry Jake Crosby is at Foxhill. He sounds like a man who would have been of great help to me."

"I know the perfect man," said William. When Rory and Duncan appeared curious, he said, "Tom Wyatt. He grew up serving Rutherford, so he is intimately acquainted with family operations."

"What will Henry say to his son leaving Foxglen?" asked Samantha.

"What any father would say when his son is given an opportunity to advance. Go."

"Excellent suggestion. And I have the means to make repairs," declared Rory.

The statement piqued Duncan's interest. "You do? I don't recall opening the coffers. Such as they are."

Rory laughed. "While you both were gone, Tom stopped by on his way home to Nun Appleton. He retired from the army," he said matter-offactly. "He brought the payment Parliament withheld due to tensions between them and the Army. Four thousand pounds."

"Four thousand pounds!" Duncan echoed, astonished.

"Well, not all for me. It is to be split between myself and Will."

"I get two thousand pounds?"

Samantha giggled at William's stunned reactions.

"Seven years of pay," Rory clarified. He nodded to Samantha.

She pushed herself out of the chair and crossed to a desk. From a drawer she pulled out a sealed document. "This came with the money."

All eyes watched William read the document. He lowered the papers. His expression woeful. Almost on the verge of tears.

"Will?" Samantha held his shoulder.

He looked at the document for a moment of composure to find his voice. "My father died eight months ago. This is the deed to his land, business, and title; Knight of the Realm." He folded the paper. "An inheritance stained with blood."

Samantha sat on chair arm. "Oh, Will, I'm so sorry. The past is not your fault."

"No? I seriously wonder." He stuffed the paper in his pocket.

"Then go to Nottingham. It is the only way to resolve the differences. I shall accompany you. Some of the blame belongs to me," Duncan offered, but William hesitated. "Will, if you give up your inheritance, what will there be for your children? Of course, there is Foxglen, but that belongs to their mother's family." He gently touched Samantha's hair.

"Perhaps in time. At present, I cannot." William left the salon.

With a heavy heart, he trudged upstairs to his chamber. He sat on the edge of the bed and stared at the papers. His tears blurred the words. The world he once knew, gone. The papers fell to the floor when he buried his face in his hands and wept. "Lord, show me what to do!" As he lifted his head, he caught sight of his reflection in the mirror.

He wiped his eyes and crossed to the mirror. For a long moment, he stared into the glass. No longer the fresh face of a twenty-two-year-old young man who eagerly went to war. Staring back, the mature face of a twenty-nine-year-old. The light hazel eyes once filled with gaiety and wonder now looked upon the world with seasoned scrutiny. Thick brown hair and mustache unchanged in color but took on a different appearance when measured against youth.

Without thinking, he unfastened his doublet and took it off. He shed the shirt next. His face not the only part of his body that changed. His back crisscrossed with red scars from Hedgepeth's whip while his left shoulder wrinkled and scarred from the searing at Swindon.

"To think, my wife never shrank from this mangled body. Indeed, Lord, you have sent mighty challenges. This legacy is another. Just how strong I am to accept it, I know not."

Unaware, William left the door ajar. He caught sight of someone in the doorway. With stricken expression, Duncan stared at his back.

"The scars of war are not a pretty sight."

"I had no idea," Duncan weakly admitted.

"There is no reason you should. What is a scarred hide and scathed shoulder? It is still flesh that covers the more important parts of the body. Flesh wounds heal quicker than the blows to the heart." He picked up the fallen papers. "This is another blow to my heart. One that again forces me to face difficulties of the past."

"A past we shall face together." Samantha entered. She softly smiled, as she took William's arm. He kissed her cheek in response.

At the tender exchange, Duncan spoke with abashed hesitation to Samantha. "I had no idea the extent of his scars."

"I tried to tell you in Oxford."

"I deeply regret not listening."

She approached her brother. "You have since made amends. Dwell no further on it."

"That's what I told," said William. "By God's Grace, I survived death numerous times, triumphed over adversity, regained a lost friend, married the woman I love, and expecting a child. Life experiences sometimes bring a person full circle. These papers are the last chain in a particular circle. In time, and with God's strength, and my wife at my side, I will go to

Nottingham." He held out his hand, to which she returned to him. He earnestly stared into her eyes. "For now, we will return home to Foxglen. Where I will turn my sword to a plowshare and promise never to be a soldier again."

About the Author

Shawn Lamb is a multi-award-winning author of Christian fiction ranging from age 8 to adult. She is also an event speaker. Since 2010, Shawn has participated in homeschool conventions, book fairs, comic cons, and festivals throughout the Southeast, Midwest, and Mid-Atlantic regions.

As a former screenwriter for children's television, and author of numerous books, she brings over 30 years' experience dealing with publishing and Hollywood to her speaking engagements.

For more information about Shawn's books and possible speaking engagements, visit www.allonbooks.com.